THE SCARRED HEROES SERIES

THE COMPLETE COLLECTION

GWYN MCNAMEE

DEAD RECKONING

THE SCARRED HEROES SERIES BOOK 1

PROLOGUE

REAPER

The oppressive heat and humidity weigh down on my body like a heavy, wet blanket. Every breath draws hot, muggy air into my lungs, offering no relief. It's more like drinking in soup than breathing, really. Sitting in the thick, lush vegetation soaked with the recent rainfall doesn't help things, but it provides me the perfect vantage point to stalk my target. Complete cover where I can blend into the landscape and from which to deliver death.

He hasn't spotted me once since I began to follow him over a week ago, stalking him around town, assessing his every move, noting his patterns to find the perfect opportunity to strike. I could have killed him a thousand times, taken a shot that would end his life and make him pay for what he did to Evangeline. But I waited and bided my time for this exact moment. Because I knew that fucker was up to no good and that he wasn't up to it alone.

Nervous and excitable, the man practically screamed, *"Look at me! I'm doing it again,"* over the last few days. It matches the intel Cutter and Preacher provided me, suggesting he has repeated his new business venture since selling off his fiancée to human traffickers. He's found a new and easy way to make big money, and he's milking it for everything he can.

But waiting has paid off more than I ever could have hoped and opened the door for me not only to take out the fucker who betrayed Eva but also several of his contacts here in the islands responsible for the trafficking ring.

It's a win-win situation.

What more could I ask for?

This meeting place is ideal for what I have in mind to initiate his eternal punishment. The man doesn't deserve a quick death. Not when he put Eva and countless women since her through this kind of vile agony.

No, tonight he's going to pay for what he did in a way far more fitting.

First, I need to take out his buddies, the ones acquiring all the girls and selling them into their sinister version of Hell. I sight them all in my scope where they stand, talking near the rear of Danilo's car. One of them motions to the trunk and laughs.

Fuckers.

I have to bite back a growl because I know what's in the trunk. I know what my mark put there...or I should say *who* he put there. That poor girl he nabbed off the street only two hours ago before driving up here into the isolated hills to make the handoff to these assholes.

Confirmation that he's still up to his old tricks. The fact that the douchebag is still doing what he did to Elijah's girl makes this even easier. A true justification for what I'm about to do. Removing scum from the Earth has always been part of the job, but this one will taste especially sweet.

It's time for all these fuckers to meet the Grim Reaper.

I fire off five precise shots so fast the men don't even have time to react as their friends' heads explode and they crumble to the ground around each other. Danilo is the only one left standing, covered in the gore left by his soulless counterparts as they met their maker.

Surprise, you worthless piece of shit.

It takes him a moment to react. Long enough that I police my brass and am already on the move down the hill toward him before he finally manages to pull his phone from his pocket frantically. I reach into mine and press the button on the device that will jam the cell phone signals for miles around us.

He isn't getting help from anyone. Not up here. Not *ever*.

The man is so engrossed in trying to get his phone to work that he doesn't see me coming until it's too late. His head jerks up just as I reach him, and I grab him by the throat and pin him against the car.

His phone clatters to the ground as he scrambles and scratches at my arm, and I calmly lower my rifle to lean it against the car. His resistance doesn't faze me, barely even registers against the type of pain I'm used to enduring.

I meet his terrified brown gaze, his eyes free of any remorse for what he's done or empathy for the woman he has in this damn trunk. Only concern for himself fills them.

The desire to tighten my hold, to watch him gasp and claw at me while he struggles for a breath he'll never take again, surges through my veins. But that isn't the plan. I need him conscious enough to understand the message I'm about to deliver before taking his life.

I plaster on a wicked smile, the one I so enjoy using before I take the life of someone who doesn't deserve to have it. "Hello, Danilo. Eva sends her regards."

His eyes widen slightly, and he shakes his head, still clawing at my wrist, his nails digging at the flesh there.

I lean in to him and sneer. "There's no use fighting this. It's time for you to get what you deserve."

Truthfully, even this is too easy for a man like him—for *any* of these men. But I don't have the time to do what I really want, to break him down over days, tear him apart physically and mentally, draw out the death he knows is coming until he's literally begging for it.

So, this will have to do.

I grab my Yarborough knife from my boot with my free hand and drive it into his stomach in one smooth motion, then saw the blade back and forth as I pull it up and out, ensuring it does optimal internal damage and causes the most pain possible.

He opens his mouth to say something or to scream, but all that comes out is a strangled gasp and groan. I loosen my hold on his neck slightly, enough to allow him to take in a tiny breath.

"If-if you let me go, I'll tell you where you can find the others."

His words send ice shooting through my veins and goose-bumps spreading across my skin despite the warmth of the night air.

The others?

Of course, there had to be more girls somewhere. An operation as big and well-put-together as the one that held Eva captive wasn't just some small upstart. It was established.

I've been hoping Danilo would lead me to any women being held here during the time I've been watching him, but it seems he's just a street supplier and not privy to any of the major workings of the organization behind this. So, I highly doubt he would have any useful information.

"Bullshit. You don't know anything."

He nods his head against my hold on his throat. "I-I do." He struggles to get the words out. "I heard them talking."

"Tell me." I shove my knife into his stomach again, ensuring the pain remains fresh and extreme as an incentive to be honest.

Another nod and gasp are all he can manage. "New York. Russians. Some club. I don't know the name."

"Russians?" I glance at the five dead men on the ground. "All your friends here are Filipino."

He gives a quick nod. "They-they're the suppliers. Get the girls onto the boats. But they work with these Russians from New York. And I also heard maybe some Albanians out of Chicago."

I growl and slam him against the car again, my anger flaring to life and heating the blood rushing in my ears.

These fuckers will create ties with anyone for a price, it seems.

That second part fits with what Cutter told me when he called to ask me for this favor. His crew had raided an Albanian boat on Lake Michigan filled with women who had been trafficked on their way to Chicago to be sold to the highest bidder. While Cutter assured me they took care of things on their end with the head of the family in Chicago to get things shut down there, this mission to locate Danilo and anyone on this side of the world who may have been involved fell to me.

But the Russian twist is unexpected.

It creates a new wrinkle in my plan. The mission was just supposed to be to take out this fucker, to make him *pay* for what he did to Evangeline, and maybe save a few more here in the process. But I can't stop knowing there are other innocent women out there, ones potentially being held and sold on US soil. Not when I can do something about it.

I jab my knife into him again, twisting and slicing, and he cries out, the sound echoing through the still night air. But out here, there isn't anyone to hear him. No one to hear the shots I took. No one to discover the massacre, perhaps for several days. Their choice of remote meeting spots sealed their fates tonight even though I've had them marked for death for far longer.

"You...said...you wouldn't kill me..." He barely manages to get the words out around the blood flowing out of his mouth.

I grin at him and stab again. "I said no such thing." Rage fills me as I spit in his face and watch it slide down over his blood-stained mouth. "You're getting what you deserve."

The second I release my hold on him, he crumples to the dirt, and I make my way to the trunk and pop it open. The girl lies bound and blindfolded, trembling, still in the school uniform she was wearing when I watched him lure her into his car back in the city before I followed him up here.

I reach out a hand to her arm, and she kicks out violently with her bound legs, some fight still in her despite what she's already been through at the hands of this monster.

"*Huwag kang magalala.*" My Tagalog is absolute shit, but I hope she understands what I'm trying to say to her, my assurance that she's okay and that I won't hurt her.

She freezes and turns her head toward me even though she can't see anything. Her bottom lip quivers, and tears slip from beneath the blindfold covering her eyes and down her cheeks.

I gently lay my hand on her arm. "Do you speak English?"

She offers a tiny nod.

"I'm gonna lift you out of the trunk and set you onto your feet. The men who took you can't hurt you anymore. You understand what I'm telling you?"

Even in the trunk, she must have heard the shots that took out Danilo's buddies, and she likely caught some of what I said to him, even if it was only muffled bits and pieces.

The girl is right to be scared of me.

She nods, trembling uncontrollably despite how suffocatingly hot it must have been in the trunk.

"Good." I reach in and scoop her up into my arms like she weighs nothing.

Her entire body vibrates so badly that when I set her onto her feet, I have to use my hand to steady her for a moment before she can get her balance. Using the same bloody knife that killed Danilo to cut the bindings at her ankles and wrists feels almost poetic, but when she reaches up to grab the blindfold, I capture her wrist with my free hand.

"Leave it on. Count to 200. Then get into this car and drive to the first police station you can find. You understand?"

She nods.

I can't take the risk of her seeing me and describing me to the police. I'd never get out of the country if they were looking for me. She seems to understand exactly what I'm saying without having to explain it further, though. Perhaps she can sense she's been saved and wants me to get away clean, even knowing what I just did.

This poor girl can't even comprehend what would have happened to her had I not been watching and planning this already. If I had come next week, she'd be on a ship bound for only God knows where a day from now.

My heart tightens in my chest, and I release a deep sigh. I rest my hand on her shoulder, and she flinches. Rubbing gently, I lean into her. "You're going to be okay. I promise."

It isn't a promise I can make and definitely not one I can help keep in any way—that's one hundred percent on her and how she lets what happened affect her long-term—but I hope it's true. Like Eva, I pray she's able to move past what's been done to her and find a normal life with someone who loves her.

Not that we all get that. Some of us never will.

I glance at Danilo's cell. "There's a phone on the ground right near you. In case you need it. Tell them it belonged to the man who took you."

The man I came to the Philippines to kill lies bleeding out on the ground, gurgling and gasping for breath.

Mission accomplished.

He won't last long enough for any help to arrive, but it's still too good a death for him. It would have been nice to have a few days or even a week with him, to make him suffer and take him apart piece by piece. But I'll take this win, even if it isn't exactly how I wanted it.

Things rarely are. I've learned to accept that they never will be.

I give him one hard kick in the stomach. He cries out, and his former captive flinches and shifts away from the sound slightly but starts counting. "One. Two. Three. Four…"

Shit.

I never meant to scare her more, just needed to get in one last good one before I grab my gun and make my way back out across the small clearing to disappear into the darkness of the jungle.

It'll be like I was never here.

Get in. Get out. Nothing but bodies behind.

By the time she's done counting, the carnage will be the only evidence I was ever here.

A ghost.

A reaper on a mission to right this particular wrong.

It's the only thing I'm good at.

Except, it seems this is only the tip of the iceberg. Next stop—New York.

1

VIKTORIA

The deep bass thumps through the floor and straight into my temples, threatening to bring on a migraine I can't afford right now. I need to be one hundred percent on the ball tonight if I have any chance of catching something that might help the investigation. If what Hank said is true, breaking this case wide open will require absolute focus.

But just being in B66 makes unease coil around my spine and tighten with every passing minute. And it isn't just because Hank asked me to come here with him during off-duty hours, without a formal open investigation, on what appears to be some sort of shady tip he received from some "mystery" source.

I'm all for using who I need to on the streets to gather intel, but infiltrating a club owned by the Russian Bratva carries a risk far higher than anything else I've been involved with since becoming one of NYPD's finest.

I joined the force so I wouldn't end up in a place like this —like so many of the girls I grew up with who had big dreams but ended up slinging drinks and sucking dicks just to make ends meet month to month, or feel like they belonged somewhere.

This club is a magnet for desperate women like them and men with too much money and lacking any morals. No wonder Hank suspects it's the center of the human trafficking ring we've long known runs here in NYC.

So, while I may have fought hard to stay away from places like B66, knowing what might be happening here to innocent women means taking one for the team and coming to see what I can spot, regardless of how uncomfortable it may make me.

Though, truth be told, maybe it's more than this space and the people in it making me uncomfortable. Like the man at the end of the bar across from us.

Tall.

Muscular.

Dark.

And despite there being any number of threats in the club —gangsters carrying unregistered, loaded weapons, women selling themselves, and drugs, the potential for a familiar face —I can't seem to drag my attention away from *him*.

He's new—if he were a player in town, I would recognize him. He has one of those faces you can't forget—strong, stubbled jaw, piercing blue eyes visible even from this far away— and despite my best efforts to keep my focus where it needs to be tonight, something about him keeps drawing my attention that way.

And it isn't just how handsome he is.

Something's off about him, and it has been since the minute he walked in here and took a seat on the stool.

His gaze never stops moving—from the door to the patrons, up to the balcony from where Yankovich runs his empire. He scans the club like he's looking for someone or waiting for something to happen. Dozens of scantily clad women work the floor and try to sidle up next to him, offering everything from drugs and drinks to sex, but the guy doesn't seem interested in the slightest. He offers them a little half-smile that doesn't reach his eyes and says something that has them scurrying away quickly. Yet he remains almost completely still, calm and casual—at least, to the untrained eye. But to me, it's clear—he's here for something else.

Maybe the same thing we are.

The rumor is they're still trafficking women brought in from all parts of the world. Innocents snatched off the streets and even straight from their homes, then thrown on huge cargo vessels to live in squalor for weeks or even months, making their way across to the States where they're sold into sexual slavery to the highest sick bidder.

I nudge Hank with my elbow and incline my head toward the mystery man while making it look like I'm just leaning in to talk over the loud music. "The guy at the end of the bar."

Hank raises an eyebrow and surreptitiously glances at him over his shoulder while he takes a sip of his beer. "What about him?"

"I think he's here looking to buy." And I don't mean drugs.

"What makes you say that?"

I continue to keep my eye on the man while pretending to laugh at something Hank said. It's important we blend in here. If we get made as cops, this could end with a lot of bloodshed. And while I wouldn't mind seeing some of Yankovich's men in body bags for what they've done, I prefer to keep Hank and myself out of them. "Watch the way he's looking around. He isn't paying any attention to the girls on the floor. He's searching for something or someone in particular."

"Yankovich?"

"Maybe?"

It would make sense if he's here for the same reason we are. Yankovich runs this place and the bratva in NYC. He's the one who will be in charge of any trafficking that's happening. The man who will need to approve all buyers.

"I haven't seen him come down from the second floor once since we got here, though."

Nor would he.

Yankovich is smart enough not to get his hands dirty, especially somewhere as public as this. Anyone could walk in off the streets and witness deals handled up on that balcony. He won't want to be seen doing anything that could get him put away.

I fucking hate smart criminals.

They're the hardest to catch and usually the ones getting away with the nastiest stuff. The kind of stuff that keeps people like me—who have to clean up after it and deal with the aftermath—awake at night.

Hank wraps his arm around me and leans in close, both of us trying to make it appear like we're here as a couple and so we can ensure our conversation isn't heard by any curious ears near us. Though, with as loud as it is in here, that's unlikely, anyway. Perhaps the *one* positive note to the noise pounding on my brain relentlessly. "What you want to do? Want to grab him?"

I place my hand over his on my shoulder and brush my mouth against his ear while peeking at the man out of the corner of my eye. He hasn't moved from his perch at the bar, and his disinterested demeanor hasn't changed, either. "Watch him. See if we can get any confirmation of what he's doing here."

There isn't much else we can do at the moment. We haven't witnessed anything illegal yet, other than girls disappearing down the back hallway with bar patrons. But what happens behind the closed doors back there is the least of our worries. The girls on the floor here are doing it willingly and aren't our primary concern. While I'd love to get them out of this life, help them clean up and get decent jobs that don't require them to spread their legs or gag on cock for money, it's the women who don't choose it and are bought and sold who are our focus tonight.

A nod of his head confirms Hank agrees with the plan to wait and watch. So, we pretend to flirt and slowly sip at our drinks while maintaining a close watch on the man and the rest of the patrons in case anyone else interesting shows up.

With Michail Yankovich safely tucked up in the private balcony on the second floor, overseeing his kingdom but keeping his distance from the action, it won't be easy to nail him on anything. But if we can get an insider, someone who will feed us information, or someone we can put the screws to for cooperation, we just might be able to bring down the man responsible for so much misery.

Maybe it's wishful thinking on my part, but I have to believe good will triumph over evil, or I couldn't do this job day in and day out. Seeing what we do every day, the destruction and vileness humans show to each other, weighs on my soul in a way I never imagined it could. It's the only reason I agreed to Hank's off-the-books trip here tonight in the first place, but now that I'm here, I can't just walk away without *something* to show for it.

And that moment might have finally just come…

"Hold on." I tighten my hand on Hank. "Alexei Kosofik just came out of the back hallway, and the guy grabbed him."

Hank chuckles. "He has some balls to lay his hands on Kosofik."

"Or he's really stupid."

Something tells me that's not the case, though. This guy is too careful. Too meticulous in how he's leaning against the bar, how he's watching everyone, how he moves and doesn't put his back to the front door.

Something is definitely off here.

REAPER

I SIP at my tonic with lime and scan the bar for what feels like the hundredth time since I arrived. Definitely isn't the type of place I want to be spending my evening and hanging out. But when I got to New York and started talking to the people in the know, all streets led me here. And to Michail Yankovich.

"They can get you anything you want. Their auctions are the best I've ever been to."

I cringed having to hear the way the people I pretended to befriend talked about these women...children even. Like they're a commodity to buy and sell and broker to the highest bidder rather than human beings with families and lives and hopes and dreams that were destroyed when they were taken. But I can play the part. I can play *any* part to get to my end goal. So, I smiled and nodded and said the words I needed to get me here—to B66, the center of the bratva's activities in the city.

Now all I need to do is find Alexei Kosofik, Yankovich's underboss. The bastard hasn't shown his face here the last three days I've been hanging around, and the rumor mill suggests another auction will be happening soon. That means I don't have a lot of time to fuck around. He's likely busy making final preparations, but if I want to get to the girls before they're sold out from under my nose, I need to *find* them first. That will only happen through *him*.

I turn and lean back against the bar so I can appear to

casually glance up at the private loft where Michail Yankovich always stays—just out of reach of anyone except those he deems worthy. I haven't seen him set foot down here once, even though this is his place. The man uses his balcony like a throne to lord over his kingdom, not caring about the fact that what he's doing to these women is destroying not just their lives.

He doesn't pay any attention to me watching him from below, just scans the crowd, then returns to the leather couch against the wall to drink and chuckle with his cronies.

Fucking asshole.

Men like him are the reason I joined the military in the first place, only I never expected to find them on US soil. At least now that I've been forced into retirement, I can stay busy using the skills good ole Uncle Sam gave me to eliminate fuckers like him and ensure innocents aren't caught up in his enterprise of filth.

I turn back to the bar and take another sip of my drink while I survey the club. The brunette across the bar, who I've caught watching me a few times, locks green eyes with me for a second before she darts her gaze away with a sweep of her long, dark hair and leans in to murmur something to the man next to her.

He wraps his arm around her as if they're a couple and he's drawing her closer, but the body language is all wrong. I snort and crunch on a piece of ice. They're clearly cops. It couldn't be any more obvious if they had a neon sign above them pointing down that read, *"The Fuzz."*

And likely, they're here for the same reason I am—because the Russians are up to no good. The girls are just one very small portion of their business, but it's a lucrative one. One I intend to use to get my foot in the door and the information I need.

Speaking of doors...

The one that leads down the back hallway opens. Private rooms lie beyond it, and I keep seeing the dancers and waitresses disappearing down there with customers. Alexei Kosofik steps out, adjusting his cock behind his zipper.

This might be my only chance.

Before he can make it too far past me, I reach out a hand and grab his arm, stopping him in his tracks.

A stupid move for anyone, but intentionally so on my part.

It has to appear that I'm an idiot who doesn't know what he's doing. Some Midwestern farm boy who made his way here to purchase something very specific but who is naïve and clueless about the ways of this very dark world.

I plaster on my most idiotic smile. "Hey, are you Alexei Kosofik?"

He shoves off my hand and steps in to me with a snarl, puffing out his chest. "Who the fuck is asking?"

I retreat a bit, shrinking back and holding up my hands in surrender, trying to appear intimidated by his display even though I could kill him with my bare hands in ten seconds right where we stand. "Got your name from an old friend. He said you might have what I'm looking for. Potentially in red?"

Kosofik eyes me for a moment, from my dirty boots, up over my jeans and black T-shirt. "Who is this old friend of yours?"

I shrug and glance around but don't see anyone paying us much attention aside from the brunette. "He asked that I not use his name. You know, given the circumstances. But I have money. Whatever it takes to find what I'm looking for. It's hard to come by where I'm from."

He makes a scan of the club, then inclines his head to the bartender, who hands him a leather-bound menu. Holding it up, he leans into me. "You tell me what you're looking for, then you give me your cell phone number and I'll text you with the time and location."

Progress!

I smile at him and grab the "menu" from his hand. Acid climbs up my throat as I flip it open and read the pages. Of course, they aren't stupid enough to make what they're selling obvious. It's disguised as a "wine" list, with characteristics of the girls described in terms that any layperson would never think suspicious.

Red blend – 2014 vintage. South American grown fruit.

The lime tonic water churns violently in my stomach.

A fucking seven-year-old child.

I have to force myself to stay unaffected and close the menu slowly. Handing it back to Kosofik, I smile. "The red blend from 2000, Romania, would be lovely."

He nods and grabs a napkin and pen from the bar, and I hastily scribble down the number for the burner phone I bought.

"What's your name?" The question holds every ounce of suspicion he still has about me, so it's time to really turn on my act.

"Adam Jones. From Minneapolis." The lie rolls off my tongue easily. And I know enough about Adam's life before he died to answer any questions this guy might have when he undoubtedly checks up on me before sending me any further information.

I'm sure Adam wouldn't mind my using his identity for this good cause. He died protecting the innocent, and now, his name can help save others.

Rest easy, brother.

Kosofik nods toward the front door. "I suggest you leave now."

I hold up my hands and back away. "I'll wait for your text."

He scowls and watches me leave. Giving him my back feels wrong and foreign and goes against everything I've ever been trained to do when it comes to the enemy, but it's a necessary action here. He has to believe I'm too stupid to do anything to interfere with their operations—just some farm boy completely out of his element in the big city looking for something only they can supply.

The second I step out the door into the not-so-fresh city night air, I light a cigarette and make my way toward where I parked the rental truck down the street. Footsteps follow behind me—light and casual. Someone who knows what they're doing and likely wouldn't be noticed by anyone else.

As I near the end of the building where the alley starts, the man with the brunette darts around me and steps out to block my path. The footsteps behind me stop, and I glance over my shoulder to find her only a few feet back, at the ready should I make any attempt to flee.

I take a drag off my cigarette and twist back to raise an eyebrow at the man in front of me. "Can I help you with something, officer?"

He scowls at me and glances toward the front door of the club, probably concerned someone heard what I just said, but we're too far from it for anyone to have been alerted to who and what he is—that is, if they didn't already know given how obvious it was to me in the club.

I drop my cigarette to the sidewalk and grind it out with my boot.

His gaze follows the movement, and he raises an eyebrow at me and inclines his head toward the woman behind me. "Cuff him."

Shit. I do not *have time for this.*

I sigh and roll my eyes. "What's the charge, officer?"

The cop sneers at me as his partner grabs my wrist and jerks it behind me. My first instinct is to knock her back, take them both out, and hightail it out of here before they know what hit them, but that would only put a target on my back from the NYPD. That's the last thing I need when I'm on a mission like this.

He steps forward and reaches down for the cigarette butt on the sidewalk. "Littering. In violation of New York City Administrative Code Section 16-118."

Smug fucker.

I smirk at him as his partner secures the cuffs to my other wrist.

This is annoying and will eat up valuable time when I could be gathering more information and preparing for what I'm going to need to do, but at least it will be entertaining to fuck with New York's finest.

2

VIKTORIA

"Something is so off about this guy." I stare at the screen showing the video feed from inside the interrogation room where we're holding the man we grabbed from B66.

Roderick Dixon—at least according to his ID.

Hank glances up at me from his phone, which he's been glued to since the moment we got back. "Why do you say that?"

I sigh and slouch down into my chair. "We've been letting him stew in there for two hours and he's barely moved. He's just sitting there, like a damn statue. Most people would be restless, sweating, nervous. But not this guy."

"So, what are you thinking?"

I sigh and push to my feet. "I don't know yet, but I'm going to find out what the hell he was doing at B66."

Hank shifts uneasily and peeks at his phone again. "I, uh, need to go make a phone call. You start with him. You're always good at getting under the skin of these types."

Making a phone call instead of interrogating our potential way into B66? What the hell are you up to, Hank?

I narrow my eyes on him. It doesn't make any sense for him not to want in on this questioning. The whole stakeout was his idea in the first place, his deal. Something is going on with my partner, too, but I can only handle one man at a time. And right now, the one in that room has to take priority. I can deal with Hank and make him fess up later. "Make your call quick."

He inclines his head in acknowledgment before I head down the hall to the interrogation room. Whatever Mr. Dixon's deal is, he's going to come clean to me tonight. It's too important for him not to. If what Hank suspects is right, there are innocent girls out there who need to be found —fast.

Even when I unlock the door and push it open, Dixon doesn't flinch. Doesn't even look my way, just stares straight ahead like he's sleeping with his eyes open. For all he seems to care, he could be sitting on a beach, relaxing under the sun instead of stuffed in here, with no windows, very little airflow, on a rickety chair.

The door closes behind me with a click, and I slowly lower myself into the chair across from him. Blue eyes meet mine, but they give away nothing. Perfect glassy pools I could swim in—but blank.

How the fuck does he do that?

I shove his pack of Marlboros and his Zippo across the table to him. "Thought you might want one of these. You've been in here quite a while."

He smirks at me, the first sign of any emotion I've seen from him since we grabbed him outside B66, and reaches out to take what I've proffered. Large hands deftly light a cigarette, and my focus follows as he brings it to his mouth and takes a drag from it with his perfect lips.

Shit. I'm staring.

It's hard not to with a guy like this. There's just something about him. The way he carries himself. The way he speaks. He's the kind of man who could be lethal to a woman's libido, and likely in other ways, too.

I force myself to meet his eyes, and he raises a brow at me, waiting for me to speak. "What were you doing at B66, Mr. Dixon?"

Dixon releases a plume of smoke into the air and leans back in his chair casually, crossing one arm over his barrel chest, causing his dark T-shirt to pull tightly across his well-formed pecs and biceps. "I thought you arrested me for littering."

Smartass.

"We did, and you'll be charged with that, but it doesn't mean we can't chat about something else."

He offers me a casual shrug that I know is anything but. It's all an act, one he does well. "I was there for a drink."

Lie.

"No, you weren't. The bartender poured you tonic and lime—all night. He never put a drop of alcohol in anything that you drank."

A grin he fights tugs at the corners of his lips, and he takes another drag, releasing a smoke ring that slowly dissipates in the air between us. "You were paying attention. I'm impressed."

I snort and shake my head, fisting my hands on the top of the metal table. "Why is that so shocking? A woman can't be a good, observant cop?"

His brow furrows, and he shifts forward slightly to tap his cigarette into the ratty-looking ashtray on the table. "No. Because I figured you had more important things to worry about than what I was drinking, like Yankovich."

Yankovich.

My heart thunders against my rib cage. I certainly hadn't expected him to bring up the man we were there for, but it gives me the opening I'm looking for. "What do you know about him?"

Dixon shrugs again and takes another drag, blowing the smoke out the side of his mouth. "Just that he owns the place."

Bullshit.

A man like Dixon doesn't just hang out at a place like B66 for shits and giggles, ignoring the girls and *not* drinking. And I don't like dancing around the truth, let alone being *lied* to. "What was in the leather menu Alexei Kosofik handed you?"

The blue of his eyes darkens slightly as he leans toward me and snuffs out the cigarette in the ashtray. "A drink menu. So I could order something a little more interesting than tonic water."

Fucking smartass. This isn't going anywhere.

I scowl at him, shove away from the table, unlock the door, and storm out of it, letting it click closed behind me, locking him in. We've barely gotten started and he's already rattled me. Instead of me getting under *his* skin, he's managed to worm his way under *mine.* And I can't lose my cool in there with him. That would get us nowhere fast— even more *nowhere* than we already are, that is. I need to figure out who and what this guy really is so I can come back better prepared and break down that wall of smug machismo he exudes.

Entering the squad room, I spot Hank down the hallway toward the bathrooms on his phone and motion him over to our desks.

He ends his call and approaches me, eyebrows raised. "Well?"

I drop into my chair and slam my fist on the desk. "Nothing. But he definitely knows something."

Hank grabs a single sheet of paper off my desk that I hadn't even noticed. "Not much on his criminal history check."

I grab the sheet that must have been dropped off after I went into the interrogation room and scan it quickly.

Nothing. Literally nothing.

There isn't a single speeding ticket, arrest, not even a damn *parking* ticket listed on this guy.

"*This* is all we have on him?"

No one is a ghost. No one. Everyone has a past. Everyone has skeletons hiding in their closets—even me. And with the way Hank is acting, it sure seems like he might, as well. All I need to do is find Dixon's and I'll have a way to get him to talk.

Hank shrugs. "Apparently so."

"Impossible…unless…"

Unless someone cleaned *up anything so no one would ever find anything.*

"What are you thinking, Vik?"

"Special ops, maybe?" I fire up my computer and grab the phone off my desk to call in a favor. "I'm going to see what I can dig up on this guy."

"Do you want to cut him loose?"

"No. Give me some time to see what I can find."

Hank motions toward the interrogation room. "Let me go see if I have any better luck with him in the meantime. We can play bad cop/good cop."

I snort and shake my head. "Which one am I?"

Hank smirks at me and shrugs. "Remains to be seen."

He makes his way toward the interrogation room as I dial a number I know by heart. I don't like asking for favors when it can get someone in trouble, especially the *illegal* kind, but there's only one person I know who has access to military records.

Anya answers on the second ring. "Vik? What's up?"

I glance around the room to ensure no one is within earshot. It would be very bad if anyone overheard the request I'm about to make. "I need info on someone I think is special forces, may be active, potentially retired."

She sighs. "And I suppose you don't want me to tell you how I get it?"

"Exactly."

Using Anya to get information that would otherwise be unavailable isn't at the top of my list of favorite things to do. I've only asked for her help once before, and it's weighed on my conscience ever since. I'm a good cop who likes to do things by the book, but special times call for special measures, and something tells me Roderick Dixon won't be easy to nail down—at least, not by any legal means.

"Give me what you have, sis, and I'll see what I can do."

REAPER

I TAKE a drag off my cigarette and fiddle with my lighter—flicking it open and closed, the click of the lid the only sound in the room while I wait...again. The familiar feel of the metal in my hand threatens to bring up memories I can't possibly deal with right now.

It would be dangerous to let them come to the surface while I'm in a place like this and need to maintain my cool. Despite their best efforts to get me off my game and rattle me, it won't happen.

This is too important to fuck it up. The memories of how I got this lighter and what it's been through with me will remain buried under years of scar tissue intended to keep them at bay for as long as is humanly possible.

Hopefully, forever.

I wouldn't be surprised if they left me in here that long. They likely would if they legally could. Those two seem the type to think letting me stew will get me to break. That thought brings a smile to my lips as I take another pull off my cigarette. So does remembering the flash of anger in the brunette's eyes when I refused to give her what she wanted. That woman's passion simmers barely beneath her restrained surface, ready to burst.

The doorknob turns, only instead of the sexy brunette entering, it's her partner who walks in with a sneer on his lips. He smooths a hand over his beard, meeting my gaze with a hard one of his own.

Well, this is a surprise. I thought she would come back for round two.

I raise an eyebrow and lean back in my chair. "Your turn?" I cross my arms over my chest. "You two really got a thing for littering, huh?"

He pulls out the chair across from me that his partner occupied less than an hour ago and slowly lowers himself into it. This would be much more enjoyable with the pretty brunette, but it seems they've decided to play good cop/bad cop with me.

Though, I'm not entirely sure which one is supposed to be which.

His sexy partner was definitely annoyed and flustered during our brief conversation, but she wasn't hostile or aggressive. More like hot and bothered—though maybe that was just me bantering with her. Our interaction definitely did *good* things to my body.

I guess that means this man is the "bad cop."

He leans back in his chair, crossing his arms over his chest, matching my position. It's probably meant to be intimidating, but this guy is anything but. Cops don't scare me.

Not much does anymore after everything I've seen and done. After that much blood, that much violence. The violent nature of the human race. What madmen will do for power. I thought nothing *could* affect me anymore.

Until now...

The thought of those girls getting sold off to sick fucks who will use them for all sorts of depraved torture brings up a fear I've never experienced. That poor girl from Danilo's trunk back outside Manila. The way she shook uncontrollably. Her flinching away from my touch even when it was meant to help and comfort her. It got to me, more than I'd ever admit out loud to anyone.

"Cut the shit, Dixon, or whatever the fuck your name is. The only hang-up my partner and I have is that we're both desperate to keep the streets of New York clean, and I'm not referring to your fucking cigarette, but I think you already know that."

Of course, I do.

They wouldn't have been at B66 if they didn't already suspect something shady was going on there; though, what they actually know remains to be seen. My information about the ring came straight from the source—Danilo pointed me in this direction before I left him to die, and there isn't any question he was involved with it since Evangeline made it clear who sold her. Then my people here only confirmed what I already knew.

What these cops know is another story. I'm sure they have their own sources, people they may trust, but that doesn't mean *I* trust them or the information they might have.

Detective Grayson uncrosses his arms and leans forward, propping his forearms on top of the metal table. "I think you and I aren't all that different. Hell, I think we were both at B66 for the same reason."

I quirk an eyebrow. "You looking for a piece of ass, too?" I angle my head and tip my chin toward the door. "If that's the case, the next time, you might want to leave the arm candy at home."

There was no way he was going to get anywhere with Yankovich or Kosofik with a woman like his partner hanging all over him. The men they *want* at their auctions, buying their women, aren't going to show up with one as poised and beautiful as Detective Garin to make a fucking purchase.

He clenches his fists on the table and nods, the evidence of his annoyance and frustration building just like it did with his partner when she was in here.

I bet he doesn't even know I can tell he's biting the inside of his cheek.

"That's good advice, and I might buy that you were in there looking to get laid if you had paid an iota of attention to the bitches hanging on your arm, but you dismissed every one of them. I saw the exchange with Kosofik."

I raise an eyebrow at him again. "And?"

I'm not about to offer him the information he's so obviously fishing for. He doesn't know jack shit and has nothing on me to keep me here once they issue the "littering" charges that I can no doubt easily have dismissed after paying a simple fine.

"*And* you're wasting your fucking time. My father wrote the book on vigilante justice, man. He helped take down Yankovich's two brothers, but it took him years to do it. You're in over your head, and I don't have time to waste on you, so you have a choice to make. Either you stand the fuck down and drop whatever it is you're doing, or you tell me what you know, and we nail this guy to the cross before any other girls go missing or get hurt."

Stand the fuck down? Who the fuck does this guy think he is?

There's no way I'm letting him or his partner get in the

way of my mission. We may have a shared goal, but I made a promise to Cutter that I would make Danilo and everyone else responsible pay for what they did to Eva. Cutter came to me for a reason—he knows I won't stop until every single one of them who had a hand in it is six feet under.

Cops only fuck things up. Their hands are tied by rules and regulations. Worries about superiors and the law. Nothing will hold me back when the time comes, and I can't have them fucking things up with their ethical bullshit.

Detective Grayson pushes back his chair and stands. "I can't keep you here. But I can promise you that if you get in my way, there is an army of people who have no fucking problem making you disappear."

I snort and chuckle. "I'd like to see you fucking try."

This guy has no idea who he's dealing with. But if he interferes with my mission again, he's soon going to learn what I'm truly capable of.

He reaches into his jacket, pulls out a business card, and lays it on the table. "If you want this guy so badly, you're going to have to go through me." He nudges the card toward me. "Choose wisely, Dixon."

The door shuts behind him, and I reach out and grab the card, turning it slowly in my hand.

Choose wisely.

It sounds like something Dad would have said to me before I left the house on a Friday night as a teenager. But it's clear, it wasn't just a warning. It was a threat.

Detective Grayson may have more balls than I thought.

If he has even an inkling of who I am, threatening me takes on a whole different meaning. He's putting a target on his back, one I can easily hit...even with my fucking eyes closed.

Game on.

VIKTORIA

I lean back in my chair at my desk and release a heavy sigh into the phone, staring at the stain on the old, warped ceiling tiles I've watched slowly grow over the years. "Thanks, Danny. I appreciate you trying."

"Sorry I wasn't much help, Vik."

"Not your fault. I'll talk to you later." I end the call and toss my phone onto my desk a little too hard, sending it skittering across the marred wooden top.

Another dead end.

I don't know why I thought my friend over at the FBI might be able to find something I couldn't on Dixon, but I had to pursue every avenue available while I wait for Anya to work a miracle. Then again, if my suspicions about him are right, then maybe Danny *did* find something and just can't or won't tell me. Government secrecy and all that shit. Either way, my frustration has built enough to start a throbbing in my temples.

Maybe Hank is having more luck with him.

It might be our only hope of finding out what his interest is in Yankovich and B66.

I push away from my desk to check on the interrogation, but my ringing phone makes me turn back. Anya's name flashes across the screen.

Please have something...

Dropping back into my chair, I grab my phone and answer, "Hey, did you get anything?"

"You were right."

I grin and lean back, rubbing at my temple with my free hand. "I typically am, but what about this time?"

Anya snorts. "This guy you asked me to look into. I assume you don't want to know how I got the information."

Guilt churns the acid in my stomach. "I don't." I drop my hand and glance around the squad room to make sure no one is within earshot. "What did you find?"

"He joined the army at eighteen, right out of high school, and by the time he was twenty-two, he had been moved to the Combat Applications Group at Fort Bragg."

"Combat Applications Group? I don't get it."

"That's one of the code names for Delta Force."

"Shit. So, I was right?" It certainly explains a lot.

"Yeah, so it looks like he was a member of that unit for the last ten years or so. Retired about six months ago."

"He seems pretty young to retire."

The sound of her clicking on a keyboard floats through the line. "Looks like a medical discharge. I haven't been able to get into any more specific files because those things are locked up tighter than Fort Knox, but it's possible he was injured."

"He sure looked healthy and fit to me..." The way his hard muscles flexed under his T-shirt with every little move he made at the club and in the interrogation room definitely suggests a man in good shape.

But what the hell is a former Delta Force operative doing at B66 and getting tied up with Yankovich?

"Were you able to get anything else?"

Anya scoffs. "Do you have any idea how difficult *that* was to get? How about a thank you?"

I rub my eyes, trying to combat the growing migraine building behind them that seems to have migrated from my temples. "You're right. I'm sorry. Thank you. But did you get anything else? Anything I might be able to use? Maybe where he came to New York from or something that might be able to get him to realize he needs to talk?"

"Vik, this guy likely has resources you can't even imagine. Even retired, he has a skill set and training that make him more than capable of handling an interrogation from a New York City cop. And he likely has access to all sorts of different identifications, passports, and travel documents. Even if I tried to track him or where he's been, there is no way to know what name he was traveling under."

"Shit." I slam a palm against my desk and get a few looks from some people in the squad room. "I hadn't even thought about that."

"Who is this guy? Why are you so interested in him? Is he a suspect?"

Is he?

He was definitely acting suspicious at B66, and his little talk with Kosofik suggests he may be looking for the girls. But *why* is less clear. He doesn't strike me as a buyer, but that doesn't mean he isn't working for someone who is—perhaps picking up the "package" and delivering it to the sick fucker making the purchase.

"I can't tell you. Even if I wanted to. Which I don't." It's bad enough I dragged her into a case by asking her to look into him—through illegal means. I don't need her being any more involved in this. "So, please, don't ask again."

Anya sighs again, that same annoyed sound she's always used since childhood when she gets frustrated with me. "Vik, I'm worried about you. This isn't the kind of guy you want to tangle with."

"I can handle it. Handle *him*."

She snorts and chuckles. "I've heard that before."

I lean back in my chair and scan the squad room for anyone potentially eavesdropping. "I gotta go. But thanks for the info. This conversation never happened."

"Of course not. I'll keep digging, too, to see if I can find anything useful."

"Thanks."

I end the call and glance down the hallway toward the interrogation rooms. Still no sign of Hank, so he must be in there with Dixon. I flip on my computer screen to try to peek in on their conversation through the live feed, but the feed from the room I left our suspect in is black.

"What the hell?"

"Something wrong, Vik?" Pete peers over my shoulder at my screen.

I motion toward the blank screen. "I was trying to check on an interrogation, but the feed isn't showing anything."

Pete leans over and uses my mouse to click on another feed which instantly pops up, showing Detective Jacobson interrogating a suspect in a different room. "Looks like the other feeds are working. Maybe a malfunction on this one? Check the equipment."

Shit.

If Hank is having any success with Dixon, none of it will be on video or audio, which makes it ten times harder if we bring a case to trial in the future.

I push away from my desk, head back toward the interrogation rooms, and almost run directly into Hank as he comes around the corner. "Did you get anywhere with Dixon?"

Hank stops and rubs the back of his neck, glancing behind me toward the squad room. "The guy stonewalled me just like he did to you."

"Well, I just got confirmation from a source that he *is* former Delta Force. It doesn't surprise me that he's being difficult. But maybe I can use that information to get under his skin."

"I let him go, Vik."

"What? Why the hell did you do that?"

I wasn't anywhere near done with that man, and we still don't have any of the answers we need. Given a bit more time, I might have gotten something useful out of that handsome hardass man.

Hank motions back toward the room where I sat across from Dixon not so long ago. "Because the littering charge was bullshit, and you know it. He would've gotten it dismissed if the DA even decided to charge it. And that's not the type of guy you want pissed off at you."

Anger tightens my hands into fists at my sides. "I could've broken him, Hank. I could've found out what he was doing at B66. What his interest is in all of this."

"I don't think that guy breaks for anything, Vik. Except maybe a deer in the road. Just let it go, and we'll continue our investigation."

What the hell? Let it go?

If I weren't standing right here and hadn't heard it with my own ears, I wouldn't believe those words just came out of Hank's mouth. He's never been the type to let things go. Neither am I. It's why we've always worked so well as partners. We aren't willing to let things slip through the cracks.

But for some reason, he was willing to let Dixon go without getting any answers when we could have kept him at least a few hours longer and pushed him harder. The man never even asked for an attorney after we read him his rights and brought him in. We had free rein...at least for a little while longer. And Hank let him walk.

The blank footage flashes at the forefront of my mind. "I tried to watch the interrogation footage from when you were in with him, but it was blank. What happened?"

"Oh, yeah?" Hank glances behind him toward the room and rubs his neck again. "I couldn't get the equipment to work."

Bullshit.

In all the years we have worked together, I've never seen Hank so fidgety, averting his eyes, trying to brush off my concerns.

He's lying.

Whatever happened between Dixon and Hank in that room, he didn't want it recorded, and then he rushed our suspect out of here before I could question him again. That was intentional. There isn't any doubt in my mind.

The question is...why? Why would Hank help someone who is clearly involved in the shady shit happening at B66?

Hank's focus centers on something over my shoulder. "Shit. Sorry, Vik, Tiffany is here for some reason. I gotta go talk to her and make sure Brady is okay."

You have got to be fucking kidding me...

How convenient that his ex-wife appears right when I'm about to grill him for more answers about Dixon.

Hank is up to something, and whatever it is, it isn't good.

I never thought I'd say it, but I'm starting not to trust my own partner.

REAPER

I FLICK open my Zippo and light up a cigarette, but sucking in much-needed nicotine to my system doesn't help the growing frustration tensing my body. Detective Grayson let me go over twenty-four hours ago, and there still hasn't been any word from Kosofik. Plus, all I'm getting from my other sources in the city is dead end after dead end.

Whatever is happening with this auction, anyone who knows anything is staying tight-lipped. Which makes my mission nearly impossible. Typically, it's pretty easy to shake loose the information I need—sometimes with the use of force—but all I'm getting now is stonewalled no matter what I do.

It's possible my appearance at B66 sent out a warning signal to Yankovich's crew that made them lock down everything tightly and issue warnings against anyone who knew anything. But more likely, it was Detectives Grayson and Garin. They stood out like a damn lighthouse signaling "we don't belong here"—at least to me. And if any of Yankovich's men caught on, too, then they're sure to be in crisis mode.

I take a drag off the cigarette, close my eyes, and the image of the "menu" flashes against my lids, making me wince as if someone punched me straight in the gut.

The sounds of the city surround me out on the fire escape. Honking horns. Yelling. Laughter. With over twenty million people in the New York metropolitan area, finding those innocent women is going to be impossible without some help. Which means I need more boots on the ground, more people to help crack kneecaps and put the screws to anyone who might have any information about the auction or where I can find the girls.

And there are only two people I can trust to do that without a second thought. The men who have held my life in their hands while I have held theirs in mine. More like brothers than friends, they'll come without question and do whatever it takes. And when they learn about what's happening here and how my little favor for Cutter got me in this position, they'll show up armed and ready.

Yankovich and his crew are precisely the type of men we've spent years fighting against and taking out. The men who have caused us to lose other brothers and end up soaked in their blood. They're the people we've dedicated our lives to eliminating. So, they'll come. No question.

I drop my cigarette and grind it out with my boot on the metal stair below me as I dial Chaos. While it rings, I lean forward and rest my elbows on my knees, sucking in a breath of air filled with all the smells of those millions of people.

Chaos picks up on the second ring. "Yep."

"It's me. You busy?"

Something metal bangs in the background before the phone jostles and he returns. "I got a minute."

"I need you in New York. Going to text Mouth to see if he can come."

More jostling crackles through the line, then a heavy sigh I know better than to take personally. "I'm kind of in the middle of something. What's going on there?"

I run a hand through my hair and toss back my head to stare up at the night sky even though I can't see any stars here in the city. So different from so many places I've been, places with endless desert or jungle and no cities for hundreds of miles. "Cutter called and asked me to take care of an extermination in Manila."

Chaos chuckles low. "He told me about that last week when we talked. Sounds like it went well, though, so why do you sound so pissed?"

"That part of it did, but I learned we have a bigger vermin problem."

"Shit."

"Yeah." I fight back the memory of the girl I pulled from

that trunk and what I did to Danilo to get the information that led me here. There isn't any need to get into specifics over the phone. Chaos and Mouth both know I wouldn't call if it wasn't important and necessary. "It's bad."

"What are we looking at?"

"A whole lot of vodka-drinking rats."

"Shit. I'm not sure how long this will take me to clean up."

"Just get here as quickly as you can. Things are complicated. There's...a woman cop who stuck her nose where it doesn't belong."

Chaos bites back a laugh. "A woman, huh? Never known you to get bent out of shape over a skirt."

"Yeah, well, you'll see why. Let me know when you're on your way."

"Stay out of trouble 'til I get there."

I bark a laugh and end the call, then immediately pull up my messages and fire one off to Mouth.

> Vermin problem in New York.
>
> Need you here.

Almost immediately, the three little dots that let me know he's replying pop up.

> Give me a few days.

My chest tightens, and I rub at it with my free hand.

The girls might not have a few days.

Yankovich's auction could be happening right now, and I wouldn't have any fucking way of knowing. If Kosofik made me, he'll never send the message giving me the information, and the girls could be gone before I can even make a move.

All I can do is keep pounding the pavement and putting

the screws to my sources, hoping something pans out while I wait for Chaos and Mouth to get here to help.

I'm just one man in a city of millions. But when they get here, the three of us together will be a force to be reckoned with. The Russians have no idea what's coming for them, and we will succeed. As long as Detective Grayson and his beautiful partner, Detective Garin, stay out of our way.

Grayson and I may share the same goal but teaming up with him will be the last resort. If I can't dig up anything useful in the next day or two, I'll see what he's willing to share with me.

Until then, I'm ready to do whatever it takes to find those girls and get them home safely—no matter how much blood I have to spill.

4

REAPER

"Fucking shit." I end the call, toss my phone into the center console, and slam my fist against the steering wheel before pulling out into traffic to make my way to the meeting I absolutely thought I would never fucking arrange. "Motherfucking hell!"

I can't believe I just called the damn cop.

Bringing Detective Grayson in on this goes against all my training. It could interfere with what I'm going to have to do. Having the fucking cops tagging along or inserting themselves will limit my actions in a way I can't afford. But after almost two days of digging until my fingers practically bleed, I still haven't been able to find out where Yankovich holds the girls, and Kosofik hasn't contacted me on the burner phone with a time and location. Yet, the rumor mill is still spouting off talk about an auction happening—and soon.

That means either Kosofik isn't ever going to give me the info—because he saw through my act or maybe saw the cops grab me outside—or that it will happen so last-minute that I won't be able to get in there and free the girls before the place is swarming with even more security *plus* scumbags there to buy them like cattle.

It means I'm getting desperate—something that never happens.

Time is ticking away for those girls. That's the only reason I called Detective Grayson and asked to meet him. Even with Mouth and Chaos agreeing to come to NYC to help me, it won't mean anything if we can't get a location on the girls. Mouth, Chaos, and I know how to follow through on a tough mission, so if Grayson doesn't have what I need, then I may have to resort to more bloody means of obtaining the information. But I worry that will only alert the men behind this that I'm coming for them. They'll move the girls and go into hiding before I can do anything. That would only make things worse for the victims.

Such a clusterfuck.

Even taking out Yankovich won't end this. As much as I'd love to believe that whole "take the head off the snake" bullshit, he has men like Kosofik who will step right up into his role and keep this sinister train moving. In order to *really* end this, we need to take them *all* out. And we can't do that if we can't fucking find them.

Something Detective Grayson can hopefully help with...

I pull up to the meet location at Roll N Roaster and park beside the building, scanning the streets on either side of the corner restaurant. The smell of frying oil smacks me in the face through my open window, turning my stomach, but not as much as the idea of what's happening to those girls does.

Detective Grayson climbs from a truck a few spots over and walks past my vehicle and toward the rear of the restaurant, apparently expecting me to follow him around the back. This late, it shouldn't be easy to spot us together, which is good for both of us given the circumstances.

Still surveying the area, I climb from the truck and make my way after the cop. The crisp fall air would be a lot nicer if I could smell anything other than the food from this place and the dirt of the fucking city.

I turn the corner to find him standing next to the dumpsters and grease traps, hands shoved into his pockets.

Fucking great. I guess I just won't breathe during this meeting.

He nods at me as I approach, then quickly scans the parking lot and street. "Glad you made the right choice, Dixon."

I snort and shake my head. "I haven't made *any* choice yet, Grayson. Don't take my request for this meeting as a statement that we're now buddies or that I plan on working with you on anything."

A scowl turns down his lips, and he takes a step toward me. "Then what the hell did you call me for?"

I shove a hand through my hair and check the small strip of street visible behind Grayson for anyone who might be close enough to hear anything we're discussing. This topic of conversation certainly isn't anything we want to share with members of the public. The area appears clear aside from a group of teenagers walking down the sidewalk away from the restaurant.

Still, I take a step closer to him, so I can keep my voice down. "If what you said at the precinct is true and we're looking for the same thing, then we have a real problem. My sources around town and here on the East Coast tell me an important auction is happening soon. Like *real* soon. And I have been striking out in terms of finding a location where I might be able to intercept the *'lots'* before they're sold to the highest bidder."

"Fuck. An auction?" He shifts and glances over his shoulder before returning his attention to me. "We knew they were trafficking, but an auction wasn't even on our radar."

"They're very well organized, which means we don't have a lot of time to fuck around."

"It also means Michail has flipped the fucking script."

I narrow my gaze on him. "If you know anything that could help me find them, I need you to tell me now. My hands aren't tied the way yours are. I can do whatever needs to be done. Nothing is off the table."

He considers me for a moment and opens his mouth like he's about to respond when the roar of motorcycle engines fills the night air around us, rumbling deep in my chest the closer they come.

What the hell?

Four bikes roll up on the street behind Grayson, and my hand automatically moves toward my weapon at my hip.

Grayson scopes out the new arrivals and holds up a hand while sliding his other into his pocket. "Hold it. They're with me."

I narrow my eyes at him and keep my hand exactly where it is. This doesn't feel right, and there's no way I'm letting down my guard when he's springing fucking surprises. For all I know, this fucker is setting me up to get taken out by these assholes so it won't tarnish his badge.

He wouldn't be the first dirty law enforcement officer I've come across, and he sure as shit won't be the last. Though, I don't believe for a second that Detective Garin knows what he's up to. She's too straight of a shooter. A rule follower. No way she knows he's meeting with me or is tied to a fucking motorcycle club.

Hand on my gun, I quickly check my back to ensure no one is coming around the other side. A brief flash of movement gives me pause, but the sound of advancing heavy boots makes me whirl back toward him. "Want to tell me what fuck is going on?"

"Hear me out." He turns to face me while the four guys climb off their bikes, the lights from the restaurant making their Satan's Knights patches visible on their cuts, and amble toward us. "They can help."

Even though every fiber of my being is telling me to high-tail it back to my truck and out of here, the face of the girl I pulled from that trunk back in the Philippines flashes in my head. It's the only thing that keeps my feet cemented to the pavement.

Grayson motions toward the man at the front of the group of bikers. "This is Jack Parrish, the former president of the Satan's Knights."

Parrish gives me a dirty look and sneers. "Who the fuck are you?"

Like I'm going to tell this asshole anything.

I don't know what the fuck the cop is up to setting this meeting with these guys and not warning me, but I don't like it one fucking bit. These are the kind of situations that get you killed.

And these are the kind of men I don't offer anything to. "You can call me Reaper."

Grayson turns back to Parrish. "He's Delta Force. I brought you both here because I think the only way we're going to get this cunt is if we all work together."

Seems the detective knows more than I gave him credit for about my history. Someone must have been doing some digging since I was released.

Grayson or his pretty partner?

Parrish fixes a glare at Grayson.

The cop seems undeterred by the threat in the look. "You got the past, but Dixon's got the present. Come on, Jack, do you really think I'd tell you to come here if I didn't think this guy was legit? He checks out."

Grayson may have checked me out, and I had Preacher run him before I ever made that call to set up this meeting, but I don't know anything about these guys except they're criminals—for all I know, he brought them here because they're involved in this whole fucking thing with the girls in the first place.

I keep my hand on my weapon. No matter how friendly or non-threatening they may appear to be at the moment—and really, they're both—these are the kind of men who can turn on you in an instant. It's easy to recognize someone so much like me, and I see it in every single one of these fuckers.

Parrish clucks his tongue against the roof of his mouth and steps to the side, allowing me to get a good look at the three men behind him. "This is Cobra—"

Pop! Pop! Pop!

Gunfire erupting from the street behind me interrupts the introductions, and I reach for my weapon and dive for cover.

VIKTORIA

GODDAMMIT!

I wouldn't believe it if I weren't watching it unfold with my own eyes—Hank, Dixon, and the Satan's Knights... together. Conspiring. I didn't *want* to believe it. Yet, deep down, I *knew* Hank was up to something. This just confirms the uneasy feeling I've had for days since the minute he asked me to go to B66 and not start a formal investigation.

It was a red light flashing right in front of me, yet I

ignored it because I *trusted* Hank. Because we were talking about the potential of there being innocent women out there who needed our help. Women we *couldn't* help without more information and actionable evidence. Then I allowed myself to brush off the unease because of the way Dixon got under my skin. I blamed it on the fact that he got me off my game. But I was right to suspect Hank was hiding something and lying to me.

Trusting my gut has never led me astray before, and I should have trusted it and confronted him right away—the moment he stepped out of the interrogation room and told me he let Dixon walk.

Going to B66 unofficially should have been enough to make me question it. His releasing Dixon should have been another nail in the coffin. And couple that with what I discovered after, what Hank had *done* to cover his own tracks, it was clear Hank has been keeping some serious secrets.

There's no way the video *and* audio feeds to the interrogation room just happened to malfunction while he was in there with our suspect. Not when they had been working perfectly fine when I was in there with Dixon only hours before...and continued to work fine when I tested them *after*.

The system was tampered with—intentionally—by the one person I'm supposed to be able to trust with my life on a daily basis. Whatever went down between the two of them in that room, Hank didn't want me to know about it.

And now, he's lied to me *again* and snuck out of the precinct—apparently to meet with a bunch of criminals.

What the hell is he doing with the Satan's Knights? And why the fuck *is Dixon here with all of them?*

The information Anya finally came through with this morning about Dixon let me know I was spot-on with my suspicions. He has seen some serious shit as a member of one of the world's most elite special forces groups.

You don't just walk on to Delta Force. They only recruit the best of the best, the cream of the crop, the most talented operators in the armed forces, which means that man is more dangerous than just about anyone on the planet. And not just because of his sexy smirk and striking blue eyes.

He's lethal and coupled with a dirty cop and a criminal MC, this is looking really fucking bad. The code he lived by in Delta must have stopped existing once he was discharged. It's not unheard of, I guess, going "bad" after serving time overseas and doing the kinds of things he likely had to. Men are changed when they live that way, do those things, and some of them come back lacking the basic ability to humanize. It can make them do things completely out of character.

But that idea just doesn't sit well in my stomach. Even with all the evidence otherwise, something tells me Dixon isn't the type of guy who would get involved in something shady. He has a *code*. Maybe not the same one they swear to when they're active duty. But he has one. One he *believes*. One I can't see him breaking just to make some money off selling women.

A cop, a one-percenter motorcycle club, and a former Delta Force member walk into a bar...

It sounds like the start of a bad joke, and that's exactly what this is feeling like right now, watching it go down in front of me. If I could get closer, I might be able to overhear something that could shed some light on what's happening between these people who have no business being together. However, given where they're standing, I'm not sure I can without someone spotting me.

I need to try, though...

If I'm going to confront Hank about this, I need all the ammunition I can get. I need to know what they're up to, what they have planned. Because it may be worse than I even think. It isn't something I *want* to believe possible for a man I thought I knew almost as well as I know myself, but this could end our partnership. This may be something I need to go to IA about.

Shit. I hope not.

For better or for worse, Hank is my partner. He has my back, and I have his. That's why what he's been doing the last few days is so upsetting. Either it's so beyond what's right that he knows he could never tell me, or he doesn't trust me enough to fully fill me in. Both possibilities hurt more than I'd like to admit, twisting at my gut like I took a knife to it.

I need to know the truth. Here. Now.

Inching my way toward the group where they stand at the back of the restaurant, I stay low and against the building wall to try to maintain my cover. If they see me, I'll never get any answers. But I still can't hear what's being said and can only catch glimpses of them for a split second before I have to take cover again.

Desperate times call for desperate measures. I take a chance and dart from next to the wall to behind a large garbage can even closer to the group.

"You can call me Reaper." Dixon's deep voice reaches me, sending a shiver down my spine.

Reaper?

Hank's voice rises above the noise from the street. *"He's Delta Force. I brought you both here because I think the only way we're going to get this cunt is if we all work together. Come on, Jack, do you really think I'd tell you to come here if I didn't think this guy was legit? He checks out."*

All work together?

Hank wants to bring the Satan's Knights and Dixon in on taking down Yankovich. That explains the meeting, but it doesn't explain *why*. We could do this through proper channels, stake out the locations we *know* are connected to Yankovich until we see something we can use. We could pull in his guys until someone talks. We could do our *jobs* the way we're supposed to—legally and by the book. We could bring them down and ensure their faces are splashed across every paper in the country and they're exposed for what they're doing.

Before I can hear anything else that might answer my question, the sharp crack of gunfire shatters the night and a sharp slice of pain in my right side knocks me to the ground.

Agony blurs my vision as I try to search the street at the end of the alley for a shooter, and I struggle to reach for my gun at my side. My arm doesn't want to cooperate, but when I finally get it down there, my hand comes away covered in warm, sticky blood, and I collapse back against the concrete.

Shit.

The gunfire continues, seemingly coming from both the street and where everyone was meeting around the side of the building. The restaurant's position on the corner means they're exposed to attack on more than one side.

And I'm exposed here. The rounds ping off the concrete around me and the metal trash can behind me relentlessly while I lie on the damn ground, bleeding like a stuck pig. Which means no one is coming to help me. They can't. There isn't any way anyone could get here without getting hit, even if they wanted to and tried.

Given I wasn't invited to this little chat, my guess is no one will bother. If I'm going to get out of here alive, I need to do it myself.

Get the fuck up, Vik. Move!

I try to push myself up onto my elbow, but a searing burn sends me back down roughly, and I press my hand against the seeping wound at my side. Blood oozes out around my fingers, and darkness starts to encroach on the edges of my vision.

Stay awake. Don't close your eyes.

Gunfire grows closer.

Muffled yells.

A deep voice near my ear.

Someone over me.

"Fuck!"

Strong arms lifting me.

Squealing tires.

And then, nothing.

5

VIKTORIA

Strong arms close around me. The world spins. Something tightens around me. A warm palm presses hard against my side. Pain surges through my body, threatening to make me retch. The squeal of tires fills my ears. Voices bounce around my head. Honking horns. Broken conversations. Distorted words fade in and out with a darkness that threatens to completely drag me under.

A soft touch brushes the hair away from my face. All I want to do is lean into it…escape from the agony…

"She goes in and out of consciousness. The bleeding looks like it might be subsiding."

Dixon?

His words come from directly above me, his chest rumbling against me.

"And you?"

Hank?

"I'm fine." Annoyance and anger taint Dixon's clipped

response. "I'd be better if we got to wherever it is we're going, though."

Where are we going? Where are they taking me?

The movement stops, and I shift and groan at the pain that shoots through my side. But then I'm being lifted, jostled, though the arms I'm wrapped in try to cushion each movement.

Darkness reaches out to me again...

Angry voices...

Yelling...

"Can you people do this shit later?" Dixon issues a low growl of warning to someone. "She's starting to come to again."

My back hits something hard, and without the warm arms cradling me, the agony I was already in redoubles. I squeeze my eyes shut and cry out through clenched teeth, wrapping my arms around myself to try to hold my body together when it feels like it's shredding apart.

"Do you have anything to give her for the pain?" Hank snarls his question to whoever we're with.

"This ain't a fucking triage unit, man," someone hisses. "We don't got morphine; we got whiskey."

"Give it to her." Dixon's clipped order hits my ears.

"You heard the man." Hank's agreement has me turning toward his voice.

"Hank?" My voice comes out soft, full of all the agony I'm feeling.

"Right here, Vik." He pulls my hand into his and squeezes gently. The familiar touch and just knowing he's here relaxes me slightly...

Until someone unwraps something from around my waist and probes at the wound at my side.

Fuck!

I flinch and grit my teeth to keep from crying out or

smacking away whoever it is, but I force open my eyes to meet Hank's. "I was shot."

"Yeah, you were, but you're going to be okay. Celeste is a nurse, and she's going to patch you right up."

"The good news is it looks like the bullet went straight through." The woman, who must be Celeste, lifts her focus from my side to meet my gaze and nods to a bottle in the hands of Jack Parrish, the notorious former president of the Satan's Knights. "Now might be a good time to give her some of that."

Shit. That doesn't bode well for me.

Hank slips his hand under my head and lifts it gently, bringing the bottle to my lips.

"What's this?" I probably shouldn't be blindly trusting what one of the Satan's Knights is giving me, especially someone with such a bad rep.

Hank smirks. "Whiskey. It'll help with the pain while she closes the wound."

I hesitate for a second, scanning the space around me through blurry vision. Lying shot and vulnerable in a room full of criminals isn't where I imagined I would find myself today. Every fiber of my being wants to run—to head to the precinct or the hospital to let the proper people know what's happened. But Celeste does something at my side that shatters any resistance I have, and I howl and wrap my hand around Hank's wrist to guzzle from the bottle.

"Whoa!" A redhead standing to the side of us raises her eyebrows. "I want to party with her one day."

After finally chugging what I hope is enough to slightly numb the pain, I push away Hank's hand and the bottle and settle my head back against the table. The movement coupled with the booze is enough to send my stomach rolling, and I wipe my mouth with my hand and take in all the people surrounding us while Celeste does something to the wound that sets my entire body on fire. The strange, mixed crowd brings back the memory of the conversation I overheard before the shooting started.

I glare at Hank while Celeste works on my side. "You want to tell me what the hell is going on? Why are you working with the Satan's Knights?" I glance over my shoulder to Jack Parrish. "No offense or anything. I appreciate the fake doctor performing surgery on me, and the whiskey is pretty potent, too."

"Only the best for our brothers and sisters in blue." Jack winks at me. "You should visit us when you're not shot and bleeding all over the place. We're a good time."

Un-fucking-likely.

I narrow my eyes on Dixon, who has remained suspiciously quiet, standing against the wall, taking in everything and everyone around him with a shrewd gaze, his bloody hand pressed against his upper arm. "And what's he doing here?"

"You're welcome." Dixon practically growls the words at me.

Scoffing, I raise an eyebrow at him. "Excuse me?"

What would I have to thank him for? Getting me shot?

"Maybe she should take another shot," the redhead suggests.

"Look, Vik…" Hank sets his hand on my arm. "I'll explain everything, but right now, you need to calm down. Here, take another swig."

Trying to get me drunk so I won't ask questions. No fucking way.

"Not until you start talking, Hank."

Something *major* is going on here. Major enough that my own partner has blatantly lied to my face—repeatedly. Major enough that he's willing to risk his badge by meeting with the Satan's Knights and one of our suspects he released. Major enough that we got *shot at* and rather than report it and go to the hospital, he brought us wherever the fuck we are. He better have a damn fucking good explanation.

Hank sighs and runs a hand back through his hair. "Fine, Parrish is the one who gave me the intel on Yankovich. It wasn't an anonymous tip."

Before he can get another word out, the tray of supplies crashes to the floor, causing everyone to turn and stare at the redhead. She watches Hank with wide eyes. "I'm sorry, but did you say Yankovich?"

Two of the Satan's Knights guys rush to her side, and one pulls her into his arms and forces her to tear her shocked gaze away from Hank. Mumbled words reach me from across the room. He's telling her about Michail and the operation we suspect he's running.

"So Yankovich shot her?" the girl stammers, glancing back at me.

"We don't know who shot her, Ally," Parrish interjects. "But we're going to find out, and we're going to take down Michail just like we took out his brothers."

"Hold on." I try to push myself up but pain and Celeste's strong hand on my chest keep me down. "You're going to *take him out?*" I turn to Hank. "We're cops, Hank. We ride on the side of the law. What the hell are you doing?"

How can he think this is okay? That I can just let him help Parrish murder people?

Hank stares at me for a moment, the wheels churning in his head. "Vik, we took an oath to serve and protect the people in our community, but you know that sometimes even the good cops—hell, even the best—need help from the outside. We're not going to catch this guy on our own. We don't have the department backing us, and even if we did, it wouldn't change things." He pauses and turns to the blonde.

"She's living proof the system is broken. If you don't believe me, ask her yourself."

"What the fuck are you doing?" Cobra—according to the name on his cut—snaps. "Ally's been through enough shit. She ain't reliving it to ease your conscience or your partner's."

"Jagger," Ally calls, placing a hand on his arm. It must be his real name—confusing as fuck when you're in massive amounts of pain. "It's okay."

"No, it's not." The other member who comforted her earlier, Deuce, shakes his head. "Cobra is right. This ends here, or you can patch your girl up yourself."

"Both of you need to quit it," Ally shouts. "I can decide what I want to share and what I don't. That's the beauty of being rescued. I get to be my own person again, and you two need to stop hovering." She turns and looks at Hank for a moment, then focuses on me. "Your partner is right; the system failed me. I was fourteen years old walking from the neighborhood pizzeria when a white van pulled up to the curb. A man rolled down his window, and he appeared distraught. He said he had a daughter my age and that she was missing. At the time, all I could think of was my dad. If something had happened to me, I wouldn't want him roaming the streets, begging people to help him find me, so I got inside his car. The man was Vladimir Yankovich. It didn't take long for me to realize my mistake. As soon as he put the full-face helmet over my head, blocking out my cries for help, I knew I was done. I stopped praying for someone to rescue me and started wishing my death would be quick and painless."

"Fucking hell," Cobra hisses.

"I was forced to give a blow job before I ever even had my first kiss. I was used and abused, and then I was sold to a man just as vile as Yankovich, and that guy turned me into a junkie. He kept me a prisoner for years. My parents…"

"Ally, baby, come on." Cobra reaches out to her, but she brushes off his touch. "You don't have to do this."

She shakes her head and keeps her focus on me. "My parents never gave up on me. They gave all their trust and all their faith to the detectives in charge of my case, but they never found me. They never even named Yankovich as my captor. When my case went cold, my dad hired a bounty hunter." Her gaze cuts to Hank. "Your dad."

Hank shoves his hands into his pockets and nods.

Keeping her eyes locked with mine, she sighs and continues. "He is the one who put two and two together and realized Yankovich had taken me, but by then, it was too late. I was already in Rush's possession, and Yankovich had killed my parents." She pauses and lifts her gaze to Jack, the corners of her mouth curling as she gives him a sad smile. "If it weren't for Rick Grayson and the Satan's Knights, I'd be dead." She turns back to me. "I don't know what the hell is going on, but if this Michail guy is anything like his brothers, you need all the help you can get because if even one innocent girl slips through the cracks, that's on you. Will you be able to live with that weighing on your conscience for the rest of your life?"

Well, shit.

As if the physical pain of being shot and then poked and prodded by Celeste isn't bad enough, Ally's story certainly makes this a lot more complicated and painful.

In this job, there's a line I don't want to cross, one that would bring me into that gray area that leads even further into the blackness that turns so many good cops bad. I've always prided myself on staying on the right side.

But here, there isn't one. Not when innocent women are being sold like cattle and abused in ways I can't fathom.

Hank is right that we'll be restricted by the badges we wear, by the very law we fight so hard to uphold and enforce.

That truth weighs heavily on my chest as I let Celeste finish patching me up, alternating between clenching my eyes shut to keep from throwing up and locking gazes with Ally, Hank, and Dixon.

When my "doctor" finishes and finally steps back, I inhale a long, deep breath and blow it out before looking at my partner again. "I'll keep this quiet from the department. For *now*. But only because I know they'd pull us both off duty and probably fire you for working with the MC."

Hank nods his agreement. "Probably." He glances around the room at the members of the Satan's Knights and still-quiet Dixon. "But working together, I think we can all get this fucker and ensure no more innocent women suffer like Ally did."

I sure as hell hope so because if we fail, we won't be able to explain away what's already happened. We'll lose our badges, our jobs, and we could end up in prison ourselves if we have to do what I think we will. Squeezing my eyes closed, I try to force all the worst-case scenario possibilities to the back of my head. If I dwell on them too much, I might do something I will regret, something that could get those girls killed or worse.

Releasing a deep breath, I open my eyes and meet Hank's concerned gaze. "I'm in. I'll call in sick for a few days at work so no one suspects anything, but for now, I just want to go home, Hank. Drive me?"

Hank raises an eyebrow. "Home? No, you should stay here a while. Let Celeste watch you and make sure you're okay."

I shake my head and grit my teeth as I try to sit up and fail miserably. "I'll be fine. Just get me to my apartment. Give me a few days to recover while you all figure out the specifics of our plan."

He looks ready to argue with me, and when I look to where Dixon has been leaning against the wall, the spot is empty. I scan the rest of the room, but he isn't anywhere in sight.

Where the hell did he go?

It doesn't matter. I'm too exhausted to worry about where that brooding man ran off to at this moment. Even if the memory of his touch, the way he held me in the car on the way here, the soft brush of his fingers across my skin still warm me more than the whiskey ever could.

REAPER

THE TOTAL DARKNESS surrounding me might make some people uncomfortable, but I've embraced the dark for so long, it's more of a home than anywhere else in this world. I've never stayed anywhere long enough to make it feel like one, and darkness can be found anywhere, everywhere, really. It makes it easy to come back to it whenever I want.

But this is different. Because of *her*. Even in the pitch black, her light flowery scent permeates the air, invading my lungs with every breath. The feel of her limp in my arms weighs heavily on my chest. Her whimpers of pain ring in my ears.

I absently flip the top of my lighter, the rhythmic motion so familiar, it takes me back to another place. Another time. When I was doing the same thing in a dark room, surrounded by my brothers in arms. Before the whole thing went to shit.

Flashes of light and booms that shook the entire building

still rattle through my body even now, and I clamp my hand around the lighter so hard that it hurts. But I barely realize I'm doing it until a key slides into the lock, breaking through the memory and the absolute silence of the room I had been enjoying prior to the past rearing its ugly head.

The deadbolt clicks, the sound echoing through the room seemingly as loud as the explosion that shook that night, and the door pushes in slowly, allowing in a sliver of bright fluorescent light from the hallway. It cuts across the hardwood floor, but before it can reach me and reveal my presence, Viktoria closes the door behind her and sags back against it with a grimace I can see even in the dark.

She sucks in several deep, painful-sounding breaths mixed with groans before pushing off the door and staggering forward. Her legs wobble, and she reaches out for a side table but misses, her hand finding nothing but air. She starts to fall forward, but I rise from the chair I've been sitting in for the last half an hour and grab her before she can hit the hard floor and injure herself further.

"What the fuck?" Viktoria jerks her head back to see who caught her and tries to yank herself from my grasp, but I tighten my hold on her upper arms.

Gritting my teeth, I bite back the torrent of curses that want to flow out at her jerking movements that are the last thing she should be doing after being shot and patched up haphazardly at an apartment above a fucking bar. "Stop fighting me, Viktoria, or you're going to end up face-first on the damn floor."

The blood loss she suffered tonight will be affecting her for a while, making her weak and unstable on her feet. She should have stayed at the clubhouse so Celeste could watch her for at least another day or two and ensure she rebuilt her strength before coming home alone. But Viktoria is far too stubborn to admit when she's weak and needs help. This woman would rather go down in flames than acknowledge a little smoke.

She freezes, her eyes finally adjusting to the darkness enough for them to focus up on me. Her bow lips twist into a scowl, and she tries to pull free from my hold again, though with far less fight in her—either because she doesn't have the energy anymore or because she knows I'm not a real threat. "Reaper? What the hell are you doing in my apartment?"

"Apparently, keeping you from face-planting."

Her lips press together in a hard line, her body tensing. "I could have *killed* you!"

I snort and shake my head, which only adds fuel to the fire dancing in her gaze. "Unfuckinglikely since you can barely stand up."

As if to prove me wrong, she tries to yank her arms from my hands, but she only manages to hurt herself—the exertion and twisting movement likely pulling at her stitches. She grits her teeth and winces, then takes a long, slow deep breath, trying to regain her composure.

"Get out." She lifts her head and scans the apartment behind me. "How the hell did you get in here, anyway? Or know where I live, for that matter?"

Too fucking easily.

After I slipped away from everyone at the club, I called Preacher to find Viktoria's address. In less than two minutes, I had what I needed and was in a cab on the way here to ensure I cleared the place before she came home.

And getting in was a piece of fucking cake.

The fire escape leading right up to the window of her bedroom couldn't be a greater invitation to someone with ill intent, and the ancient lock on the old wooden frame didn't last twenty seconds, allowing me to easily climb right into her most intimate space.

If I had been here for any other reason, she'd be dead or worse by now.

"You need better security."

"*You* need to leave." Her voice holds firm conviction but underlying it, a tiny waver brought on by her weak physical state, belies her deep fears, the ones she doesn't want to acknowledge. The fact that if someone did break in right now, she wouldn't be in *any* shape to defend herself against an attack.

I drop my head until my eyes align with her unfocused green ones, ensuring she sees the conviction there. "Not a chance in fucking hell, sweetheart."

She glares at me, her lips twisting again. "Do I need to call Hank to have him physically remove you?"

Like he could.

"Hank would agree with my being here to watch over you —I'm fucking confident of that. And I'm not leaving anytime soon because I'm worried about you, and not just because this place is a shithole with zero security that anyone could basically just walk right into if they wanted to hurt you."

"Why would anyone want to hurt me?" Her gaze darts down to where my hands grip her upper arms, probably a little too hard.

Point taken.

I relax my hold on her slightly, waiting to release her until I'm confident her legs aren't going to give out from under her. She wobbles slightly, squeezing her eyes together, and reaches out for me to stabilize herself. Her hands press against my chest, and a rush of heat spreads out through my body from the point of contact like a fire has been lit over my heart.

Shit.

"I'm-I'm fine, Reaper." She drops her head and sucks in a painful breath. "Go."

Damn stubborn woman.

"You're not fine, Viktoria. Not by a longshot."

This woman clearly has no clue what's going on. She's a good, observant cop, who saw through me at B66 in an instant, yet she somehow managed to miss what was completely obvious to me.

"Do you really not know you were the target in that shooting tonight?"

Her head snaps up, her green eyes wide. "What? No. That doesn't make any sense. Why would anyone shoot at me?"

"That's a good fucking question we need to answer. It could just be someone you arrested who got out trying to get a little payback, or it could be something more." Like maybe the Russians made her at the club the other night and want her gone before she can interfere with what they're planning. "Until we figure it out, I'm not leaving you alone."

A low, tiny growl rumbles in her chest, anger flashing in her gaze despite the fact that she's about ready to pass out. "I don't need you protecting me, *Reaper*." She tosses my nickname at me like she's firing a bullet. "I can take care of myself."

The words barely leave her lips before she winces and reaches down to press her right hand against her side. When she pulls it away, blood covers her palm, and a dark-red stain spreads across the fabric of her shirt.

Shit. Now she's really done it.

No doubt Viktoria is a strong woman who is good at her job, but if I hadn't jumped in to shield her during the shooting and then drag her out of there, she'd be dead. And if I weren't holding her up right now, she'd likely be spending the night on the floor, bleeding out.

"Like hell, you can." I scoop her up before she can object, ignoring the twinge of pain in my arm where I was hit and the little gasp of surprise slipping from her lips. "You're dead on your feet, and you're bleeding again."

She opens her mouth to object but then winces and wraps her arms around my neck. Either she's given up on arguing with me, or her body is doing it for her. It doesn't matter to me, as long as she stops fighting. The more she does, the worse it will be for her.

I easily carry her to the bedroom, the dead weight of her body in my arms enough to drag up memories I'd rather keep buried. Ones I managed to push away when she returned home.

This isn't that.

No matter how many times I try to remind myself that that's true, it doesn't stop the anxiety that tightens my chest. I'm no longer in a war zone, but the truth is, I just traded one type of war for another. All I've ever been is a soldier. The only skills I possess gave me the name Reaper, and now, I have no choice but to use them to do what's right—no matter how difficult. I just never expected a complication like this beautiful, feisty woman getting in my way.

I lower her to the bed and pull away the blood-stained shirt from her side, pushing it up around her breasts. Several of the stitches Celeste put in have come out. Not because Celeste did a bad job but because Viktoria is too damn stubborn. She should've stayed. They could have protected her and watched over her while she healed and was well enough to actually come back here.

But it seems she has to fight everyone on everything. And something tells me she's going to fight me the whole way, too.

It's a good thing I thrive in war.

6

REAPER

"Take off your shirt." My words come out gruffer than I had intended, but the frustration building with every argument that comes from her mouth is starting to bubble to the surface of my usually cool demeanor.

I've always prided myself on my ability to remain unaffected in *any* situation—it's one of the things that made me so good at my job. But this woman…

Christ, this woman…

She brings out something I didn't even know existed. I've always protected my brothers in combat, and doing Cutter this favor means putting myself in the line of fire for the innocent women being trafficked. But Viktoria is something else.

This *need* to decimate anyone who would even *think* of laying a hand on her seems to want to overpower my reason in this situation, and I'm fighting a losing battle against giving in to my base needs right now.

Her eyes widen at my command, and her mouth drops open with a surprised gasp. "What?"

Ignoring her indignation, I push off the bed and duck into the small bathroom to gather what I need to clean her up. I'd rather not have to drag her back to Celeste, and I managed to patch up my own arm when I got here with what little Vik had in her cabinets. God knows I've handled a lot worse injuries than ours—more times than I care to count.

"I *said* take off your shirt."

"Uh, no. I'm fine—"

I duck my head back into the bedroom and point at her. "No, you're not *fine*. Take off that *bloody* shirt so I can get you cleaned up, or I'll come take it off for you."

She scowls at me from where she sits propped up against the headboard. "You wouldn't!"

A low growl slips between my clenched teeth before I can bite it back. "Fucking try me, Vik."

Her hands fisted at her sides, she looks ready to argue again, but I narrow my eyes at her, giving her my best "you better not even think about it" look, silencing her immediately. Maybe she'll stop fighting me for five fucking seconds.

Or maybe Hell will freeze over.

Something tells me that would be more likely than Detective Garin just relaxing and letting me take care of her without opening that pretty mouth of hers with backtalk.

Returning from the bathroom, I almost step on the bloody shirt in a pile on the floor—probably tossed there with spite—and let my gaze travel up to her exposed skin and a lacy black bra that barely contains her breasts.

Fuck.

My cock twitches against my jeans even though this is clearly not the time nor the place for it to be making an appearance. But it's been a long fucking time since he came out to play, and Viktoria is a strikingly beautiful woman, even in her current state.

I'd have to be blind not to notice the way the light from the bedside lamp shimmers on her almost flawless pale skin —marred only by the nasty bleeding wound at her side—and the way her breasts swell and rise over the cups of that delicate bra with each huffy breath she takes.

Too bad she's pissed and injured because I can think of a few ways to help relieve some of the pain and stress from this day—for both of us.

She doesn't make eye contact with me, just stares out the window into the night with anger turning down her lips as I sit on the edge of the bed next to her and set down the supplies I found. It isn't ideal, but I'm used to making do with what's on hand in shittier places than this.

I tuck a towel under her side, grab the hydrogen peroxide, and pour it over the reopened wound.

She jerks her head toward me, gritting her teeth. "What the hell?"

Her natural response is to try to pull away from me, but I press a firm hand against her hip, holding her in place. "We need to make sure it stays clean before I close you back up."

Those green orbs dip down to the gauze I have pressed against her side, blood already seeping through it. "Shit." She shoves at my shoulder and tries to push my hand out of the way to take the gauze. "I can take care of this. Go."

"Like hell, you can. If I hadn't been here, you'd be out there napping in blood on the fucking floor. If not worse."

She tries to shift to sit up more, but I press my hand against her exposed chest, forcing her back. My fingers linger against the warm, soft skin there a little too long, but for some reason, I can't drag them away, and she doesn't make me.

Our eyes lock. Something sizzles between us. Something

other than the anger and annoyance that has seemed to be constant since we first met outside B66. Something far more dangerous than either of those things.

I swallow thickly. "Let's get one thing straight, Vik. I'm not going anywhere until I'm sure you're safe."

"Safe?" She searches my face for something, but she isn't going to find it. It died a long time ago.

I pull my hand away from her chest and the other from her wound and examine the damage. "I'm going to have to re-close this."

She glances down. "With what?"

I hold up a needle and thread I found in her linen closet next to the bathroom.

Her eyes widen. "You can't use that."

"Watch me. I've used worse to close wounds a hell of a lot nastier than this." And the same setup worked just fine on my arm an hour ago when I arrived. Luckily, she seems to have a lot of sewing supplies.

She huffs and narrows her eyes on where I work to tie off the thread. "And they probably died from infection."

I grit my teeth and finalize the knots. "It wasn't from infection. And they didn't all die."

Just most of them.

Thinking about the number of friends I've lost over my last fifteen years in the service would only further heat my blood and drag me to that painful abyss at the bottom of a bottle I refuse to go back to.

She rests her hand over mine, and I glance up to find her soft gaze filled with compassion. "I'm sorry. I didn't mean—"

"It's fine." I cut her off before she can try to do any more digging into my psyche. Nothing good ever comes from that. I grab the prescription bottle I brought from the bathroom. "Found this in the medicine cabinet. You should take one."

It looks like she wants to say something else. Her lips

open and close again before she accepts the bottle from me. "Vicodin. Left over from when I had my wisdom teeth pulled last year."

"This isn't going to feel very good, and you're going to be in a lot of pain the next couple of days. You'll want some of those. Though, be careful."

"You sound like you're talking from experience."

I freeze and glance up at her, trying my best not to give anything away. This woman has already gotten under my skin; the last thing I need is her delving any deeper into my soul or my weaknesses. "You could say that."

Her gaze drops to the bottle in her hand, and she removes the lid and pops one into her mouth, swallowing it with no problem, even without water. An uncomfortable silence stretches between us as she rolls the bottle in her palm. "I-I know you were Delta Force. I can only imagine what you must have seen and—"

"And that's exactly why you should listen to me when I tell you you're in danger."

She shakes her head. "I don't understand why you think that."

I nudge her to get her to lie back, then position the needle to make the first stitch. She nods that she's ready. Maybe if I keep her talking, the pain won't be so bad for her.

"Vik, those guys didn't start shooting until you showed up. You and I were the only two hit for a reason—because *you* were what they were aiming at and I covered you and got in the damn way."

I shove the needle into her skin and through to the other side of the wound.

She grinds her teeth together and sucks in a breath. "I suppose you want me to thank you for that."

Fucking smartass.

I make another stitch in silence, letting her comment

hang in the air between us. Another one should close her back up and prevent any more bleeding. And I'd be lying if I said I wasn't enjoying the little jab of pain she's feeling with each stitch more than I probably should.

Some might call me a sadist, but it's not that I get off on causing her pain. I just know that it often helps me focus and see things I might not when my mind is clouded with other thoughts. Focusing on the pain means ignoring the other shit in my head. If that's true for Vik, too, she might be able to see what I'm trying to protect her from.

Finally done, I lean back and set everything on the nightstand before I examine my work. Not half-bad considering the circumstances and the less-than-cooperative patient.

Viktoria finally relaxes slightly and releases a long, slow breath. She keeps her eyes closed and her head dropped back against the headboard. It gives me an opportunity I don't need to stare at her perfect breasts in that damn tiny piece of lace that barely covers her nipples. As it is, the almost sheer fabric shows them reacting to the slight chill in the fall air, letting them poke out toward me.

My fingers itch to reach out and twist them as much as my mouth waters, thinking about sucking on them and lapping at them with my tongue.

Fucking hell...Not again.

To keep myself from touching her, I adjust my swelling cock and rest my hand on the mattress near her leg to nudge her. "So, about that thank you."

VIKTORIA

IS HE FOR REAL?

I open my eyes and watch him where he sits just to my

right on the edge of my mattress. One of his dark eyebrows rises, waiting for some sort of response from me while amusement dances in eyes that seem to see all the way into my soul, to that part of me that wants to throw caution to the wind and do something that feels good even though it's so, so bad, for once.

Heat creeps up my leg where it touches his wrist and makes its way straight to my core. Like fire licking across my skin, it creeps over my exposed breasts, up my neck, and to my cheeks the longer he looks at me with that damn smirk.

No. No. No. No! This is not happening, Vik.

It doesn't matter how handsome he is or how strong the desire to climb him like a fucking tree might be. I can*not* be attracted to this man. He's a killer. An assassin trained by the damn government. He literally came to town to *murder* people. Bad people—but still...*murder!*

He's the kind of person I've fought hard to get away from, leads the kind of life I never wanted. I can't trust him to do what's right. He's always going to do whatever he wants, whatever he can justify in his own head, even if it's wrong and may hurt someone else.

Mainly me.

As soon as we take down this trafficking ring, he'll be gone again, off gallivanting around the world, doing whatever the hell it is he's doing now that he's retired. I don't even want to think about it—about what a man with his skillset does with them once his actions are no longer sanctioned by Uncle Sam.

The word *mercenary* keeps coming to mind, but even that feels wrong. With a name like Reaper, my guess is he's too good for a word like that.

"I'm not going to thank you, *Reaper*."

His other eyebrow wings up to join its counterpart. "Oh, yeah? Why not? That's kinda rude."

I scowl at him and cross my arms over my exposed chest, suddenly *very* aware of how nearly naked I am on top. "Because I wouldn't have gotten shot at in the first place if it weren't for you showing up in town and stirring shit up."

He barks out a laugh and shifts closer to me until his side presses against my thigh. "How do you figure that?"

"Hank and I had things under control at B66. We would have found out what we needed to through *legal* means and had everyone involved locked up within a few weeks."

"A few weeks?" He snorts and shakes his head. "Sorry, sweetheart, but that wasn't going to happen. If I could make you two as cops that easily, so could any one of Yankovich's guys. You two were never going to get anything or get anywhere close to wherever they're holding those girls. I'm the only chance they have."

I shake my head and try to ignore the desire to lean closer to him and the warmth he radiates. "I don't believe that. Even if they did make us, we would have used our sources and resources to find the girls. We don't have to resort to killing people."

"Sometimes that's what it takes to get the job done, Vik. I only do what I do because the authorities are either useless or have their hands tied."

Anger flares through my blood, and I lean forward with a slight wince. Despite the drugs taking the edge off the pain and making the world a little foggy around me, I'm still feeling what happened today. "So, I'm useless? We should just let vigilantes run around killing whoever they deem to be worthy of a death sentence?"

Reaper moves even closer, his shoulder almost touching my breast, and he reaches up to brush a strand of my hair away from my face.

The memory of the same soft touch after I was shot and

was bouncing in and out of consciousness sends a shudder of anticipation through my body.

"You're far from useless, Vik. But your hands are tied by the badge you wear, and some people deserve death for what they do. It's as simple as that."

Is it really?

It's not something I ever considered at length before. Growing up, all I knew was I wanted a different life and was determined to make it for myself, one free of the crime and drugs and sketchy behavior that ran so rampant in my neighborhood. I was able to break away from it, but Anya wasn't so lucky, or more accurately, she just didn't care enough to do it. She was content to do dirty work—at least digitally— for anyone willing to pay her. And while I appreciate her entrepreneurial spirit and ability to use her skills to make a living, it's certainly not what I would have chosen for her.

But at least she isn't doing what *he* does. She isn't out there pulling the trigger and being the judge, jury, and executioner.

"I can't let you just go around killing people, Reaper. I took an oath. It's my job to uphold the law."

He raises a dark eyebrow at me. "Yet, you had no problem breaking it by lying about the shooting and hiding your injury from the department?"

Guilt climbs like acid up my throat, and I have to swallow past it to respond. He called me out, brought to the surface the things I've been trying to justify in my own head. "That's different."

Reaper snorts and crosses his arms over his chest. "So, you pick and choose when you get high and mighty?"

"We're talking about *murder*, Reaper. You want to go in there, guns blazing, and kill anyone who gets in your way. We should be letting the police know where the girls are and where the auction is happening if we find out so they can come in and make arrests. Those men should have their day in court. They should go to prison and face justice."

His jaw clenches, anger blazing in his blue eyes, darkening them in a way that sends another shiver through me, though this one is different than before because I see the *real* danger staring right back at me. "I *am* justice. They're getting exactly what they deserve, and I'll do whatever it takes to make sure those innocent women are free and can't ever get hurt by bastards like Yankovich and his men again."

Before I can open my mouth to argue with him, he leans in, pressing his hands onto the bed on either side of my hips, making me sink back even farther into the mattress.

His warm breath flutters over my face, the heat of his body radiating into mine while anger rolls off him in waves. "I can't stop, Vik, and I won't let anything or *anyone* get in my way."

If Reaper thinks I'm going to back down on this, he couldn't be more wrong. But with him this close, it's hard to think of anything but grabbing him and pulling him even tighter against me, despite my injury. My body doesn't seem to care how weak I might be or that my inhibitions might be suppressed slightly by the damn Vicodin. Every part of me still yearns for his touch, his mouth, his hands...

Something about this man drives me wild—in the best and the worst ways. But the truth of who and what he is prevents me from acting on what I may want. While we share the goal of having these trafficking scumbags pay, we're on opposite sides when it comes to how to handle this fight.

I swallow thickly and try to stop myself from shaking before I respond to him. "Is that a threat?"

Reaper shifts even closer, his lips a mere hairsbreadth from mine. "No, sweetheart, that's a promise. One I intend to keep."

He brushes his mouth against mine, slow and soft at first, but when I release a tiny gasp and open my lips for him, he growls low and captures my face in his palms, angling my head up and allowing him to sweep his tongue inside and against mine.

I should push him away. I should say *no* and remind him I'm hurt and we're arguing and on opposite sides of the law, but I don't want to. Because Reaper has come unleashed. That control he exhibited in the interrogation room is gone, and all that passion we've been arguing with seems to now be focused on this kiss. The one that's stolen my breath completely.

When he finally pulls away, he shifts back and off the bed. "But I'm also going to keep you safe. Whatever it takes."

Whatever it takes to keep me safe.

The words should be comforting, knowing someone has my back and is protecting me. But somehow, it feels like even more of a threat.

7

VIKTORIA

Somehow, I managed to fall asleep after what went down with Reaper the other night. It was likely the mix of physical exhaustion, adrenaline dump, and the narcotics he made me take that finally did me in.

The last thing I remember is Reaper's hard eyes watching me like a hawk from where he sat in the little chair in my bedroom while I fought against heavy eyelids.

And when I woke yesterday morning...he was gone.

No sign of him. Not a single drop of blood. All the supplies and evidence of his patch-up job on himself and me vanished as if he were never even here in the first place.

It shouldn't surprise me. Not given his background. He's trained to disappear into the shadows without leaving a trace of his presence. But there was one thing he couldn't erase... the feel of his lips pressed against mine.

I reach up and brush my fingers over the exact place he kissed me. Even in pain and with the meds starting to take effect, that moment lives in vivid memory, almost like I can still taste him. Even after more than a day and half since he was here, his scent still invades my every breath.

Shit.

This man is turning into a major complication—personally and professionally. What I told him before he disappeared was true. I won't let him run off to slaughter Yankovich and his men without definitive proof they're doing what we think they are, and if it is at all possible to save the women caught up in the trafficking ring while still sending the men through the proper court process, I'll leap on that before I accept vigilante justice at the hands of Reaper, the MC, or anyone else.

And if I'm going to get in any deeper with this plan, I need to know exactly what and who I'm working with. Hopefully, Anya can provide me with some of that when we meet for lunch today, more than the very basics she was able to uncover initially.

I'll just need to be careful meeting her to ensure no one else sees me out and about, not after calling in and taking a few days off. It definitely raised some eyebrows with the boss, but better he not expect me for a couple days and be annoyed at my absence than be searching for me.

The way I'm still feeling today, even after resting and staying in bed all day yesterday, it would be difficult to hide that something is very wrong. Pain still slices at my side every time I move, and while Celeste and Reaper did an excellent job patching me up, the packing around the wound still bears the evidence of my injury—pale red seeping through in spots.

Shit.

I do my best to clean it up again, wincing and gritting my teeth when I lift my arm. My phone buzzes on the counter, and I glance down at the screen and the text from Hank I've been expecting after he checked in with me around the same time yesterday.

You doing okay today?

I'm good. See you in a few days. Keep me updated on anything urgent.

Will do. Call me if you need me.

I won't. At least, I wouldn't admit it to Hank—or anyone else, for that matter—if I did need help.

It was bad enough I had to rely on the MC to patch me up when I was shot and then Dixon to save me from ending up on my ass when I came home that night, so I don't have any plans to end up in that vulnerable position again.

Reaper seems to think I was the target of the shooting, but I'm far from convinced. It's more likely I was just in the wrong place at the right time and Dixon or someone from the MC was the real target. Getting caught in the crossfire makes more sense than someone targeting me out of the blue.

But still, I'll watch my back as best I can before I rely on someone else to do it again. While I can understand why Hank did what he did, he's broken a trust I'm not sure can ever be repaired.

I'll see this case through to ensure those girls don't suffer. But when the smoke clears, I may have to reevaluate where I stand with my partner.

There isn't any time to dwell on it now, though. I only have half an hour until I have to meet Anya. Which means I need to get moving even though I want to crawl back into bed and binge watch something sappy on Webflix.

I don't have that luxury today. Not if I want answers about the man who let himself into my apartment the other night and who left an indelible mark on my memory with that damn kiss.

My body heats just thinking about how close he was. How his large, calloused hands felt against my soft skin. The way his lips pressed into mine with a force that left the message undeniable—he doesn't intend to go down without a fight, and he won't disappear just because I don't want or need his protection.

That means even though he was gone when I woke this morning, he won't be for long. I need to get to my meeting with Anya before Reaper does something to interfere.

I slide on my jacket, wincing at the pull on my side, slip out the door, and lock it behind me. The hallway is silent this time of day—everyone is either gone at work or engrossed in their soap operas.

The elevator ride down seems to take forever, the ancient, creaky car shifting in a way that always makes my stomach lurch into my throat even after five years of living in this damn building. They'll never fix it, no matter how many times I complain, so it's just one of those little quirks of living in an old building in New York I have to live with.

So is the polluted air that hits me the moment I step out onto the busy sidewalk. Exhaust from traffic. Smoke from pedestrians' cigarettes and vapes. It makes me pause and cough, and I have to grab my side and clench my jaw to keep from crying out at the pain and drawing unnecessary attention to myself.

After a few deep breaths, I'm finally able to right myself and step out into the flow of people walking back and forth, always in a hurry.

The restaurant is only a few blocks down. Close enough that I was sure I could make it no matter how shitty I might feel. Each step seems like more and more work, though. As if my shoes are weighted and my body is failing.

Dammit.

Being weak like this pisses me the fuck off. I became a cop so I could be in control and always be able to protect myself. But now, it feels like every set of eyes is on me, every car is slowing to stare, every person on the street might be a source of danger.

I'm letting Reaper get into my head now. That can't happen.

I shake off the paranoia creeping into the edges of my mind. I'm almost there. The restaurant is only half a block up on the opposite side of the street. Even from here, Anya's crimson bob is visible at one of the tables on the front patio.

The stoplight changes to red, and I pause, waiting for the sign to change. A tall man in a black peacoat steps up next to me. His dark gaze darts over to me briefly, and a shiver rolls through my spine.

The light changes, and I let him cross the street in front of me to the opposite corner where he turns right when I need to cross another street to the left to finally reach the restaurant. With her back to me, Anya hasn't seen me coming yet, but I spot the waitress chatting with her as I wait for yet another light change.

Almost there.

It will feel so good to sit down for a bit. I never could have anticipated how wiped out I'd be after such a short walk.

The light changes to green, and I step off the curb. A hand closes over my mouth and a strong arm wraps around my shoulders, dragging me back and toward a white van to the right before I can even react.

My instincts kick in immediately, and I reach back to try to eye-gouge my attacker, but somehow, he manages to shift his head away and wrangle me toward the open rear sliding door.

Don't let him get you into the van. Don't let him get you into the van.

But it's too late.

Strong arms maneuver me into the vehicle, and a black hood is shoved over my head as I kick out and swing wildly with my fists. My foot connects with something—someone—and a muttered curse fills the space, but before I can act again, my ankles and wrists are bound by skilled hands.

The van shakes with my captor's movements, and tires squeal as we move away from the curb at a breakneck pace.

Shit. So much for watching my back.

REAPER

WATCHING Viktoria make her way down the sidewalk, caught up in the throngs of people on their way to and from lunches and appointments, makes my stomach turn. Combined with my knee that won't stop bouncing wildly under the steering wheel, I am feeling decidedly unsteady compared to the other hundreds of times I've surveilled someone.

She couldn't have just stayed in bed another few days?

At least in her apartment, I know she's safe—relatively speaking. Nailing her bedroom window shut might have been overkill, but it was the only way to know for sure she wouldn't become the victim of someone who figured out how easy it was to get in, just as I had. She was so messed up when she got home that night, she hadn't even noticed I had done it, though I imagine the first time she goes to open it, there will be a few curses thrown my way.

But it's only a temporary fix for the greater problem—which is figuring out who wants her dead.

I need more time. Time to get fucking help here, time to look into why she would be the target for someone, time to locate the girls before this damn auction happens. It's too much to handle alone while simultaneously trying to make sure she doesn't do something stupid.

Like leave her fucking apartment when she was shot less than forty-eight hours ago.

This fucking woman...

My cock twitches, and I shake my head to try to clear the memory of how soft and sweet her lips were, even with all the pent-up tension and animosity between us. She kissed me like she wanted it. More, actually. Like she *needed it.*

And I had to force myself to move off her bed and settle in the chair across the room, or I would've done something that would've been very bad for both of us.

Even sitting across the room from her while she slept, keeping watch over her like some dark guardian angel, I couldn't quell the thoughts plaguing me.

Thoughts that were *not at all* angelic.

Far fucking from it.

They haven't dissipated in the day and a half since I left, when I have barely taken my eyes off her fucking front door except to get a new vehicle while I was sure she was asleep. I kept hoping she wouldn't leave. I fucking *prayed* to a God I don't believe in that she would stay put, give herself some time to recuperate.

But that woman is too damn stubborn to do that. She has to walk out onto the street like somebody didn't just try to kill her. Stumble out is more like it, actually. Her slow, deliberate steps prove she's not ready to be up and out, even if her life weren't in danger.

Yet, there she fucking is.

She makes it to the corner across from me and pauses at a red light, pressing her left hand into her side. I flinch and grit my teeth, practically experiencing the pain she must be in for myself.

Because I know what that feels like. Far too well. It's no fucking fun, no matter how tough you are or pretend to be. Pain is pain, and while it's absolutely possible to push through it when you need to, it hits you eventually.

Which means whatever got her up and out must be pretty fucking important. At least, it better be. Because now she's exposed to anyone who might want her hurt or worse.

Scanning every person on the street and passing cars, all I can see are potential threats. The problem is, half the fucking people visible look suspicious. People with shifty, angry eyes. People with hands in their pockets. People with phones to their ears who could be calling for a car to snatch her right off the street. The entire situation makes my shoulders tense.

A sketchy-looking guy with dark hair wearing a black peacoat steps up next to Viktoria. She glances over at him, her eyes drifting up his much taller frame. Her entire body tenses, and she takes a half-step away from him, closer to the curb.

He makes her nervous. That can't be good.

Vik is smart enough to sense danger. To know it when she sees it. She sure as hell did with me. And if she's getting a bad vibe off him, that likely means there's a reason—one we both should be wary of.

The light changes, and Vik allows the man to walk in front of her.

Smart move, Vik. Keep him in your line of sight. Don't let anyone you don't trust get your back.

She moves slowly to ensure she doesn't catch up to him, and once he hits my side of the street, the man turns to the right without looking back at her while something catches her eye to the left.

What has your attention, Vik?

Whatever it is, she turns her back to the man in order to cross the opposite corner. The glance he casts over his shoulder at her might not be caught by anyone else. It may not appear suspicious to anyone not watching for it. Nor would the twitch of his hand near his waist warrant concern for most people. But I can see it for exactly what it is.

"Fuck." I slip on the black balaclava sitting on my lap and jump from the van before I can talk myself out of it.

If I don't intervene now, Vik is likely to end up in the back of a dark SUV speeding away to her doom.

Her continued distraction with whatever is across the street allows me to slide up behind and clamp my hand over her mouth, silencing any cry for help while keeping a watch on the man behind us. Before he can react, I drag her toward the van, throw open the side door, and climb in with her.

True to form, Vik kicks and lashes out with her hands and feet as I slide the door shut behind us. Despite her physical protests and the scream she releases stinging my ears the moment I move my hand from her mouth, I manage to get the black fabric bag over her head and secure her wrists and ankles with zip ties that should hold her long enough to get where we're going. But then her feet connect with a very sensitive area of my body.

"*Fuck!*" I mutter a litany of other curses as I climb into the driver seat and take a quick survey of the area around us to ensure nobody saw what just went down.

But it's exactly what I anticipated. No one on the street saw it—too preoccupied with where they're going, or who they're talking to on their phones—or if they did, they don't give a shit. And the man who was watching her darted away, either disinterested or to alert whoever employed him that the target was just taken off the street by someone else.

I throw the van into drive and peel away from the curb, my cock and balls aching bad enough to make me want to throw up the cup of coffee that was my breakfast this morning.

Fucking woman...

Tearing off the mask and tossing it onto the seat beside me helps me suck in a few deep lungfuls of air, which somewhat quells the nausea. But Vik kicking and thrashing around as much as she can in the back tightens my chest again.

That woman can fight all she wants. She won't get out of those bindings, which is good for me because she'd probably try to gouge out my eyes and tear off what's left of my balls.

But there will be hell to pay when I get to where we're going.

8

VIKTORIA

L eft.
Right.
Sharp left.
Another left.

The familiar rumble of a train crossing the raised track above us.

This van the dickhead shoved me into speeds up, shifting me across the floor of the back.

Traffic whizzes by, then we slow.

Construction equipment.

Blaring horns and weaving that makes my stomach turn.

We've hit the BQE.

The sounds of the expressway overwhelm the air in the van for several minutes while I hold my breath, doing my damnedest to listen to every single noise.

A deeper form of darkness overtakes us for what feels like forever while the sound of the traffic around us changes. I tilt my head to angle my ear toward the wall of the van.

The Battery Tunnel. It has to be.

Even with this black cloth bag pulled over my head, preventing me from seeing anything about where we're going, that doesn't mean I can't gather as much information as possible with my other senses.

It might be essential to my escape when given the opportunity. I need to keep track of where we're heading. And as soon as the asshole who grabbed me tries to get me out of this piece-of-shit van, I'm going to make my move.

My body may be weak, but my will hasn't been affected by being shot by some soulless asshole. I will fight with whatever strength I have left to ensure this fucker doesn't get me somewhere I can't escape from. I've already let him move me from the location where he grabbed me, and I can't let it go further than that.

Who the hell does he think he is, anyway? Snatching me off the street in broad daylight. I'm a cop, for fuck's sake.

The entire NYPD is going to be looking for me. Maybe not until tomorrow since Hank already did his daily check-in with me today, but as soon as he can't get a hold of me in the morning, he's going to send every fucking officer in the Tri-State area on a manhunt.

And that creepy guy who crossed the street in front of me has to be connected. I don't get that *vibe* from just anyone. Only when I'm around someone who truly represents a threat.

He was probably sitting, watching my apartment this entire time, waiting for me to be stupid enough to step out onto the street where he could snatch me. And I played right into his hands. I got distracted when I saw Anya waiting for me at the restaurant and gave him my back even though I knew he was up to no good and was bad news.

It was fucking stupid and careless—something I'm going to blame on the pain, the meds, and lack of good sleep the last few days. But I'm not going to make any more stupid mistakes, not when it could cost me my life.

The fact that whoever grabbed me didn't kill me right away means they need me *for* something or need something *from* me. That might buy me a little time to find a means of getting the fuck out of these bindings and away from that asshole.

Honking horns and the bustling sounds of Manhattan fill the van.

Stop.

Go.

Stop.

Go.

Lunchtime traffic can be a real killer, yet he headed straight into it.

Where the fuck is he taking me?

We inch through the streets, moving slowly while I wait for anything, like a noise or a smell, that will tell me exactly where we are. Manhattan for sure, but precisely where is less clear.

Then, the sound of the road under us changes again. Definitely a bridge.

Maybe the GW?

It definitely smells like the Hudson.

So, he's taking me to Jersey?

We come down off what I assume was the bridge, and the sound of the road beneath us changes again. He makes a hard right turn a little too fast, slamming me against the side of the van, sending a jolt of pain through my side. Grimacing, I try to push myself up, but it proves futile with my wrists bound.

After another couple of minutes pass, the van slows, and the sound of metal grating against metal fills the air around me—almost like an industrial garage door opening.

Shit.

If he pulls the van inside somewhere, that eliminates any possibility of someone seeing me being dragged from the vehicle and coming to my rescue. But that's okay.

I'll fucking rescue myself.

This fucker is going to have to try to grab me, and even though my ankles are bound together, I still know how to aim for where I can do the most damage—his nuts.

If I connected with them earlier like I think I did, a second strike could do untold damage. And I'm more than ready to battle.

The van jerks to a stop, and I slide against the driver seat with an *umph.* If they're trying to keep me alive, this guy might want to drive a little bit more carefully. After being shot, the last thing I need is to be jostled around violently by a shitty driver.

A muffled grunt reaches my ears before the driver's side door opens and then slams closed, rocking the whole van.

I turn my head to place my ear toward the door.

No talking.

No sounds of people moving around.

Dead silence. So quiet, I can hear my own heart beating in my ears.

Wherever he brought me, we're alone.

Is that a good thing or a bad thing?

Probably a little bit of both. On the one hand, that means it will be a lot easier to take him out, but it also means his focus is likely one hundred percent on me. That could make my escape harder.

But there isn't any time to contemplate the situation further. The door slides open in front of me, and I tense, preparing myself for what I'm going to have to do if I want any chance of surviving this.

Watch out, fucker. Here I come.

REAPER

EVERY STEP I take around this van on my way to open the sliding door sends a zing of sizzling pain through my balls that's strong enough to make me fight back the need to wretch—again. And here I thought I had finally regained my faculties while making the drive from Vik's place in Brooklyn out to the safehouse in Jersey.

Vik got me good when she kicked out after I got her bound. If it weren't so agonizing, I might be able to admit how proud of her I am for fighting tooth and nail despite the fact that she's probably still hurting so badly from being shot.

Instead, I pause for a moment, my fingers curled in the handle of the door, and suck in a deep breath to prepare myself. She's going to come out kicking and screaming. There isn't a fucking doubt in my mind about that. But I don't want her to hurt herself trying to get away from me. That would defeat the entire purpose of this endeavor.

Rescue her only to hurt her more. That would be my fucking luck.

Patching her up once was more than enough for me. The memory of her bleeding in my arms has blended with other bloody ones to haunt even my waking hours. I don't need to go through that again, especially with her.

I tug open the door and barely have enough time to dodge to the left to avoid her bound feet flying out at me with all the force she can muster in her position on the floor.

Fucking knew it!

Pride wells in my chest as I wrap my arms around her thighs, and when she swings out to hit me with her hands fisted together, wrists bound in front of her, I swing her up over my shoulder like a sack of potatoes. I've carried men twice her size through IED-filled deserts dodging bullets. This, I can handle.

She releases a weak little squeal of protest, and I grit my teeth to bite back the need to apologize. That probably hurt, but it's far better than letting her do worse to herself.

"Knock it off." I smack the side of her thigh to emphasize my point.

She freezes instantly, shifting to twist her head toward the sound of my voice. "Dixon?"

Shit.

I hadn't intended for her to know I was the one who snatched her yet. Not until she had some time for the adrenaline to wear off a little bit so she could think more clearly. It was the only chance I had at getting her to see this situation without a red veil of anger coloring her view of it.

Well, she can speculate all she wants until I'm good and ready to reveal myself. Which isn't now. I stalk across the garage and into the freight elevator on the far side.

"Dixon, if that's you, I swear to God, I'm going to fucking kill you!"

Her shapely hips attempt to buck up, but she can barely budge with my arm wrapped firmly around her. Her hands connect with my lower back, but she doesn't have the angle to actually hurt me.

Thanks for the nice massage, sweetheart.

Biting back a snort of laughter, I reach up and jerk down the metal door, securing us inside the elevator cab before jabbing my thumb into the button for the second floor where the converted loft living spaces are.

Old machinery cranks to life, groaning in protest. The high-pitched whine of the motor and grinding of gears fills the air, and she shifts on my shoulder violently, still trying to get the leverage she needs to inflict any damage on my back or push herself up from dangling upside down.

"Dixon, you better let me the fuck down right this moment."

I don't bother to hide my snort of laughter and tighten my grip around her thighs, making her struggling even more fruitless. The elevator car jerks to a stop, and I raise the cage and carry her, kicking and hitting, across the room to where one of the two bedrooms sits.

She isn't going to like this, but I'm doing it for her own good. The windowless room is only temporary digs until she's willing to acknowledge how much fucking danger she's really in and I can trust her not to do something stupid like try to leave.

If that ever happens...

Locating who shot at her while also tracking down where the girls are being held has proven beyond frustrating, and I can only hope the trajectory of this mission changes quickly.

Stopping in front of the bed, I give her legs another squeeze. "Stop fucking fighting, or you're going to hurt yourself."

I lean over and lower her onto the mattress, releasing her to bounce slightly across the surface toward the wall it's pushed against.

"I swear to God, I *am* going to kill you, Dixon."

She can sure try.

It's not like she'd be the first to try. Or even the hundredth. None of them succeeded, so I doubt the feisty, beautiful, and infuriating Detective Garin will have any better luck.

I reach out and tug at the top of the black fabric bag on her head, yanking it free and sending her dark hair out around her in a staticky, disheveled halo. Viktoria is anything *but* an angel, though. The fire that blazes in her green eyes might as well be the flames of Hell.

Only she thinks *I'm* the Devil.

She keeps her wrath-filled gaze on me while I slip my knife from my boot and cut the ties at her ankles and wrists, then step back before she can use her new-found freedom to her advantage.

Vik is going to have to face the reality that no matter how she might feel about me, I saved her damn life. She owes me a thank you—*another* one. But I'm going to give her some time to simmer down before I get into it with her.

I don't trust myself in here with her otherwise.

"Take some time to cool off. We'll talk later."

"You *kidnap* me and now you're leaving me in here?" She makes an attempt to leap off the bed, but I throw up a hand to stop her.

Thankfully, she complies; otherwise, I'm not sure where the fuck this would lead.

"It's for your own good. You'll thank me later. And stop calling me Dixon. It's Reaper."

9

VIKTORIA

Pale morning sunlight filters through the tiny crack under the door, the only real slice of freedom or the world that I can see.

If it's morning, that means he's had me locked up here for at least eighteen hours—maybe far more. Without a damn way out. I had planned to stay awake and jump him to attempt an escape when he opened the door again, but I must have dozed off because the plate with a sandwich and chips was sitting on the small nightstand beside the bed the next time I opened my eyes.

That bastard snuck in here, and I didn't even wake up.

I'd be a lot angrier with myself if I didn't know how stealthy and well-trained he is or how badly my body needed the rest. It's not like trying to attack Reaper to get out of here would have worked, anyway. He would have made sure of that—all those skills focused on keeping me locked up instead of against our common enemy.

And other than getting up to use the small bathroom attached to the room, I haven't moved off this bed, the exhaustion of fighting against my "attacker" making me so tired, it felt like I had taken a step back in my recovery rather than one forward.

All because of fucking Dixon...Reaper...whatever the hell I'm supposed to call him.

First, he terrified me by breaking into my apartment. Then, he patched me up and kissed me until I could barely breathe. And now, he's kidnapped me and thrown me in this room like he somehow owns me.

Fucking jerkface.

A shadow blocks the light, the knob turns, and Reaper pushes open the door and steps inside the room, closing it behind him with a finality that sends a chill down my spine at the same time it brings a heated fury raging through my blood.

He stops a few steps back from the bed, arms crossed over his chest in his signature stance. "Are you ready to have a calm, rational conversation about this, or do you need a little more time to cool off?"

Calm, rational conversation?

"Are you fucking serious right now? You *kidnapped* me!"

He points a finger at me, his eyebrows raised. "Hey, I did it to save your ass."

"That doesn't make it any less illegal, asshole."

"Now, that's just splitting hairs. Would you rather I had let that creep on the street nab you and then wait around for a ransom call or to find your body in the Hudson?"

I scowl at him even though it doesn't seem to impede anything he does.

He watches me with icy, hard eyes. "You could say thank you. It would be a lot easier than arguing with me."

Leaning back against the wall the small bed is pushed against, I fist my hands so tightly at my sides that my nails dig painfully into my palms. Flashes of the man in the peacoat and the unease that crept over me take over my mind.

I had assumed he was the one who nabbed me, and while, in reality, it was Reaper, it could just as easily have been that man...or anyone else, for that matter. "You can't know he was going to grab me."

Reaper barks out a laugh and shakes his head. "Yes, I can. After you passed out the other night, do you know what I did?"

Heat spreads up my neck and over my face at the memory of the kiss. The way his lips moved fluidly against mine. His warm palms cupping my cheeks. That smug smile tilting his lips when he told me he wouldn't quit.

I shift uncomfortably on the bed under his assessment—the way his eyes bore into me like he can see I'm reliving that moment and the way my body is reacting to that. "I know you stayed for a while."

He nods slowly. "And you were so out of it that you didn't even notice that I nailed your goddamn window shut."

"You what?"

His nostrils flare, his jaw clenching. "Vik, it was so easy to get into your place, a child could have fucking done it. So, after I made sure no one else was getting in, I secured a new vehicle, came back, and sat and watched your place for the next day and a half."

"They have a term for that, you know..." I raise an eyebrow at him. "Stalker."

He snorts and shakes his head again, that cocky grin turning up the corner of his lips. "I was thinking *hero*."

Scoffing, I roll my eyes. "You would."

Annoyance tightens his shoulders, the muscles bunching like he's trying desperately to contain his desire to lash out at me. "You want to know what I saw during those almost two days, Vik?"

"A lot of angry New Yorkers?"

"Well, yeah, that, but I also saw a dark SUV sitting across from your place for hours on end. Then a new vehicle would show up and they'd switch places. Almost like they were doing shifts. You want to know what that was?"

I scowl and give him my best glower. "I'm not an idiot, Reaper. I'm a damn cop. It was obviously surveillance."

"Right. Probably the same fuckers who shot at you. Probably connected to the guy in the black coat who was going to nab you off the street before I did." He inhales a deep breath like he's trying to steady his nerves; though, what he has to be nervous about remains elusive. "He was watching you from the second you stepped onto the sidewalk, Vik. He only went the opposite direction once you crossed the street to let you get in front of him. He had turned his attention back to you as soon as you got distracted by whatever you saw across the street."

Anya.

"My sister...I was supposed to meet her for lunch. She's going to be looking for me."

He reaches into his back pocket, pulls out my cell phone, and jiggles it back and forth in his hand. "Oh, I've already had a lovely chat with your sister."

"You *what*?"

"I saw the multiple text messages from her wondering where you were after you didn't show up for lunch, so I texted her back, pretended to be you, and told her you were hung up with something at work." He raises a dark eyebrow. "Interestingly enough, she asked if it was about what she got you the information on. Me...I'm assuming?"

Shit.

He shrugs nonchalantly. "I told her it was nothing to worry about and I would be in touch with her in a few days. She told you to be careful."

Dammit.

Sometimes, we'll go weeks without talking to each other, so she won't suspect anything not hearing from me for a while, especially if he told her I was working on something. It's not unusual for me to go deep into a case, shut out the entire world for a while.

But she isn't the only one in my life.

"What about Hank? He's going to be looking for me. So is the precinct."

Reaper grins. "Hank, I can handle." He crosses the room and holds out my phone to me. "The department...you're going to."

"Like hell I am."

He squats down to face level with me, his eyes hard and determined as he holds up the phone and shakes it in front of me. "You're going to call them and tell them that you're sicker than you thought and that you're going to take two weeks off since you have so much built-up vacation to ensure that you are one hundred percent before you come back."

"Fuck you, Reaper. No way. You're not keeping me locked up here for two weeks."

"Didn't say I was. Just until we get this sorted out. But I want to make sure I bought us enough time, just in case." He reaches out and wraps his free hand around my wrist, turns up my palm, and sets the phone in it. "Make the call."

Where his palm connects with my skin practically sizzles with electricity that travels up my arm, over my chest, and straight down between my legs.

What would those calloused palms and fingertips feel like in other places?

I lick my lips and glance at his involuntarily.

"Viktoria…"

Crap.

I let my gaze meet his again.

"Make. The. Call. I can't be spending my time ensuring your safety and do what I need to do to locate the girls and get *them* to safety. I can't be constantly worrying about someone dragging you off the street or breaking your fucking windowpane to get in. I can't be wondering if you're collapsed and bleeding on the damn floor of your apartment."

"Shit, Reaper." I plaster on a saccharine sweet and fake smile. "It almost sounds like you care."

Silence hangs between us for a second, his hand never moving from around my wrist. I meant it as a joke. A jab at the fact that he's so stony and impossible. But he seems to have taken it literally, and it appears to be making him very uneasy. He squeezes my wrist gently, then swallows thickly and shakes his head.

"Shit. I do, Vik. That's the fucking problem." He releases me, pushes to his feet, and points to the phone. "Make the call."

I scowl at him but dial the number for the precinct despite my anger and reluctance and confusion over what just happened between us. While I may not agree with his tactics, he has a point. If what he says is true and people have been watching me, waiting for an opportunity to strike, it's quite possible that man on the street today was one of them and that they're connected to the shooting.

And I can't only think about my own anger and animosity toward the situation—and the man who put me in it—right now. Not when there are potentially dozens of innocent girls somewhere in the city who need the help that only someone like Reaper can provide.

It would be selfish of me not to do this.

The man I need to talk to answers on the third ring. "Captain Miller."

"Hey, it's Vik. I'm going to need two weeks off…"

REAPER

VIK ENDS the call with her boss and jabs her finger into the phone with so much aggression, I'm surprised the screen doesn't crack. I step forward and hold out my hand for the phone.

Her jaw drops incredulously, her green eyes darkening with her anger. "Seriously?"

I raise an eyebrow. "You think I'm going to let you keep your phone? How dumb do I look?"

"Dumb enough to think that you could keep me locked up here and that I would just comply."

Like I ever fucking thought it would be easy.

With a sigh, I snatch the phone out of her hand with a little too much force. "We have to figure out who wants you dead and why. The faster we can do that, the sooner I can let you go." I slip the phone back into my pocket. "Did you recognize the guy in the black coat?"

Vik closes her eyes for a second, likely running through the events of yesterday in her head. "No." She opens her eyes and shakes her head. "I didn't. But that doesn't mean anything. I've arrested a lot of shitheads, any number of whom could want revenge."

"Anyone in particular with a vendetta against you? Someone whose sentence may have just been completed and they got released? Someone you sent upriver who has an angry family?"

She shakes her head again and pulls up her knees against her chest with a little wince. "Not that I can think of off the top of my head."

"Which makes me think this is connected to B66."

Her brown furrows. "What makes you say that?"

I pace the small room, running through what we do know in my head. "Because someone had enough manpower and resources to have a car sitting on you for two days in shifts. Who else would spend that kind of money and time?"

"True. And while the guy wasn't familiar, that doesn't mean he isn't one of Yankovich's minions. His network is huge and spreads out across New York and the surrounding boroughs, so he's bound to have hundreds if not thousands of foot soldiers I've never seen. Which is probably why they used him specifically. So that I wouldn't suspect anything."

"But what I don't get is...why would the Russians want you dead?"

Her eyes widen slightly. "Shit..."

That doesn't sound good at all.

"What is it?"

She chews on her bottom lip, her eyes meeting mine with a mild hint of panic in their depths. "Nothing. Never mind. Just being paranoid."

"No, you're not, Vik. I have to know *everything* if we want to figure out *anything*."

With a long sigh, she drops her head and runs her hands back through her long, dark hair, squeezing her eyes closed. "I guess it's possible I was recognized at B66."

I freeze mid-step and turn to fully face her. "What the fuck do you mean *recognized*?"

Vik slowly lifts her head and opens her eyes. "I grew up with those people, Reaper. Not Yankovich specifically but his type. And everyone knew his family. I'm from Brighton Beach. I became a cop so that I wouldn't get sucked into that life the way so many of the girls who were working at the club have been. But a lot of my friends didn't get out and ended up in places like that. People I haven't seen or talked to in over a decade, maybe more. I guess it's possible…"

Fuck.

I sigh, rubbing at the tension building in the back of my neck. "It's possible someone you grew up with still recognized you when you were there with Hank."

She shrugs slightly. "It hadn't occurred to me when he asked me to go. I thought I was far enough removed—physically as well as in time—that no one would identify me, or it wouldn't cause a problem if they did."

"But if someone *did* recognize you, and they knew you became a cop…then they would also know you weren't at B66 to enjoy the nightlife and were likely snooping around and that you might cause a problem for whatever is about to go down."

Her lip disappears under her teeth again, and she nods. "It's a definite possibility."

"Shit." I shove my hands through my hair. "That would explain them coming after you specifically. Maybe they didn't make Hank out as a cop and just thought he was a boyfriend or someone you dragged along as cover. It makes sense *you'd* be the target. The one they for *sure* knew was a threat to their business."

"Oh, God…" She sucks in a breath and presses her hand to her side. "It's my fault I got shot." Her panic-filled gaze meets mine. "That *you* got shot."

Oh, hell…

This looks like the beginnings of a full-on panic attack.

I drop onto the bed next to her and push her hair back from her face, tangling my fingers in the soft tresses I have no right to be touching. "Don't do that, Vik. I'm fine. Just another scar to add to dozens of other ones. And you will be fine soon enough."

She doesn't respond to my words, just watches me with unshed tears shimmering in her eyes.

"Do you see now why you need to stay here? Why you need to stay hidden?"

"No." Indignation flashes in her gaze. "I caused this. I need to be out there helping you, doing what I can. I need to get my feet on the pavement to help locate what we need to save the girls even more now."

Christ, this woman is stubborn.

I shake my head and tighten my hold in her hair, forcing her face to angle up to mine. "You might be the most frustrating woman I've ever met."

The corner of her mouth twitches, like she's fighting a smile or potentially the desire to slap me. "I could say the same for you."

Despite knowing how dangerous it is, I can't fight the smirk that pulls at my lips. "That I'm the most frustrating woman you've ever met?"

That earns me the tiniest crack of a grin from her. "You drive me fucking crazy. You know that?"

I nod slowly. "I sure as hell do, Vik. The feeling is more than mutual."

"And you're not going to let me out of here, are you?"

Shaking my head, I lean in closer until my lips barely brush against hers. "Not until I know you're safe."

Her hands come to my chest, but rather than push me away, she curls her fingers into the fabric of my shirt, using it to drag me tightly against her. "And what if I fight my way out?"

A low chuckle rumbles in my chest, pressing it harder against her ample breasts. "I'd have to tie you up."

Her heart thunders against mine, her breath coming hot and fast. "Don't threaten me with a good time, Reaper."

Fucking hell.

I tug her hair harder, tightening my grip to a point that must be painful for her. A warning I hope she understands before she pushes this any further. "You wouldn't survive a good time with me, sweetheart."

10

VIKTORIA

Reaper's lips crash down on mine so fast, it steals my retort and my breath, along with any ability to continue to fight the draw I feel toward this man who's all kinds of wrong for me.

Just yesterday, this killer, this criminal willing to take a life rather than allow me to do my job, literally kidnapped me. Yet, for some reason I can't even begin to understand, I trust that he would never hurt me. At least, not intentionally.

And the way his touch ignites the tiniest fibers of my being, all I can think about is how damn good it's going to feel to have his rough hands work over every inch of me.

Slowly. Softly. Brutally.

It won't matter. I'll take it all.

Anything and everything he has to give me.

Reaper doesn't disappoint. He wraps one of his arms around my waist and squeezes firmly to drag me up to straddle his lap, careful not to touch my other side. Even if he did, any pain I'm feeling is so easily pushed back behind the need overtaking my entire being.

Our lips wage the same battle we've been having verbally since the moment we met, while our tongues dance in a duel for supremacy. But neither one of us is going to win this one. Neither of us will give in or give up power. If anything, he's made that even more clear since he brought me here. He sees it as his responsibility to keep me safe and save those girls, and mine is to those girls, too, but also to the law and to ensure its upheld for everyone living in the city.

None of that matters at this moment. Not in this tiny, windowless room—wherever the hell we might be in fucking Jersey. All that does is the brush of his calloused fingertips up my spine and the roll of my hips to grind down against his hard cock between us in just the right spot.

A tiny whimper falls from my lips and into his mouth, and he sucks it down greedily, shifting his hands to the hem of my shirt and tugging up until I reluctantly pull back enough to let him move it. I release my death grip on the fabric of his tee, and he drags mine up and off, letting it fall to the floor beside the bed.

His blue eyes, darkened to almost navy by his lust, focus on the red blush spreading over my chest. This isn't the first time he's seen me like this—with nothing but a thin layer of lacy fabric covering my breasts—but somehow, it feels like I'm exposed more now than I was the other night when I was perhaps at my weakest. Now, it seems almost like his heated gaze blazes right through what little physically separates us and past the skin that should protect me, like he's burrowing his way deep to expose everything I try so hard to hide.

My need to prove myself.

My desire to win.

The pulsating need I feel for him.

He reaches out a hand and pulls the fabric of my bra

down, exposing my nipple to the chilly air of the room. Rough fingertips twist it, sending a jolt straight to my core and making it clench in anticipation.

Fumbling between us, I manage to find the hem of his T-shirt while he releases my aching breast and undoes his belt. I tug up at the soft cotton, and he lets me pull it over his broad shoulders and head. The black fabric falls to the bed beside me, but my focus is on what's directly in front of me.

Rock-solid muscle.

Sun-bronzed skin marred by too many red, angry, puckered scars to count.

But Reaper doesn't give me a chance to consider them long because he flips me onto my back and kneels between my legs, pulls off his belt, and jerks down his pants, letting his thick, hard cock spring free.

I swallow thickly and dart out my tongue to wet my suddenly dry lips.

His fingertips tickle the sensitive skin along the edge of the waistband of my yoga pants. Back and forth. Back and forth. Sending flutters of anticipation through my body and building the heat growing between my legs.

The pressure there urges me to arch my hips, seeking some sort of friction, some sort of release, and almost as if he knows what I need, he slides his hand down and drags his thumb up the seam of the stretchy black fabric to my clit. My pussy immediately spasms in response, and I drop my head back and squeeze my eyes closed against the flutter of need growing from that very spot.

"Fuck…" The word tumbles from my mouth, and I clutch the bedspread beneath me in my fists. But instead of urging him to move us to where we both want to be, my distress seems to only make him more determined to torture me.

Oh, great. Kidnapping and torture.

One side of his lips turns up smugly, and he rolls his

thumb there, languidly, so damn slowly that he's ensuring I feel every tiny brush, every little change in pressure, making me squirm under his touch. I force open my eyes again just in time to see him take his cock in his other hand and stroke it, never taking his crystal-blue gaze off me.

At least this isn't just torment for me. The white-knuckle grip Reaper has on his erection as he draws his palm along his length and the tense, coiled muscles in his arms and chest tell me he's just as on-edge as I am.

Yet, he seems intent on dragging this out, brushing his thumb over my clit and swirling it slowly until I can feel how soaked the fabric between my legs is. Embarrassingly wet, really. The kind of wet virgins get when they're touched this way for the first time, not how a grown-ass woman who has had her fair share of lovers does when she's looked at the right way by the wrong man.

If he doesn't tear these pants off me soon, I might spontaneously combust...

I release my death-grip on the bedspread and move my hands to the top of my pants, curling my fingers under the edge of the material.

If that doesn't give him the hint, then nothing will.

With a grin playing on his lips, he releases his hold on his dick and shifts his hand from between my legs to grasp my waistband and peel the fabric, along with my thong, down my legs and off my feet, letting it fall unceremoniously into a pile on the floor.

His darkening eyes flicker straight between my legs, zeroing in on the spot I want him so badly. Desire blazes in his gaze, only eclipsed by the anger still lingering at me or at the situation, the same anger I keep pushing deep down so I can get what I want without second-guessing it.

He leans forward and brushes his left hand against the

bandage on my skin while he glides the other up between my thighs and slips a finger inside me.

"Oh, God."

His hand at my side presses there firmly, and it almost numbs the lingering pain, or maybe it's the way his finger moves inside me then pulls out as he swirls his thumb around my clit that makes euphoria the only feeling I can manage to process even though a million are raging within me right now.

Propping himself on his elbow, he kicks his jeans free while he continues to work me over with his hand, forcing me even deeper into becoming a needy, quivering mass. With his eyes locked on mine, he asks me a million questions without ever voicing one, and I answer with a single look.

He kisses up my neck until his warm lips brush against my ear. "Tell me if I'm hurting you."

I manage a groan of response and a slight nod before he pulls his hand from between my legs and pushes his cock into me so fast, there's barely any time to prepare myself. "Fuck, Reaper!"

Not that I could have ever prepared myself for this man.

I never saw him coming.

And I never stood a chance...

REAPER

FUUUUUUUUUUUUUUCCCCCCCCCCCCCCCCKKKKKKKKKKKKKKKKKKKKK!

Vik clenches her pussy tighter around my cock, wraps one hand around my neck, and digs the nails of her other hand into my bare chest. The move only urges me to push in even deeper until I bottom out inside her and capture her surprised gasp with my lips.

She groans against my mouth, clasping my flesh inside her as I draw back my hips and slam in again. Her hot breath rushes out, and I drink it in the same way she does mine with each pant.

Despite her injury—or maybe *in spite* of it—she doesn't tell me to stop. To go slower. To be gentler. To take my time with her. That isn't what she wants.

This isn't making love. I haven't done that in so long that I'm not even sure I remember what that feels like anymore. But this isn't *that.* This is hard and demanding. This is fucking away the tension we've felt every time we've been in the same room together. This is both of us proving a point. That I'm in control here but she's never going to back down from me or any challenge. Neither of us is willing to break, both determined to come out on top.

I complete every mission—including this one. And right now, making her come is at the top of my priority list. I find a rhythm and angle that has the head of my cock dragging against that perfect spot inside her. Her nails score the skin on my chest and the back of my neck, and I roll my hips, grinding my pelvic bone down against her clit with each thrust.

Her lips fall away from mine, and she drops her head back, exposing her long neck, dark hair spread out around her on the pillow. "Oh...fuck..." She wraps her left leg around my hip and digs her heel into my lower back. "Right there. Fuck! Just like that."

There isn't any hiding the deep rumble of satisfaction in my chest when it's pressed to hers. Vik writhes under me, her hips meeting mine fluidly, like we're meant to move and fit together this way. And she's wound tight. So damn tight. That was my intent with the way I teased her earlier. I had to get her ready and primed well because I knew once I was inside her that there was absolutely no way in *hell* I would last long enough to do her properly.

Not when it's been this long.

Not when it's *this* woman.

Her anger. Her touch. Her righteous indignation and unwavering defiance. It's all so beautiful and toxic at the same time. The perfect mix to create an epic explosion now that we've finally come together like this.

And every thrust of my cock inside her wet, welcome heat drives me closer to losing control, to taking this beyond what she can handle after what she just went through.

She shifts her hand down my neck, over my shoulder, to my back, her fingertips brushing over the jagged scars there —reminders of the last things I want to be thinking of while like this with Vik. It drives me into her with a renewed force and determination to push us both to the brink of insanity.

A familiar, warm haze encroaches on the edges of my vision, making Vik's face come in and out of focus, and I take her mouth with mine again in a vicious, bruising kiss.

"Come for me, Vik." I grit my teeth, the muscles in my neck and jaw straining with my effort to hold back what my body demands. "Fucking come!"

Vik hates anyone telling her what to do or how to live her life. She's proven over and over again that she needs to be the one in control, but the moment that final word leaves my lips, her entire body seizes like something otherworldly takes hold of her.

She gasps and clutches at my back and neck, pulling me even closer while I pound into her rippling cunt. Every drive in, her body tries to keep me there, and it fights me on each withdrawal.

It doesn't take long—only a few more thrusts—for the tsunami I've been holding back finally crashes over me. The pleasure and pain. The truths of where we are and what we've done to get here. It all threatens to drown me in her wildly bucking hips until I finally empty myself inside her and she collapses beneath me, her hands falling away from my warm, sweaty skin.

Jesus...what the hell was that?

I roll to her right side, putting myself between her and the door, and drop my arm over my eyes. No matter what just happened between us, I don't trust her. This woman wouldn't think twice about using this as an opportunity to sneak away from her "cell."

My chest heaving, my breaths coming out in hard pants, I do my best to slow them down, to regain control over my body and my mind. Because I clearly just lost it. Giving in to whatever the hell this is with Vik makes this all so much harder. So much more complicated. It makes what I'm going to have to do hurt more than it ever should. More than I should ever *let* it.

Vik shifts next to me and rolls onto her side, lifting her hand to drag her fingers over the still-fresh wound on my arm and the scars on my chest and side. Her featherlight, almost reverent, touch sends a chill of dread through me that I haven't felt in a really fucking long time.

I shift away and sit on the edge of the bed, running my hands back through my hair, squeezing at the tension in the back of my neck and shoulders that suddenly feels like it's about to snap me in half.

It should have been an obvious move to tell her to leave me alone, to back the fuck off if she knows what's good for her. I should have known this woman *never* cares about what's good for her.

That soft touch flutters over the scars on my back. Slowly. One by one. It takes far longer than it should for anyone still breathing to get through them all. Sometimes, it surprises me that I still am. Often, I wonder why I, of all people, survived what I have when so many men more worthy of living died so tragically.

It's why I avoid situations like this. When people will ask questions I don't want to answer. When they'll make assumptions about my wounds and how I "earned" these scars. When they'll look at me like I'm a hero when all I feel like is a fucking fraud most days. The "lucky" one who got away relatively unscathed when those better than me fell.

I push to my feet to escape her touch and avoid looking back while I grab my clothes from the floor. But I don't *have* to look to know she's watching me...and being uncharacteristically quiet for Vik. It's in her cop nature to ask questions, to want to know someone's background and what makes them tick. It's how she gets into the heads of the people she interrogates. She reads them like open books and plays them until they fold in her favor.

But that won't happen with me.

If she hasn't learned that by now, she's going to at this moment.

I jerk on my jeans but don't bother buttoning them before I head for the door.

"Where are you going?" Her question holds every bit of incredulousness I would expect her to have after that.

"To have a fucking smoke and make some calls."

"And you're just leaving me here?"

I suck in a deep breath, keeping my back to her as I open the door. "It's where you belong..."

My foot crosses the threshold out into the loft, but I pause and turn back, finally letting my gaze land on her. Spread out across the small bed, propped up on her elbow, naked and practically glowing with my fucking cum still inside her, Vik locks her hard eyes with mine, waiting for me to say the words she knows are coming.

"Since you clearly can't be trusted not to get into trouble. Even in here."

11

VIKTORIA

The scalding-hot water in the tight shower in the minuscule bathroom attached to my "cell" can't warm me from the freeze that settled over me when Reaper's icy gaze fell on me from the doorway.

He had shut down completely. Any connection we made in that bed ended the moment I touched his scars. It was like flipping a switch. And now that I've seen a glimpse of why they call him Reaper, I don't know if I can ever shake this chill.

Because I saw it in those blue depths. The detachment. That is what allows him to do it. That is the man who can so easily say he'll wipe out anyone involved with this trafficking ring rather than let the law handle them. The man willing to spill so much blood and have it on his own hands.

Another shiver rolls down my spine, and I reach out and crank the water even hotter until it stings, pelting my hypersensitive skin.

I knew it was there. Knew what I was getting myself into

when I agreed to be involved with this mission instead of running it up the food chain like I should have. But I let Hank and Reaper convince me to go along with it, anyway. Knowing it went against everything I believe in and fought for my entire life.

Shit. What the hell am I doing?

I slam my palm against the old mint-green tile, my frustration boiling over again.

This entire situation is just...unbelievable. I never could have anticipated it would lead to this—being locked up in a room by a man I can't stand and can't seem to control myself around at the same time under some misguided plan to protect me.

Maybe it was stupid to think no one would recognize me at B66, but I left that life behind so long ago, went to community college, then got my job with the Department as soon as I graduated, and never looked back, never even set foot in Brighton Beach again to ensure I made a clean break from everyone associated with that life. It hurt Mom and Dad while they were alive that they always had to come to see me rather than me go to them...but they also understood it. Because it was what they wanted for me, too, ultimately. To get out. To have all the success in the world they never did, no matter how hard they worked.

But now, I've been sucked back into the world, and while Hank and Reaper and the Satan's Knights might be arguing that this is all for the greater good, that part of me that's always strived to not become those people I fight so hard against, those who don't respect or abide by the law, doesn't want to fully accept that. *Can't* accept that.

My chest tightens uncomfortably just thinking about what's coming in the near future, and I turn and drop my head forward, letting the water hit the back of my neck.

Reaper may be right about his having to watch and

protect me being a distraction from our greater focus, but it doesn't mean he needs to keep me locked up here and away from being involved with the search and rescuing of those girls.

I have to be.

If I let them fully cut me out of this, it won't be possible for me to intervene before things are taken too far, before I can steer them in the lawful direction. Because there's still hope at this point. There's still a *chance* there might be a way to do this without breaking every code I live by and every societal rule I stand for.

But maybe that's just wishful thinking on my part. Because those codes didn't seem to mean anything a few moments ago when Reaper was inside me. They didn't seem to mean much when I was urging him to keep going and relishing every movement under his hard, tight body.

So, perhaps I'm a fraud. Perhaps I am too far gone to bring us back from this dark path we've started down. Because what we just did changes everything, whether or not we try to deny and attempt not to let it.

Reaper said it himself—I even get into trouble in this room.

And he's the kind of trouble I don't need, the kind of trouble that leaves a permanent mark—maybe not visibly like the scars that mar his body, but on your soul, one you feel for a lifetime burning there, searing and reminding you of your mistake.

And since the water is doing nothing to make me feel better, I turn it off and step out onto the cracked tile floor, wrapping myself in the towel hanging from a hook on the wall. Another shiver runs down my spine despite the heavy, warm air, and I reach up and wipe the fog from the cheap, dingy mirror.

What the hell are you doing, Viktoria?

A complete stranger stares back at me with cloudy, tired, green eyes. So much has happened in the last week, so much that I never thought could. So much that has changed everything.

My partner lied to me and betrayed my trust. I was involved in an off-books investigation and shooting I kept a secret from the police department. And ultimately, I agreed to help a group of vigilantes take down an organization that should be dealt with through the proper channels.

The Viktoria who looks back at me isn't the one I thought she was. She never would've ended up in bed with Reaper. Yet, my entire body still tingles, remembering his touch, and my pussy clenches at the memory of what he felt like thrusting into me with such force, such aggression and passion. It's hard to say I don't want to be that girl, the one who could just let go and take what she wanted for once without thinking about the consequences far off in the future.

But I don't think my conscience will let me do that. Thinking about it alone weighs so heavily on my chest that I can barely take a breath.

I have to look for an opening—a way to get what is about to go down into the hands of the FBI or the Department, someone who can control it and ensure no innocent bystanders—or Hank or Reaper—get hurt or worse.

They might have the best of intentions. That's one thing I don't question about Reaper. That man believes wholeheartedly that what he's doing is right. The problem is he won't draw any lines and is willing to go to any lengths, and it's just not something I can let happen. Even if Reaper admitted he *does* care about me in *some* way. It's not enough to give up everything I've ever stood for.

REAPER

ANOTHER DEEP, long inhale off my cigarette sends nicotine coursing through my system. It's exactly what I needed and yet not nearly enough to calm the anxiety building inside me. I flick the lighter open and closed, the familiar rhythmic clicking sound doing little to soothe me the way it normally does.

And it isn't just about what just happened between Viktoria and me; it's knowing what will happen as soon as we get the information we need to locate the girls.

Mouth and Chaos should be here in a matter of days, and by then, either Hank or the MC or I will hopefully have the information we need to take immediate action. I trust my brothers with my life, but doing something like this on American soil is a lot different than anything we've done before. It holds a lot more risk, much deeper ramifications if we get caught.

I'm not afraid to face those because I know what I'm doing is right, and I can handle anything anyone can throw at me. But Viktoria is another matter.

She has ideals. Ones that can never withstand what she'll need to do if she's involved with this or with me. What just happened between us can't happen again. Not if we want to maintain focus and be able to walk away from this unattached and her still holding her job.

And that's the only option.

Because when all this is finally over, she'll be back to being a pit bull detective hunting down New York's worst scum, and I'll do what I do best—disappear somewhere I can live my life on my own terms without having to answer to anyone anymore. That ended when Uncle Sam said I could no longer do my job properly. And honestly, the way things were six months ago, they were probably right.

Keeping her locked in there is the only way to ensure she doesn't get in too deep. When we finally get the location and move on it, Vik won't be there. I can't expose her to that kind of danger—to herself or her career.

Not after I already did that in her bed.

Being with me is the most dangerous thing she's ever done.

I drop the cigarette onto the grates of the fire escape and grind it out with my boot as I slip the lighter back into my pocket. The sounds of the street below fill the air, and I'm tempted to remain out here to avoid the tension of what's inside. But I can't ignore the reality forever, no matter how much I'd love to.

There is work to be done.

Dirty work.

Things are about to get bloody.

I step inside the loft, and my back pocket buzzes.

Fuck.

That better be someone with some good news because anything else will only stretch my already-thin control to its breaking point. What happened with Viktoria was only the tip of the iceberg, a brief, small glimpse of what I'm capable of when I'm unleashed.

I pull out my phone, but the screen is black. "Shit."

It must be Viktoria's.

The deception with her sister may have worked in texts, but if she's calling now, Viktoria isn't likely to cooperate and get on the line. Not after I just walked out and locked her back in there.

My pocket buzzes again, and I grab Vik's phone and glance at the screen to find a flurry of text messages from Hank asking if she's okay that started hours ago.

Fuck.

While we were getting busy in there, he's been trying to get a hold of her and can't, so he's panicking.

> Really, Vik? Two fucking weeks?
>
> What the fuck is going on?
>
> Come on, answer me goddamnit.
>
> Text me.
>
> Call me.
>
> If I don't fucking hear from you in one minute, I'm coming over.

Shit!

That was almost an hour ago. Which means Hank may already be at her place, or at the very least, on his way there.

Almost as if on cue, her phone dings with a notification from her video doorbell. I press the button for the camera and find Hank banging on the door like a fucking madman.

Fuck. This is just what I don't need right now.

He's liable to start a manhunt for her if I don't intervene —and do it fast. I scroll through her contacts to find his name and hit send before bringing the phone to my ear.

Hank answers on the first ring. "Vik? Where the hell are you? I've been texting you and calling you. I'm in front of your place."

"It isn't Vik. It's Reaper."

"Dixon? Why the hell do you have Vik's phone? I think Vik is missing. She's not answering my texts or taking my calls. I'm outside of her apartment—"

I scrub my hand over my face and sigh. "She's fine. I have her."

"You *have* her? What does that even mean?"

"It means that she's safe and you don't need to worry about her."

"The hell I don't." Hank's indignation comes through the phone loud and clear, and I can't say I blame him for it. "I don't know what the fuck you're doing, Dixon, but I don't fucking like it. Put her on the damn phone. Now."

I settle onto one of the stools at the kitchen counter. "Now isn't a good time. But trust me when I say this was necessary. I saw a car surveilling her place."

""Back up. Why the hell were *you* surveilling her place?"

"That doesn't matter. She left to meet her sister for lunch and I noticed someone was following her. He looked suspicious as fuck—"

"Hold on. She left to meet her sister?" The fucker just cut me off, but his response tells me we're on the same page about how stupid it was of her to be leaving so soon after being shot. "Never mind. That's irrelevant. Continue. What happened?"

"I had to intervene. I grabbed her."

"Is she okay?"

The vivid memory of her screaming my name while I pounded into her flashes through my head, stirring my cock. "Yep. A little pissed off by what I had to do, but she'll get over it. I couldn't put her at risk like that."

She's already put herself at risk by going to B66 in the first place, thinking no one would recognize her. It was reckless and stupid. She could have gotten herself killed.

Why do I care so damn much?

The only way I've survived this long is by never allowing myself to care about a woman. I couldn't and continue to do what I did. Couldn't be away for weeks or months at a time, knowing she would worry and be miserable. Couldn't leave behind a widow when I inevitably didn't come home.

This is no different. I can't let her get under my skin anymore. It isn't good for either of us.

Hank blows out a long breath. "So, with you being preoccupied with Vik, I guess you don't have anything new on Yankovich."

"Nothing worth mentioning."

"Well, I may have made a dent. Long story short, Parrish gave me a tip, and I checked it out. Michail has a place in Williamsburg where he's keeping Vlad's wife, Anastasia, and her two kids. I followed her for a couple of days and made contact. First at a coffee shop she visits regularly, then when that proved to be a bust, Parrish and I cornered her at her kid's school. It was the only way to get close without her guards. We tried talking some sense into her, but the woman is stubborn as shit and dead set on protecting her brother-in-law. If we can get her to flip, she might clear the path to Michail, or at the very least, lead us in the right direction."

It's a good lead, one that definitely has potential. "You think she might know where he's keeping the girls or holding the auction?"

"I'm not sure, but she knew who I was and was pissed. Made me think that she knows something."

"Well, now that I know Vik is safe, I can get back to pounding the pavement and talking to my contacts to see what I can find out." And hopefully, they'll be more forthcoming once I have more firepower here. "I have two buddies coming into town to help. They should be here soon. Then, hopefully, we can plan our next move more easily."

"And what about Vik? Do we know who the guy sniffing around her was?"

I glance at the closed and locked door keeping her contained. "I'm pretty sure it was one of Yankovich's guys and that they were who took a shot at her the other night, too."

"Fuck. Why her though? Why not me or the Satan's Knights?"

"She said she might have been recognized at B66. Did you know she grew up in Brighton Beach?"

"Well, yeah, but to my understanding she hasn't been back there since before college. So let me get this straight, she thinks someone from her old neighborhood placed her at the club, told Yankovich, and he sent someone to silence her. Should we be worried?" "I'll handle Vik."

"I've known her a lot longer than you, Dixon, and fair warning—it's a lot harder than you think."

"Trust me," I growl, "I'm more than aware of how hard she is to handle."

I end the call and shove the phone back into my pocket, my gaze automatically darting back to the locked door across the open loft space.

I'm not in any position to be trying to deal with her again right now. She needs more time to cool off, and I need time to figure out my next move without her in my orbit, fucking with my head and my ability to think clearly.

It's time to get out and see what I can shake loose.

12

REAPER

The blood pooling at my feet should probably concern me. It should be pushing me into action, to move, to step out of it, to do *something,* but instead, all I can think about is how peaceful Vik looked when I opened the door to her room to leave food for her before I left earlier.

Either she was passed out, or she's one hell of a good fake sleeper. Either way, her chest rose and fell in that steady rhythm, the fabric of the T-shirt she slipped on after we fucked unable to conceal her nipples straining against it. Her lips slightly parted, practically begging me to storm across the room and kiss them.

And I almost did just that.

Forcing myself to walk away rather than take her again was harder than what I'm doing to this asshole. That was nearly impossible. This...this is fucking easy in comparison. If I can get my head back in the game.

Focus on the mission. Forget the girl.

I tighten my grip on the knife in my hand and stab into his gut again.

A strangled cry of pain and distress floats out his open mouth and through the warehouse rafters, but there isn't anyone here to hear him or answer his pleas for help. That's why I chose this place. The perfect location to get what I need without drawing unwanted attention.

I squat in front of him, determined to push Vik from my head, reach out with my free hand, and tug on his hair, forcing his head up until his half-closed eyes meet mine. "Let's try this again, shall we?"

He releases a strangled groan, and blood trickles from his lips, down to his bare, cut and bruised chest. "I-I told you…I don't know what you're talking about."

"And I told you that I know you're lying."

This fucker came out of B66 with Kosofik, laughing and joking like old pals. There's no way he doesn't know what's happening with the auction. I don't believe that for one fucking second.

I release his head, and it immediately drops forward, his body too weak to even hold it up. If I'm not careful, I could push this too far to ever get the answers I need. "I'm going to ask you one more time before I switch to another type of persuasion. And if you don't like this"—I flash the knife under the bright overhead fluorescent lights—"you sure as hell aren't gonna like that."

A gurgling objection slips from his lips, and he shakes his head and manages to lift it enough to meet my gaze. "No. No more."

"Then tell me what I need to know."

"Okay…" A rattling, painful-sounding cough makes him double over as much as the bindings allow. If he weren't tied to the chair, he would probably be face down on the ground right now. "I don't know everything. Just that it's happening before the end of the month."

The end of the month?

That doesn't give us much time. Two weeks tops. But it does explain why I haven't gotten a text from Kosofik with the information yet. They likely haven't even decided on a location to hold it or are waiting until the last minute to send instructions to avoid any leaks to the police.

I grin at the man and raise my knife to press my finger against the tip directly in his sightline. "I don't believe you don't know where they're keeping the girls."

Knowing when the auction is going to happen is important, but it doesn't get me to the innocent victims. I need a location, and this guy is going to give it to me.

"You want to know why I know that?" I raise an eyebrow at him. "Because you're buddies with Kosofik, and he runs the show for Yankovich so the big man can keep his hands clean. My guess is, you're his go-to guy, and that means you know every little detail."

Pushing to my feet, I click my tongue and shake my head. "I gave you one opportunity. You're still holding things back from me. Not a wise decision on your part."

One that is going to make this much more painful for him. It's not that I relish this, inflicting pain on others. But when it's a total scumbag like this, I certainly don't feel guilt over it, either.

I grab the bucket of water from the side of my captive's chair and tilt him back to drop his bare feet into it before I snag the jumper cables attached to the car battery sitting on the floor. He sees them and screams, the sound echoing through the vast space but falling to the cold concrete below us without anyone hearing it.

"You can scream all you want." I attach one of the heavy metal clips to his left nipple. That alone is painful enough that he screams again. "Let's see if this changes your coop-eration."

I attach the other one to his right nipple, allowing the current to surge through him, his body jerking and twisting painfully as the electricity fries him like an egg from the inside out. His bladder releases in a rush of piss that mixes with the blood on the concrete around the chair.

This type of torture is never pretty, but sometimes, it's necessary to spill some bodily fluids to get some answers. Still, I need him alive enough to give me what I need. I pull one of the cords from him, cut the power, and he sags forward again.

Squatting, I drag his head up by his hair. "Let's try this again. Where are they holding the girls?"

Saliva and blood drip from his lips, and he opens and closes his mouth several times before he finally manages to speak. "I-I-I don't know."

"Really?" This douche canoe is stronger than I gave him credit for. Most men would have broken with the stabbing. Those few who still hung on would have caved to the elec-trocution. But this fucker still wants to play the game.

I drop his head and reach to reattach the cable to him again, ensuring my motion is still in his line of sight.

His eyes widen, and he sobs and spits. "All I know is it's a warehouse near the docks in Jersey."

A slow smile pulls at my lips. It might not be an address, but it's enough to get me where we need to be. Simply staking out the area around the docks should give us a specific location. The girls need to be fed and kept relatively healthy if they want top dollar for them, so Yankovich's men will need to come and go. That kind of activity can't be hidden easily from someone looking for it specifically.

I reach out and slap the side of his face. "There's a good boy. Was that so hard?

He opens his mouth to answer or say something else, but I reattach the clamp, allowing the current to flow through him again, and wipe the knife off on his jeans before sticking it back into my boot.

"It's been nice knowing ya."

I got what I came here for, and now, it's time to leave. Only what I face when I get back to the loft may be fucking worse than what I did to this guy.

VIKTORIA

I KICK against the door near the knob for the thousandth time and release another angry scream when all I get for my efforts is pain shooting up my leg and a twinge in my side. Pressing my hand against the healing wound, I pace away from the door and peek down at the tiny crack between it and the concrete floor.

What lies beyond that door is a mystery, but it seems whoever built this room, they designed it to keep someone in. The solid, sturdy door hasn't budged despite my best efforts to find a weak spot. It's as unwavering as my anger toward Reaper. And not just because he locked me in here but because he did *it* again...managed to sneak in and leave more food for me while I was passed out.

It's almost like he has some sixth sense when to come in here so I won't have the chance to confront him. And even though I've been banging and screaming for what feels like hours, I haven't heard a peep from out there or seen any sort of shadows move in front of the door, which means he probably left me here while he went out to do something no doubt nefarious.

I let out another frustrated growl, wander back to the bed, and plop down on my back.

Bad move.

The entire bed smells like sex. Smells like *him* and what we did...

All the things I don't want to be thinking about right now —not if I want to stay angry.

I need to stay angry.

It's far better than the alternative. Far less dangerous to my heart and sanity.

A low rumble shakes the bed beneath me, and I jerk upright and tilt my head to listen.

The garage door...

It must be right below this room. Wherever he went, he's back. Which means it's time to get myself together.

I jump from the bed and race to the wall by the door, pressing my back flat against it. If he decides to come in here to check on me, I'm going to take advantage of it the only way I can think of.

It may not work. It may not do anything other than piss off Reaper even more, but I still have to try. I can't let him remain in control of the situation, in control of *me*. I have to start thinking of him as what he is—my abductor and a killer —instead of as the man who makes my heart race and my body heat.

Muffled grinding and groaning of the ancient elevator make it through the crack under the door, and then his heavy boots thud on the floor outside the door. A shadow blocks out the light coming under it, and I prepare myself for a fight.

You can do this, Vik. Stay strong.

The lock clicks, and the doorknob turns slowly before the door itself pushes in. I lash out with the only weapon I have in here—my fist. With my police training, I know how to throw a punch. And if it were anyone else, I might have stood a chance, but Reaper's large hand snaps out and wraps around my wrist, stopping it in midair, nowhere near connecting.

He whirls on me and pushes me against the wall so fast that it forces all the air from my lungs in one giant whoosh.

"What the fuck do you think you're doing?" His words come out more growled than spoken. "Did you think that was going to work? Did you actually think you would be able to hurt me enough to get out of here?" A sneer twists his lips. "You clearly don't know who the fuck I am."

I lock my gaze to his, refusing to give even an inch to him as he continues to keep a death-grip on my wrist and pin my other arm between our bodies. "I know exactly who and what you are. You just proved it earlier."

He snarls and leans in until our mouths are only inches from each other. Anger flashes in his blue eyes, making what could be calm pools to swim in tumultuous and stormy. "Then you should know this was a bad move."

"Thinking I won't keep fighting because you fucked me is a bad move on your part."

His brow furrows, his eyes darkening even more. "Is that what you think? That I fucked you to try to stop you from fighting me?"

The incredulous tone in his question tightens my throat, but I force out a response anyway. "It's certainly the way it seems."

He shifts in even closer until we're sharing the same space and breath. "I *fucked* you because I can't get you out of my head. I *fucked* you because even *after* fucking you, I can't get you out of my head. When I needed to focus. When I needed to do my damn job, all I could think about was how fucking beautiful you looked with my cock buried inside you."

My breath catches in my throat, any words I had intended to hurl at him with fury suddenly refusing to leave my lips.

It isn't romantic. It isn't a declaration of love or even that he gives one iota of shit about me or that he keeps me locked up in here like *I'm* the damn criminal. It's a statement about lust—pure animal need. But it's enough to ignite another fire in me that mingles with the anger already burning through my veins and threatening to sear my soul.

Something about this man breaks through the hard exterior I was forced to create to start a new life in a very difficult profession for a woman. I've fought for so long to hide my desires, my needs. To push them down and only give into them in secret when I reached my breaking point. But around Reaper, they flare to life and quickly rage out of control.

I promised myself I wouldn't do this, that I wouldn't let him get close enough to touch me, that I would push him away if it came to this again, but when his lips descend on mine, I don't question it.

Even if I wanted to, I can't...

Instead, I moan into his mouth and issue a low needy-sounding whimper that would make me cringe under any other circumstances.

His hard cock brushes against my hand pinned between us, and I shift my arm the best I can to rub it. He releases my wrist so he can jerk down my pants while I undo his and free him.

He lifts me easily, and I wrap my legs around his waist so he can drive up into me, slamming me back against the wall and shattering any hope I ever had of getting out of this with my heart intact.

VIKTORIA

E verything that happened in the last ten minutes blurs into a blissful cloud. But coming down from the orgasmic high, reality slams into me hard and cold despite Reaper's warm body still pressing mine against the wall.

Dammit.

I want to be furious at him. For what just happened. For *everything* that has happened since he entered my life. But that wouldn't be fair. I'm just as much to blame for the situation I find myself in—with his still-hard cock buried inside me, my chest heaving, and my heart aching.

This shouldn't have happened...again, and I could have stopped it at any time. But I didn't even try because as much as I hate him, I also *needed* this. I needed *him* to give me this release from the stress and turmoil and pain of the last few days, even though he's been a major cause of all of it. I need him to remind me that I'm *alive.*

Something about the tension that always builds between us makes it feel like we're two caustic chemicals that combust when we're thrown together. It's violent and harsh and painful but also brilliant and addictive, like watching a train barreling down the track toward a car stuck there and knowing there isn't any way to stop it yet not being able to look away.

I can't look away from Reaper. I can't give up the way he makes me feel with his body against mine, inside me and enveloping me. But the thought that he might have been gone the last few hours, doing something I should be arresting him for, yet I just did *that* with him, won't let me hold in the question that keeps floating through my head.

Over and over and over again…

And I can't just let it go.

I swallow against my dry throat and turn my head until my lips brush against his ear, where his head is still buried against my neck. "Where were you?"

His entire body goes rigid, and he slowly pulls back his head until his hard eyes meet mine. He raises his hand from my side and captures my face in his rough palm, brushing his thumb across my cheek. "My dick is still inside you and you're asking where I was?"

Shit.

The last thing I expected was to hear hurt lacing his words. Anger—yes. Reaper seems to harbor a lot of that. But the fact that my question might actually put a ding in the armor he wears so diligently never even crossed my mind. Not after he walked away and locked me back up in this room earlier today.

Such an easy dismissal of what happened between us left me unnerved and bitter. Still, I never imagined it had affected him in *any* way. He certainly never showed it before now, only acted like it didn't mean anything to him other than a way to get a needed release. I never intended to hurt him, even though he hurt *me* by disappearing.

Why couldn't I keep my mouth shut for one damn minute? Enjoy a few moments of peace and revel in the afterglow of really hot sex?

I glance down, avoiding his penetrating gaze, and my focus goes right to his boots…and the dark stains splattered on them. It's a stark reminder of why I asked the question in the first place. Because I know enough about Reaper to know he wasn't out on a walk, enjoying the scenery and people of the Garden State while I was locked up in here.

My resolve returning, I lift my head and meet his stare. "Yes, I want to know where you were and how you got blood all over your boots."

A low growl rumbles in his chest and vibrates through mine straight to my heart. Heat blazes in his blue eyes, far different from what was there before. This heat is born of fury.

At me asking or because of what he did?

He shifts slightly, his cock still buried inside me, and I squeeze around him instinctively and issue a low groan.

His hand tightens on my face, drawing me closer to him. "I just spent a few hours of quality time with one of Yankovich's men to get the information we need, and even while I was there, doing things that would make you cringe, even *then,* I couldn't get you out of my fucking head."

I couldn't get you out of my fucking head…

He's trying to distract me. Get me to focus on *those* words and what they might mean instead of the other part of that explanation, the part that goes to my very important question.

"Yankovich's man? What did you find out?"

Reaper watches me for a moment, searching my face for something he apparently doesn't find because he releases a heavy sigh and moves his hand from my cheek to the wall behind me. "The auction is happening at the end of the month. And I have a pretty good idea where the girls are now."

My breath catches in my throat. It's exactly what we've been looking for, what we need to finalize our plans and make a move. We can finally free these innocent women, but Reaper's comment from earlier still lingers at the forefront of my brain with the visual of the splatter on his boots.

A few hours of quality time...

I glance at his hand against the wall, and while there isn't any blood on it, that doesn't mean anything with this man. He knows how to clean up after himself, how to do a dirty deed and not leave anything that will tie him to it. I'm sure his clothes and boots will end up in some incinerator in the bowels of this building as soon as he pulls his dick from inside me.

"Did you..." I swallow and force myself to hold his gaze, even though doing so makes my heart thunder against my ribcage violently. "Kill him?"

His anger returns, flaring to life, darkening his eyes and tensing his shoulders. "So what if I did? He was a piece of shit who got what he deserved. That's all you need to know. Everything *I* needed to know before I took care of business."

Took care of business.

"Are you admitting to a cop that you just murdered someone?"

A cold grin tilts his lips. "I'm not admitting anything. You can draw your own conclusions, but what are you going to do?" One of his dark eyebrows rises. "Turn me in?"

Would I? Could I really turn him in for killing some piece-of-shit lackey of Yankovich who is involved in a human trafficking ring and likely even worse?

For a brief moment, I consider saying no, but then the entire reason I became a cop in the first place slams into my brain, altering my response, which comes out with more bite than I intend, unable to restrain my incredulity.

"Yes, Reaper, I would." Tightening my grip on his shirt, I tug on the fabric to emphasize my point. "Who made *you* judge, jury, and executioner? What gives *you* the right to decide who is guilty of what, what their penance should be, and then complete their ultimate sentence?"

Reaper leans in slowly, and the absolute calm that overcomes his face sends a chill through my spine, making me shiver. The movement only shifts his cock still buried in me even deeper, and I bite back a whimper rather than admit how good it feels while we're having this argument.

His lips brush against mine, just barely, enough to leave me wanting more but not giving it to me. "*I* did, Vik. And I'm more than qualified. I've spent my entire adult life hunting down threats to this country and threats to innocent people all over the fucking world. I know evil when I see it. I can *smell* it coming from them while I watch them in hiding. I can *feel* it in my gut when I look into their eyes. These men deserve to pay the ultimate price for what they've done. And if the big man upstairs has any issue with what I'm doing in my life, He can tell me Himself when I finally head to the pearly gates...or, if I find myself in the nine circles of Hell, I'll have my answer."

He brings his hand back to my face and squeezes my jaw.

"Until then, Vik, I'm just going to keep doing what I can to make this world a safer place. If you want to stop me, you can certainly try, but you won't get very far or be very successful. I think I just proved that."

To emphasize his point, he drives into me hard, pushing his cock as deep inside as humanly possible and completely stealing my breath or any response I have.

Instead, a small gasp tumbles from my lips, and I fight the urge to beg him to go. To move. To fuck me hard again.

Don't give in, Vik. Don't let him take this control.

I force myself to open my eyes and hold his searing gaze. "Turning you in or stopping you would require me getting out of here, and you don't seem inclined to let that happen anytime soon."

His lips twitch as he fights a smile. "No, I am not so inclined."

"But you know where the girls are. Let me help you plan a way to get them back safely."

He shakes his head, leaning in again until his warm breath flutters against my lips. "I have all the help I need. What I need you to do is stay here and stay safe."

"Hank will be looking for me."

"I've dealt with Hank."

"What?"

"I took care of him."

Any hope I had for rescue deflates with that revelation. "So no one is coming for me…"

"It certainly appears that way."

"And you're just going to keep me locked up here."

He tightens his hold on my jaw. "I'm going to do whatever I have to with you to make sure you keep your ass alive and out of trouble."

"Don't you think it's a little late for that?"

I don't know if I'm referring to what already happened with Yankovich and his men or what just happened a few hours ago between Reaper and me, what is *currently* happening between us.

It seems his answer is the same either way. "Damn right it is."

REAPER

I GROWL the words at Vik like a rabid dog about to bite, barely restraining my desire to lash out at her even more, but I don't care how menacing I may look or sound right now. It's necessary. Her pussy clenches around my cock, practically begging for more, and the woman *still* can't stop arguing with me.

She just isn't getting it.

Viktoria just can't seem to understand how bad this is for both of us, but especially for her.

"You've been nothing *but* trouble since the moment I met you, Vik. First, letting your partner drag you to B66 without the department knowing or having any backup, a place you knew there was a possibility you might be recognized. Then, you two tried to grab me, thinking you would get something from me and wasted time you could have used investigating the real criminals. *Then*, you had to follow Hank and get yourself *shot*. Then, you didn't stay at the club where Celeste and the Knights could take care of you, and instead, you went home where you would've bled out had I not been there. A home that is so easy to break in to that it was a fucking *joke* to think you'd be safe there. And then you did the stupidest thing you could have. You let me *kiss* you."

My dick twitches inside her at the memory of the first time I got a taste of her, that first press of my lips to hers. I capture her face between both my palms and tilt her face up to ensure she's one hundred percent with me on how *stupid* she's been.

"And let's not forget that you *then* got yourself kidnapped."

Her eyes widen slightly. "By *you!*"

"Again, you're fucking welcome for that. But even kidnapped, even knowing your life is in danger and *why* I took you, you just can't seem to stay away from trouble."

Instead, she runs headlong into it and deals with the

ramifications only after the fact. But it's time I force her to really think about what she's doing, what we're doing, and what it means for her future.

Her mouth falls open, and a gasp slips from those lips I want to kiss so badly. *"You're* the one who kissed *me."*

True...

But I'm not about to take all the responsibility for this. "You could've said *no.* You *should* have said no...because I'm trouble, Viktoria. You already know that. You've known it since the moment you saw me in that bar. And yet, look where we are...again."

I drag back my hips and plunge into her again just to prove my point. Even though we just fucked five minutes ago and I haven't pulled my dick from her warm cunt, I still haven't had enough of her. I don't know that it's even possible to.

She groans, dropping her head back, and tightens her hands in my shirt, clinging to me.

"We just *fucked,* Vik, and I'm still *inside* you and we're arguing about what I just did to one of Yankovich's men and whether or not you're going to turn me into the damn police." I shake my head. "This isn't healthy or normal at all, Viktoria. *I* am not healthy or normal. I'm fucked up and volatile, and I would *destroy* you."

It's the only warning I can give her. The only way I can try to make her understand what she's doing to herself by being with me like this. If I told her what it's doing to me, how it makes me weak to have a blind spot where she's concerned when I need to stay focused on my mission, it would only confuse things more. This needs to be about *her,* about how wrong this is for *her* and how it will decimate her future.

Her glassy eyes meet mine. "Maybe I want to be destroyed."

"Fuck." I fight the desire to fuck her silent, stopping my hips from pulling back and driving into her relentlessly until she can't breathe, let alone speak. "Don't say shit like that to me, Viktoria. You think you know what I can do, but you can't even fathom what I have done in my past. You need to stay as far away from me as you can."

Run away...

I swallow through the strange emotion clogging my throat. "I'm dangerous. To you. To your career. Because I'm not going to stop. I'm not going to stop taking out these assholes who deserve it. I'm not going to stop doing what I can to protect people who need it. I'm not going to put you in a position to have to choose between your morals and *me*. I could never forgive myself if you chose me over everything you've worked your entire life for." I shake my head and squeeze my eyes closed. "I'm not worth any of that, Vik. Not even fucking close."

A silence lingers between us, heavy with the weight of all that I've just confessed to her. Then her soft, warm hand releases my shirt and presses to my cheek, and she forces my face up. I open my eyes to find hers shimmering with unshed tears, and I start to pull away from her, from the wall, to put some distance between us. But she reaches up and clings to the back of my neck with both hands, wrapping her legs more tightly around me, keeping me buried inside her.

"Shouldn't I be the one who decides what you're worth? Isn't it *my* life and therefore my decision?"

She rolls her hips and squeezes my dick tightly in her wet heat. I grit my teeth against the very real desire to drive into her hard again, to somehow show her how dangerous I can really be. How badly I can hurt her.

Her soft lips brush against my cheek. "Does what I want not matter? How I feel not matter?"

"Fuck. Of course, it does. I'm trying to keep you from throwing away your entire life. Why can't you see that?"

She pulls one hand down from around my neck and presses it over my heart. "What I see is a man who has been scarred by what he's had to do in his life. A man who has such a tainted view of the world and the people in it that he can't even see the good anymore. But I also see a man who would never hurt me."

My chest tightens, my breaths suddenly harder to drag in. I shake my head. "Don't be so sure about that, Viktoria."

"I *am* sure. And maybe there isn't a future for us. Maybe when this is all over, you'll disappear and I'll go back to being a cop with a heavy weight on my conscience. But that's *my* decision to make, not yours." She drops her forehead against mine. "I get to make the choice of what's good for me or what isn't. And in this moment, I choose you. It might be different tomorrow, might be different the day after that, but it's my choice and mine alone. So, please, Reaper…fuck me."

"Christ, Viktoria." I pull my head back and lift her chin, swiping away a single stray tear from her cheek with my thumb. "You don't know what you're asking me for."

"Yes." She nods slowly, her bottom lip trembling. "Yes, I do."

She's asking me to break her. To demolish everything she stands for in this world to have a few minutes of comfort and bliss in each other's arms. She's asking me to do this, knowing we can't have a future, knowing that when this is over, I'll walk away and never look back.

Even with all that assured, she still leans forward and presses her lips to mine slowly, tentatively, almost like she's expecting me to pull away and run.

But I don't have the strength for that left. Not by a fucking long shot.

14

REAPER

The consistent soft rise and fall of Viktoria's chest assures me she's asleep, but I still wait a few minutes, watching her, just to be safe, before I gently pull my arm out from under her and climb from the bed to hastily tug on my jeans and slip from the room.

I close the door quietly but don't bother locking it this time. I'm not going anywhere today. Too hard to do what I need to do in daylight. Plus, I don't think Viktoria would make the mistake of trying to escape again.

Not after what happened the last time she tried something so stupid.

Scrubbing my hands over my face, I try to rub away the visuals of how she looked at me while I had her pinned against the wall, and splayed out on the bed, and bent over the end of it. It doesn't work. They're burned into my retinas and mind forever. I force my eyes open and stare at the chipped paint on the door.

What the hell are we doing?

I don't even know. Part of me screams to go back in there, climb into bed with her again, and take her as many times as possible before I have to make the next move in my mission. But the bigger part of me is telling me to lock the door and keep it locked this time. Because if she's in there and I'm out here, *that* can't happen again. And the more it *does* happen, the harder it's going to be to walk away when this is all over. The harder it's going to be not to worry about what it might do to her career when we finally have to pull the trigger on these guys.

But I can't worry about that right now. I need to get in touch with Hank and let him know what I got from Yankovich's guy and try to find out when Chaos and Mouth will get here.

First, I need a fucking smoke.

I cross the loft to the far side, unlock and push up the old window, and step through it out to my usual spot, where I've found myself more times than I can count since I first met Vik and her nosy partner. The fire escape is the only spot in this entire place where I can't smell her, where every breath isn't full of that soft, flowery scent that makes me taste her on my tongue.

Even the heaviest drag from my cigarette and holding the smoke in my lungs can't erase that.

Why do I even try?

Instead of contemplating that question, I pull out my phone and call Grayson. The sooner I get him updated on what I learned, the quicker I can focus on finding the exact location and creating a plan of attack that might bring those women home to their families alive.

The determined detective answers on the third ring. "Dixon? Is Vik all right?"

Her screams from earlier fill my ears again, and I clench my jaw but manage to grit out a response through my teeth. "Fine. I got something. I know where the girls might be."

"Talk to me. Where?"

"A warehouse in Newark, looks like somewhere near the Jersey docks. I don't have an address, but that narrows down our search by a fucking lot."

"Makes sense. Still a pretty large scope, though. The waterfront is adjacent to the airport. You got the Port Newark Container Terminal and the Redhook Container Terminal there, too. Easy access to move the girls after the auction. You want me to have the Satan's Knights recon the area?"

"No. I have a few buddies coming in to help. Let us do it. No offense to your friends on the motorcycles, but they're not the most inconspicuous group."

Hank grunts as I take another drag off my cigarette and blow smoke out into the air.

"It shouldn't be hard for us to find the right warehouse fairly quickly. The auction is happening at the end of the month, so we have time to determine the exact location, get any blueprints we can of the building, and plan before we go in there."

"How sure are you about the auction being at the end of the month?"

"Why?"

"Well, I got Anastasia to cooperate. I can't take all the credit, though. I think Parrish put the fear of God in her. The woman doesn't want her kids to have to relive the shit they witnessed when Parrish and the Knights took out their father, so in exchange for their protection, she's been talking. Told me Michail mentioned a charity gala to her, but she doesn't buy it. And after doing some research of my own, neither do I. "

A charity gala?

Seems a bit odd for someone like Yankovich, but it sounds like Hank knows even more. "Explain."

"Well, when he first mentioned this gala to her, she got suspicious because he's never committed to one specific charity. Any donation made is for tax purposes. Now, all of a sudden, he's hosting one? I checked out his financials, and she's right. I also looked into each specific charity he's donated to, and not a single one has a gala on their calendar. I've been to a couple of these fundraisers for the Sergeants Benevolent Association, and I can tell you, not only do they advertise the fuck out of them, they charge per plate. She also said Michail beefed up his security. He took the two guards he had detailing her and the kids and put them on him."

"So you think the gala is a front for the auction?"

"It could be. It could also be a fucking decoy. Ana overheard him and Kosofik talking about me and the Knights. That's how she knew who I was when I approached her. If he thinks we're onto him, he could be staging this gala to coincide with the auction. He sends Kosofik to the warehouse in Newark while he wines and dines the elite at B66. That gives him an alibi and me no arrest. The sale takes place, and he gets off."

"Fuck."

"Yeah, that's why I'm asking you if you're sure this auction is set for the end of the month because Anastasia called me last night from the burner phone I gave her and said the gala is in four days."

"If your theory is correct, then we need to be ready to strike."

"We need that location."

"I'll get it."

"Are you—"

"I said I'll get it."

"Fine." Hank pauses for a beat. "You share any of this with Vik?"

"She knows what she needs to know."

"Oh, yeah, how's that going for you?"

I pinch the bridge of my nose and shake my head. "She wants to be there, but I told her there wasn't any fucking way I was letting her near this raid."

He laughs. "I bet that went over well."

"Of course not. But I'm not about to let her tank her career to help us with this. You were already in bed with the Satan's Knights. Whether that move was right or wrong, you made the choice yourself. Vik was kind of dragged into this kicking and screaming. You know this doesn't sit right with her, even if the reason behind it is valid."

He sighs, the sound just as heavy with frustration as what I'm feeling. "Yeah, I know. If you can keep her away from this, then do it. You're right. When all this comes to a head, I'm going to have a big mess with the department on my hands, and I'd rather take that heat than have her do it."

At least we're on the same page.

Protecting Vik is just as important at this point as finding the women being held by the Russians.

And I fucking hate myself for it.

How could I let a woman get into my head like this?

It's a weakness I could never afford and one I managed to avoid for a decade. Yet do one favor for an old friend and I somehow find myself drowning in unwanted feelings that only complicate the job I came here to do. A job made all that much harder when I'm doing it alone while keeping my eye on the loaded pistol locked in that bedroom.

"My buddies should arrive in the next day or two, and I'll start without them. We'll get the precise location ASAP, and I'll keep you updated."

"Sounds good. If I get any more intel on the gala, I'll reach out."

I end the call and immediately send a text to Mouth.

> ETA?

Tomorrow sometime. Chaos?

> Calling him now to confirm but should be around the same.

It can't come soon enough.

Maybe with the boys around, it will provide the distraction I need to keep my hands off and my dick out of Viktoria.

I dial Chaos and wait for him to pick up, taking several long drags off my cigarette before he finally answers.

"Yep."

"ETA?"

"Just wrapping up a few things. Tomorrow, day after at the latest."

"Good. I need the backup."

He chuckles. "For the vermin or for the girl?"

"Shit." I shake my head and toss it back to stare up at the clouds passing slowly in the blue sky. "This girl, man...you'll see what I'm talking about when you get here."

He barks out a laugh—wherever he is, he clearly isn't concerned about making noise. "If she's got *you* this twisted up, she must be something."

"Oh, she's something, all right. A big fucking pain in my ass."

"If that were true, you wouldn't be so worried and twisted up."

"There's nothing to worry about as long as I can keep her out of trouble."

"That sounds ominous. Can't wait to hear about what's going on. See you soon, brother."

He ends the call, and I set my phone on the step beside me and finish my cigarette, trying to relax as much as possible and enjoy the last smoke I'll have for a while since I need to start recon.

As soon as it gets dark, I'll head out to the area around the docks and see if I can narrow down and exclude the warehouses until the guys get here.

Which means locking that door I just came out of again.

Something twists in my gut at the thought of doing that to her, but it's the right thing to do. The only way to keep her safe—at least from the things on the outside that could hurt her.

When it comes to me, it seems that door and lock just aren't enough.

VIKTORIA

A BIG FUCKING pain in my ass...

Reaper's words echo through my head even though he ended the call a few minutes ago, and anger only continues to tighten my fists at my sides where I'm pressed against the wall beside the open window that leads out to the fire escape.

It's not that I'm surprised to hear he feels that way—after all, he's basically said the same to my face—but whoever he's talking to doesn't know me, doesn't know the situation we're in. And while I only caught the end of the conversation, it's clear their only opinion of me is going to be formed based on the less-than-flattering statements Reaper just made.

As if it isn't bad enough he's planning on keeping me away from the rescue of the girls, now his friends are going to think it's because I'm some idiot who can't watch her own back or protect herself.

The fact that Reaper was so easily able to grab me off the street and keep me locked up here doesn't help my case.

But that was *then*, and this is *now*.

I'm physically and mentally stronger. More determined to help those girls and prove myself to Reaper. Ready to face whatever consequences may come from whatever actions I have to take.

And while I may have been on the fence about that not too long ago—wavering between ratting the guys out to the department before anyone gets hurt or joining them in their mission—I'm one hundred percent convinced now about what I have to do.

It's the only thing I can *do.*

Reaper thinks he's keeping me from danger by locking me up in that damn room, but all he's done is awaken a sleeping giant. He's made me more intent than ever to prove what I'm capable of and use my skills to help those girls.

I force myself to uncurl my fists to avoid making my palms bleed, and the sound of Reaper moving out on the old metal fire escape makes me still.

If I really wanted to, I could probably sneak back into the room and pretend to be sleeping before he even realizes I came out and overheard him, but I don't want to play games with him. The only way I'll ever get anywhere with Reaper is to face him head-on and prove I'm not going to roll over just because he puts on a show of being scary and macho.

He doesn't scare me. If anything, my heart aches for the man I can see hiding behind the scarred surface. He would rather be called Reaper than go by the name his parents gave him. He would rather be a monster, someone to fear and look over your shoulder for, than be human and everything that comes with that.

Footsteps creak the metal just outside the window, and he climbs in and immediately turns to face me.

"Not going to try to hit me this time?" His gaze darts down to my hands at my sides.

I cross my arms over my chest and square my shoulders. "No. I'm done physically fighting you because that's a battle I won't win. I'm moving on to a war of logic."

One of his dark eyebrows rises slowly. "Logic?"

Nodding, I take a step toward him. "Yes, logic. You may want to keep me locked up in there." I wave a hand absently across the room toward the open door. "But you *need* me with you at that warehouse when you finally raid it. You need as many skilled shooters as possible. And you need a woman who can talk to the girls and make sure they understand they're safe. Do you really think they'll trust a bunch of guys storming in wearing all black or Satan's Knights' cuts after they watch you slaughter whoever is holding them?"

His lips twist slightly, but he doesn't respond, just crosses his arms over his bare chest, emphasizing the hard, lean muscle and scars dotted across his lightly tanned skin.

"You *need* me there, Reaper. Whether you want to admit it or not. And keeping me locked up here won't stop you from worrying or thinking about me or whatever other lame excuse you come up with to justify it."

His blue eyes darken almost to black, his clenched jaw twitching.

Shit.

I hadn't intended to let loose on him like that, and I may have spoken a little too much truth for him to handle right now—or maybe ever. Something tells me Reaper isn't a man who likes to be forced to face anything involving "feelings" or to have his authority questioned.

And I'm certainly doing that right now.

Maybe to my own detriment. Reaper could literally

throw me over his shoulder—again—and toss me back in that room and lock it without a look back.

He more than *could,* actually. He probably *will.*

But instead of going all caveman on me, Reaper sucks in a deep breath and blows it out slowly, like he's trying to rein himself back in and contain his desire to lash out at me like he has before.

I raise an eyebrow at him in question, waiting for him to respond.

Finally, he shakes his head. "Even if I agree with your assessment—and that is a *big* if—you're forgetting the fact that you're a cop. You're going to ruin your entire career for *this?*"

What's he talking about? Me and him or my involvement with this entire case?

Either way, my answer remains the same.

I hold his hard gaze, letting the silence linger between us a few moments longer than I normally would, trying to find any hint that might tell me what his question was about. But just like always, Reaper remains stoic, hard, never giving away anything that's going on inside his head. The momentary crack in the wall he's built up around himself that I saw earlier has closed up as if it never existed.

But I know it did. I saw it. Saw the way he snapped and lost control. The way we both did.

"It's worth it."

That's all I can think to say because the more time I spend with Reaper, the longer I contemplate what those girls must be going through, the more confident I become that this is the right course of action.

Of course, seeing the scumbags responsible have to face a courtroom would bring a certain sense of justice, but it wouldn't put an end to what's happening. Not with the size of network Yankovich has. If we don't prove how serious we are about shutting down this trafficking ring, if we don't spill blood, someone else will just pick up in his place.

We need to make a statement. Prove that we're willing to go to any means to make these men pay and protect the innocent.

If that means I lose my badge, so be it. I'll do everything in my power to keep it, but I'm not going to kid myself into believing that anything we do is going to be by the book or even legal.

"I'm ready to face the consequences, Reaper. I'm ready to do whatever it takes." I point back toward the open door of the bedroom. "You've had me in that room for days, and you want to know what I've been thinking about in there?"

He watches me with hooded eyes, his arms still crossed over his chest that somehow seems bigger now than ever. The corner of his mouth twitches, giving me a clear indication of what he *thinks* I've been thinking about.

I push my finger right in between his hard pecs. "Besides how *mad* I am at you, I've been thinking about what it must be like for those women locked away somewhere, knowing what fate awaits them and what terror it will be. At least here, I know you won't hurt me and that I'll get released after a while. But they know the opposite is true for them. And as distraught as I've been, it pales in comparison to what they must be feeling."

My stomach clenches even considering the pain and terror they're living in, and I press my palm flat against his warm skin.

Reaper freezes under my touch but does nothing to push me away, even as my fingers brush over a scar.

"Let me help you free those women. I have to do this."

His lips twisting, Reaper watches me for a moment, searching my eyes for fear or regret, for anything else that might tell him I'm second-guessing this decision, but he won't find it there because there is no second-guessing it. This is what *has* to happen.

"Don't fight me on this, Roderick. You know I can help."

Using his real name might be playing dirty, especially combined with my hand over his heart and stepping even closer into his space. But finally, after what feels like an eternity, he uncrosses his arms from in front of him and reaches up to cup my cheek.

"If I let you do this, if I let you come with us, I need you by my side the entire time. Where I can see you. Where I can *know* you're okay. I'm not going to take any chances with you. If I tell you to get the fuck out, you get the fuck out."

I open my mouth to argue with him, but he shakes his head and tightens his grip, using it to drag me up against his firm body.

"Don't argue with me, Vik. This isn't something I'll change my mind about. It's the only way this is going to happen, so either you accept my terms, or you go back in that room to keep fighting me only to have nothing change."

"I don't want to fight with you." I bring my other hand up to rest over his steadily beating heart. "Not when I feel like fighting is all I've been doing my entire life. First, against what the neighborhood expected of me. Then, against Mom and Dad and Anya when I left to find a better life. Then, against the men at the precinct who didn't think I could handle my job. Now you. I just want to stop fighting."

"No." He shakes his head again and leans in, brushing his lips against mine. "Don't stop fighting. Just change who you're fighting against. We have a common enemy, Vik. So, let's take them out together."

15

REAPER

It's strange to come back and see the bedroom open. Having it closed since I brought Vik here has given me a much-needed barrier against all the turmoil that woman brings to my mission and my body. The non-stop bombardment of sass and sexiness from her drives me to want to simultaneously pin her against the wall and fuck her silent again or lock that door permanently. But I left it open when I took off to recon the warehouses in the area around the docks. Vik isn't going anywhere. Not after I agreed to allow her to help with the mission.

Hearing her words, seeing how much being involved and helping those girls means to her, I couldn't deny her that, even if it means having to keep an eye on her while decimating the Russians. But that doesn't mean I was about to let her come with me while I was trying to zero in on our target. Not when she still has one on her back.

The fact that she didn't fight me when I told her she was

staying almost felt like some sort of trick, like she was playing a game with me. Yet, for some reason, I trust her. She won't interfere with our plans. Whatever reservations she had about our mission have been erased by the time she spent in that room.

It wasn't my plan, but it is a nice side effect.

Because she's right. Having another trained shooter along will be invaluable. As long as she stays on my six and doesn't run off to play hero and end up getting herself hurt again.

I couldn't live with that—seeing her in pain and bleeding again. Even thinking about it makes my ribcage feel like it's tightening around my lungs, making it impossible to breathe.

Whatever is going on between us, it's affecting me more than I want to acknowledge, deeper than I ever want to explore.

Just knowing she would be here, waiting when I got back, sent a strange warmth through my entire body while I was sneaking from building to building, checking for any signs of Yankovich's crew.

Is this what it felt like for the guys who had women to come home to?

All those years, all I ever thought about was how much it would hurt someone who loved me to have me gone. To be constantly worrying and wondering if I was all right. To not know for days or even weeks at a time that I was alive and breathing. The devastation it would cause if I didn't come home.

Keeping those worries at the forefront of my brain made it easier to walk away from all the women I slept with. It made it possible to prevent myself from letting anyone get close. But it never crossed my mind that the good might outweigh the bad. That having someone care about you that deeply could offer you something you can't find anywhere else—a reason to live. And somehow, that woman, the one tearing my world apart from the inside out, has made me question everything.

It doesn't keep me away, though. I'm drawn toward the sound of the running water in the small bathroom attached to the "prison" that's become hers. I kick off my boots and cross the floor into the room, listening for any signs she's been alerted to my return. But all I hear is the rush of the shower and a low, melodic hum from deep in her throat that goes straight to my cock.

I hope Vik got some sleep after I left because things are going to get a lot busier and a lot more complicated very soon. Our time together will end as soon as Yankovich is taken care of, and I'm not about to waste one minute of it. These moments need to last me a lifetime.

All I can think about while I undress is getting under that cascade of water with her, how beautiful she'll look with it trickling over her breasts and down between her thighs. Taking my hard cock in hand, I step into the small steamy room. The frosted glass door offers me the perfect view of all of Vik's luscious curves as she turns her back to the water and tilts her head under it.

Fuck...

My cock aches to be inside her again, and I stroke it slowly, watching her rinse her hair while she hums to herself contently.

"Are you just going to stand there jerking off, or are you going to join me?"

Her question freezes my hand, and I can't fight off the grin that pulls at my lips.

Such a smartass.

It's okay, though. I'll just fuck it out of her.

And enjoy every fucking second of it.

I slide open the shower door and meet her bright-green eyes, dancing with amusement. She knows what she just said is likely to set me off, and she doesn't care. Vik likes poking the bear.

She raises an eyebrow at me, the water pelting her back and steam rising around her. "How did it go?"

Stepping in, I shake my head. "Good. But I don't want to talk about that right now."

I close the distance between us and wrap my arms around her slick body, letting my hands drift down to grab her ass.

She brings her arms up around my neck and drags my head down to press her mouth to mine. "Oh, yeah, what do you want to do?"

Her tongue probes playfully at my lips, and I grind my cock against her stomach and enjoy her little mewl of need filling the tight space. I drop my hand between her legs and feel the slick heat of her pussy, so wet and ready for me.

Driving inside her right now sounds incredible, but there's something else I need to do first. She wraps her hand around my cock, and I drag my mouth back from hers and shake my head.

"Not yet, Vik."

Before she can protest too much, I drop to my knees onto the cracked tile of the shower and slide my tongue where my fingers just were.

Good God.

Her arousal coats my tongue and makes me almost come on the spot. Even after fucking Vik a half a dozen times over the last couple of days, I'm still dancing along that razor-thin edge of losing control like a fumbling teenager the first time he touches a woman's cunt.

But I won't embarrass myself by reaching the end before she does. Determined to make her come hard and fast, I lap at her relentlessly, savoring her taste and committing it to memory.

She gasps and grabs my shoulders to hold herself steady, but I plan on devouring this woman so well she won't be able to stand, so I push her backward until her shoulders and ass press against the wall. With the hot spray beating against my back, I dip my head down to taste her again. She moans and digs her nails in my shoulders, the sharp bite of pain making me groan against her wet flesh and drive my tongue into her while I slip my thumb up across her clit.

Her hips buck against my face, pushing herself tighter against me, seeking the very thing I'm just as desperate to give her.

I could eat this woman forever and never have my fill. I don't care if I suffocate like this. At least I would die a happy man.

Yet, it still isn't enough. I grasp her thighs and lift her to settle them over my shoulders, spreading her pussy wide open right in front of my face, exactly where I want it. But she needs more. I pull my tongue from inside her and replace it with my fingers, curling them to find that perfect spot inside while I swirl my tongue on her clit and allowing her the ability to roll her hips and drive up against my mouth and hand.

She offers a little mewl of approval as I suck her clit between my lips and flick my tongue against it. One of her hands moves from my shoulder to dig into my hair, grasping at the short locks, searching for something to cling to.

I chuckle against her pussy, the vibration sending her wild, her hips seeking the release she's so close to—that I'm so close to. My cock aches so badly, it can't be ignored anymore. I reach down with my free hand and grasp it, stroking it hard and fast as I eat her like she's my last meal.

Because this very well might be the last time we get to do this.

Once Chaos and Mouth get here, things will move quickly, and I'm not ready to stop until she comes all over my face and screams my name loud enough that the echo will remain with me forever.

VIKTORIA

Whatever has suddenly gotten into Reaper, it's both terrifying and exhilarating at the same time. He once told me he will always complete his mission, and it seems his mission now is to drive me to the brink of insanity without giving me release.

He lashes at my clit with his tongue while he pumps his fingers into me, but it isn't enough. Not nearly enough. I need him inside me. I need that feeling of completeness, of being whole and filled that only his dick can give me. But Reaper doesn't seem inclined to offer me that. Just torture me.

And damn, is he good at his job.

Squeezing my thighs around his head, I drag him closer, desperate for more friction, more force, more everything, and when he sucks my clit between his lips in that pulsating rhythm, my body detonates like an atom bomb going off. My pussy clenches around his fingers, clasping and seeking what it really wants. His moan of approval against my skin only makes my orgasm surge on longer, and Reaper refuses to offer me any reprieve from the relentlessness of his mouth.

I claw at the back of his head, simultaneously wanting to draw him closer and push him away because of the intensity of the feelings flooding my system. Every muscle vibrates, spasming with pleasure and need and something else I've never felt before.

When the orgasm finally subsides and I sag back against the cold tiles, Reaper looks up at me with a hooded gaze filled with promise, his lips glistening with my release. He darts out his tongue across them, his shoulder bunching and flexing under my thigh as he strokes his cock.

His blue eyes locked with mine, his jaw tightens, and he comes on a low groan, hot spurts hitting my ass where it's dipped down low against the tile.

Fuck. Why is that so hot?

Reaper got so turned on by going down on me that he just came without even getting inside me. But the look he's giving me now suggests we're far from through. He slowly slides my legs from his shoulders, lowers my feet to the tile, and holds me steady with a solid grip on my hips as he rises to his feet, his breathing heavy.

"Christ, Vik…"

I don't even know how to respond, but I don't have to because he captures my mouth in a searing kiss and grinds his still-hard cock against my stomach.

"Turn around."

It isn't a request. It's an order. And I do it on shaking legs to press my hands against the tile and arch my back, offering myself to him.

He grips my hip firmly with one hand, aligns his cock with the other, and slams up into me, pushing my chest against the wall while the hot water still beats against his back.

I gasp and press my cheek to the cool tile surface, a startling juxtaposition to the heat of his body against mine and filling me. He leans forward and places his hands over mine, twining our fingers as he drills into me, hitting exactly the right spot to make me lose control all over again.

His warm lips kiss a trail up my neck and across my cheek until his hot breath flutters against my ear. "Whatever happens, we'll always have this."

My heart thunders against my rib cage, the rush of the water falling filling my ears while his cock continues to drill into me like there is no tomorrow.

Maybe that's what his words mean.

He knows this might be our last time together. That thought makes tears form in my eyes, but I don't want him to stop, especially not now. Not when my body tingles with the rise of another orgasm. Not when I'm so damn close.

One of his hands pulls free of mine, and Reaper captures my chin and turns my head back to meet his gaze. "Look at me when you come."

The low growl of the words sends a jolt straight to my clit, and almost as if he can read my mind, he releases my chin and reaches down there, working his hand in time with the pace and punishment of his cock.

That's exactly what I need to release another cataclysmic orgasm that leaves me gasping and shaking as he pumps into me harder and deeper and finally comes again deep inside me, never taking his eyes off mine.

I sag back against him, this tiny shower suddenly feeling far too large, like there's too much space between us, and he wraps his arms around me and buries his face against the crook of my neck.

He places a kiss there, and I release a tiny, contented sigh that's interrupted by loud clapping filling the bathroom. We both jerk our heads toward the steamed glass door, two shadowy figures barely visible through it.

"Wow. That was hot. Way to go, man."

Reaper issues a low growl and turns to place his body between me and whoever is standing out there. "Get the fuck out of here, you asshole."

I glance up at him. "Who the hell is that?"

He sighs and squeezes closed his eyes. "That was Chaos."

"Chaos?"

Somehow, that name doesn't seem to bode well for what's to come.

16

REAPER

They're on me the second I step out of the bedroom and close the door behind me, not giving a shit about the fact that I'm standing in front of them buck naked.

Chaos motions behind me. "Whoa, dude, you didn't tell me you were banging her or that she was so hot."

I glare at him as I make my way to the other bedroom to grab some clothes, both of them hot on my trail. "You didn't have to be a total prick about it."

"Sorry, man." He holds up his hands even though he doesn't mean the apology and chuckles. "I can't believe you didn't hear my bike outside when I pulled up, or the garage door, or the elevator coming up."

I pull a pair of jeans from a drawer and jerk them on, then do the same with a T-shirt. "I'm suddenly regretting giving you guys keys to this place."

The safehouse was meant to be somewhere we could all use when needed, not a place for them to come give me shit when I finally manage to get it in with a beautiful woman after six months of self-imposed celibacy.

Chaos chuckles and leans against the door jamb while Mouth watches from just behind him, a smirk curling his lips.

I point at Mouth. "You could have given me some warning."

Like a fucking text saying they were going to arrive soon...

He shrugs and shakes his head as if to say, *"What the hell was I supposed to do?"*

A fucking text would have been nice.

I wave them off and intentionally bump shoulders with Chaos as I make my way out of the bedroom and into the main living space of the loft. They follow me to the kitchen, and each takes a stool at the counter while I grab a bottle of water from the fridge and chug it. "I would offer you two fuckers a beer, but..." I shrug.

Chaos' lips twitch. "Still doing the whole sober thing?"

My hands itch to smack the half-grin off his face, but I crumple the empty water bottle between them instead. "I don't have much of a choice. You know what that shit did to me and what it cost me. It's not anywhere I ever want to go back to."

Those few months before and just after I was discharged are nothing but a blur of bad decisions and hangovers. It wasn't pretty, and they both know it since they were the people who helped pull me from the bottom of the bottle—but not before I lost my spot on Delta and got medically discharged due to "mental health."

Still, I know they'd enjoy a cold one after traveling here. I grab them each a bottle of water and set them in front of them. It's the least I can do.

Chaos rolls it between his hands. "So, who's the girl?"

I glance at the door to ensure it's still closed and rest my palms on the granite, leaning forward slightly. "Detective Viktoria Garin of the NYPD."

They both raise their eyebrows.

Chaos snorts. "Then I'm even more interested in why you wanted us here. Considering any reason I can think of consists of things you don't want the fuzz knowing about."

I sigh and run a hand back through my damp hair. "She and her partner, Hank Grayson, were looking into the Russians and the same human trafficking ring. We bumped into each other at a club called B66. Turns out, this guy, Michail Yankovich, is holding monthly auctions for these girls."

Mouth's lips twist into a sneer, and Chaos clenches the water bottle tight enough that his knuckles whiten.

"Fucker."

"I share the sentiments. Anyway, while I was meeting with Grayson off the books to exchange information to try to advance either of our investigations, we got shot at."

Both of their eyes widen. Since all of our discharges, we've been dabbling in various endeavors that often require us to use the skills we were taught by Uncle Sam, but rarely are we dodging bullets anymore.

Chaos shakes his head. "Who was dumb enough to shoot at you?"

"The Russians. At least, I'm pretty sure it was them. Only, Grayson and I weren't the targets." I incline my head toward the bedroom. "She was."

"What?" Chaos stops fiddling with his bottle of water and raises an eyebrow at me. "Why?"

I release a deep sigh, the annoyance at finding out the information from Vik returning. "Apparently, she grew up in Brighton Beach, where there's a huge Russian population and thinks she was recognized at B66. Anyway, she got hit, but her partner had a buddy's girl patch her up. Then someone tried to nab her off the street, and I brought her here to keep her safe. And well…"

Chaos chuckles deeply. "You thought your dick would keep her safe?"

Asshole.

I chuck the empty water bottle at him, and he ducks to avoid it hitting his head. "Shut up, fucker. Show her some respect."

"Oh…" He holds up his hand. "Respect? Damn, you are really twisted up about this girl."

"Fuck you, man."

The last thing I want to be discussing with Chaos and Mouth is my situation with Vik. It's complicated enough without them tossing in their two cents when they know absolutely nothing about her and could never understand how easily she gets under my skin.

Chaos chugs half his water and smacks his lips. "So, what's the plan? What do you need us to do?"

I open my mouth to respond just as the door cracks and Viktoria peeks her head out. All eyes turn in her direction, and both Mouth and Chaos smirk.

This is going to be a shit-show.

The guys have never seen me with a woman—at least, not one who wasn't stripping on a pole. Giving each other shit is just part of our friendship, but when it comes to Vik, my protective instinct seems to go beyond keeping the Russians from putting more bullet holes in her.

Though, I can't keep her from the boys forever.

No matter how much I may want to.

I wave for her to join us, and she slips from the door into the loft and slowly makes her way over to the kitchen. "Guys, this is Detective Viktoria Garin." I motion toward Chaos, who looks even worse than usual with his dark hair disheveled and blue eyes rimmed with dark circles from lack of sleep. "Viktoria, this is Kalen Riggs, but you can call him Chaos, and this is Jude Lawson"—I point toward the brick house with the haunting gaze that seems to bore right through anyone he looks at—"but he goes by Mouth."

They both incline their heads toward her in recognition, but neither says nor does anything else to acknowledge the fact that they just watched me fuck her in the shower.

Given how they arrived and the first impression they made, the need to defend them to Vik rises before I can stop it. "I trust these guys with my life, and you should, too."

She joins me on my side of the counter and offers them a tight smile. "Nice timing, boys."

I bark out a laugh that echoes around the loft space. Leave it to Vik to have a smartass comment after being caught in the act. "I was just about to fill the guys in on the plan. I scoped out the warehouses, and I've excluded a few where there were clearly no signs of anyone being there recently. But I haven't pinpointed it yet. The boys and I will do some more recon tomorrow and nail it down. Then I'll get a hold of Hank, and we can all meet and finalize the plan."

Based on what I saw, any of the warehouses should be fairly easy to get in and out of, but Yankovich's men are armed to the teeth wherever they are, so it won't come without a lot of bullets flying. That means this needs to be organized carefully, and I need Chaos and Mouth and Vik to all be on the same page.

The guys are rock solid. No questions there, but something tells me despite Vik's insistence, some reservations still linger—the kind that could get someone killed.

VIKTORIA

"JUST WHAT EXACTLY IS THE plan? Besides getting the girls out of there."

Reaper exchanges a look with his friends and glances at me. "Am I giving you the law-enforcement-appropriate answer or the truth?"

His question makes acid rise up my throat, and I swallow it back and glance between the three men. If the other two are anything like Reaper—which I assume they are, or he wouldn't have asked them here to be involved in something like this—then they aren't going to hesitate to pull the trigger if necessary.

Even though I resigned myself to the fact that the vigilante-style of justice that will be happening might be necessary in these dire circumstances, and that getting the department involved would likely only complicate things in a way that could cost these women their lives, it doesn't mean the cop in me doesn't still feel a bit uneasy about all of it.

Still, I made my decision and laid all my cards on the table with Reaper. There isn't any way to go back now.

"The real answer. I have to know what to expect."

Reaper leans his hip against the counter, addressing me, scanning my face to see if I really mean it or if I'm just placating him. "If we arrest these guys, what are the chances of them actually getting convicted and doing any time? What are the chances that while they are in there, someone else doesn't just pick up the business?"

Pretty slim.

It's the unfortunate reality of the court system and the power men like Yankovich have. Money and connections often mean justice isn't served and the perps walk. Frustrating for a cop who spends months or even years building a case and for the prosecutors, but even more so for the victims.

I just need to keep reminding myself who I'm doing this for—those innocent women and girls.

But Reaper doesn't wait for me to respond, clearly intending those to be rhetorical questions—or maybe because he's worried about what I'll say, especially in front of his friends.

"We need to take them out, Vik—each and every one of them. We need to make a statement that this type of trafficking isn't going to happen without repercussions. The only way to do that is to spill as much blood as possible." He pauses and narrows his eyes on me. "You have a problem with that?"

I look from him to his friends, waiting for one of them to show even an ounce of hesitance or guilt. "None of you do?"

A smile plays on Chaos' lips, but Mouth, who still hasn't said a thing, sits stoically on his stool, his elbows resting on the counter.

Well, I guess that answers that question.

Not that I expected anything different, but the fact that people can take lives so easily still unnerves me. I can't let it affect this situation, though.

I turn back to the man I just let destroy me in the shower, my body heating at the memory and with the returned embarrassment of knowing Chaos and Mouth witnessed at least the end of it. "I guess I can't expect anything else from a man called Reaper, can I?"

He crosses his arms over his chest and shakes his head. "Don't make the mistake of thinking I *like* doing this, that *any* of us get off on taking lives. Sometimes, it's just necessary, Vik." He glances at his friends. "Believe me, I had no idea what I was walking into when Cutter asked me to help take out the man responsible for his friend's girl being trafficked. I had no clue it would lead to all of this. But I couldn't just walk away then, and I can't walk away now with these guys still breathing. Not when the criminal justice system is so fucked up. Between payoffs and plea deals, some or all of these guys could end up walking, and then, where would we end up? With another warehouse full of girls."

Chaos leans back slightly. "But we don't know exactly where they are?"

Reaper returns his focus to him. "I found a source who said they were in a warehouse by the Jersey docks. Scoping it all out, I was able to exclude a bunch of them, but we have to do some additional recon, and of course, see if we can get the plans to the building. Then, we'll meet with Hank and the Satan's Knights in a couple days when we're ready."

"The Satan's Knights?" Chaos raises an eyebrow. "As in, the motorcycle club?"

I nod and release an annoyed sigh that draws a knowing look from Reaper.

He shakes his head and addresses Chaos. "Their involvement is a long story I'll tell you later. Just know we're all on the same side of this."

All on the same side.

I wish I could believe that was true. But it's hard to think of myself as being on the same side as criminals and vigilantes. Still, I guess that's where I am. Where I've chosen to be. Because, like it or not, the only reason I'm here is of my own choosing.

Of course, the alternative is to be locked inside that room until this is all over, but I need to do good where I can when I can—even if it means eating away at my own conscience a little bit.

If Reaper and his friends think the only way to end this is putting a bullet or ten into the men behind it, then maybe they're right. They've spent their entire careers defending this country and innocent people against threats all over the world. I may not agree with their methods, but maybe I'll just have to learn to live with them.

Like I'll have to learn to live with what I've done with Reaper.

Involving myself emotionally with a man as cold as he is ruthless is just setting myself up to have my heart broken. Just like he'll pull the trigger on Yankovich, he's going to pull the trigger and end whatever this is between us when his mission is all said and done.

I'll be left to wonder what might've been if we had met under different circumstances or if I've made a huge mistake. To be haunted forever by the memories of his rough, calloused hands touching me, his warm lips pressed against the most intimate spots of my body, his tongue...

A shudder rolls through me, one I'll likely experience every day of my life going forward, remembering this time we had together.

Not the smartest move, Viktoria.

No, not at all.

17

VIKTORIA

The Satan's Knights clubhouse looks a hell of a lot different when there are still hints of sunlight on the horizon and I'm not drunk on whiskey and in excruciating pain after being shot.

It isn't much of a clubhouse at all, really, just a dive bar that apparently allows them to use a room at the back. Not exactly what one expects when they picture the home of a one-percenter MC. Though, it isn't really my department, so while I was familiar with the group prior to our fateful meeting, I can't say I've ever really spent any time considering where they do their business. And when they dragged me here to patch me up and Hank brought me home after, I wasn't really concerned with where the makeshift surgery had occurred.

But now that we're here to meet with Hank and the Satan's Knights to plan what could very well be a raid that ends my career as a cop, I can't help but feel the guilt, knowing I've gotten involved with these guys.

Their reputation precedes them, and now, I'm entering the lion's den, with three mercenaries hot on my heels—one of whom I'm sleeping with. Or more like fucking and getting very little sleep with.

Christ, how did you get in this situation, Vik?

Each step feels like marching toward my doom. Likely because the former president, Jack Parrish, stands at the end of the long, narrow hallway in front of an open door and motions for us to step inside.

Reaper urges me forward with a warm hand firmly at my lower back, and somehow, despite all the reasons it shouldn't, his touch there is like an anchor keeping me grounded in this moment and instead of overthinking everything like I want to.

And it's a good thing, too, because if I did truly stop to think about what we're about to do in this backroom, I would probably turn the other way and walk right out of here.

As it stands, it's only Reaper's physical presence at my back that keeps me moving forward in the room that isn't at all what I expected. Several tables from the bar have been pushed together to form one long one in the center, and Satan's Knight's insignia occupy all the wall space. But it isn't nearly as intimidating as I anticipated. Maybe I've mentally psyched myself out for no reason whatsoever.

Then my eyes fall on the man at the head of the table. His cut says "*WOLF*" and bears the patch reading "*President.*" He must be the man who took over from Parrish when he stepped down…and he doesn't look too pleased with this meeting.

Reaper leans in and brushes his lips against my ear. "Just stay cool, Vik."

Stay cool?

I shoot him a dirty glare over my shoulder, but he just

grins and urges me toward an empty seat on the near side of the table. Parrish motions for us to sit, and Chaos and Mouth drop into seats on the other side of Reaper while the rest of the Satan's Knights settle into the other empty chairs, leaving only one open and one very important person missing from this meeting.

"Where's Hank?"

Almost as if on cue, he hustles through the door, looking slightly disheveled and exasperated. "Hey, sorry I'm late." His eyes land on me, and he sighs in relief. "Vik, are you all right?"

The look he casts at Reaper tells me he hasn't been all that comfortable with the situation despite his conversations with the man and likely has a thousand questions I'm not sure I want to answer about what's been happening while I've been with our mercenary friend.

I glance around the room at all the hard eyes watching us and nod. "I'm good. We'll talk later."

Hank seems to catch the drift and settles into the empty chair on the opposite side of the table.

Parrish leans forward in his chair and rests his elbows on the table. "Now that we're all here, let me introduce you to Wolf, our current prez."

Wolf inclines his head toward each of us, a snarl on his lips. "Let me be clear; I don't take kindly to being kept in the dark about shit like this." He turns his beady eyes on Parrish and fixes him with a glare. "Getting in deep with cops and mercenaries is not how this club operates anymore."

Parrish rolls his eyes. "If this is the part where we whip out our dicks to see who the bigger man is here, I feel I should remind you there is a lady in the room." He spits out his toothpick and crosses his arms against his chest. "We all get it, brother; you're in charge. But Yankovich is personal."

"Damn straight he is, but that isn't exclusive to you. The

Yankovich family has inflicted pain on everyone with a fucking patch. Need I remind you, who shot my son while you had me tied to a fucking chair?"

"Pop," the guy with the patch that reads *"NICO"* calls from across the table. "Not the time."

"Yeah, Scotto," Parrish interjects. "That's old fucking news. The Satan's Knights involvement in this operation is justified no matter how you spin it."

Hank clears his throat. "With all due respect, can you two handle this after we get the girls to safety because time is not on our side?"

Wolf regards Hank with a look. "Our club is at your disposal. Whatever resources you need—men, ammo, a place to crash while this is all going on—it's all yours."

Parrish uncrosses his arms and slaps his palms against the table. "Great, now can we get the fuck on with it? What's the plan?"

Reaper shifts next to me and leans forward. "I've located the warehouse where they're holding the girls. Chaos, Mouth, and I sat on it all day yesterday, and we have a good feeling of their schedules and what we can expect going in when it comes to resistance. We also grabbed the blueprints that were filed with the city when it was built, so we have a good idea of the internal layout and structure. What we don't know is how many girls there are or how much help we'll need getting them out of there."

Hank shifts uneasily in his seat, his gaze darting from Parrish and over to us. "That's going to be a problem."

Reaper raises an eyebrow at him. "Why is that?"

"We have to get Anastasia and the kids to safety. If we go in for the girls and Yankovich somehow gets wind of that, all he has to do is call the guard he has watching her and she's done."

Parrish leans forward. "Yeah, and if we get her and the

kids out first, he's going to lock that warehouse down tight. He might even move the girls before we can get them. We're fucked either way."

Shit.

While this Anastasia woman has tried to assist us since Hank first made contact, I never thought about the fact that we'd have to worry about her, too, when the bullets started flying.

With an annoyed sigh, Reaper leans back in his chair and shrugs. "We hit them both at the same time. You and the Knights get Anastasia and the kids, and Chaos, Mouth, and I will go into the warehouse."

Oh, hell no!

"You, Chaos, Mouth, and *me.*" I lean forward and turn until my gaze meets his. "Don't think you're leaving me out of this raid, Reaper."

The corner of his mouth twitches. "I wouldn't dream of it. If we hit them both at the same time, no one can issue a warning. We should have a chance of getting everyone out safely."

A chance...

Those words don't instill a lot of confidence. Unease coils and tightens around my spine, making me shift uncomfortably in my seat.

Hank apparently shares my worry. "Are you going to be able to do it with just four of you?"

Reaper exchanges a look with his buddies. "We've handled worse."

Somehow, I don't doubt that. I've seen the evidence of it permanently marked across his skin and in the way his buddies' eyes constantly dart around the room, taking in every detail and missing nothing.

Still, it seems like a tall order for the four of us to take on potentially dozens of men at the warehouse alone, even if we do have the best-trained men in the country on our side.

There has to be more we can do. More *I* can offer to this mission.

"What if we stack the deck in our favor?"

All eyes in the room turn to me.

Hank shifts in his seat and narrows his gaze on me. "What do you mean?"

"Well…" I cast a hesitant peek at Reaper, who has gone stock still next to me. "We suspect I was the target of the shooting, right?"

Everyone nods their agreement.

I swallow and avoid looking at Reaper when I finally lay out my plan. "So, we know they would be interested if I showed up at the warehouse, right? Maybe I should draw them out of the building. It makes them easier targets if they're out in the open on the docks."

REAPER

"ARE YOU FUCKING *INSANE*?" I don't bother trying to hide the anger from my voice. Even if I had made an attempt to, I would have failed. Miserably. As it stands now, I wouldn't be surprised if steam were coming out of my ears like in the old cartoons as I stare at Viktoria. "You *must* be completely unhinged if you think there's any way in *hell* I'm going to let you be *bait* for the guys who tried to *kill* you once already."

How can she even suggest such absolute lunacy?

Fisting my hands on the top of the table, I wait for her to offer some sort of explanation for her crazy, ridiculous, absolutely stupid suggestion.

Hank snorts from his place across the table and holds up

his hand to point at me. "I actually agree with Dixon. That's not happening."

Viktoria has the nerve to look shocked by our reactions. "What? Why not? We know they want me."

I slam my fist onto the table, making several people twitch in their seats. Maybe an unwise move around these guys. "Because I'm not going to put your life at risk *again* any more than we have to."

Hank clears his throat. "Neither am I, Vik. I'm the one who dragged you into this. I'm the reason you got shot and you're risking your badge. I'm not going to let you be bait for a madman, too."

At least Hank and I are in agreement with this insanity. If he backed her idea, we might have a very serious and bloody problem on our hands. As it stands now, Vik will undoubtedly tear into me at the first chance she gets once we're somewhere private. But I can handle her, especially when I have her partner backing me—along with everyone else in the room, which I have to assume is true since no one is jumping in to say her plan has any merit.

Vik scowls and glances from Hank to me, shooting daggers at both of us with hard eyes, her arms crossed over her chest. "I'm a big girl and capable of making my own decisions on this."

I slide my hand onto her leg and squeeze her thigh as I lean in. What I'm about to say isn't for everyone's ears. "We had a deal, Vik. You would stay by my side or at my fucking six so I can keep an eye on you the entire time if I was going to let you out of that room. Your idea isn't the deal, and it isn't happening. End of fucking discussion."

Her mossy eyes lock with mine, defiance flashing in their depths.

Just fucking try me, Vik.

I won't think twice about tossing her over my shoulder

again, throwing her right back into that room, and keeping her locked up until this is all over.

And it looks like she's more than ready to argue and fight this out. She opens her soft, pink lips to do it when Wolf bangs his meat mallet "gavel" against the table.

"I don't know what the fuck is going on with you guys, but if anyone gives a shit, I'm in agreement that it's best if we go in unannounced." He shakes his head and narrows his gaze at Parrish. "And this is why we don't do business with these types."

Chaos finally speaks up from beside me. "This is what we do best, guys. We can handle it." He cuts his gaze to Viktoria. "*Without* putting anyone at unnecessary risk."

Her entire body goes rigid, her leg stiffening under my palm, and I know what she wants to say—that all of this is an unnecessary risk—but she bites back her comment and settles in her chair, huffing and re-crossing her arms over her chest angrily.

Parrish chuckles from his spot across the table. "Well, since that's settled…it looks like we all have some more specific planning to do." He looks at Reaper. "You let us know if you guys want any additional men or resources."

Wolf shoots him a dirty look, but Parrish either doesn't see it or doesn't care. Whatever is going on with those two, I wouldn't want to be stuck in the middle of it. Nor do I anticipate needing any help from the Satan's Knights. After what Chaos, Mouth, and I saw when staking out the place, I'm confident we can get in and out without too much trouble.

I nod and squeeze Vik's leg. "We'll be fine."

And I will have a *serious* conversation with Vik when we get back to the safehouse about the little plan she suggested. One she is definitely not going to enjoy.

Everyone pushes back from the table. I place my hand at Vik's back to steer her from the room, but she glances over her shoulder at me with a scowl and inclines her head toward Hank.

"I need to talk to my partner for a minute. *Alone.*"

Her brush-off shouldn't bother me. Hank has been her partner for a long time, and they had a relationship long before I was in the picture in any capacity. But still, the edges of my vision go green as she rounds the table and approaches him, dragging him to the far corner of the room where they can talk in private.

Is this what jealousy feels like?

It isn't anything I've ever experienced because I've never allowed myself to care enough about any one woman to give two shits about who or what she does when she isn't with me.

Hank wraps an arm around her shoulder, and I fist my hands at my sides to keep myself from crossing the room and doing something very unwise to Detective Grayson.

Chaos claps me on the shoulder. "You might want to wipe that sneer off your face if you want any chance of that woman ever letting you do what you did to her in the shower or what I heard you two doing the last few nights ever again."

Fucking asshole.

I turn toward him and flip him off. "Fuck you, Chaos. What the hell would *you* know about how to deal with a woman, anyway? Didn't your ex-wife leave your ass high and dry during your first deployment?"

Shit. Maybe that was going a bit too far.

He stills, and his lips press into a firm line as he leans in so the men lingering in the room can't hear whatever he's about to say—likely a good thing. "Don't pretend to know my personal business, Reaper. You don't have the first fucking clue about anything."

This isn't the time to delve into his complicated personal

life, even though I stand by my assertion that he perhaps isn't the best person to be offering love life advice.

I shrug off his hand from my shoulder and turn toward the door. "You're right. My bad." I try to shake out the tension building in my shoulders, but another glance at Hank and Vik whispering in the corner only tightens my muscles even more. "I just want this whole thing over and done with."

Chaos raises an eyebrow at me, following my gaze. "What? The raid or your time with Viktoria?"

Fuck if I know.

And that's the entire problem.

18

REAPER

The cool breeze off Newark Bay flutters Vik's hair around her where she crouches down next to me, gun in hand, eyes laser-focused on the warehouse in front of us. Despite the river being right there, that damn scent of summer flowers invades my breath, tightening my hand on my weapon.

How the hell can she still smell like that when she doesn't have her things at the safe house?

It's just how she smells, and it's fucking with my head in ways we can't afford right now.

Leaning into her only makes it worse, but I can't risk being heard. I brush my lips against her ear. "I told you to put your fucking hair up."

Vik turns her head toward me until our lips almost brush. "And I told you to fuck off."

I grab her upper arm and drag her chest up against mine. "We don't need any distractions, including your goddamn hair tickling me in the fucking wind."

Even though it isn't in Vik's nature not to argue back, she relaxes slightly and inclines her head toward mine in acknowledgment. "You could've just fucking said that."

She hands me her gun, quickly pulls up her hair into a messy bun with a hair tie around her wrist, then settles back in next to me and holds out her open palm. I slap the gun into it with an annoyed glare at her before I return my focus to the warehouse.

The big, dark-blue conversion van they use to deliver late-night food to Yankovich's men every night since we started watching the place pulled in a few minutes ago, and the food was unloaded and brought inside quickly. Now, all we have to do is wait for the agreed-upon signal to go in.

Viktoria shifts next to me. "You really think this is the right time to go in?" She glances at me with concerned eyes. "We shouldn't wait 'til there are fewer men inside?"

It isn't the first time she's expressed her concern with the plan Chaos, Mouth, and I came up with. She wanted to go in while the two guys who always grab the food were gone, but we shot down that idea pretty damn fast.

I shake my head and lean into her again. "Like I told you before, when they're eating, they're not going to be paying attention. Ten distracted men are better than eight men on full alert."

She nods her understanding and shifts in her squat again, though whether she's uncomfortable in the position or her nerves are getting to her remains unclear.

I scan the entire area around us, focus moving from building to building and the quiet docks that are basically empty this time of night. What we're about to do could draw a lot of unwanted attention, and there's a good chance one or all of us may end up in cuffs on the way out of here. But it'll be worth it if the girls are safe. Whether because we set them free or because the cops show up at the sound of gunfire and intervene.

The former would be preferred, but either way, this might be the last moment I get alone with Viktoria—maybe ever. I didn't want to think about it last night when she straddled me and slowly rode up and down on my cock. I didn't want to think about it when she leaned down and kissed me, her dark hair falling around us like curtains against the world outside, keeping us in that moment just a little longer so we could pretend that the private world we have been living in wasn't coming to an end the next day.

Not thinking about it allowed us to ignore what we did over and over and over again until we both collapsed so exhausted we could barely move then wrapped around each other. It allowed me to keep ignoring the reality of what tonight would bring.

It was the best damn night's sleep I've ever had in my entire life. In the arms of a woman who simultaneously makes me want to strangle her and kiss her senseless. A woman who hates everything I stand for and stands for everything I believe in. A woman who's ready to go into that warehouse with us, guns blazing, to rescue innocent women and ensure that they're safe, even if it costs her the badge she's worked her entire life for.

I glance at her out of the corner of my eye. "Be careful, Vik. Remember, stay with me at all times—at my side or on my six."

She opens her mouth to say something but then quickly presses her lips together and nods. It's too late for any further reservations or concerns. We're too far in to go back now. We don't have time to scrap tonight and regroup. Not with the auction coming up so fast.

It's now or never.

The light over the dock door where they pulled up the

van goes out, a sign they've finished bringing in all the food and won't be back outside the rest of the night unless something draws them out. It's also our signal to go in.

If all goes as planned, they'll be so distracted eating that they won't know what hit them until it's too late for them to respond and formulate any sort of counterattack.

What I said in that meeting yesterday was true. Chaos, Mouth, and I have seen shit and faced odds a lot worse than this. I'm not worried about us, though. I'm worried about those women and Vik. One stray bullet is all it takes to end the life of somebody who doesn't deserve it instead of the bad guys. Which is why we're going to be careful and stick to the plan.

I raise my hand and signal to Vik that we're moving. She sends off a text to Hank to let them know to move that just says "now," then we dodge out from around the buoys where we've been taking cover at the side of the dock and make our way through the shadows toward the warehouse where the Russians are holding the girls.

Vik stays directly behind me, her soft footsteps barely audible to anyone but me. But even if I couldn't hear her, I would feel her. Whenever that woman is within a hundred feet of me, my heart races, and my body responds.

It's more dangerous to both of us than whatever lies inside this building. Yet, I can't bring myself to regret anything that's happened since the day I met her in that club. Not when I have felt things with her that I never thought possible. It's why having her with us tonight ups the stakes so much. Because it isn't just about rescuing these girls and making sure the fuckers pay for their sins; it also means protecting this woman to ensure that when this is all said and done, she still has her life and her job.

God willing...

If I still believed in the big man upstairs, I might actually send up another prayer for what we're about to do, but my faith in a higher power died a long time ago with my friends on a sandy road across the fucking world. It didn't help them, and it didn't keep Vik from leaving her apartment the other day, either.

We reach the side of the building and duck into the shadowy recesses of a side door. While Vik keeps her eyes on what's happening behind us, I quickly pick the lock. These idiots didn't even upgrade the security doors on this place. They're so fucking confident no one would ever come at Yankovich that they've gotten complacent.

That just makes things easier for us.

Hopefully...

According to the blueprints we found for the building, this door leads to a small hallway filled mostly with janitorial closets and other small storage. There shouldn't be any reason for any of Yankovich's men to be back here. More than likely, they'll be in the kitchen or doing God knows what with the girls, who we assume are being held somewhere in the main warehouse area.

I would've loved to have gotten eyes inside somehow before we came in tonight, but we had to work with what's available. Which isn't much. Still, with Chaos, Mouth, and Vik with me, I'm confident we can get these girls out of here safely.

As long as all goes as planned. And unfortunately, one thing my time in Delta taught me is that even the best-laid plans can go to shit in an instant.

Tightening my grip on my weapon, I ease open the door, listening for any noise on the other side, but all remains quiet. Only the sound of Vik's soft breathing behind me fills my ears.

I signal for her to follow me, and the determined look she shoots encourages me that she is one hundred percent on her game. Her bullet wound has healed well, and any lingering pain from it seems to be a long-forgotten memory.

Just like I'll be once this is over and I leave.

But I can't get ahead of myself. It's essential to stay in the moment when we have such an important job to do first.

The dark hallway in front of us might seem ominous to some, but it gives us the cover of darkness to enter the building. We make our way in, pausing at each door and clearing several small storage rooms. Chaos and Mouth will enter from the opposite side and meet us at the rendezvous location, assuming no one runs into any resistance before then. And the sound of laughter trickling down the hallway seems to suggest we won't.

Our plan is to hit them when their guard is down and they're concentrating on something else, like eating, and it seems as though we correctly assessed the situation. Nothing hints at them being aware we've breached the warehouse walls and are almost on them.

They have no idea what's coming, and once we unleash it on them, there won't be any escape from our wrath.

I pause a few feet from the open door to the kitchen, light and voices pouring out to the dark hall. Viktoria stops behind me, the warmth of her body radiating against my side, reminding me she's safe—at least for the moment.

Chaos and Mouth approach stealthily from the opposite direction and pause just on the other side of the door, weapons at the ready.

Here we go.

I hold up three fingers and take one deep breath before starting the silent countdown.

Three...

Two...

One...

VIKTORIA

THREE...

Blood rushes loudly in my ears, like waves crashing against the shore, while watching Reaper start the countdown. Everything around me moves almost in slow motion. Three fingers. Then another one slowly goes down. I hold my breath, my own inhalations sounding almost deafening with us trying to be so silent.

All my senses are heightened. The scent of something spicy reaches my nose from inside the kitchen. The chill in the air raises goosebumps across my exposed arms.

Two...

Reaper's eyes flick over to meet mine, and I get lost for what feels like forever swimming in the sea blue. Then he returns his focus to the door and lowers the second finger.

One...

He closes his hand.

It's go time.

Reaper and Chaos both turn to face the door and begin firing. This isn't a mission to take prisoners or ensure we'll be able to question anyone. They have one goal—take out anyone who stands in the way of us freeing those girls, at any cost.

Excited yells in Russian fill the air, mingling with gunfire exploding all around us, too muffled for me to make out what they're saying. Reaper and Chaos move into the room, leaving Mouth and me at the door. The silent but clearly deadly man moves in immediately after them, weapon blazing, and I take my position just inside the jamb to watch the hallway and ensure no one else is coming to join the melee.

Heavy footsteps come from my left, and the moment

Yankovich's man turns the corner, I unleash on him, firing three shots straight to his chest. He drops before he even has a chance to pull his weapon, and I glance over my shoulder to take in what's happening behind me in the small kitchen.

The shots have stopped, and Reaper, Mouth, and Chaos appear to be checking the bodies of the men down on the peeling linoleum floor. Blood pools under them, and the splashes of it across the already dingy walls adds another dash of evidence of the pure violence that has been unleashed in the room.

These guys decimated them. Took out what appears to be seven men in less than thirty seconds. And watching the way they work—so precise, so skilled, no reservations—sends a little shiver of appreciation through my body that I never thought I'd feel.

Reaper is a killer. A man trained to be absolutely lethal and one who takes his job seriously. A man who carries out his work easily, without a second thought.

Knowing it's true and witnessing it in person are two different things. While I probably should be more worried about the ramifications of what they've just done, instead, a sense of pride blooms in my chest at how fucking badass Reaper really is.

Mouth collects weapons from the bodies, and Reaper pushes up from the squat he was in over one of the bodies and turns toward me, his jaw hard.

"Yankovich isn't here. Neither is Kosofik."

I glance up and down the hallway. "You think either of them is in the building?"

Reaper approaches with Chaos and Mouth directly behind. "Kosofik was here last night when we came after our meeting at the Knights' clubhouse. And he was here the night before."

"Maybe he just hasn't come yet?"

Chaos offers a half shrug. "It's possible, or he might be tied up somewhere else tonight."

A low growl rumbles in Reaper's chest. "I was hoping we could take out that fucker here. But let's keep moving. We need to find the girls."

The reminder of our mission replaces that tiny sense of dread, and Reaper pushes past me out the hallway to the left. I follow behind him without even thinking about it, his command to stay with him still blaring through my head.

Even last night, as he gripped my wrists together above my head in one of his large, calloused hands while he drove into me slowly, almost sweetly, he reminded me of our deal. Of the fact that I would never leave his side.

I wondered then, and I still wonder now, whether he strictly means that in terms of today or if there was some broader hidden meaning to his words that neither one of us were ready to consider last night—or maybe *anytime* in the near future.

God knows I'm not.

Making our way toward the end of the hallway that splits off in two directions isn't the time to do it, either. Reaper signals for Mouth and Chaos to go right, and I follow him to the left, down a long, poorly illuminated hallway. One of the neon lights that is actually lit flickers randomly, casting our path in an eerie and ominous glow. After the explosive gunfire in close quarters, the strange silence surrounding us leaves my heartbeat flooding in my ears, the only sound besides our soft footsteps.

It's unlikely anyone outside heard the shots, though. This portion of the docks is largely quiet and unused this time of night, and when the boys scoped out the other warehouses, the vast majority of them were dust-covered and empty, unused for a while.

But one thing being a cop for all these years has taught

me is to never make assumptions. That's the kind of thing that gets you killed. If the girls are here, they should have heard the shots. There isn't any way to hide that kind of carnage. They're likely hiding and terrified, unsure of what's happening. Just like we could be rescuers, we could just as easily be someone even worse than Yankovich's men attacking the facility to get their hands on them.

I try to put myself in those women's shoes, to consider what I might be thinking if I were trapped here in this moment, locked up and likely restrained for God knows how long—potentially months or years if they've been brought from elsewhere like most are. The thought raises bile in my throat, and I swallow it down as we reach the jamb of a cracked door to our left.

Reaper pauses and signals to go in and clear it. He pushes it open all the way, and we step into a small, dark office with an old metal desk and ripped leather chair occupying one corner. Papers litter the desktop, some words in English jumping out, but most of it in Russian.

He motions for me to watch the door while he approaches the desk and shifts around some of the papers until his eyes narrow. He grabs one and lifts it to read in the darkness of the room, only illuminated by the faint moon-light coming in from the solitary window on the far wall.

"What is it?" I ask the question as quietly as possible, but it still sounds deafening after the silence of making our way down here.

He approaches and holds it up for me to see. "A list. I assume of everyone who should be here." He swallows thickly, his hard gaze cutting over to me. "And prices they want to start the bidding at."

"Shit." I check the hallway again, tension tightening my back. Even though Reaper held that "menu" in his hand, seeing a version of it for myself makes our mission even more urgent.

"Let's move." Reaper brushes past me through the door and then sweeps out, checking both directions down the hallway.

I follow him again, trying to match his pace while keeping my steps as light as possible, and we make our way toward where the blueprints said the main warehouse would be. Though, any number of changes could've been made to the building since it was first constructed decades ago. The plans gave us a nice basis to go on but expecting the unexpected is all part of a mission like this.

The closer we move down the hallway toward the warehouse, the thicker the crackle of energy in the air grows, making the hair on my arms raise.

I don't like this.

It's not often my gut warns me to back away or turn around, but every nerve in my body screams at me to get the fuck out of here right now. That isn't an option, though.

I shake my head to try to clear it and stop behind Reaper at the opening of one of the doors to what should lead to the warehouse. Reaper glances back at me, his hard blue eyes sharp as ice.

It looks like he wants to say something, but he remains frozen, looking at me for what feels like forever, though it's likely only a few moments, before he gives me a simple nod and then turns.

The sound of the gunshots comes so fast, I don't even have time to react to it, and Reaper crumples to the floor in front of me.

19

VIKTORIA

No! All the air whooshes from my lungs, my breath stalling as my chest tightens.

No. No. No!

I turn the corner the rest of the way, stepping over Reaper's legs, gun ready to nail whatever fucker shot Reaper, but instead of unleashing a torrent of bullets, I freeze with my finger on the trigger.

Oh, my God...

Row after row of metal-framed beds fill the entire interior of the dimly lit warehouse, dozens, maybe a hundred of them, and too many terrified eyes to count watch me from the gloomy darkness. Metal chains glint in what little light the failing overhead lamps provide, leading from the frames to frail wrists and ankles of more women than we ever anticipated.

It's worse than we could have ever imagined. Far more women on a much larger scale than we planned for. There might be a hundred women and young girls here, maybe more. All frightened. Maybe one armed.

Is it possible one of them somehow got a weapon from one of their captors and used it against Reaper, assuming he was one of Yankovich's men entering?

No matter how far I try to gaze into the gloom, I can't locate a weapon or anyone who could have possibly taken a shot at Reaper. Either one of these women has a gun, or the person who does is using the sea of trafficking victims as an opportune hiding place.

My skin pebbles with anticipation of something. Anything. I scan the room the best I can, keeping my eye on them as I kneel beside Reaper's prone body. Flat on his stomach, his face turned toward me, blood starts to pool out from under him, thick and red.

No. No. No. This can't be happening. This isn't the plan.

We didn't get this far just to have it end like this.

Gunfire sounds from somewhere else in the building, behind me and to the right, which means Chaos and Mouth are tied up elsewhere and won't be coming to give me any backup—at least, not in the immediate future.

I need to handle what's happening here on my own.

Pull your shit together, Vik.

This isn't any time to let nerves get the better of me. Not when Reaper's life and the lives of all these girls are at stake. I reach out with my free hand, check his pulse at his neck, and release a sigh of relief.

It's low and thready...but still there. That means there's hope. As long as I can get the bleeding to stop, he might have a chance. But it's impossible to focus on saving his life when I don't know who is threatening it or mine.

Keeping my eyes on the warehouse, I nudge Reaper's shoulder. "Reaper."

Instead of his usual smartass and growled response, I get

nothing. And the room remains silent. No one moves or says a thing. In the dim lighting, it's hard to make out everything, and my gut clenches at the thought of the danger lurking in the shadows.

Still, I can't wildly shoot at what I can't see. If I hit any of those girls, I would never forgive myself. Not after everything we went through to get here and save them. Not after everything *they've* been through waiting for someone, *anyone,* to do the right thing and release them.

But the job is far from done. And I need the man lying at my feet as much as I need to take my next breath.

Please wake up. Please!

I shake Reaper again, harder, with more force than I probably need to or should use, but desperate times call for desperate measures. No movement or reaction.

Fuck you, Reaper. Don't leave me like this!

I pull my hand back and smack his cheek facing me, and this time, he sucks in a harsh breath and groans, wincing.

Thank fuck.

I push on his shoulder and roll him onto his back so I can better assess his injury while trying to keep one eye on the warehouse. He grits his teeth, pressing his right hand against the growing wound in his left shoulder.

Two inches to the right, and he would have taken the shot straight to the heart. Whether he moved at the last minute or whoever pulled the trigger just has shitty aim, either way, it probably saved his life. But he's still losing a lot of blood, and if we stay here much longer, he won't walk out of here at all.

"Get up, Reaper." I glance down at him, and his eyes flicker open but move, unfocused. "Get up!"

This time, my sharp order echoes through the space, louder than I had intended it. Something shifts in the darkness to my left, but before I can turn, the cold muzzle of a gun presses to my temple.

Shit.

"Viktoria Garin..." Kosofik's heavily accented voice floats through the still, humid air of the warehouse and sends a chill down my spine. "To your feet." He presses the muzzle harder against my temple. "But you leave your weapon on the floor."

Shit. Shit. Shit.

I chance a glance at Reaper again. With his eyes closed, he appears to have fallen unconscious again, which means I'm on my own.

Fucking hell.

Slowly, I set my gun on the ground and push to my feet, then turn to face Kosofik, the barrel of his gun now pointed directly at my chest. The corner of his lips twitches, and he motions for me to move away from my weapon. I take two steps toward him, and he scans the room behind him briefly before returning his focus to me.

"I would say I'm impressed you finally located this place if I weren't so angry you succeeded in breaching it." Hard dark eyes meet mine. "My men let down their guard. But if I had been with them instead of in here checking on the girls, you never would've made it this far."

I fist my hands at my sides hard enough to make my nails bite into my palms. "But we *did*."

He glances down at Reaper bleeding on the cold gray concrete and smirks. "A lot of good that did you and your friend who calls himself...what was it? Adam Jones? I'll admit, I believed him for a moment. And I likely would have given him the location for our auction in a few days had you not moved in. He's a true professional. You"—he raises an eyebrow—"on the other hand. The fact that you thought you could walk into B66 and not be recognized just shows the arrogance you share with your brothers in blue."

"We don't know each other." I hold up my hands in hopes

that it might convince him I'm willing to give up, even though that's the furthest thing from my mind. "You had already moved well beyond the neighborhood by the time I was born, so I know you weren't the one who recognized me."

He chuckles and shakes his head. "No. The girls are very loyal. Inessa recognized you immediately and alerted us within five minutes of you and your partner stepping into the club. From there, it was only a matter of keeping an eye on you to ensure you didn't interfere with what we had coming up." He offers me a smile that *almost* borders on kind. "I'll admit I never anticipated you getting this far or this close." He glances down at Reaper's body, unmoved, and I follow his line of sight. "But whoever your friend is clearly has skills you don't."

No doubt Anya could've located this warehouse just as easily as Reaper did with brute force, using her considerable hacking skills, but I had no intention of dragging her deeper into this than I already did by asking her to look into Reaper's background. And I'm not about to let Kosofik know about her involvement because if he knows who I am, then he knows I have a sister.

"Just what did you hope to accomplish here, Viktoria?" He raises a dark eyebrow and swings his free hand out toward the sea of women around him. "Did you think that you would actually get past all of us and free them? Did you think you would kill me?"

Anger tightens my fists as I lower them to my sides, suddenly unconcerned about whether he thinks I'm compliant or not. I'd rather go down fighting than go down giving up. "I thought maybe we could save them from this horrible life you forced them into."

He barks out a cynical, evil-sounding laugh that echoes around the place, making several of the women cower further behind the beds they're strung to. "Rescue them? From what? From men who would give them roofs over their heads, who would offer them food, shelter, and some even the chance to become life partners in a way most of these women could never even dream of. That's what *you're* trying to take away from them."

"Are you really so twisted and demented that you don't understand this is all in your fucking head? These women didn't choose this. They don't want to be slaves to grown men who have nothing better to do with their money than to buy humans. These women had lives. They had families, and you ripped them from them."

An evil grin twists his lips as he eyes me. "Maybe that's true. But it's too late to stop me. And despite what will undoubtedly be your initial reluctance, I have a specific client in mind who I'm sure can break you, given enough time."

REAPER

THE WORLD RETURNS IN A RUSH, slamming into me with gut-turning pain and a voice I hoped I would never hear again.

"But it's too late to stop me. And despite what will undoubtedly be your initial reluctance, I have a specific client in mind who I'm sure can break you, given enough time."

Fucking Kosofik.

He was here, lurking in the shadows, waiting for an opportunity.

"I will never break, Kosofik. You have such a low view of women, of what they can accomplish and what they deserve, that you underestimate me. And underestimate *them*." Viktoria's anger hangs on every word.

He chuckles, a low, deep sound that makes me want to leap up from the floor and pound him into it with my bare fists, but the screaming agony in my shoulder and the fact that he undoubtedly has a weapon aimed at Viktoria right now keeps me prone.

Kosofik isn't the type of man anyone should fuck with, yet Viktoria seems intent on aggravating him until he finally snaps and unloads on her.

"I don't underestimate you, Detective Garin. I have a very clear view of what you can accomplish. Which is nothing. You standing here without a weapon with your associate dead on the floor beside you with no way to escape...you've lost."

"*Have* I?"

Oh, hell. I know that voice.

The indignation. It's the same she's shown me since the moment I met her. It could get her fucking killed.

She shifts where she stands only a foot from me, the movement sending her scent wafting over me. "Our gunshots are sure to have alerted someone to what's happening here, and I've already called in the cavalry. The entire NYPD will rain down on this place so hard in the next minute that you won't know what hit you. You'll wish you stayed back in Russia rather than setting foot here, thinking you could pick up doing the dirty work you did there so easily."

He barks out another laugh that echoes around the warehouse that I only got a glimpse of before he hit me with that bullet.

But why didn't he take out Viktoria the moment she rounded the door?

"You're lying, Detective Garin. The NYPD has no idea

what you're up to. If they did, a SWAT team would have burst into this place and overwhelmed us with force a long time ago. Instead, you and your friend arrived alone, which tells me that you're also working alone outside the law." He chuckles. "I guess it shouldn't surprise me for a girl from Brighton Beach. No matter what anybody does to try to escape it, it's inevitable."

"Fuck you, Kosofik."

That's my girl.

Pride swells in my chest to join the pain there, and I risk a quick glance to my side to assess the situation, barely opening my eyes enough to see a sliver. A mere foot from me, Viktoria stands tall, her shoulders back, eyes focused on the enemy where he stands in front of her. But he's alone. The only one of his crew left. I have no fucking clue where Chaos and Mouth went, but at least I know Kosofik's by himself. And that gives us the upper hand.

Watching through squinted, barely cracked eyes, I keep my focus on Kosofik and shift my hand, gritting my teeth at the pain moving my left arm causes, and curl my fingers around the back of Viktoria's ankle to let her know I'm awake and moving.

She freezes, going stock still. "I'll give you one more chance, Kosofik. Give me the weapon and surrender so I can set these poor women free."

His laughter booms around the warehouse again, along with the excited chatter of the women who must've overheard Viktoria. "You must be delusional, Detective Garin. All it would take is a flick of my finger against this trigger to end you. The only reason I haven't was because I needed to ensure that the NYPD wouldn't be coming. I've long suspected the NYPD is a bunch of useless assholes who think they're above the law because they pretend to enforce it. If you only knew how many of your men I have on my payroll, how many of them watch and wait and feed me all the information you have. I suspected the department knew nothing because I haven't heard anything, but you've just confirmed it for me, which means I no longer have any use for you. Except if I'm going to sell you."

"Over my dead fucking body."

Viktoria's rage vibrates through her words and into me, making adrenaline surge through my body. The weapon I was holding when I was hit lies to my right, and there isn't any way I can grab it without Kosofik noticing my movement. But the gun Viktoria laid on the ground sits a few inches from my left hand, and her body blocks most of mine.

I'll only have one chance at this. One opportunity and one shot before Kosofik unleashes his own. If I fuck it up, I'll lose her and bleed to death on this cold, hard concrete floor while the victims of Yankovich's trafficking ring watch their only chance at freedom disappear.

I squeeze Viktoria's ankle three times.

Please, Vik, understand what I'm saying...

This will only work if we're on the same page completely —something the two of us have failed at repeatedly basically since the moment we met. Unless we were in bed.

Three...

Two...

One...

I grab the weapon from the ground as she dives to the side, and I fire, unloading the entire magazine in Kosofik's direction before the pain and blood loss finally suck me back down to the concrete and under to the familiar darkness.

REAPER

A familiar scent drags me from what feels like the deepest sleep I've ever been in—blooming flowers on a summer day. The rest of my senses come back to me slowly. A clattering, banging of metal from another room. The weight of a blanket over me and the soft brush of a hand against my cheek.

Where the fuck am I? And why does it feel like I got hit by a fucking truck?

I force open my heavy eyelids to a dimly lit room and blink them until they finally focus on a familiar ceiling. My room at the loft. Another soft brush of a hand on my face makes me turn my head toward it.

Viktoria sits in a chair beside my bed. "Welcome back."

"Shit. How long was I out?"

She glances at the clock on the nightstand and releases a heavy sigh. "About twelve hours, which doesn't surprise me after the blood you lost and the drugs Chaos and Mouth pumped into you."

I try to move and groan, the bone-deep pain in my shoulder keeping me down. But the agony and her words bring a barrage of memories to assault me. Memories broken by long blank periods. "What happened?"

Viktoria offers me a little half-smile. "You don't remember?"

No matter how hard I try to drag up what happened in that warehouse, all I get are bits and pieces. I shake my head and run my right hand over my face, rubbing at my sore eyes. "Not everything. The last thing I remember was you standing down Kosofik."

Her free hand tightens into a fist, and she pulls her palm from my cheek and runs that hand back through her dark, silky hair, releasing another waft of that scent that would make me weak in the knees if I were standing. But considering how I feel, I'm pretty sure I'd collapse onto the floor if I even attempted it right now.

She presses her lips together in a firm line, her anger clearly not abated. "That fucker." She shakes her head and inhales sharply. "After you squeezed my ankle, I dove out of the way and you emptied the magazine."

"And I killed him?"

Viktoria snorts and leans in. "No. You didn't. Three of your shots hit him, but that fucker was still breathing and on his knees, so I grabbed your gun from the other side of your body and put one straight into his fucking heart to ensure he would never do something like this again."

"Holy shit. You killed him?"

She brushes her lips over mine gently and then pulls back. "I did."

A war wages in my chest, between being proud of her and being terrified of what it means. I try to push myself into a sitting position and only manage to get up a couple of inches before I have to drop back down and grit my teeth. "You could've called it in, Vik. Gotten an ambulance there and maybe saved his life so he could be charged and put on trial."

Viktoria presses her lips together and considers me for a moment, turmoil turning her green eyes even darker. "I could have, but that would've meant exposing you, too."

She did it to protect me?

The reality of what that could mean slams into me harder than the bullet Kosofik shot did.

"And you're okay with that?"

She sighs and shakes her head, relaxing back in her chair slightly. "Honestly, I don't know. After I did it, I rushed to your side to try to stop the bleeding, and then Chaos and Mouth appeared. They pulled you out of there and brought you back here to patch you up. The bullet was through and through and didn't appear to hit anything important. You're lucky."

"No shit." I glance at the bandage over my shoulder and try to move it but instantly regret that decision when agony burns down my arm and the entire left side of my body. It's far from the first time I've been shot, but Chaos and Mouth know I wouldn't want any drugs beyond what they had to give me to dig around in there. So that means this time, waking up is a lot more painful than any other. "So, what happened after I passed out?"

She pushes to her feet and paces, the reality of reliving what happened making her antsy. "Once I was sure they were long gone with you, I called it in."

"What happened when the cops showed up?"

The look she casts me could melt ice, and she shakes her head. "I'm going to have a lot of explaining to do when I meet with my boss later today. I just told them that the warehouse was full of women who have been trafficked by the Russians and that they would find a lot of bodies inside."

"How are you going to explain all of that?"

One of her dark eyebrows raises in question. "You mean without ratting out you, Chaos, and Mouth?"

I feel like an asshole even thinking it, which is why I didn't ask, but she inclines her head.

"I get it. I do. And I'll figure it out."

"What about Hank and the Knights?"

"They got Anastasia out. That's all I know."

"What's the deal with Hank and that woman, anyway?"

She sighs and shakes her head. "I don't know. Hank gets overly invested in these things, and now there's a pretty woman involved. When I talked with him at the Knights' clubhouse the other night, he tried to blow it off as nothing, but I've known him a long time—there's definitely something he's not saying. I'll see Hank this afternoon at our meeting. I snuck away from the scene last night to come back here to you. It was chaotic enough that I could easily, but I need to have answers at this meeting, ones that are going to be hard to come up with."

The anxiety over what she's going to have to do practically vibrates through her and into me, and guilt climbs up my throat. There's only one choice here, one thing I can do.

"Give me to your boss."

"What?" She freezes and whirls back to face me.

"He'll never believe you did all that, took them all out alone. There were too many different guns, too many different trajectories, too many men for you to have done it solo. And you protecting us is going to cost you your job. So, give me to him...and save yourself since I couldn't fucking do it at that warehouse."

VIKTORIA

"Are you out of your ever-loving mind?"

Maybe I misheard him. I must have.

There's no way he just volunteered to throw himself on the pyre for me. He knows what would happen if the District Attorney or God forbid the United States Attorney found out a former Delta Force operative was killing people on US soil.

I drop onto the chair next to his bed and glare at him, hoping it's enough to burn the insanity out of him. "If I give you to my boss, you're going to end up in prison for a very long time, maybe forever."

He shakes his head, his blue eyes softening with an affection I wasn't so sure he was capable of. "I failed at that warehouse. Failed to protect you. I couldn't even take out Kosofik. And now, I'm lying here like a useless piece of shit and you're about to sacrifice yourself for me."

"Cut the woe is me fucking bullshit!" Anger rises in my blood, making me clench my fists at the side of the bed. "You were half fucking dead and still managed to shoot the guy three times before you passed out. I may have saved our lives by ending it, but you sure as hell started it."

He continues to glare at me, his frustration with the situation building as fast as my annoyance with his attitude.

"I was exactly where you are not long ago, so I know what it feels like to be in your shoes. You hate being weak. I get it because I do, too. But you need to take some time to recover from this, and I'm not going to let you do that in a prison cell."

He snarls at me and pushes himself up with his good hand, grimacing but leaning toward me, a sneer on his lips. "You're not sacrificing yourself for me, Vik. I won't allow it."

"*Allow?*" I raise an eyebrow at him and snort. "You don't have a fucking choice, Reaper. This is *my* life, *my* career. And Hank and I will walk in there and tell our boss what he needs to hear. If I lose my badge because of it, so be it. Those girls are free now. I don't know what more I could ask for."

Except you.

I bite back those final words as I stare him down, waiting for him to continue to argue with me about it. But he can talk until he's blue in the face, and it won't change what's about to happen. I'm going to walk out of here and go to that meeting. I'm going to sit there with Hank and have to explain to Captain Miller what we did. And why. And I'll do it without naming names. That will no doubt bring IA breathing down my neck and cost me my badge, but so be it.

The future is uncertain in so many ways...and not only with my career. I don't know if Reaper will even be here when I get back. The man is trained to disappear like a ghost, vanish without a trace, and even shot up, something tells me he can still do it so quickly I wouldn't even see the dust he kicks up on his way out.

But I can't bring myself to tell him how much I don't want him to leave. How badly I want to crawl into this bed with him and just stay there.

Instead, I swallow back those words and press my lips to his harshly before I push on his chest. "Lie back down. Get some sleep. I'll be back...if I can."

I rise to my feet and walk to the door, intent on not looking back unless he asks me to stay, but his silence speaks volumes. Enough to make me pause at the doorway but keep my focus on the kitchen where Chaos and Mouth struggle to cook something for themselves.

They probably saved his life as much as I did, but those men are just as lethal as Reaper. Only he hasn't just killed hundreds of men, he's also destroyed my soul because I don't know how I'm ever supposed to be with anyone else when all I will do is compare them to that man lying in the bed behind me.

Stop, Vik.

This isn't the time to think about it. Not when I have such an important meeting. I force myself to walk out and close the door behind me, essentially sealing my fate with Roderick Reaper Dixon.

VIKTORIA

Now I know how the suspects I question must feel when we sit on the opposite side of those crappy tables in the interrogation rooms. I shift in my seat under Captain Miller's scrutinizing gaze and cast a glance at Hank, where he sits beside me in the hard, uncomfortable wooden chairs in front of the captain's desk.

The moment I entered the precinct, the captain unceremoniously ushered me into his office, where Hank was already waiting. Which means my partner and I haven't even had a chance to talk before the inquisition begins.

Finally, after what feels like hours of sitting with nothing but awkward, uncomfortable, heavy silence between us, the captain leans forward and rests his elbows on his desk, clasping his hands together. "I honestly don't even know what to say, Garin. I expect this kind of shit from Grayson, but from you?" His hard gaze cuts through me like a knife. "You went into a warehouse, knowing it was likely filled with Yankovich's armed men as well as dozens of potential trafficking victims without calling it in. Then after discharging a weapon and killing several men, you did call it in and then fled the damn scene and left all of us to pick up the pieces and wonder what the fuck happened."

He releases a heavy sigh and leans back.

"Then *this* guy shows up and walks in with Yankovich in cuffs and says he has the evidence we need to charge him."

"What?" I jerk upright in my seat and turn to Hank. "You arrested Yankovich?"

I never got any details of their portion of the mission other than a text that the woman and her kids were safe. Yankovich never came into the conversation.

Hank raises an eyebrow at me and clears his throat. "As I was just telling the captain, you didn't have any choice but to act. And I made it clear to you that you had to. There wasn't any time to wait for backup. The lives of all of those women depended on it. I explained that all of this was my fault. That I knew once I arrested Yankovich, word would get back to his men at the warehouse and they would likely kill the girls so that none of them could testify. I sent help for you, and you were completely unaware of the identities of the men who then left before the police arrived."

Oh, my God. What in the hell is he doing?

He's taking the fall for me.

Oh, oh God. No. No. No. No. No. No. No. No.

I open my mouth to object, to tell the captain that I knew exactly what I was doing and made the conscious choice to get involved, but Hank shoots out a hand and wraps it around my wrist.

"It's okay, Vik. I have to own up to what I did. Tell the captain the truth."

The hard look he offers me tells me exactly what he wants me to say. He wants me to cover my ass and go along with the story. He wants to take the fall completely, even if it costs him his badge.

Fuck. Fuck. Fuck. Fuck. Fuck.

I can't believe only a few days ago, I was questioning whether I could ever trust Hank again, and now, here he is, ready to fall on his sword even though I made a very conscious decision to help him, knowing the risks.

"I-I'm sorry, Captain, that I didn't phone it in right away. I happened to be in the area, right around the corner actually, and Hank knew I could get there fast."

Captain Miller raises his brows. "And you couldn't pick up the fucking radio and call it in?"

"I wasn't in a squad car. I didn't even have my gun on me since I've been on my little vacation. Hank said someone would meet me there to assist. I'm sorry. I didn't even get the guy's name."

Hank squares his shoulders. "And you're not going to, either, Captain. I'm perfectly prepared to face the ramifications of what I've done, but the people who helped me did so to save those poor girls. I'm not about to let them all go down for that when I can protect their identities."

Good God. He's really taking this all the way...

The captain releases another heavy sigh and leans back in his chair. "You'll likely be criminally charged." He cuts his gaze to me. "And internal affairs is going to be all over both of you like white on rice."

Hank inclines his head. "I know, sir."

I do the same. "I'll tell them whatever they need to know and cooperate with any investigations. But I can't offer you any names if I don't know them."

That should protect Reaper, Mouth, and Chaos from any criminal prosecution, assuming there isn't additional evidence somewhere that can be tied to them. But I'm not even worried about that.

They're true professionals who know what they're doing. After Chaos and Mouth took care of the few remaining men elsewhere in the facility, they did a full sweep to ensure nothing was left behind before they came to locate us. If there was anything to find, they would've found it and ensured it was taken care of. I have zero doubts about that. Which means they should be in the clear.

Hank, on the other hand...

He still sits, shoulders back, head held high despite the fact that he's tanking his career. And he's doing it for *me.*

I can barely find the words, but the captain stares at me, waiting for me to say something. "I'll take whatever punishment IA deems necessary for what I've done."

He shakes his head and scowls. "You could lose your badge over this, Viktoria." Another heavy sigh slips from his lips. "And I would ask you if it's worth it, but I've seen those girls. I heard about the conditions they were living in and what those fucking Russians intended to do with them. So, I know it was worth it. As angry as I am about the entire situation, I can't fully fault you for what you did." He turns his attention to Hank. "Now, Hank, I'm sorry to have to do this."

"I know, sir." Hanks reaches for his waistband and sets his badge and gun on the desk.

Is this really happening?

"Viktoria?" The captain raises an eyebrow at me. "I'm going to need yours, too. At least until IA finishes their investigation and determines if any further action is required."

I incline my head. "I understand."

Pulling out my badge and gun that I stopped at my place to grab on the way over here feels surreal, and my hand shakes so violently, it's almost embarrassing.

The captain nods to both of us. "Expect to hear from them soon."

I push up from my chair and follow Hank from the room in a trance, the last few minutes playing through my head like a bad horror movie. The moment we're far enough down the hall, I grab his forearm. He turns to face me, and I release my hold on him and scan the hallway to ensure we're alone.

"Are you insane? Why did you do that? Why would you—"

He steps up to me and embraces me in a very un-Hank-like hug. "I did it because you don't deserve to go down for any of this. I, on the other hand, knew the risk going in. I accepted it. Made peace with it. I can get another job, Vik. What I can't do, is watch you lose everything you worked so hard for all because your partner got a wild hair and went fucking rogue."

"Jesus, Hank…" I shake my head and pull back from him. "I really wish you hadn't done that."

He smirks at me. "I know, Vik, but I had to. Just stick to the story, and you'll be fine. You might get a mark in your file, and I wouldn't rule out a temporary suspension, but they won't fire you. This city needs good cops more now than ever. You're one of the best."

"What the hell are you going to do?"

Hank glances over his shoulder down the hallway and offers a shrug. "Maybe I'll join a motorcycle club." He tosses me a wink. "Right now, I'm going to go check on Anastasia and the kids to make sure they're settling in."

"You really like her."

He shrugs again, his eyes darting around the hallway, purposely avoiding mine. "It's complicated."

I snort. "You totally like her." I shake my head and sigh, "It can't be any more complicated than things are between me and Reaper."

He smirks. "Yeah, I bet. The two of you are like oil and

vinegar. So, what's the deal? Is he planning on sticking around?"

"I wish I knew."

Fuck, I really wish I knew.

REAPER

I SHUFFLE out of the bedroom, scrubbing my hand over my face, and find Chaos and Mouth sitting at the counter with what looks like might actually be edible pasta half-eaten in bowls in front of them.

"Hey, man." Chaos turns toward me on his stool and leans back against the counter. "Good to see you up. How you feeling?"

Mouth inclines his head toward me, then returns to his food.

I offer Chaos an annoyed look and heave myself onto the stool next to him with a grunt.

"That good, huh?"

"Fuck you, man. When was the last time you were shot?"

He rubs his jaw and pretends to think about it even though all three of us know exactly when it was. "Twelve months ago."

"Maybe you're due."

He shakes his head and chuckles. "I'd like to keep myself bullet-free for the foreseeable future."

"Wouldn't we all?"

Mouth snorts and nods, polishing off his meal.

Chaos opens his mouth, likely with another smartass remark, but we all freeze at the whine and rumble of the garage door downstairs going up. "Sounds like your woman's back."

I scowl at him. "She's not my woman."

He pops a piece of bread in his mouth and chews. "Sure seems like she is." With a shrug, he shoves away from the counter and motions for Mouth to follow him. "Going to grab a smoke out on the fire escape. Catch you later."

They climb through the open window onto the back fire escape, and I sigh and run a hand over my face while the elevator makes its way up with one very big complication inside.

I didn't know what to say when she left earlier. How to tell her that I might not be here when she got back. And honestly, if it weren't for my arm in a sling and a hole in my shoulder, all three of us would probably be long gone by now.

Watching her stand at that door with her back to me felt like waiting for a piece of myself to walk away, but I just couldn't get out the words I wanted to say. Not when I don't know what she wants. Not when our lives are so completely different. When *we're* so different.

The elevator reaches the loft, and Viktoria pulls open the metal gate and steps out. Her eyes lock with mine as she slowly makes her way across the room and settles on the stool next to me, her dark hair flowing around her so soft it makes my fingers itch to touch it.

"Where are Mouth and Chaos?"

I incline my head toward the fire escape. "Having a smoke."

She nods and blows out a long, slow breath like she's releasing all the stress of her day. That suggests her meeting did not go as planned.

I'm almost afraid to ask. "How did your meeting go?"

"About as well as can be expected. Especially because Hank threw himself on the proverbial sword and took the fall for everything."

"What?"

She nods, the exhaustion of the last few days creating dark bags around her eyes. "He told our captain that this was all him. That he called me with the location of the girls because he knew I was in the area and wanted them secured while he arrested Yankovich so that nobody would harm them."

"He arrested Yankovich?"

"Yep." She pops the *P* and leans forward, resting her elbows on the counter and shoving her hands back through her hair. "Surprised the hell out of me, too."

"So, you're getting at least half of what you wanted. He'll go to trial."

She shrugs. "Maybe. We'll see." Her gaze darts to me and softens slightly. "How are you feeling?"

I offer a little shrug, then wince and instantly regret it. "Pretty good."

Lightly drumming her nails on the counter, Vik swallows thickly and casts a glance in the direction the boys went. "When are you guys taking off?"

I sigh and run my hand through my hair, turning on the stool to face her. "I don't know. What's going to happen to you?"

She squeezes shut her eyes and releases a frustrated groan. "IA will be up my ass. I'm supposed to meet with them tomorrow, and then…" One of her shoulders rises and falls, and she finally opens her eyes to peer at me with a look that forms an ache in the center of my chest. "I don't know."

"Is there a chance you might keep your badge?"

"I hope so."

I clear my throat. "And…if not?"

She releases a long, heavy sigh and runs her hands through her hair, tugging at it gently. "I don't fucking know, Reaper. I feel like I don't know anything anymore. The last few weeks have been nothing but one mind-fuck after another."

"Is that what I am? A mind-fuck?"

Where the hell did that question come from? And why the hell do I sound so defensive?

It doesn't matter. It's hanging out there between us now, thickening the air with tension I could cut with the knife I keep in my boot.

She freezes and turns to face me, throwing up her hands —but whether in anger or frustration…it's impossible to tell. "I don't know *what* you are, Reaper."

"Yes, you do. You said it yourself…I'm a heartless killer."

"You're not heartless." She shakes her head and leans to brush her fingertips along my cheek and her thumb over my lips. "You try to hide it, but I can still see it in there under all those scars you don't want me to touch or tell me about."

Fuck…

There comes that damn tightening in my chest again, and I pull away from her touch, averting my gaze from her toward the window to the fire escape—where I would much rather be enjoying a smoke than having this conversation.

"You don't want to hear about that, Vik. You don't want to hear my horror stories."

"I wouldn't ask if I didn't want to."

"What happened last night at that warehouse…" I glance at her and tighten my fist on the counter. "It's nothing compared to some of the things I've seen, some of the things I've done."

The reasons for the scars and the drinking that eventually got me discharged. The reason I never go home to see Mom and Dad—that I can't look them in the eye, knowing what I've done and continue to do.

Vik slides from her stool and nudges my legs open until I turn to fully face her again and let her step between them.

She captures my face in her palms and tilts it up toward her. "I don't know if I'm going to be a cop anymore or not. What I do know…is I want to know *you*. I want to know Roderick Dixon. *And*…I want to know Reaper. I want to know what turned you *into* Reaper. Why you'd rather be him than Roderick. I want to know everything you're willing to tell me. Everything that's happened in your life is what brought you to me, to this moment in time. One I don't want to let slip past us."

Her words cut me deeper than any knife ever has. It's the thing that I've always secretly longed to hear but have always been terrified of at the same time. "That's what you want? For me to stay?"

"Or go…" The corner of her mouth twitches up. "And I'll come with you."

"You would leave? Just like that?"

"I don't even know if I'll have my badge anymore, at least here in New York."

If it were only that easy, riding off into the sunset together. "What about what I do, Viktoria? You told me there is no place in this world for vigilantes who act outside the law."

She offers a little halfhearted shrug. "I may have taken a hard line on that when we first met, but after what's happened with Yankovich, I think vigilantism could have its place. And I also don't think what we did over the course of the last few weeks is what you're doing every day."

Pretty bold assumption on her part.

We haven't exactly discussed what I was doing prior to appearing in New York, aside from my little mission in Manila that brought me to The Big Apple.

I swallow thickly. "I haven't been doing much since I was discharged. Some favors for some friends, and that's about it."

She can make her own assumptions about the types of "favors" I've been doing, and something tells me that by now, she won't be far off from the truth.

One of her hands slides from my cheek, down my neck, to press against my chest. "And will you continue to do it? Favors for friends?"

If I told her *no*, I would be lying. And I don't want to make promises I can't keep.

"I've been thinking about setting up a business. Private security firm with Chaos and Mouth and maybe a few other guys who are about to get out. We would likely still do some work and *favors* for people, but a legitimate security firm would bring in a nice stream of income."

A grin plays on her perfect lips. "That sounds perfect for you."

"It might be." I suck in a deep breath, building up my nerve to say these final words to her. Words I never imagined saying to anyone before. "It would be perfect if you're by my side."

Her hand freezes on my cheek, green eyes sparkling with unshed tears. "Is that really what you want?"

It's the same question I've asked myself a thousand times since I first kissed her. The one that has rattled around my head so much that it left permanent marks. But after so long not knowing the answer, now, it seems so obvious.

"All I know is I want you, Viktoria. I want your smart-ass mouth, your attitude. I want you to challenge me and fight with me so that we can make up the way we have been. I want to be able to sleep at night, and the only time that's ever happened is with you. That's what I want. If you do, too."

She doesn't answer me, just leans in and presses her lips to mine in a kiss so sweet that it's almost sickening. But instead of rejecting it, rejecting her and protecting myself like I always have for my entire adult life, I wrap my good arm around her and pull her up against me, ignoring the bite of pain it causes as I devour her mouth and deepen our kiss.

I knew a reckoning was coming, that someone would have to pay for what they had done to Eva, to *all* those girls. I just never imagined I would be coming out feeling more alive than I ever have been and with the woman who could have ruined the entire mission.

The woman who now holds my heart and my future.

Keep reading for *Off Course*, Chaos' story and the second book in the Scarred Heroes Series.

OFF COURSE

THE SCARRED HEROES SERIES BOOK 2

PROLOGUE

CHAOS

The perfectly still, quiet, dark night, lit only by the millions of stars and the partially cloud-obscured moon, shatters in an instant.

A planned cataclysm.

Deliberate devastation.

Total assured destruction.

Methodical chaos.

The well-executed explosion rips through the dilapidated building, sending handmade mudbricks and mortar flying skyward and out in a tidal wave of debris. Bits and pieces of the structure plunge to the ground like rain from the heavens, but unlike the water this desert so desperately needs, it doesn't quench a desperate thirst and feed life into the crops and animals; the stuff falling from the sky will kill you with its force.

If I've done my job, there won't be anyone alive in there to feel the rubble striking them, though.

And I always do my job well.

I used enough C4 to destroy a building twice that size. Some might argue I overdid it. That using more than necessary wastes resources. Some might say it's overkill. But when it comes to eliminating a threat, I always go all-out.

It's the one thing I'm good at. The one thing the guys can always count on. They call me in when they need chaos, and I bring it. I ensure the enemy is nothing but dust in the desert wind.

Reaper watches the fallout through his night vision goggles next to me, silently assessing every inch of visible real estate in front of us. The village remains still despite the blast.

Smoke billows high into the night sky, flames leaping up and dancing merrily as if in celebration of my achievement. Even after all these years and countless missions, it never gets old seeing the orangey-red glow of my success.

Only, the internal celebration is short-lived.

An eerie silence falls over the small desert village just rocked by my hand. A slow, cold tingle spreads through my body, sending the hairs on the back of my neck up and putting me on high alert.

Something's wrong.

I don't even have time to call out a warning before gunfire tears through the smoky night air and slams into me.

Fuck.

Pain explodes through my side, and I roll to my left toward Reaper just in time to avoid another fusillade of bullets hitting where I was just lying. "Where the hell is that coming from?"

Reaper scans the village and focuses to the right and up. "Three o'clock."

I wince and press my hand against my side. Warm blood seeps between my fingers, a bullet having hit one of the spots not covered by my body armor. I pull off my night vision goggles and examine the wound as best I can. "Where the hell is Mouth?"

"I'm here, guys. Repositioning," Mouth's voice comes through our com.

Reaper peers over at me. "Are you hit?"

I try to take a deep breath but end up coughing—whether it's from the smoke in the air or because the bullet hit something vital remains to be seen. "I'm fine."

"That doesn't answer my question. Were you fucking hit?"

"I'm *fine*." I barely manage to grind out the words through clenched teeth as we wait for Mouth to do his thing.

Without him to provide cover, we'll be trapped here, sitting ducks for whoever managed to escape the explosion and now seems intent on ensuring we don't make it out of this hellhole alive.

I watch the building at our three o'clock for any signs of movement. Whoever was shooting has momentarily stopped, but they're likely just reloading or adjusting positions. "How the fuck did anyone get out?"

When we scouted the village, almost all the residents had fled, leaving it in the control of the insurgents we're here for, and those fuckers had chosen a central location within the small cluster of buildings to act as their headquarters. It was our primary target, and given everything we'd seen during our recon, they all should have been there and long asleep before it blew.

One calculated strike to remove a pesky problem for the forces in the area—or, at least, it should have been.

Reaper shrugs as he surveys the village. "Who the fuck knows, with these guys. Might not even be one of them. Might be some villager who didn't get the fuck out in time who picked up a weapon they found lying on the damn street."

"Ready to light 'em up, if you are, motherfuckers." Mouth's cheery sing-song voice cuts through the com.

Having him up there doesn't mean we're safe down here, but it's better than the alternative—trying to get back to the exfil spot with someone trying to peg us off.

I push myself up slightly to check the building where we last saw the threat, clouded in smoke from my explosion. "You have the shooter?"

"Movement in the north window. He's either reloading or jerking off."

Reaper's gaze shifts up, trying to see what Mouth can from his position. "Do you have the shot?"

"Negative."

I scan the town square in front of us, searching for the rest of the unit. "Where are Mayhem and Flash?"

Mayhem's voice cuts through the com. "Coming up on your six."

Flash and Mayhem make their way over to us, moving silently through the outskirts of the village, eyes on the building containing the shooter.

Mayhem settles next to me. "We had to circle around to avoid the town square."

"Any resistance on your side of town?"

He shakes his head. "Nah. We saw your handiwork but not a living soul."

Where the fuck did this shooter come from?

It's like he just popped up out of nowhere—a ghost with an assault rifle and a hard-on for killing American troops.

Flash takes position next to Reaper and inclines his head toward the east, where the rising sun will break the horizon in only a couple of hours. "We need to get the fuck out of here and to exfil. Mouth?"

"Still no shot."

Reaper glances to where Mouth is perched atop the roof

of another mudbrick building, waiting for his opportunity to pick off the shooter so he doesn't use us for target practice when we try to make it to where the helo will pick us up. "We're gonna have to draw that fucker out." He points to me. "Chaos stays here. Mayhem, you're with me. Flash…do your thing. He's gonna have to choose a target and should bring himself into Mouth's sights."

Reaper, Mayhem, and Flash head out in the respective directions—each keeping to the darkest of the shadows until the exact right time when Flash's speed comes into play.

The man moves faster than a damn lightning bolt and has managed to outrun any bullet that's ever been fired at him. He will again tonight. With Reaper, Mayhem, and me providing cover, Flash will draw the shooter to the window where Mouth can end this.

I shift into a better position, sharp pain slicing at my side. My vision blurs slightly, the smoke and darkness of the night creeping in at the edges, but I shake my head and force my eyes open.

Gunfire erupts from my three o'clock. Reaper and Mayhem both return fire. The wind kicks up, pushing more smoke lingering from the explosion through the town square, further obscuring the view for anyone without the benefit of night vision.

The crunch of footsteps behind me makes me whirl in that direction, weapon ready. A tall lone figure approaches in the faint moonlight, holding something long pointed in my direction.

I fire, and he cries out and stumbles forward, then drops to the sand.

Almost instantly, a blast from behind me, in the center of town, propels me forward. The rock-hard ground knocks the air from my lungs, and I struggle to keep the world around me in focus, blinking rapidly to clear the bright spots from my vision.

The night sky erupts with a towering blaze and more smoke that's sure to draw in others from the surrounding mountains. We won't be alone here for long.

I focus on the body on the ground ten yards in front of me. A form huddles over it. Another figure. Someone who wasn't there only moments ago.

Wailing carries through the night.

A woman.

Pieces of her words reach me.

Broken but enough for me to translate.

My son!

I stagger to my feet as Reaper's voice comes through the com.

"Mayhem is down. I have him. They just shot a damn rocket into the fucking building where Mouth was set up."

His words register slowly, like my brain has been soaked in high-octane bourbon.

"Mouth? Mouth?" Flash's breathing comes ragged and heavy, like he's running hard again. "I'm going in after him, but we have company. We're going to be shooting our way out of here."

The woman in front of me finally seems to sense I'm there and turns toward me. She cries out, reaching for whatever her son had in his hand.

Metal glints in the moonlight.

Gun.

"Where the hell is Chaos?"

I cough and try to respond to Reaper as I struggle to bring up my weapon with weak arms. It's like being under water. Drowning and not being able to see the surface. Every breath filling my lungs with fluid. She aims the weapon in my direction, stepping closer through the smoke.

Somehow, I manage to fire off a single shot, the sound sharp and final.

She crumples to the ground next to her son, the gun in her hand clattering to the hard, compacted earth. I drop to my knees, my legs no longer able to support my weight. My breaths come ragged. Wheezing and wet.

The world darkens…

Shit.

Avery is going to be fucking pissed.

1

FOUR YEARS LATER

AVERY

I jerk the wheel to the right to avoid the car I didn't even notice was in front of me in my lane. My phone tumbles from my center console and onto the floor on the passenger side. A horn blares, and the man driving the car I almost just side-swiped to avoid hitting the *other* car flips me off.

Fuck.

The world blurs, my hot tears making it virtually impossible to see the road or anything else. I wipe at my eyes, trying to clear my vision, but it doesn't help.

Just get home.

Just get home where you can think and figure out what to do.

You just need to think.

I keep telling myself that, repeating it *ad nauseum* the entire drive, somehow hoping the more I say it, the more I'll believe it and the greater the chance it might be true. It's wishful thinking at its finest, but it's all I have left to cling to after what I just saw.

My hands won't stop shaking, though, because deep

down, I know it won't be okay. Getting home won't help anything. I'll still be in the same damn position, just sobbing on my couch instead of in my car, seeing the same thing over and over again in my head, reliving it every waking moment and refusing to sleep so it doesn't visit me there, too.

It's a mistake.

It has to be.

Another lie I keep telling myself—one I want so badly to believe because the alternative—that I *really* saw what I did, that it really means what I think it does—is just too horrific to accept.

But I know what I saw.

I just want to pretend this was all some bad dream, some hallucination, some sort of warping of my mind brought on by the time of year and the turmoil it always dredges up from the past.

It's just an awake nightmare brought on by stress, nothing more.

Yeah, keep telling yourself that, Avery.

I quickly swipe the tears from my eyes to try to clear my sight again and suck in a deep breath, but concentrating on what's happening outside this car, outside the vivid visions playing in my head, becomes harder and harder.

How could I have been so stupid?

So blind?

So trusting?

I've always prided myself on my ability to see through bullshit. To see people's true intentions, deep into their souls. Or at least, I did. Before Kalen. Combined with what just happened, it's abundantly clear that my radar is so far out of whack that it can't ever be fixed. I'm apparently a very shitty judge of character, and now, my failure has gotten me into this mess.

What I thought was a green light at the upcoming intersection flips to red, and I slam on my brakes and skid to a screeching stop, barely avoiding careening into the intersection and cross traffic.

Holy hell.

My heart thunders against my ribcage, and I press my hand over it, sucking in short gasps of air that seem to do nothing to help clear my head or fill my lungs.

How did I miss that turning yellow?

That's twice now, in the last five minutes, I almost killed myself because I can't see straight enough to drive. I'm supposed to be getting *away* from danger, not driving myself right into it.

Get a grip.

If I don't, I'm going to end up dead on this damn road and none of this will matter, anyway.

Traffic flows past in front of me, the good people of Baltimore making their way home after a late dinner or a long day at the office.

It's the time of night that bad things happen.

I should have known better than to be there.

Vivid, fresh memories flash before my eyes, the very thing I'm running from refusing to give me quarter for even a moment, and I squeeze them closed for a minute, hoping to will away what I saw with that simple action.

It doesn't work.

I reopen them, and the darkness of the night makes my skin crawl. Even with the headlights, the streetlights, and the buzz of movement surrounding me, there are too many shadows. Too many unknowns. Anything can be hiding out there. Anyone...

It's something I've never really thought about before, how truly vulnerable we all are at any given time, likely because I always had Kalen looking out for me, protecting me and making me feel safe...until he didn't. But now, I can't shake the feeling of eyes on me, of someone or something watching and waiting for the opportunity to strike.

With the light still red, I lean over and try to reach around the floor well on the passenger side for my phone. My fingers brush hard plastic, and I scoop it up and glance down at the screen.

Shit.

The little one percent on the battery indicator taunts me, red and glowing, the same color as the blood I can't get out of my visions.

So much blood...

I sit back up and settle into my seat, dropping my phone into the cup holder again. Almost instantly, blinding headlights hit my rearview mirror. A large SUV or truck barrels down at me from behind. Still half a block away, it doesn't appear to be slowing down as it approaches rapidly, ready to ram into my car and send me out into the cross traffic.

Shit. They're going to hit me.

The traffic light remains red, and traffic whizzes in front of me, a river of cars I can't make my way across. If this asshole doesn't stop, there's nowhere to go except into the middle of the intersection to be T-boned.

I throw my wheel to the right and floor it, hoping to squeeze between the curb and the oncoming traffic just as the SUV clips the back of my car. It sends me careening sideways into the fray. My side of the car slams into something, whipping my head to the left. I lay on my brakes, and the SUV that hit me continues straight into the intersection, smashing into a large truck with a sickening bang and crunch.

Gasping, my brain fogged and heart beating a rapid tattoo, I fumble to put my car into park and turn my head to observe the disaster behind me. The SUV that struck me sits in the middle of the intersection, its entire front end collapsed against the passenger side of a sedan that was also rear-ended by another car. Smoke rises from both vehicles, obscuring my view.

Shit.

Is everyone okay?

I reach for my seatbelt but pause with my hand on it as the passenger door of the SUV swings open and a familiar figure steps out on the pavement which is littered with shards of glass and pieces of metal that have been violently torn from the various vehicles involved.

"Oh, my God…" My stomach turns, the acid threatening to make its way up my throat. "No!"

I crank the gearshift, trying to get it into drive, and the back window just behind my head explodes, glass flying everywhere, hitting the side of my face. Sharp bites of pain aren't enough to stop me from understanding what just happened.

He's shooting *at me!*

Another shot pings against the door, and I slam my foot against the gas, but nothing happens. The engine revs violently, but I don't move—frozen in place, watching the man advance, still shooting.

I fumble with the gear again, finally getting it to move from neutral to drive as two more bullets strike the car.

Fuck.

I floor the gas, and this time, the vehicle complies, barreling away from the curb, leaving the accident, other angry drivers, and the apparent death squad sent after me, behind.

Sobs tumble from my lips, and the tears come so fast, there's no way to stop them even if I wanted to try.

What the hell am I going to do?

Not go home.

If I do, they'll show up eventually—likely quickly if they

were concerned enough to send *that* man after me so fast tonight.

They know I know.

They know I saw.

They can't let me live with the information I have.

I reach a shaking hand for my phone. "You know what you need to do."

My own voice mixing with the noises of the street and the city outside coming into the car from the broken window helps me develop some clarity.

"There's only one person you can call, Avery."

I can't. I can't. I can't.

I glance in my rearview mirror to see if anyone else is following me, the accident now so far behind me that I can't even see it anymore. The road remains empty, the traffic blocked by the cataclysm at the intersection.

"You don't have a choice."

It's the same thing I told myself all those years ago, that I didn't have a choice, that he was *forcing* me to make the decision I had to that changed so much.

I open the phone and dial the number I still know by heart, the one he said to only use in emergencies, one I hope he still answers. It's been so long that it's likely disconnected by now, all ties cut the same way he slashed everything and everyone else out of his life.

Still, I have to try.

It doesn't even ring before the familiar recorded voice hits my ear. *"Leave it."*

Hearing him after so long draws a violent sob from deep in my chest. I swallow past the rock lodged in my throat and try to blink away the rapidly falling tears so I don't end up crashing into something else. "Kalen, I'm in trouble. I don't know what to do. I need you—"

My phone issues a sharp beep in my hand, and I pull it away from my ear and glance down at a black screen.

"No! No! No!"

It's dead.

And so am I.

CHAOS

MY FIST CONNECTS with the hard jawbone of the motherfucker strapped to the chair in front of me, the force vibrating up through my arm in a satisfying sting as his head snaps back.

This fucker deserves so much worse.

He recovers from the blow, slowly shaking his head to try to clear the stars he's no doubt seeing after the way I've been working him over the last few minutes.

I squat, resting my forearms on my knees and watching the blood trickle from the corner of his mouth and nose. "I told you you didn't want to mess with her again, didn't I? I gave you a fair warning, and what did you do? Not even two weeks after we had our last chat, you thought showing up at her work was going to fly?"

A strangled groan slips from his lips, but I can't tell if it was meant to be a word or just a reaction to the agony he must be in. Hopefully, the latter. He's hanging just at that edge of blacking out, but that would be too good for him, too easy.

I won't let that happen.

Not until my job is done.

I reach forward and grasp his hair, forcing his head up until his unfocused muddy-brown eyes meet mine. "You really thought I wouldn't be there? Watching her? Protecting her? Making sure your punk ass didn't show up to cause more trouble?" I bark out a laugh that echoes in the empty, dilapidated boathouse. "You are one dumb fucker, aren't you? You just couldn't stay away."

My chest tightens slightly, knowing how hard that can be, and I push up to my full height, release his hair, and cross my arms over my chest.

The moment Robyn showed up at the office, asking for protection, and told us the history with this douchebag, I had a feeling it wouldn't be quick to resolve. Unlike a lot of our jobs—get in, get out, leave nothing but bodies behind—obsession is a whole other animal.

It twists the mind. Makes people irrational. Causes them to act against their own best interests. Makes them forget completely about self-preservation.

And Ryan Andrew Long is one obsessed man.

That creepy shrine to Robyn in his houseboat was all the proof I needed to know he wouldn't stop even after the first warning, which is why I never took my eyes off her and caught him tonight in the one place he should have stayed miles away from.

It's why he's suffering now.

Why he *deserves* to suffer.

Still, killing him is off the table for a variety of reasons. Robyn would know. The police could become involved and dig due to the restraining order she has against him, and she isn't trained to hold up under questioning. The firm's name would fall from her lips, and they'd end up on the doorstep with a warrant and questions we can't answer—at least, not without going to prison for a *very, very* long time.

Since my favorite permanent way to ensure our clients remain safe isn't available, that means coming up with new, creative strategies.

I scan the old boathouse that clearly hasn't been used in

years. The half-crumbled roof lies in pieces on the broken concrete floor. Rats scurry in the shadows. The water of the Patapsco River laps against the moorings in the empty boat slip. Combined with the moonlight streaming in from the holes in the roof, it provides the perfect ambiance for what I have to do.

Squatting again, I wait until Ryan lifts his head to meet my gaze. "Do you have a favorite movie, Ryan?"

"Wh-what?"

I raise an eyebrow. "Do you have a favorite movie?"

"Wh-why? I don't—"

"Because I'm about to make a point here, Ryan. Let me tell you about *my* favorite movie." I examine the blood on my knuckles and smile. "*Casino Royale*." Looking back at him, I wait for the connection to click in his head, but he remains almost passive, his face gaunt and pale, the blood still falling to the concrete below him from various places. "Have you not seen it?"

He shakes his head slightly. "No…I mean…yes…a l-long time a-ago."

"Well, it's absolutely *brilliant.* Not only did it launch Daniel Craig as the new Bond, but it also has one of my favorite movie scenes of all time—where Bond is tortured by *Le Chiffre.*"

I let the words hang in the damp, chilly air between us, giving him a moment to absorb where I'm going with this, but it doesn't seem to register.

"In that scene, *Le Chiffre* strips Bond naked, ties him to a chair with no seat on it, and then whips his junk with a large rope."

Ryan's head jerks up, and wide, frantic eyes meet mine. Things have finally fallen into place. He finally understands.

I grin at him and reach down to grab the old, weathered mooring rope beside the seatless chair he's strapped to.

"Now you know why you're naked." I push to my feet and lean in. "I want to ensure you feel every damn bit of this in the place it will hurt the most."

"No! No! Please! I-I won't go near her again. I won't—"

Liar.

I swing the rope and whip the knotted end up and under the chair to slam against his dick and nuts. He cries out something unintelligible and lurches forward against the restraints keeping him upright.

"If you can't stop thinking with your dick, then we need to take it out of play."

If I can't take him *out of play, I can at least punish him in a way he'll feel forever.*

Very real, very permanent damage is likely—and would be most welcome. But it still isn't enough to ensure he won't continue to stalk Robyn and make her live in fear. And that's not something I'm willing to let happen to any innocent woman.

I take another swing, this time adding an exaggerated flick of my wrist at the end to ensure it gets up high and connects with one hundred percent of the force I intend it to.

Bloody vomit spews from his mouth, out across the floor and over my boots. I glance down at them and groan.

Dammit. These are so comfortable and broken in.

"Now I have to replace my boots, Ryan." I shake my head. "That doesn't make me very happy."

He chokes and gags again, heaving out breaths that are becoming more and more ragged. "I-I can-can't breathe…"

"I imagine not."

I know what it feels like to be gasping for breath. Not being able to fill your lungs. Your body struggling for oxygen, for what it needs to keep functioning. I've been there one too many times, and it's much more pleasant being on this side. But another blow like that might make him lose consciousness, and I need him alert to hear my words and understand them.

Gripping his hair again, I tug his head up. "Now is the time to listen and really pay attention, Ryan, since you didn't when we had our first chat…"

A strangled groan is the only response I get, but his eyes are open and somewhat focused. If I wait any longer, my message may be lost in his fogged brain.

"You will be leaving Baltimore." I twist my fingers in his hair tightly. "I will personally escort you out of town, and you will keep driving until you hit the Pacific. Then, you can drive straight into the water for all I care, but what you will *not* do is ever come back to Baltimore or the East Coast at all. Ever. It's off fucking limits to you. Do you understand me?"

He opens his mouth to speak, but only a struggled rush of air comes out.

"What did you say?"

I lean slightly toward him, tilting my head to the side to try to hear what he's saying. He swallows thickly, the sound wet with his own blood and saliva.

"I-I ca-can't leave. My job. My parents—"

"Are none of my fucking concern. What *is* my concern is the safety of Robyn Hall, and I'll be watching you, ensuring you keep to your side of the fucking country. And if there are any other *problems* like what happened here and other women being harassed, my face will be the one you wake up to just before you take your last breath. Are we clear?"

He coughs and sputters, the rattling sound in his chest more pronounced than before. "O-okay."

A smile pulls at my lips, and I release his hair, letting his head drop and his body sag forward against the ropes keeping him bound to the chair. "Then we're done here."

I walk away from him and out to the edge of the water, inhaling the fresh air while I pull my phone from my pocket and turn it on to call Reaper with an update on our client's problem. Ryan may look bad, but none of his injuries will prevent him from packing up and leaving town tonight. I made sure of that.

My phone glows to life, and the little red voicemail icon sits in the center of the screen.

What the hell?

No one has this number except Reaper, Mouth, and a handful of other guys from the unit. None of them would leave a message, and the number it came from isn't familiar.

I press the button to make it play and put the phone to my ear, staring at the glistening lights across the river.

A strangled sob floats through the line, driving straight to my heart. The agonized sound I've heard before from the same lips. Ones I used to kiss. "Kalen, I'm in trouble. I don't know what to do. I need you—"

The voicemail cuts out, and I tug the phone from my ear and call the number back.

"Hi, you've reached Avery Mills. I'm not available to take your call right now, but leave a message, and I'll get back to you as soon as I can."

Beep.

That sharp sound pierces my ear, and I end the call as I try to suck in a breath against the vise suddenly tightening around my chest.

My always-steady hand shakes as I call Reaper and wait for him to answer.

He picks up on the second ring. "You done?"

"I need you to come meet me here to take care of the package. Avery's in trouble. I have to find her."

2

CHAOS

The door to the condo stands slightly ajar, but no light trickles out from inside. This time of night, the area's quiet, still.

It should be comforting.

If any of the busybodies in the neighborhood watch heard or saw anything suspicious, they would have contacted the police, who would be here by now. Given the number of stickers and signs in windows around here, there are plenty of people watching, yet the night remains silent. Everyone completely oblivious to whatever went down at Avery's place.

Anyone else might have missed the door being open that fraction of an inch, might have walked by on the street and glanced up at it and not have noticed or given it a second thought. But I don't miss things like that.

When I do, people die.

Shaking off that thought, gun in hand, I nudge open the

door and make my way inside. Her familiar scent hits me instantly—light, flowery, sweet. Perfect.

Just like her.

Overturned furniture…

Drawers dumped out…

Avery's belongings scattered around the living room…

And the kitchen…

I slowly make my way down the short hallway, listening for any signs that whoever did this might still be here, but the dead silence makes my blood run cold.

She isn't here, but someone else sure as hell was, and they may have left with what they wanted. The same thing I always wanted but never deserved and never should have had.

Fucking hell.

Her bedroom smells even *more* like her, and as I clear it, I inhale deeply, relishing what might be my last chance to experience it again.

I never thought I would after that night.

And if she hadn't called, I never would have.

The apartment is a wreck, but there isn't any trace of her or whoever might have done this.

Son of a bitch.

It's only been an hour since she left the message, so she's still close—assuming she called from here.

I hustle back to the front of her condo, close the front door, flip on the lights, and pull out my phone. Hers goes straight to voicemail again.

Shit.

The phone is likely dead or turned off; otherwise, she would have called me back. But her car wasn't parked out front. I need help finding her, and there's only one person I know who has the skills to do it.

I quickly dial Preacher, and he answers on the third ring.

"Chaos, long time no talk."

It has been a while, but I don't have time for idle chit-chat or catching up with old friends. What I need is his very specific skillset.

"I can't find Avery." The words burn in my chest, and I absently rub at it. "I think somebody grabbed her."

"What happened?" All the humor and good cheer his greeting held flee instantly. "Tell me everything."

"She called me and left a message saying she was in trouble. Then it cut out. I'm at her place, where she moved after the divorce. No sign of her, but it's trashed."

"Oh, hell. What do you need?"

"Can you track her phone or her car? I'm texting you her number."

The sound of his fingers flying across the keyboard hits me. "Give me five minutes."

It's five minutes too long.

Every second that ticks by makes things more dangerous for her—a truth Preacher knows as well as I do.

I send him the number and lower myself onto the couch, squeezing the bridge of my nose. The continued clicking of keys offers me a brief glimmer of hope that he might find something, and it's the only thing preventing me from completely going off the rails.

"Nothing on the phone. It's probably turned off or dead—"

"Shit."

"—but I got into the DMV database and located her car, then got the GPS tracker number from the dealership where she bought it. Wait a second…"

I hold my breath as more typing ticks in my head like a damn clock counting down.

"Got it. Traveling West on US 66 near Wellington."

I jerk my head up. "Are you sure?"

"Yeah. Why, do you know where she is?"

There's only one reason she'd be up there. Only one place she could go. And it makes complete sense. If she were in trouble, if she knew she couldn't come home, or if she came home to this, she would have taken off and headed somewhere she felt safe. Somewhere she believed no one could find her—except maybe me.

"I know where she's going."

"Do you need assistance? I'm sure Cutter can get out there if you need him."

As much as I love the thought of having Cutter Jackson at my side again, there isn't any time to wait for him to get here from Chicago, and Reaper and Mouth are tied up cleaning up Ryan and getting him out of town for our client. I'm on my own tonight.

"No. At least, not right now. I don't know what's going on yet. But as soon as I find out anything, I'll let you and Cutter know."

"If you need anything, just call." The sincerity in the computer genius' voice helps ease the tiniest bit of tension in my body. "And hey, Chaos?"

"What?"

"I hope your girl is okay."

I end the call.

My girl.

Avery hasn't been my girl in a long fucking time. And with good reason. The last words we spoke to each other were in anger. Awful, terrible, hate-filled words neither one of us can take back, said while lawyers sat at our sides and we signed the divorce papers.

Yet…she called *me*.

She didn't call 9-1-1. She didn't call the people you're supposed to call. She called the number I gave her all those years ago when we were still together and told her to use if she ever needed something, if she were ever in trouble.

I never thought she would. But she reached out.

Things must be really fucking bad for her to come to me.

I push to my feet and give the living room one last scan. My eyes land on a framed photograph of her on a beach smiling bright, her auburn hair floating in the wind around her.

Damn. She looks good.

Even though I shouldn't, I walk over and pull it from the shelf. Examining it, for a moment, a twinge of jealousy heats my blood.

Who took this picture?

A boyfriend?

I swallow down that thought and quickly return the frame.

It doesn't matter. She needs *my* help, or she wouldn't have called.

I switch off the light, step out, and close the door behind me. I'll have to tell the guys to come back and get this cleaned up before anyone else discovers it and alerts the cops.

The last thing I need is them meddling in whatever this is and fucking up my chances of getting her back safely.

Scanning the street, I hustle down the stairs and back to my bike parked at the rear of the building. Straddling it, I pull on my helmet and take one final look at the place she settled when we split.

Not exactly the way I had hoped to see it.

But it wasn't like she was inviting me over for friendly chitchat after what went down.

I fire up the bike, knock up the kickstand, and tear out of the parking lot.

She may think she's heading somewhere safe, that no one

else can ever find her, but if *I* know she'd be there, someone else can easily figure it out, too.

Jesus, Avery, what have you gotten yourself into?

A million possibilities flit through my head as the cool wind whips around me, each worse than the last.

Whatever it is, I'm going to get you out.

AVERY

THE FAMILIAR NEON sign glowing in the distance makes me release the breath it feels like I've been holding for the last few hours while driving.

I made it.

Someone here will have a charger. I can get my phone working again and call Kalen to tell him where I am.

He'll just abandon you again, leave you twisting in the wind.

That tiny voice has been harping at me since I left the message for him, eating away slowly at the certainty I had that he would come to help me fix this horrible mess I've gotten myself into.

Kalen isn't the man I fell in love with. He hasn't been for a long time. All I really know is he has a history of letting me down, of failing me, of failing *us* so badly that it ended things.

I blink away another round of impending tears as I approach the gravel driveway for the diner. My stomach rumbles violently, a reminder I haven't eaten all day. The lack of calories mixed with the adrenaline coursing through my veins is finally starting to catch up with me. I can't ignore the lightheadedness I've been fighting for the last few miles.

As uneven and treacherous as the rest of the trip is from here, I definitely can't drive like this, but Bernice's chicken soup and homemade biscuits might just give me a tiny piece of comfort I need so badly after everything that's happened.

I put on my turn signal, even though the road is quiet and desolate behind me, and turn in to the almost-always empty parking lot.

This place is never exactly bustling. I can't recall it ever having more than five or six cars in the lot at any given time, except for maybe Christmas Eve. For some strange reason, that's when all the loonies from up the mountain come down for a drink.

Do they still do that?

It's been years since I've been up here, but everything still looks the same. The same chipping paint on the door boasts "hot coffee and pie — best in three counties," and despite everything that's happening, I find myself smiling because it really is.

Bernice's cooking can bring a smile to anyone. I'm proof of that. I should be a sobbing, shaking mess—and I *am*—but just imagining that familiar taste is enough to give me hope that this will somehow all work out.

I park facing the highway and inhale another deep breath to try to keep myself in control. If I walk in there looking like this, Bernice will know something's wrong, and she cares enough to call the cops if she thinks I'm in any danger.

She would think she's helping, believe she's doing the right thing, but getting the authorities involved will only complicate things more.

It's why I need Kalen.

You don't need Kalen. You need Chaos.

My hands tighten around the wheel. That's a realization I don't want to consider right now. Not when Chaos is what changed him and destroyed us.

I look back at the broken window behind me and then at

the diner, ensuring it isn't in view. If she happens to look out, she won't see the damage to my car, so I'm in the clear.

At least with that…

Keeping myself from blurting out the reality of this mess once I see her will be harder than this drive was. Bernice has a way of drawing things out of you, things you never thought you'd reveal.

Not today, Bernice.

All I need is soup. Not a heart-to-heart.

I climb from the car, phone in hand, and beeline for the glass door. Pulling it open, bells jingle overhead and a familiar head of white hair lifts from behind the counter to examine the newest arrival.

"Well, Avery Marie Mills, is that you?" Bernice grins at me and races around the counter even though I haven't answered.

I swallow back the sob that threatens to climb up my throat and instead force a smile. "Hi, Bernice. It's good to see you."

"Oh, honey." She pulls me into her arms, gifting me a warm hug I haven't felt in years. Pulling back, she examines me, pressing her palms against my cheeks. "Honey, you look upset. Is something wrong?"

"No, no, I'm okay."

If I believe it, so will she.

She narrows her shrewd russet gaze on me. "What are you doing up here now?" Her eyes dart to the clock. "And this late! It's been what…five years since you've stopped by and you decided to at midnight?"

"About that, yeah." I offer a shrug I hope comes across as nonchalant. "I just needed to spend some time up here."

"Well, I'm glad you stopped." She drops her hands to my shoulders and gives them a squeeze. "I just made a fresh batch of your favorite soup. And I have an apple pie about ready to come out of the oven."

True warmth spreads through me for the first time tonight, flooding me with good memories of times when things felt so certain and safe. "That sounds great." I hold up my phone. "Do you happen to have a charger that would work on this phone?"

She examines it and chews her lip. "You know, I'm not quite sure. All this technology stuff is way beyond me." She flits a hand. "But Russell is working in the kitchen, and he knows a hell of a lot more about this than I do. Let me go check with him while I grab your stuff."

"Thank you. I'm going to go use the bathroom."

An icy-cold splash of water on my face will do me good. Even though my hands have finally stopped shaking, knowing Bernice and her grandson are here with me, I still feel on edge, like a single word from her will break me open and I'll spill all my secrets.

That can't happen.

She winks at me. "Well, you know where it is."

"I sure do."

Almost fifteen years of spending summers up here at Grandpa's cabin made it like a second home, and coming to the diner for some soup and pie a few times a week while I was up here was an unbreakable tradition.

Part of me always suspected something was going on between Grandpa and Bernice all those years ago. The old widower and the old widow spent an awful lot of time together and shared a look every once in a while that I was too young to understand then, but now, looking back on it, I'm glad Gramps had someone like Bernice in his life.

It's hard going it alone, not having anyone to rely on or confide in.

Please don't fail me, Kalen.

I cast a quick glance out the big front window toward the road that brought me up the mountain. A pair of headlights approach, traveling the same direction I just was, and I hold my breath. The vehicle moves closer and closer, and anxiety coils coldly around my spine. Finally, the car hits the driveway for the diner, but it drives past it without slowing and disappears up the two-lane county highway farther up the mountain.

Oh, thank God.

My relieved sigh rushes from my lips, and I make my way to the short back hall that leads to the bathrooms and the rear exit. I push into the bathroom, do my business, and step out to wash my hands.

No wonder Bernice said I looked upset. Red rims my eyes despite my best efforts to stop the tears, and blotchy skin and wind-tangled hair from the broken car window make me look like something that just crawled out of the swamp.

Hell...

I wash my hands and splash cold water onto my face, then run my wet fingers through my hair, trying to tame the beast it has become. It doesn't do much good, but I look more human than I did a few minutes ago. Not even close to perfect, but it's the best I can do.

Bernice's soup and pie will help, too. The kind of cooking that can make any rainy day—or murderous one—better.

I step out of the bathroom to return to the main portion of the diner, and a hand wraps around my waist tightly from behind while another flattens over my mouth, stifling my attempt to scream.

AVERY

I try to scream again, but the large hand over my mouth muffles any attempt to cry for help to Bernice or Russell. My attacker drags me backward, and despite my best attempts to grip the door frame and keep him from doing it, he yanks me out the rear exit of the diner easily, as if I weigh nothing and my thrashing doesn't faze him.

But he's not going to take me easily.

Never.

After all that's happened in the last few hours to get me here, I refuse to let this asshole win.

I reach back toward his head and try to find his eyes with my thumbs to gouge them as I kick his shin with my left foot with all the strength I have. He squeezes his eyes shut against my assault, and his hold doesn't loosen even a bit with the strike to his leg, but our movement stops just outside the door.

Warm breath floats across the back of my neck and right ear, making me shudder and gag against the hand.

"I taught you well. That would have worked on anyone else." Kalen's deep, husky voice rolls over me like a soothing balm, bringing with it years of memories—of promises made and broken, of a love I thought was going to last forever but crumbled so easily under the weight of the world he carried on his shoulders as Chaos.

The hand around my mouth slides off, and he squeezes me around the waist once and releases me. I whirl around to face him and meet his ice-cold blue stare.

So many years have passed since I last saw his face, and then, it was through a haze of tears. But the ones burning my eyes now aren't of despair like they were that night. They aren't from fear of him even though he looks harder, like life has beaten him up over and over again and left him barely hanging by a thread. They're because he's really *here*. It's *him*. It's Kalen.

And once—what feels like not that long ago, standing here with him so close—he was my entire world.

"Oh, my God! Kalen!" I launch myself at him, throwing my arms around his neck as his strong ones wrap around me and hold me tightly. A sob slips from my lips, and I fight another one as a million words try to race out at once. "How did you find me? My phone is dead and—"

"*Shh.*" He pulls me against the side of the diner and takes my face between his palms abruptly. "Quiet."

It's an order—clipped and direct.

He scans the area where we hide at the rear of the restaurant, assessing every noise, every movement of an animal in the woods behind us, searching for threats.

The hair on the back of my neck stands on end, and I whip my head around, trying to see what he does. "W-what's wrong?"

He leans to the side and glances around the corner of the building toward the front parking lot where I left my car.

"Just making sure we don't have any unexpected company."
He turns to me and sighs. "I found you way too easily. After I
couldn't call you back, I had a friend of mine try to track
your phone and your car's GPS."

"You can do that?"

"Not legally, but I would have figured out you were here,
anyway." His hard glare softens slightly. "Your grandfather's
cabin was always a haven for you. It's the first place I would
have looked...which means whoever you're running from
will look there, too. We're not safe here—"

What?

"But no one else knows about it. How can anybody know
I'm here?"

He raises a dark eyebrow, a move he always used when he
was biting back saying something he knew would start a
fight. "You never told *anyone* about your grandfather's place?"

"What? No, of course not." A memory flickers in my head.
Two years ago...well before I understood how much danger I
was in working there. "Oh, shit."

Kalen takes a step toward me, concern furrowing his
brow. "What?"

"I *did*. A couple of the guys in the office were talking
about going deep-sea fishing in Mexico, and I commented
that I loved to fish. They were really surprised and asked
where I had fished—"

"And you told him up here with your grandfather at his
cabin."

I nod and groan. "Yeah. Oh, my God. What if they're—"

Headlights sweep across the side of the building closest to
us, and Kalen grabs me and shoves me behind him as he pulls
a weapon from a holster at his hip.

I try to see over his shoulder, but his wide body blocks
me almost completely. "What is it?"

He peeks around the corner, steady as a rock, observing.

Assessing. Analyzing the way he was trained to. "A dark sedan just pulled into the parking lot."

Acid churns in my empty stomach and climbs up my throat. "Maybe they're just coming in for some pie."

Maybe it's just wishful thinking on my part, but if it's the people I'm running from, then I'm not the only one in danger. Bernice and Russell are sitting ducks in the diner, and I have first-hand knowledge that these guys are not afraid to get their hands dirty and bloody to get what they want. They wouldn't think twice about torturing innocent people to locate me.

Kalen makes a disgusted noise in his throat. "They're not here for *pie*, Avery. They're approaching your car."

"Shit. What do we do?"

He glances at me. "*You're* not gonna do *anything*. *You're* gonna stay *right* there. Don't move. Don't say a word. No matter what you hear."

Oh, God. No matter what I hear?

I grip his forearm tightly and tug until he peeks back at me again. "What are you going to do?"

His eyes darken from blue to almost black, his face hardening like granite. The shift from Kalen to Chaos is almost instant, and it makes me release his arm and retreat a tiny half-step.

"I'm going to do whatever the fuck I need to do to eliminate the threat."

He doesn't need to expand on that any further, and if I open my mouth with any sort of objection, it will only make things worse between us. Challenging him when he's in "Chaos mode" and intent on destruction always did.

I don't know what I expected when I called him for help, but seeing him like this—seeing *Chaos*, the part of the man that broke up everything we once shared—chills me to the core.

Wrapping my arms around myself, I shiver and fight another sob. "You're going to kill them."

It isn't a question because I know the answer. He won't give them a chance to survive, to return to their boss, to come after me again. He will *end* the threat. It's what he *does.*

He presses his lips into a hard line. "I don't know what you've gotten yourself into, Avery, but do you want my fucking help or not?"

I nod quickly.

That's Chaos.

There's the man I need in this moment.

Not the warm arms to embrace me but the cold hands that can kill easily.

"Stay here and don't fucking move. Do you hear me?"

CHAOS

AVERY NODS AT ME, her green eyes wide with fear that makes her entire body shake like the ground is quaking beneath her feet. Her bottom lip quivers, and she pulls it between her teeth, likely to try to keep herself from crying.

It's what she always did when she didn't want to appear weak or affected by something, but she can't hide it now. Not from me. I know her too well.

Whatever's going on is bad. Bad enough that she's running for her life. This isn't just some misunderstanding or some argument with a friend. She's terrified, and after what I saw at her condo, rightfully so.

Someone is after something she has, and it appears they'll stop at nothing to get it.

What the hell *have you gotten yourself into, Avery?*

Whatever it is, these fuckers seem pretty damn determined, and I need to get a better look. I creep along the side of the building to where a large glass window looks into the diner, and I can see through the front window straight into the parking lot.

The black sedan stops behind Avery's car, and the two men inside lean toward it to examine it. They exchange a few words and look toward the building.

Shit.

If they go in there, looking for her, innocent people are going to get pulled into this mess.

Knowing how deeply Avery cares about Bernice, if anything happens to her, Avery will never forgive herself, never recover, even if I manage to save her from whoever is after her.

I duck down and race below the window to the corner of the diner as they pull in and park next to Avery's car. Two men, clearly packing some serious heat, given the bumps under their shirts at their sides, scan their surroundings. One reaches in through a broken window of the car while the other watches the diner.

They're still looking for something, but it appears he doesn't find it. He rises from the window, and the two start to move across the parking lot toward the restaurant.

I fire off four quick rounds—two into each—before they even have time to react, the sound of the shots reverberating off the mountains around us. They hit the pavement almost simultaneously, and an eerie silence falls over the area. I hustle to where Avery stands near the back door, grab her hand, and pull her in the direction of the other side of the building.

"We need to move."

She glances at the building as I drag her toward the woods behind it. "What about Bernice? We can't just leave her. They'll—"

I tighten my grip on her hand to keep her from trying to slip out of my hold and go back. "They're not going to hurt Bernice."

"What?" Her voice cracks on the word, and she shakes her head. "How can you know that?"

My feet pound on the uneven ground, and she stumbles along behind me—going back through the woods the same way I came in. "Because they're *dead*, Avery."

"Dead?" She looks back toward the diner, now partially concealed by the bushes and trees. "Are you sure?"

I pause for a second and turn toward her, our bodies mere centimeters from each other. "I'm fucking *sure*, Avery, and now, we gotta go."

"Where?"

"Somewhere safe. Somewhere they won't trace back to you so you can tell me what the fuck is going on and explain what you've gotten yourself into."

It doesn't make any sense. Avery has always toed the line, always followed the rules, never even sped on the damn highway, which is how I was able to catch up to her. She's never been a rule breaker and never stepped on anyone else's toes or nosed into anyone else's business. Yet, here we are...

No matter how hard I try, I just can't wrap my head around what she could have done to have someone after her like this. But once we get to my place, she's going to tell me *everything*.

I lead her over to my bike, hidden behind a patch of thorny bushes where I left it so no one would hear or see me when I came up to the diner.

Her eyes widen slightly. "What about my car?"

I grip her wrist and draw her up against me. The low growl in my chest comes out before I can even stop it. "That's how I so easily tracked you. If they have the right resources at their disposal, they'll be able to use the GPS the same way I did. Where's your phone?"

She reaches into her pocket with a shaky hand and holds it up.

"Give it to me."

"But it's dead."

I glare at her until she hands it over, then I release her wrist and chuck it against the ground and stomp my boot against it with a satisfying crunch.

"No!" Avery lunges toward the shattered phone, dropping to her knees. "We need that."

"What do you mean?"

Bordering on frantic now, she tries to gather the pieces. "There's information on the phone. Something we need."

Fuck.

The SIM card wasn't really a problem since the phone was dead, but I couldn't have her bring it back and plug it in to charge it up.

I squat and help her scoop up the pieces of the phone until I find the memory card. Meeting her gaze, I hold up the tiny piece of plastic. "Should all be on here."

She releases a heavy, relieved sigh and watches me shove it into my pocket. I grab the remains of the phone from her hand and toss them onto the ground, except for the SIM card. That, I place on a rock and stomp on it until it breaks.

"Now, we gotta go."

Whatever is going on, the longer we stay here, the greater chance the police will arrive and tie us to the two bodies lying on the pavement in front of the diner before we're far enough away to escape them. As it stands, once they run her plates, they'll be looking for Avery. But we can deal with that later. Right now, the only thing that matters is getting us somewhere safe so she can tell me everything.

I hold out my hand, and she accepts it, letting me pull her

up from the ground. Even out here, surrounded by nature, her scent wraps around me and invades my lungs. I tried to ignore it earlier, tried to push it away and concentrate on my mission, but something tells me that's going to be nearly impossible with Avery at the center of it.

Her eyes lock with mine for a moment, and I force myself to look away and climb onto the bike. "Get on."

She throws her leg over behind me, just like she has hundreds of times, and I hand her my helmet without looking back. Having Avery with me on my motorcycle again is a dream and a living nightmare.

Thin arms wrap around my waist, and she lays her head against my shoulder blade. Her entire body shakes violently, and I start the ignition. It rumbles beneath us, and almost instantly, she relaxes into me.

Fuck.

I need to get her somewhere safe.

Somewhere away from *me*.

4

CHAOS

Trying to concentrate on the rumble of the road beneath us or the harsh wind whipping at me as we fly down the road on our way back to the city doesn't help distract me from every shift Avery makes behind me. The way she clings to me so tightly, like I'm the most important thing in the world. The same way she always used to before I ruined everything.

I never thought I'd see her again, let alone have her wrapped around me on the open road for hours like she used to be, as if no time has passed, like all the turmoil and hurt simply blew away in the wind floating around us. It's dangerous to relish it, to wish it could stay like this forever, but now that we have finally reached my place, I almost regret the ride wasn't longer, even though I know the safest thing to do is get inside and figure out what the fuck is going on.

Any delay just gives more time to whoever is after her to figure out a way to track her down. Plus, Bernice undoubtedly called the police when she heard the gunshots and discovered two bodies in her parking lot with Avery missing.

Thank fuck that old place doesn't have surveillance cameras.

Eventually, we'll have to come up with a story explaining what happened, but that isn't an immediate concern. Keeping Avery safe is.

I park my bike, knock down the kickstand, and kill the engine. Avery's death grip on me relaxes before she shifts on the seat. An awkward moment stretches out between us— neither of us saying anything or moving. Finally, I glance over my shoulder at her, and she pulls off the helmet, releasing her dark, disheveled hair.

My fingers itch to run through it, to smooth it away from her face, tuck it behind her ear, and I flex them at my sides to try to dispel the feeling, letting my gaze linger on the tiny cuts along the side of her face left from the blown-out window of her car.

Seeing the injury on her makes me want to go back and kill those fuckers again. Once I find out who is responsible, I'll be able to unleash all this anger somewhere because I don't want to direct it at Avery.

She offers me a tiny half smile. "It's been a long time since I've ridden on one of these."

That shouldn't make relief flood through my system, but it does.

She hasn't been on any other asshole's ride in the time since we split.

Thank fuck.

I couldn't handle knowing she had been. It's hard enough trying not to think about all the other things she's likely been up to since we ended things.

She shifts to slide off the seat, and I offer her my hand to help her. A ride like that after so many years off a bike is bound to have made her sore. She places her small, soft hand in mine, and a tiny little zing shoots up my arm and goes straight to my cock.

Fucking hell.

Avery always did that to me, and it appears our time apart hasn't changed anything. It takes her a moment to find her footing, but as soon as she's steady, I jerk my hand from hers and motion toward the steps on the side of the building leading up to my second-floor apartment.

"Let's go."

I climb off while I scan the street behind us, watching for anything suspicious or out of the ordinary, but the entire area is quiet. It tends to be this early in the morning, just before sunrise. None of the businesses surrounding my building will open until at least eight, and there isn't anything else to bring anyone down here this time of day.

Exactly why I chose this place.

Avery pauses at the bottom of the steps, looking to her left at the row of garage doors and the sign above them. "What is this place?

"A car and motorcycle repair shop. I live above it. Go!"

She complies without offering another comment, and I follow her up the stairs, her tight ass encased in perfectly form-fitting jeans taunting me right in front of my face with each step. I have to bite back the desire to reach up and smack it like I used to every time we were in this position before.

This isn't then, and she isn't yours anymore.

That was my choice. My actions drove her away, and I have to live with the consequences, even if it was necessary. That means ignoring the urge to touch her, to feel her against me, to take what used to be mine.

She pauses at the top of the stairs on the tiny landing outside the single door that leads to my apartment, and I pull out my keys and unlock the deadbolt, pushing it open for her to enter ahead of me.

I'm not letting Avery out of my damn sight until all this is resolved.

Avery slowly steps inside, and I usher her in farther with a hand on her lower back and flip the light switch. The single bulb hanging from the sad, ancient fixture in the center of the room flickers to life, and she pauses just inside the living room while I lock the door.

She scans the space quickly, then turns back to me with her eyebrow raised. "How long have you lived here?"

I offer a shrug. "Couple of years."

"Where's all your stuff?"

The single recliner sits in one corner, the television hanging opposite. Otherwise, the room is empty.

Just the way I like it.

I shrug again. "I have everything I need."

It's a lie I constantly tell myself, which is why I don't look at Avery when I say the words, just push past her into the small kitchen. Having her here, letting her see me live like this, so different from the warm, welcoming home we once shared, makes my shoulders tighten.

"Aren't you worried somebody might find us here and come looking for me?"

I freeze in front of the fridge and turn slowly to face her. "In order for them to do that, they would have to know who I was and how we were connected. And I bet you never told anybody you were ever married."

Her face falls slightly, and she gulps, averting her gaze to her feet for a second and shifting nervously on her feet. "I didn't."

"Exactly." I turn and grab a beer from the fridge, knock off the cap, and bring it to my lips. "So, no one knows who I am."

It's no surprise she didn't say anything about me to anyone. It isn't an experience she wants to relive, even if just through memories.

She slowly lifts her head. "I didn't tell anyone about you because it was too painful for me."

Her words hit me the same way the bullets did those two fuckers in the parking lot back at the diner, and I take a long pull from the bottle to give me a distraction from the ache in my chest. But the cool, hoppy liquid doesn't help wash away the hurt of the truth in what she said.

Like I need more reminders of how I destroyed everything. How badly I destroyed her...

I stare at the bottle for a moment, down half the beer, then pull out my phone and dial Reaper.

It only rings once before he picks up. "Hey, man. Status?"

"I'm fine. I have her, and she's okay." I glance over at Avery, where she shifts back and forth on her feet in the middle of my barren living room. "We're at my place. I need you guys to come over to figure out a plan for taking care of her situation."

"We handled our other problem. Got him out of town."

That douchebag, stalker asshole.

It would have been great to be there to watch him leave the city and drive away in agony after the way I worked him over, but given how shaken Avery is, it was the right decision to ditch the dumbass and go get her.

"Good."

"We'll be over there soon."

I end the call, slide my phone into my pocket, and take another swig of my beer.

Avery watches me tentatively, pulling her bottom lip between her teeth and twisting her hands in front of her. "Who did you call?"

I set down the bottle and lay my hands flat on the

counter, leaning against it, happy it puts some much-needed distance between us—a barrier on top of the one I've already erected through my actions in the past. "Reaper and Mouth."

She winces, and her lips twist down. "I'm really not comfortable having them involved with this."

Her reaction churns my gut for multiple reasons. There was a time when she was their friend, when she trusted them with her life the way she trusted me. But now they're the enemy as much as I've become. I was a last-resort call, and that truth makes me slam my palm against the cheap formica.

It causes her to jump, and I instantly regret having scared her when she's already so terrified, but I need her to focus and understand the position she's in.

"You called *me* for help, Avery. You don't get to decide how I do it. Now, tell me what the *hell* is going on."

AVERY

HIS ANGER IS WARRANTED. I've dragged him into a massive clusterfuck, and now I've insulted his friends. I never should have said anything, no matter how uneasy seeing them will make me.

They became everything to him when I became nothing. All he wanted was to be with them, to be Chaos as they saw him. They're the last people I want to see; still, I should keep my mouth shut about it rather than make an already-uncomfortable situation even more so by basically insulting them.

I'd love to crawl into a hole and hide now—from the reality of what's happening and from the look Kalen is giving me—but I don't have any choice but to tell him everything, to tell him what I saw.

It's the only chance I have of maybe getting out of this alive.

My hands shake as I wander over to the only piece of furniture in the room—the battered, beat-up old recliner he always loved so much. Just like us, the years have done more damage to it—the leather torn in spots and rubbed almost bare in others. Scars that match the ones we bear.

Without looking at Kalen, I slowly lower myself into it. "So...after we split, I sold the house."

"I know." His voice comes harsh and abrupt, like thinking about the home we once shared is just as painful for him as it is for me. "I wanted you to keep it."

"Well, I used the money from the sale to go back to school and get a degree in accounting. I needed some way to support myself, a job, and I wasn't qualified to do anything since I never worked before—"

"You didn't have to work. Every damn month, I sent my check to your bank account so you would always be taken care of and you wouldn't have to work."

I glance over at him, the anger burning in his gaze making me shift on the chair. "I didn't want your money. After we split, I didn't want anything to do with you. I wanted to support myself on my own. I haven't touched a *dime* of what you've sent me over the last four years. It's all still sitting in that account. You can have it."

Kalen's jaw tightens, and he fists his hands on the top of the narrow counter separating us. "What the hell, Avery?"

"I needed to do something on my own. *Be* on my own. So..."—I try to draw us away from this conversation because it's only going to get more painful if we go down that road further—"I got my degree in accounting, and I got a job at a food service company. You know, they provide products to restaurants and schools and things like that."

He nods, though it doesn't appear any of his anger or annoyance has faded.

"I was helping with the accounting. The owner also has some restaurants. It was busy. Another woman, her name was Amelia, she had been working for him for a while, and I was basically brought on to assist her."

Her kind, warm, bourbon eyes flash in my head, and I bite back a sob that threatens to slip from my lips. "Then, a month or two ago, she started acting strange."

"Strange how?"

I glance over at Kalen to find him slightly more relaxed, taking a sip of his beer. "Just…off?" I shrug. "She wasn't as talkative as usual, and she took back a lot of tasks she had previously asked me to take care of, almost like she didn't trust me to do it anymore. Now, I know what it really was…"

"What happened, Avery?"

"Yesterday morning, I went into the office like usual, and she wasn't there. That was weird because she was an early riser and always one of the first ones in. The owner, Ricardo Perez, told me she had decided to retire early and move back to the small town in Mexico where her family still lived."

"Okay…"

"But something just felt off about that. She had been telling me about how she needed to work for a few more years to really be comfortable retiring. She cared for her elderly parents and helped some other family members financially, so she really wanted a nice nest egg built up and wasn't there yet."

He considers my explanation for a moment. "So, you didn't buy what he was telling you?"

"No, but I didn't want to challenge my boss and maybe get fired, and I didn't really have any reason to suspect anything was wrong other than the *off* feeling. Until…" I sigh and brush my hair back from my face with shaking hands.

"Until I moved into her bigger office later in the day, at Ricardo's suggestion, and I found a thumb drive taped to the underside of the desk."

Kalen freezes, the bottle in his hand. "What was on it?"

"At first, I was confused. I put it into the computer and didn't know what I was looking at. It took me a while to realize she had prepared it, that it was comparisons of numbers. Inventory, sales, cash coming in from the restaurants and the customers who made purchases from the supply side of the business as well as expenses paid out." I lock eyes with Kalen. "None of it matched up."

"What do you mean?"

"There was a whole lot of cash coming from somewhere. It shouldn't have been there. There were customer names I didn't recognize. At first, I thought I was just missing something, not understanding what I was looking at. I took it home last night to examine it more carefully because I didn't want to jump to any conclusions if there was a reasonable explanation and didn't want my boss mad at me for messing up the books if there was an issue."

"But there wasn't a reasonable explanation?"

I shake my head. "Not one I could find. I Googled the names of the companies supposedly making purchases from us, but they either didn't exist or had very basic information on their websites that made it look like they weren't real. So, I went back to the office late last night. Ricardo had always been weird about that—us working late. He said he didn't expect us to and that he wanted us to have real lives. I never thought anything of it. I never really questioned why he wouldn't want anyone there after hours."

Idiot.

Naïve fool.

What boss discourages *employees from working a little harder and staying to finish things?*

Only one who is hiding something.

Kalen's jaw tenses as he listens. He's thinking the same damn thing I should have immediately. One thing he always taught me was to be aware of my surroundings, to keep my eyes and ears open for anything off. He always said intuition was our strongest weapon.

And I ignored mine.

"Ricardo's car was parked outside the building that housed our offices, but he wasn't in there. There were some more vehicles by the connected warehouse, which I found odd since I didn't realize anyone ever worked late besides him. I walked over to the warehouse to look for him and…"

"And what?"

"I—" My words catch in my throat as the memories of what I saw flash in vivid red before my eyes. "He-he was there with some of the delivery men, but they weren't working on packing the trucks with items for deliveries."

"What were they doing?"

A single tear drops down my cheek. "It just seemed suspicious, odd there would be workers there late at night. Something was off. I initially didn't see Ricardo from where I stood just inside the dock door, so I thought maybe they were stealing from the company." I let out a shaky breath. "But the truth was so much worse."

"Just tell me, Avery."

"They pulled Amelia's body from one of the freezers and loaded it into the back of a truck." I choke back a sob and squeeze my eyes closed. "There was so much blood all over her. He-he killed her because she had discovered whatever the hell he was doing."

I try to swallow another sob and force the words out, but all that comes is a wail that sounds almost inhuman from somewhere deep in my chest.

Strong, warm arms wrap around me and hold me steady.

The familiarity of his embrace, the feeling of absolute safety, makes me forget all the reasons this is the wrong place to be, that he's the wrong person to be with. Instead, I drape my arms around his neck and weep against his shoulder, letting go of everything I have left in me, everything I've tried so hard to ignore and keep inside while I fight for my life.

Kalen pulls back my head, and his hard eyes meet mine. "What's on the phone that's so important?"

I take a deep inhale. "When I realized they were doing something sketchy, I pulled out my phone, and I recorded it."

His dark eyebrows rise slowly. "You got video of them moving the body?"

"Yeah."

"What about the zip drive with the numbers? Where is it now?"

"It's still at the office. I left it on my desk."

Kalen's lips twist into a frown. "Shit. That's not why they're after you, though."

"No. I don't know how they could know I had the drive or that it even existed. They must have figured out I was watching them, or someone saw me there recording before I ran and drove away. They're trying to kill me, Kalen. One of the men from the warehouse followed me and tried to ram my car, and now, those two at the diner…"

"Why didn't you call the police or go straight to the police station?"

"Because one of the men in the warehouse was wearing a police uniform, and a squad car was parked outside the dock doors. I saw it when I was leaving."

"Fuck."

I suck in a shaky breath, fighting another sob filling my chest.

Kalen rests his large hands on my thighs and squeezes. "I'm not going to let anything happen to you. I promise."

"How can you say that? These men...they're obviously dangerous. Wherever this money is coming from, it's something bad. I—"

He captures my face between his palms and forces me to meet his concerned gaze. "I know, but I'm very good at what I do. You have to trust me."

That's far easier said than done, given our history. He's broken so many promises, shattered me in so many ways. It's hard to believe anything he says anymore.

But I'll try.

What other choice do I have?

5

AVERY

P eople always talk about adrenaline crashes. How you ride the high until you finally collapse to a crushing low and an exhaustion that permeates deep in your bones.

I finally understand what they mean.

It hits me within half an hour of walking into Kalen's place and unloading the weight of what I saw. Between being curled up in the old recliner that was always so comfortable, the last of the adrenaline that's been keeping me going wearing off, and Kalen standing vigil over me, I finally let my eyes drift closed.

I let myself go and try to forget the vivid, horrific recent memory for just a few moments. It's quickly replaced with a good memory, one of the many Kalen and I had before everything changed, before *he* changed.

The beach...

The shining sun beating down on us, warming our exposed skin...

Him kissing his way across my flat belly to my lips and

capturing my mouth in a way that says if we weren't in public, surrounded by hundreds of other beachgoers, he'd be taking me right now on the sand...

Instead, he pries his lips from mine and grins at me, his eyes covered by his sunglasses. "What are we gonna do for the rest of the day? Because I have some ideas."

I chuckle and push at his shoulder. "You're terrible."

"What?" One of his eyebrows rises over the reflective lenses. "What's so wrong with wanting to go back to the hotel and fuck my wife mindless?"

Shaking my head, I return his grin. "Nothing. Except that's all we've been doing in the last two days. And I actually want to *do* something on our honeymoon besides you fucking me mindless, if you don't mind."

"Oh, I *do* mind..." He captures my mouth again. His greedy tongue slips between my lips, and he shifts his body tighter against mine. The fact that we're on a beach in Mexico, surrounded by other tourists, doesn't seem to faze him. It seems nothing does or can...

A hard knock at the door jerks me awake, and a high-pitched scream fills the tiny apartment.

"Avery, it's fine. You're okay." Kalen lays a hand on my shoulder and squeezes gently. "It's just the guys."

Hell, that was me screaming.

I push my hair away from my face and try to take controlled breaths to keep my heart from beating straight out of my chest.

Kalen makes his way over to the door, checks the peep-hole, and pulls it open to let Reaper and Mouth walk in. Each of the men offers me a nod of acknowledgment and nothing more.

Seems the hard feelings have carried over all this time.

That shouldn't surprise me. They would back up Kalen on anything, no questions asked. That kind of loyalty is necessary in their line of work. I'm the villain in this situation because I'm the one who served him papers. It doesn't matter that he's the one who really ended things.

Kalen starts to shut the door, and an arm slips through it.

A dark-haired woman with striking green eyes shoves her way through the jamb, an exasperated twist to her mouth. "Hey, don't close the door on me, asshole."

He groans and takes a step back to let her come fully into the apartment while casting an annoyed look at Reaper and Mouth. "Really?"

Reaper shrugs. "You try keeping her from coming."

Kalen scowls at the woman who holds up a plastic bag and jiggles it in front of him.

"For your information, I come bearing basic essentials since I figured she doesn't have anything, and you would be woefully unprepared for having a woman here." She chuckles at her own joke and nudges him playfully on the shoulder as she passes by. "Am I right?"

Who the hell is this woman?

Her eyes land on me, and she offers a kind smile and approaches with her hand extended. "Hi, I'm Viktoria, Reaper's..." She looks at him with a raised dark eyebrow. "Girlfriend, I guess? I'm also a former NYPD detective, so it's not completely out of the question that I might be able to offer some assistance in this situation." She glares at Kalen, who just stomps back to the kitchen and opens another beer silently. "Despite what *some people* might think."

Reaper leans in and whispers something into Viktoria's ear.

She nods and hands me the bag. "Here. Toothbrush and clean underwear. I didn't know your sizes and didn't want to bring you stuff you couldn't wear, so anything else you need I can bring by later. Just make a list for me."

"Oh, okay. Thanks. That's really nice of you."

I hadn't even thought about the fact that I have absolutely nothing with me. Everything I own is in my apartment.

Will I ever be able to go back?

That thought brings another wave of anxiety that tightens my chest.

Viktoria reaches out and offers me a quick squeeze on the shoulder, then glances around. "Wow, Chaos, you really know how to decorate a place to make it warm and inviting."

He takes a long pull off his beer and sneers at her. "Fuck you, Vik."

She snorts a laugh. "I don't think Reaper would appreciate that very much."

Reaper waves a hand between them and leans back against the wall since there isn't anywhere to sit. "Will you two knock it off for a minute so we can talk about business?" He turns his attention to me. "This isn't exactly how I thought I'd see you again. Want to fill us in on whatever mess you got yourself into?"

These are the last guys I want to come to begging for help, but they're the ones who are probably in the best position to actually *do* something about it.

I take a deep breath. "Long story short, I'm an accountant and I work for a food company. You know one of the places that supplies product to local restaurants and has some of their own."

Everyone nods.

"The woman who headed the accounting department disappeared, and then I discovered a flash drive she had hidden with documentation that made it look like a whole ton of money was coming into the company that shouldn't be."

Reaper glances at Kalen with a raised brow. "Money laundering? Drug trafficking."

He shrugs. "Could be both."

"Okay, continue, Avery."

"So, I went to talk to my boss about it after hours, which he always discouraged, but I never really understood why. And when I got there, I saw some of his men acting suspiciously in the warehouse. Something felt off, so I started recording on my phone, and..." I suck in a deep breath. "And I saw them pull the body of my coworker out of one of the freezers."

"Holy hell." Viktoria pushes off where she was leaning on the wall. "I'm going to need one of those beers."

Kalen glowers at her but turns back to the fridge and grabs her a bottle. "Mouth, you want one?"

Mouth shakes his head and continues watching me stoically.

When no one says anything, I keep going. "I didn't know what to do. I ran, and I left the drive there."

Reaper winces. "Shit."

"But I have the recording from the warehouse on my phone. As I was basically fleeing the scene of a murder, one of the men from the warehouse tried to ram my car and almost killed me at a busy intersection. Then he shot at me."

Viktoria takes a sip of her beer and casts a worried look at the guys. "So, they know you saw them."

"We have security cameras outside, so they may have been able to look at the video after the fact and see that I was there, or they may have seen me actually in the warehouse."

Reaper gives me a grim look. "And that you were recording them."

"Maybe." I shrug, everything about last night becoming a blur the more tired I become. "I don't know what they know, just that they apparently want me dead."

Kalen nods. "She was smart enough not to go home."

I glance at him. "I knew if they were determined enough

to follow me and try to ram me with a car, then shoot at me in public, they would just end up at my place eventually."

Viktoria offers me a sympathetic smile. "Why didn't you just go straight to the police station?"

"Because one of the men in the warehouse was in a police uniform, and a squad car was parked in front."

One of Viktoria's dark eyebrows wings up. "You think he was involved?"

"He had to be because he watched them drag Amelia's body out and didn't even react. I don't think I can trust the cops. I headed out to my grandfather's cabin. He left it to me when he died, and I didn't think anyone would know about it except maybe Kalen."

Kalen steps out from behind the small counter and leans against it. "But I intercepted her at a little diner a few miles from his place. And none too soon. I had only been there five minutes before her friends from the warehouse showed up, looking for her. They won't be a problem anymore. At least, those two won't. But we need a game plan. We need to figure out who the players are and how to stop them. Get them off her back."

Viktoria looks between us. "Don't any of you think they're going to come here looking for her? I mean, you're her ex-husband. Shouldn't that be one of the first places they check?"

The look Kalen gives me makes me wince.

I shake my head. "No one there knew I was ever married."

Kalen downs the rest of his beer in one long pull. "Even if they went to the trouble of tracking down our marriage certificate, they would never find this place because my name isn't attached to it. I pay cash, and the guy who owns the shop downstairs doesn't even know my real name. This is the safest place she can be right now."

At least when it comes to hiding from Ricardo and his men.

Reaper shifts his weight, still leaning back against the wall. "We need everything you know about the business—owner, employees, customers. We have to figure out who this guy is and where this money is coming from. You never saw anything else suspicious? Anything that made you think the company wasn't on the up and up?"

I shake my head. "No, I've been there just over a year, and it all seemed great." I think back to all the interactions I had with Ricardo and the other employees, the company picnic on the beach, the lavish Christmas parties he hosted. "Looking back, maybe it was too good to be true. I got paid well. Huge cash bonuses. Had a boss who didn't want me working overtime or being there after hours. In retrospect, perhaps it should have raised some flags."

Viktoria holds up a hand. "It's okay. Don't beat yourself up over this. It isn't your fault."

"But it is." I blink away the tears welling in my eyes. "I should have known something was wrong before. Amelia would be alive if I hadn't been so naïve."

"Oh, honey." Viktoria approaches and sits on the side of the chair, wrapping her arm around my shoulders. "Don't blame yourself. It absolutely is *not* your fault. You can't think like that. What we need to concentrate on now is not placing blame but keeping you safe."

Kalen pushes off the counter and steps in front of me, squatting to get himself in my line of vision. Determination hardens his eyes. "We're not going to let anything happen to you."

Reaper nods. "I'm calling Preacher right now and filling him in on everything. He'll dig until he finds what we need." He looks at me. "Start writing down all the information you have so I can pass it along to him. Give me the video from your phone to send him, too. Maybe he can ID some of the guys from it."

Viktoria turns back to him. "I can ask Anya to help Preacher."

Reaper shakes his head. "No, there's no reason to get your sister involved in this right now. If we need her later, we can call her."

Turning back to me, Viktoria gives me a genuine smile. "I promise, everything's going to be okay."

It sure doesn't feel like it.

CHAOS

BY THE TIME Avery writes down all the information she knows off the top of her head and Reaper has spoken with Preacher, Avery is completely wrecked and can barely keep her eyes open. Her lids flutter as she talks with Viktoria, and the former cop tosses me a concerned look. She noticed it, too, and the way Reaper and Mouth are both eyeing me, it's time to let her get some much-needed sleep.

Seeing her like this tugs at feelings I've kept buried deep inside since our split, the protective instinct that I can never turn off when it comes to her, even if we aren't together.

Avery is the last person who would ever complain about anything. All the times I pulled away from her, the months I put up walls between us and pushed aside all her efforts to reach me, she didn't ever voice her concerns in a way that put the blame on me. She took all the responsibility for what was happening between us and never attacked me with the truth. At least, not until that final day.

She would never say she's exhausted and ask everyone to leave, but she looks dead on her feet. If I don't step in, she's going to crash—hard.

"Let's wrap this up." I spin my finger around. "Time to go, guys."

Reaper, Mouth, and Viktoria don't protest my call and make their way toward the front door.

Viktoria pauses and turns back to me, leaning in to whisper so Avery can't hear. "Be nice to her, Chaos. She's a mess. She needs your help and support, not you running off to blow up shit and potentially make things worse."

I scowl at her. "Don't tell me what Avery needs. You don't know a fucking thing about her or us."

"No." Vik shakes her head. "You're right. I don't. But I know what fear looks like and that girl is utterly terrified. Don't fuck it up."

She turns and follows Reaper and Mouth out and down the steps with promises to touch base after we get a few hours of rest and give Preacher time to work his magic.

If anyone can find something on the fucker behind all this, it's Preacher. There's a reason he was one of the top CIA assets during the war and often worked with Delta and other spec ops groups; the man can work miracles. And that's what we need now.

As it stands, I can't see a way out of this for Avery that won't end in a whole lot of bloodshed and her stuck in the middle of it. The cops will already be all over the bodies up at the diner, and with Avery's car there and her nowhere to be found, they'll be looking for her, too. Given what she saw at that warehouse—one of their own apparently in bed with her boss—law enforcement finding her might be just as dangerous as if the man responsible for all this does.

Scrubbing a hand over my face, I turn back toward Avery to find her curled up and almost asleep in the chair. I approach her slowly, not wanting to startle her the way the guys' knocking did earlier.

"Avery?" I squat next to the chair and watch her peaceful face twist slightly. "Babe, wake up."

"Hmm?" Her eyes flutter open and finally focus on me. "What?"

"You're not sleeping here on the chair." I rise to my feet and hold up my palm to help her up. "You're taking my room."

She stares at my outstretched hand for a moment, almost like she's afraid to touch it, and the memory of the little zing that zapped between us earlier resurfaces, heating my skin.

Fuck.

I force myself to pull back my hand and motion toward the door near the kitchen. She rises slowly from the chair and follows me, the bag from Viktoria in her grasp.

There was a time, not all that long ago, when heading to the bedroom with Avery would have had me hard as a fucking rock, anticipating what was to come, when we would lose ourselves in each other for hours or days. But that's as far from what's about to happen as we've become from each other.

Let the past stay there.

Revisiting anything—good or bad—will only complicate what I have to do...what *we* have to do to make sure Avery is safe. Staying detached is the only way to survive in this world, and that means keeping things the way they should be with her—*off* limits.

This situation is more convoluted than I ever imagined when I first got her call...and it's only going to get worse.

I flip on the light switch to my bedroom and shift to the side to allow her to enter, already anticipating how she will react. She never was one to hold back on what she thinks, and that apparently hasn't changed much since we parted ways.

Avery steps in, scans the room quickly, and turns back to me. "You don't have a bed?"

I glance at the mattress on the floor, in the exact same place and state it's been since I left the house we shared. "Don't need one."

She motions to it, her pink lips agape slightly. "That *can't* be comfortable."

Comfortable isn't anything I've worried about for a long damn time—not since I stopped sleeping with her warm body pressed against mine. I rest where I can, when I can—which isn't very often, but I don't intend to tell her that. Avery would just worry, like she always did, especially at the end.

And staring at the simple mattress on the old wooden floor, the juxtaposition to what we had when we were together looms large. The king-sized bed with the massive, tufted headboard straight out of *Better Homes and Gardens*. The luxurious mattress we sank into together each night. The super-soft, high thread-count sheets against our heated, sweaty skin. The decorative throw pillows placed precisely each morning when we woke. The comfort I still dream about when I actually *do* sleep.

It was what Avery wanted.

And whatever she wanted…she got.

At least for a while…

While I was able to give it to her…

I shrug, trying not to make a big deal about the way I've been living. It isn't any of her concern, and I don't want it to be. "It's fine."

She narrows her eyes on me, unconvinced, and I have to look away because even after all this time, the woman's penetrating assessments seem to see right through me to everything I try to hide.

Her hands propped on her hips, she twists her lips. "Where are you going to sleep?"

"I'll take the chair."

"What?" She shakes her head, eyes wide. "No. You can't do that. You'll never get any rest on that thing. It's ancient and practically falling apart."

I lean toward her slightly, my retort slipping from my lips before I can bite it back. "I've slept in some pretty shitty places in my life. I'll be fine."

She stiffens slightly at the not-so-gentle reminder of where I've been and what I've done. Even though I was never allowed to tell her the specifics of my missions, she knows enough that she understands exactly what I'm referring to now.

Maybe it was a low blow, one I shouldn't have made when she's already so on edge and suffering, but I need her to remember who and what I am. I can't have her thinking I'm the old Kalen, the one she knew *before*. Even hearing her call me Kalen instead of Chaos makes me simultaneously cringe and long for the past we can never go back to.

Avery can't confuse who we are now for who we were then, no matter how easy it might be to slip into old habits.

She takes a moment to recompose herself after my outburst and glances into the bag in her hand that Viktoria brought for her. "No pajamas."

Oh, hell.

Of course, not...

It's one blow after another—memory after memory.

I make my way over to my footlocker against the wall under the high, small window, tug it open, and grab one of my T-shirts. My fingers curl around the soft green material, and I pause for a moment, staring down at all my possessions —the only things I took with me when we split.

Avery's smile taunts me from the photo on top of the

stack of clothes. In her white dress, veil tucked into her dark hair, the memory of how her lips pressed to mine felt after we said *I do* washes over me.

No.

I tighten my grip on the shirt and push the photo into the pile of shirts to keep it hidden, where it belongs. It shouldn't be there anyway. I should have thrown it away the day she served me the divorce papers. I should have destroyed every reminder of her. And I tried, but that photo saved me more times than I could count over the years, and I couldn't bear to throw it away along with the life we shared together.

Clearing my throat of the emotion suddenly clogging it, I walk over to Avery and hold out the shirt to her. "Here."

She stares at it for a long minute—long enough that I know exactly what she's thinking.

It's impossible to forget.

No matter how hard I might try.

The way the oversized material swam around her. The soft hem hitting her thighs just low enough to cover the parts I always wanted to see.

She loved sleeping in my shirts. The way it wrapped her in my scent when I was on deployment. Even when I was home, I couldn't get her to wear anything else to bed.

We stare at each other for what feels like hours. Neither one of us says anything about the situation to acknowledge how awkward or painful it is, and finally, she reaches out and takes it from me, offering me a little half smile.

"Thank you."

I incline my head and make my way back out toward the living room before either of us says or does something we'll regret later.

"Kalen?"

Shit.

I freeze and squeeze my eyes closed for a moment before opening them and turning back to face her. "Yeah?"

"Thank you...for everything. You didn't have to do this..." She trails off and averts her gaze for a second. "After...you know..." Her eyes flick up to meet mine again. "Everything."

Christ, she doesn't get it at all.

"Yeah, Avery, I did."

I leave it at that and let her close the door behind me. The latch clicking into place makes me fist my hands at my sides until they hurt, and I grab another beer, pop it open, and down half of it in one large gulp.

Something tells me I'm going to need a lot more of these before this situation is resolved. Hopefully, Preacher has some luck with the information we sent him and the video off Avery's phone.

Once we know who we're dealing with, we can form a solid plan—one that ends with eliminating all the threats and Avery right back where she belongs...

Living in bliss, somewhere far away from this mess or any I could create.

She deserves to be happy.

She deserves to have everything.

She deserves the world.

I was once stupid enough to think I could be the one to give it to her, too, but I'm older and wiser now and know what needs to happen.

That woman needs protection, and then she needs to get the fuck away from me.

6

AVERY

Bright light streaming in the west-facing window forces my eyes open, and I shift on the mattress, turning my head away and trying to bury it under the single pillow Kalen has in this place. All the tense and awkward moments we had last night and this morning before I finally crashed out and gave in to the sheer exhaustion my body was feeling float through my head.

Even after all this time, it's still there—that buzz of electricity, that attraction that draws us together. Only now, it's tangled up with so much pain and so many unspoken words that I can't even separate it anymore.

It's one tangled mass of messed-up, just like the man whose bed I'm lying in. There's a reason they call him Chaos, and being back in his orbit keeps reminding me of it. He works his way in and then destroys everything on his way out. That was what he did to me, to us. It just took a lot longer than it does with his usual targets.

But if I dwell on it, on what happened between us, I can't

concentrate on what's important right now—figuring a way out of this situation Gramps would have called FUBAR.

If there even is one.

Kalen, Viktoria, and the guys keep telling me things will be okay, but their promises feel empty when we're facing such a huge unknown—and one apparently willing to kill to protect what's been happening right under my nose.

I just have to believe they're right and try to latch on to some of their conviction about the outcome because I don't have any of my own.

Given how high the sun is, I've slept for a while—though I'm confident Kalen hasn't. He never did sleep much after his first mission with Delta, never really relaxed enough to close his eyes and drift off. And he never would tell me why—either because he couldn't or wouldn't. Toward the end, after he got shot and almost died, he wouldn't even lie in the same bed with me.

And if I stay here any longer, wrapped up in his scent, the painful memories will only get more and more vivid. Yet, I still find myself bringing the T-shirt he gave me to my nose and inhaling deeply—taking in the familiar rich, leathery, masculine scent that's all Kalen.

The bedroom door opens before I can bring the fabric away from my face, and Kalen's eyes zero in on me like a missile, intent on destruction.

I jerk my hand away, even though it's far too late, and I've been caught by a man who never misses a single fucking detail. "How did you know I was awake?"

He shrugs nonchalantly, mug in one hand and a bag dangling from the other. "I just did."

The man could probably hear me shifting on this mattress from out there—one of the many superhuman skills he's honed over the years. Or maybe he's just still that connected to me, still able to sense me from another room like he always seemed to be able to when we were married.

"Thought you could use some coffee." He holds up the cup. "Cream, three sugars."

I push myself to a sitting position, my back to the wall. "You remember how I take my coffee?"

He shifts uneasily on his feet, averting his gaze to the window. "It's not something you forget as many times as I made it for you."

"Right." I offer a tight smile, unsure if he's complaining about it or relishing the memory of him bringing it to me every morning and climbing into bed to share it the way I do. "Of course."

There are some things you can never forget about someone you love as much as I did Kalen, but the fact that he remembered that about me after all this time makes something warm and equally dangerous bloom in my chest.

He watches me, waiting for me to make some move.

I force a smile I'm not quite feeling. "Thank you. I'd love some coffee."

It might help wake me up and offer a replacement for Kalen's scent. I shift to the side, push off the cheap sheets and comforter, and rise from the mattress. Kalen's gaze drifts down to my bare legs—his T-shirt barely reaching the tops of my thighs. My skin sizzles with his assessment, the same way he always used to look at me when I was dressed like this. Something about seeing me in his shirts always drove him wild, and we'd end up fucking against a wall or tumble back into bed for another round.

But that was a long time ago.

"Give me a second to get my jeans back on."

He stands stock still for a moment, his gaze locked on my legs and slowly drifting up before he finally clears his throat and steps back. "Yeah." He holds out a bag dangling from his other hand. "Viktoria brought you the things you requested."

"Thanks." I accept it and the cup of coffee. "I'll probably take a shower, then."

He considers me for a moment, crossing his arms over his chest. The man always could read me like an open book. There isn't any way he won't sense my distress over the entire situation, which has only been exacerbated by having to come to *him* for help. "You okay?"

Am I okay?

"Jesus, Kalen"—I shake my head at his absurd question —"someone's trying to kill me. What do you think?"

I really wish I knew.

If I had been able to read him as well as he did me back when we were married, maybe I could have made things work, figured out a way to reach him when he was pushing me away. I might have found a way to make him stay.

He watches me for a minute without responding and takes a half-step toward me—one that sends butterflies racing through my stomach. His hand rises quickly, capturing my cheek in his calloused, rough palm before I can step back. He tightens his grip on my face, urging my eyes up to forcibly meet his. Conviction blazes there, mixed with a dark intensity I've never seen before, the thing that makes him Chaos.

"I'll make sure you're safe, Avery. You know that, right?"

The tenor of his words and touch sends a sense of calm rolling through me that I haven't felt since the moment I saw what I did in that warehouse.

His thumb brushes across my cheek. "Do you, Avery? Do you understand what I will do to protect you? The lengths I will go to?"

I nod slowly, unable to form words.

A low growl rumbles in his chest. "Good."

His hand abruptly falls away from my face, and he turns sharply on his heel, stalking away and pulling the door closed behind him.

I release a heavy breath, and my hand holding the coffee shakes so badly that the hot liquid splashes over the side onto my skin, shocking me back to the moment.

"Shit."

That man always knew how to unnerve me, and he does it even better now.

I take a sip of the coffee.

Perfect. Just like I knew it would be.

Kalen always made it exactly how I liked it and woke me the best way possible more often than I can count—with his face between my thighs and a hot cup waiting on the nightstand when I could finally breathe again.

Maybe a shower will help rid me of these memories.

If I'm lucky...

I make my way to the bathroom on the other side of the room and find it just as barren as the rest of the apartment—nothing personal aside from a toothbrush and some basic essentials.

Kalen spent a long time living out of a single bag with only what he absolutely needed. Even when he was home, he never kept more than this. Never anything but what he could pack in thirty seconds and become a ghost with.

He certainly acted like one, even with me at the end.

I take a few more sips, letting the warm liquid and caffeine course through me before I strip. The bag Viktoria brought me contains everything I asked for. A few small things that might tide me over until I can get back to my apartment.

If I can get back...

A cold shiver rolls through me at that thought, but I shrug it off and grab the shampoo, conditioner, and soap. Hopefully, getting cleaned up will help me feel a little bit better, but no amount of scalding-hot water is going to wash away the tension between Kalen and me.

Nothing ever could.

Only my growling stomach eventually pulls me from the shower ten minutes later in search of food. I dress in the black yoga pants and T-shirt Viktoria brought and grab my now-cold cup of joe on my way out to the living room.

Viktoria stands at the counter, waiting for me, eyebrow raised. "Good morning."

"What are you doing here?" I scan the small space, but if Kalen were here, I'd know. Not only is there nowhere for him to hide, but whenever he's within ten feet of me, my heart and body tell me he's close. "Where's Kalen?"

"He left with the guys."

My stomach drops, and though I try my best to hide my reaction, Viktoria clearly sees my distress.

She raises her hand. "Don't worry, hon. I'm just as good with a gun as they are. I got you."

That wasn't the reason for the sudden sense of dread.

But I won't admit that to her.

"Where did he go?"

"They went to look into some of the initial information Preacher found."

"But what if—"

"They'll be all right. Those boys can take care of themselves."

They certainly can, but that never helped me worry any less that Kalen may not come home alive from his deployments. Others didn't. And while I got him back, he was never the same man. Each time he returned, it got worse and worse. Eventually, he wasn't Kalen at all.

God only knows what the years we've spent apart have continued to do to him mentally.

My stomach rumbles loudly, drawing Viktoria's sharp gaze.

"God, when was the last time you ate, hon?"

Was it really only yesterday that all this started, that I found that zip drive and sent my life into this fucking tailspin?

"Um, yesterday some time. Lunch, I guess?"

"Here." She slides a bag across the counter. "I brought some sandwiches because I assumed Chaos doesn't keep anything that's actually edible here."

Chaos wouldn't.

Kalen would have, though.

He was always so thoughtful, so caring, constantly making sure I had everything I needed or wanted, even if it meant running out in the middle of the night to get ice cream or anything else. The man spoiled me, then as soon as he saw me in one of his T-shirts, he would simply lift the hem and fuck me wherever we were, reminding me of how much he loved me and needed me.

In the kitchen...

On the bathroom counter...

Over the back of the couch...

My pussy clenches at the memory, and I squeeze on nothing and suck in a deep breath.

That was the old Kalen, the one who still wanted you. The one who promised he would never leave.

But he did.

This is who you have now, Avery.

This is what's left.

Chaos…

But Chaos is definitely the right one for the job and probably a lot safer for my heart.

CHAOS

"So"—Reaper drawls—"we're not going to talk about it?"

I glance over at him in the driver's seat and scowl. "Talk about what?"

He raises an eyebrow at me and glances my way before returning his focus to the road. "The fact that your ex-wife is at your place, who you haven't talked to in, what, five years?"

"Four years…and there's nothing to talk about."

Mouth barks a laugh from the backseat, and I twist around to offer him the same glare I just did Reaper.

"What the hell are you laughing at?"

He holds up his hands innocently and grins.

I settle back into my seat, arms crossed over my chest. "There's nothing to talk about. She needed help. I'm offering it. End. Of. Story."

Reaper snorts. "Sure, just like I was only protecting Viktoria because I didn't want her to get caught up in the middle of my mission against Yankovich."

"Definitely not the same thing."

He shakes his head, chuckling under his breath. "Whatever you say, man. You want to sit there and pretend like having that woman in your place isn't really fucking with you? You go right ahead. Just make sure it doesn't affect your ability to maintain your focus when we do what we need to do."

I grit my teeth to stop myself from launching across the center console and giving Reaper the beating he deserves for that comment. "I'm fucking good, Reaper."

His shoulders rise and fall. "Good."

I stare out at the road in front of us, busy with mid-day traffic. "Where are we headed, anyway?"

All Reaper said before they picked me up today was we

were meeting up for recon, but he never said where or of what.

He inclines his head toward a sheet of paper on the dashboard. "We're going to the first place on the list Avery gave us of the various holdings of Ricardo Perez. Avery said he seems to spend a lot of time at a restaurant he owns called *South of the Border*. It looks like it's only a few miles away from the headquarters and warehouse where she worked and saw the body of her co-worker."

"Let's hit it first, see if we can find out why he's spending so much time there. We can swing over to the warehouse later. Right now, we need to get the lay of the land a little bit."

Preacher hasn't been able to come up with much yet beyond what Avery was able to give him last night, but we have a few locations to check out while he keeps doing whatever it is he does behind that wall of computers to find information that seems impossible for anyone else to locate.

Reaper glances at me briefly. "What are you thinking?"

I shrug. "It seems as though this Ricardo guy is either laundering funds through his businesses or trafficking drugs, perhaps both. Could be connected to one of the cartels."

He nods. "It's possible. More than likely, actually. It would explain how and why they so easily took out her friend when she started to get suspicious. They can't have anyone nosing around who might interfere with what they're doing."

I swallow thickly. "Or witness any of their crimes." The words taste like acid on my tongue because I know what that means for Avery.

She's gotten herself into a completely fucked-up situation that will likely take a lot of bloodshed to fix.

"That man sent a *hit* squad after her, for fuck's sake. Whatever he's hiding, it's big, and he wants it to stay hidden."

Mouth's large hand lands on my shoulder and squeezes, silently letting me know he's with me and will protect Avery with everything he has in him. I reach up and pat his fingers, thanking him without words because my throat suddenly feels too tight to speak again.

What I told Reaper was a lie.

I'm not good.

Far from it.

Avery was my entire world for so long, and then…it was over so fast, I didn't even have a chance to look back before she was gone. I never thought I'd see her again, never thought I'd feel her touch, yet my palm still tingles from where it cupped her cheek this morning, her familiar, smooth, soft skin against my abrasive, gnarled fingertips.

Get it out of your head.

I need to be *crystal* clear going into this, or things will go sideways fast.

Reaper takes a left down Fleet Street toward *South of the Border*. The restaurant sign comes into view two blocks down, and he pulls into a lot for an empty building across the street and throws the car into park.

We all stare at the business for a moment. A few cars dot the parking lot and indicate that it has some customers. From the outside, it looks completely legitimate. Exactly as Perez likely designed it.

Reaper flips open his lighter and flicks it closed again, the repetitive sound somehow soothing after all these years of hearing it. "Do you think it's a good idea? Showing our faces in there."

I shrug. "They're not going to know us from Adam. We're just three dudes looking for some good Mexican food. That's all they are ever going to know."

We watch the place for another hour to two, waiting for anything suspicious to happen, but when all remains quiet, Reaper eventually sighs, shoves his lighter back into his pocket, then throws the car into drive and crosses the street to the *South of the Border* lot.

The spot in front of the main doors is open, and he pulls in and parks with a wink at me. "Right by the front doors to make a quick getaway."

"If we need to make a quick getaway, then we're doing something wrong."

Mouth barks out another laugh, and we all climb from the car to make our way into the restaurant casually, ignoring the four exterior cameras I count on the outside of the building facing the front lot.

A bell above the door jingles.

We each scan around us, taking in every detail of the space and everyone in it while making our way toward the front counter.

The teenage boy at the register. An older man staffing the kitchen in the back. The couple in front of him ordering— the man with his arm around the shorter woman's shoulders. A second couple at a table in the corner talking in hushed tones, holding hands across empty plates.

We step into line behind the couple at the counter, and as inconspicuously as possible, I count the interior cameras. Three facing the registers, three facing out into the dining room. One facing down a hallway to the right, likely leading to the kitchen entrance and bathrooms.

Reaper scans the menu on the wall above and behind the teen, mumbling something to Mouth, who nods. I check it out and determine my order while watching the old man through the open service window to the kitchen.

Only two employees…

Odd.

This place isn't exactly bustling, but one would think they need more than two people working here, especially near dinner time.

The couple in front of us steps to the side, and Reaper shifts up against the counter and nods at the young kid.

"Hey, man, can I get six tacos—three *al pastor*, three *lengua*, and whenever these two assholes want."

A grin spreads across the teen's face, already at ease with us based on Reaper's description.

I scowl at my best friend and incline my head toward the kid. "I'll have the same, and this guy"—I motion toward Mouth—"will have three *al pastor* and three *carne asada*."

Mouth grunts his agreement, and the teen rings it up and gives Reaper the total. Reaper pays, and the couple from the table rises to drop off their empty plates in the trash and make their way out toward a beat-up pickup in the lot, leaving us with the two employees and the couple waiting for their food near the end of the counter.

Reaper leans against the wall next to me and crosses one ankle over the other, his arms folded across his chest. "So, what's going on with you two?"

I scowl at him. "We're really getting into this again?"

He shrugs. "What else we got to talk about?"

"She's my ex-wife. That *ex* is for a reason."

"Yeah"—he nods slowly—"you never *did* tell us what that reason was, you know, just said she served you with papers when you got home from that mission."

"I didn't tell you because what happened between us is *our* business."

"Was it money business or fucking business?"

My hands fist at my sides and only Mouth's firm grip on my shoulder keeps me from decking Reaper.

Reaper's dark eyebrows wing up, and he holds up his hands in surrender. "Wow. Aren't we a bit testy?"

"I don't ask you about your sex life with Viktoria."

He shakes his head. "No, you just watched us have sex in the damn shower."

I release a hard laugh that draws the attention of the couple waiting who just steps away. "To be fair, you knew we were coming and invited us there. So…"

"So, you could have waited in the goddamn living room."

I shrug it off and give him a little half grin. "What fun would that have been?"

"Yeah, yeah."

He isn't seriously mad about it; though, he would have every right to be—unless you're into that kind of shit. Watching your buddy bang his woman isn't the type of thing we usually get into so that was a special occasion.

The old man from the kitchen hands a bag through the window to the teen, who brings it forward to the front counter for the couple next to us. They grab it and make their way out, the bell over the door jingling.

With their departure, the old man returns to cooking and the teenager at the register fumbles around on his cell phone.

Reaper glances at me. "You know, it wouldn't be so bad if you just hooked back up with your wife."

I scowl at him. "Leave it the fuck alone, Reaper."

"We know what's good for you."

We?

I glance at Mouth and raise an eyebrow. "Oh, you're in on this, too?"

He offers a half-smile and shrugs. I'd give anything to hear one of his wisecracks and completely inappropriate comments right now. We could all use a good laugh. Instead, he just leans his shoulder against the wall and watches for our food.

The old man slides three trays across the order window, and the teen grabs each one and passes them to the edge of the counter.

Reaper grabs his and smiles at the kid. "Thanks, man." He

scans the restaurant. "Hey, we've never been here before. Do your parents own this place or something?"

He shakes his head. "No, my uncle does." He points a skinny finger to the old man in the back. "That's my grandpa."

"Ah." Reaper nods. "Gotcha. Well, everything looks great."

We all grab our trays and make our way to one of the empty tables in the center of the restaurant, where one of us can watch the parking lot while the other two keep an eye on Ricardo's employees.

Keeping it all in the family, apparently.

The aroma of the grilled meats and various spices waft up to my nose, and my stomach growls. I didn't realize how hungry I was until this moment. All I've been thinking about is Avery and how best to protect her. I could have gone days without eating, worrying about that, if keeping *her* safe didn't require me to come here and actually fucking eat.

I dig into the surprisingly decent food. It goes down easily as we watch various people come in and out of the restaurant occasionally—most ordering food to go.

Halfway through my tacos, I wipe my mouth and clear my throat. "I'm gonna hit the head."

Mouth and Reaper nod their understanding, and I casually walk to the hallway that runs along the side of the restaurant. The kid at the register doesn't even look up from his phone as I pass him and make my way down—past the women's bathroom, past the men's bathroom, to the closed door on my right.

I twist the knob, find it unlocked, and push it open.

Cleaning supplies.

Another two feet down the hall, the entrance to the kitchen gives me a view of the old man bent over the flat top, humming to himself softly. The rest of the cooking area appears uninteresting. It could use a good cleaning, but otherwise, nothing suspicious.

Until my eyes land on a closed door along the back wall.

Why the hell would an office in a place like this need biometric locks and security knobs?

It doesn't make any sense, especially since *South of the Border* doesn't seem very busy. Most restaurants keep a small safe in the office. Nothing as extravagant as this setup would be necessary for that.

I poke my head into the kitchen and glance around for cameras.

There aren't any back here—not in the kitchen, not near the rear entrance to the restaurant, not near *this* door. They don't want anything that goes on inside *here* filmed. They just want to be able to see what happens on the outside of the building and in the restaurant itself. See who's coming.

Who the fuck are these people, and what the hell are they going to do to Avery if they find her?

7

AVERY

"Do you think they're okay?" My knee bounces rapidly, the constant motion somehow helping me from completely losing my mind as the minutes and hours tick by. "They've been gone a long time."

Viktoria looks at me from her spot perched on the small kitchen counter, her legs dangling beneath her, and chuckles. "You do know what they do, right?" One of her dark eyebrows rises. "You know what they're capable of?"

I swallow back the bile rising in my throat and give her a little half-nod. "Yeah. I mean"—I shake my head—"I'm pretty sure I do. None of them would have ever made Delta if they weren't the best, right?"

She offers a half-shrug and slides off the counter with a sigh. "They know what they're doing, Avery. If anyone is going to be able to sort out the situation, it's those three."

I take a deep breath and try to calm my heart which has only seemed to race more and more the longer they're gone.

The uncertainty is liable to give me a coronary or eat a hole through my stomach—maybe both. "I hope you're right."

Viktoria drums her fingers on the counter, the sound mixing with the noise coming from the television neither of us is really watching. She glances at me out of the corner of her eye, her assessment burning a hole in my cheek, like if she looks hard enough, she might find what she's searching for. "What happened between you two?"

"What?"

"What happened between you and Chaos? Why did you get divorced?" She shakes her head with a wistful look. "The way you two look at each other…"

She trails off, and I wince at the observation she's so easily made after only seeing us together for a short time.

"I wish I could explain it."

I wish I understood it.

When we were young, I thought I *did* understand it. I thought I understood *him*. I thought we were an unbreakable team, but in the end, he chose another team, another relationship over ours.

Vik leans back against the counter and crosses her arms over her chest. "Try."

Sighing, I lie back in the recliner, staring at the off-white ceiling with the dried water stains. "I don't know. We were high school sweethearts, dated junior and senior year. Got married right after. We were young, but things were really good. I knew he had planned to enlist out of high school. It was *always* the plan. He loved it. And I was actually happy being an army wife for a while."

"For a while?"

I glance over at her. "Things changed when he went to Delta." Just saying those words makes a vise tighten around my chest. "It's all he ever wanted, what he worked toward. He loved being a Ranger, but he wanted Delta. So, I was happy for him, for us, but whatever they were doing, it just…" I shake my head, thinking back to those first few assignments. "He came back different than he was—still Kalen, but he brought Chaos back with him."

Admitting that out loud to anyone for the first time feels both like a giant weight off my shoulders and a crushing blow to the gut at the same time.

"I always knew he had a special talent that couldn't be wasted. I knew he was doing it to protect our country, protect us, and to help innocent people in really shitty situations. I never had any problem with it. Until he started cutting me out."

Vik's gaze softens. "What do you mean?"

I shrug. "He had things he could never tell me. I understood that. But we stopped talking about anything that wasn't small talk you have with a loose acquaintance, and then, after the team lost Mayhem and he and Mouth got hurt, it all changed even more."

Viktoria nodded slowly. "I've heard bits and pieces of it, but obviously, it's not something they can talk about in detail."

"I got the call that he'd been hurt." Tears finally trickle down my cheeks. "I fucking panicked. I thought I was going to lose him. They said he had lost a lot of blood, that they had to give him several transfusions, that they weren't sure he was going to make it. By the time they got him Stateside and I could actually see him, he was doing a little bit better. But he wouldn't even look me in the eye. He barely acknowledged me when I went into the hospital room. He didn't want me there, had the nurses urge me out."

The pain of those moments strikes me hard, knocking the air from my lungs. I try to take a shaky deep breath but only manage a shallow, sharp one.

"It was like a switch had flipped, and he went from warm

and caring to icy cold with me. He came home and wouldn't even sleep in the same bed. He slept in this chair until I finally served divorce papers on him when he came back from his next mission."

"Wow." Vik nods slowly, trying to absorb it all. "That's pretty heavy. Why didn't you to try to work it out? Couples counseling or something? Like I said, I've seen the way you two look at each other."

I shake my head. "It wouldn't have mattered. He never would have gone to counseling. He never would have talked about it with a stranger if he wouldn't even talk about it with me. All he wanted to do was be with the boys, to be with his team. The people who understood what he was going through." A sob slips from my mouth, and I press my hand over it. "He-he didn't love me anymore."

Her sharp bark of laughter startles me upright. "I think you're wrong on that, Avery."

Tears stream down my cheeks unbidden now, and I shake my head. "No, I'm not. What you see is the same attraction that's always been there. It probably always will be. Sex was never our problem. When he came back, we had sex a lot. And I mean *a lot*. But it was like he was trying to fuck his way out of whatever memory was haunting him so badly, and then he would leave me to sleep by myself while he went out to our living room to sleep on this damn chair."

I shove away from the offending piece of furniture with a huff, even though it isn't the recliner's fault. Viktoria watches me pace the room, remaining quiet, letting me think my way through the swirl of memories and emotions threatening to suffocate me right now.

"I'm just..." I shake my head, not able to make sense of anything any more now than I could back then. "I don't know. I can't tell you what happened. I really can't."

Our life together was beautiful. It was perfect. It was what we always dreamed it would be. And then, it just…wasn't anymore.

I've never tried to explain it to anyone before, only ever mulled it over endlessly in my own head, going over every second, every minute, every hour of every day of every year we spent together to try to figure out *where* and *how* it went wrong.

Four years haven't given me any more insight into it.

I stop pacing and face Viktoria, offering one final shrug as a period at the end of my explanation. "He just…blew everything apart, but that's what he's always been good at, so I guess I should have seen it coming. I should have expected Chaos would eventually touch us, and it did more than that. It destroyed everything."

CHAOS

THE ASSHOLE after Avery has no idea we're on to him and his operation. He has no fucking clue who he's up against. Of all the women in the world to go after, he chose the wrong fucking one, and now, he'll face Chaos as a consequence.

We park in the lot diagonally across the street from the restaurant, waiting for it to completely clear out for the night. The old man leaves first, then the younger teenage boy, carrying a bag of garbage to toss into the dumpster before he climbs into his rickety car and heads home.

Time ticks by slowly as we watch for something, anything, but the building remains dark and empty.

I glance at my watch again. "Almost two. Whatever's happening in that back room has to be after hours, or they do a damn good job of keeping it under wraps if it's happening while they're open."

"What do you think?" Reaper inclines his head toward the place. "It's been an hour since the teenager left, and there's been no movement."

Whatever Perez has going on in that place, it isn't happening tonight, which makes it the perfect time to go in. "Let's go."

Reaper and I climb from the car with our weapons and my bag the guys packed before they picked me up earlier, and he signals to Mouth, where he already waits on the roof of the building next to our car. From that vantage point, he can watch every move and alert us if anyone's coming—and take out any potential threats before they can get to us.

We aren't taking any chances with this guy, not after we know he killed an innocent woman and tried to take out Avery. It isn't a question of *if* he's dangerous but simply a level of degree. And something tells me, with this guy, it's very high.

Mouth signals back from the roof, and we make our way across the street toward *South of the Border*, staying out of sight of the exterior cameras they so meticulously placed. Once we reach the pole that leads to the electrical box for the restaurant, we access it and prepare to cut the power.

We'll have five minutes—seven tops—before the security company alerts them or someone shows up here to check out what's happening.

We won't need that long.

Not even close.

Reaper snips the wire as I set the timer on my watch, and we race across the back parking lot to the rear door, which jimmies open easily without the assistance of the electronic locks on the interior door. We step inside, utilizing our night vision googles so we don't need to turn on any lights to see.

The eerie silence of the place envelops us, and we quickly

move through, clearing the restaurant and kitchen before we approach the heavily secured door at the back.

I signal to Reaper that I'm moving in and kneel to set the charge on the electronic box, which unfortunately has a battery backup keeping it locked even though we cut the power.

This charge should take care of it. Just enough to get the door open. Not loud enough to alert any neighboring businesses that anything's wrong.

We don't waste any time moving behind the cook line and detonating the device. The explosion slightly rumbles the floor, and smoke begins to fill the kitchen, but it did the trick. The destroyed door pushes open easily, and we quickly clear the room.

No windows—no other way in or out.

And no sign of anyone inside.

I pull out a chemlight and crack it, illuminating the space with a greenish hue. We push our night vision goggles up and examine the room.

Bankers' boxes stacked ten high line each wall, and a row of metal tables runs up the center, littered with bill counters, rubber bands, and paper bill wraps.

A whiteboard on the side wall lists staggering numbers that must be incoming funds, and when I pull the lid off the top of one of the boxes, the cash is stacked so tightly that there isn't any room for even a single one more.

If all these boxes are full, there's a fuckload of money in this tiny room.

Which means a fuckload of trouble.

Reaper motions toward all of it. "You think they're laundering for the cartel?"

"It would make sense. Most of these restaurants are cash businesses. Same with a lot of the deliveries they make."

"You think they're dealing out of here, too?"

I shake my head. "If they are, they're not packaging here. No scales, no baggies. No residue on the tables. And I can't see gramps and the nephew doing that, either."

Reaper nods his agreement. "So, what do you want to do?"

I glower at him. "What the fuck do you *think* I want to do?"

The tiniest grin pulls at Reaper's lips. "Burn the place to the fucking ground."

"Damn fucking straight."

There isn't any other option. If we sit idly by and let Perez continue with what he's been doing, he'll keep coming after Avery, and other innocent people will get hurt.

I reach into my bag and pull out the charges I prepared before we came, placing one on each wall before I step out into the restaurant and secure three more at the exact locations I know will create the most damage.

My radio crackles—three clicks followed by a single one.

Mouth's signal that someone's coming.

"We've got company."

Reaper touches my arm. "You sure you don't want to just let the police come in and find all this evidence?"

I issue a low growl. "So that fucker can claim he knew nothing about it, that it was his men or the sweet old grandfather or nephew working here? So he can walk away scot-fucking-free? No fucking way, man."

Reaper shrugs. "I figured, but I thought I should ask."

"This is what we do, isn't it? Exact our own methods of justice?"

"What will justice be in this situation?"

We make it to the back door, and I pause for a second and lock gazes with Reaper. "When I have my hands around this fucker's throat and watch him take his last breath as I squeeze it from him. After I've already taken everything he cherishes and loves, everything he's worked so hard for. Then, I'll be satisfied because then, I'll know Avery is safe."

Until then, I'll just keep blowing up whatever gets in my way.

I step out into the night with Reaper hot on my heels, and we hoof it toward the car. Mouth jumps from the fire escape of the building next to us and jogs over to join us, rifle in hand. We pile in and pull away, and I turn back to watch the building as I detonate the charges.

The blast shakes the car and rumbles the ground like an earthquake. Fireballs erupt into the night sky, orange and red columns of flame that feel like seeing what victory actually looks like.

Reaper glances back in the rearview mirror. "How much money do you think was in there?"

I shrug. "I don't know. Three million? Maybe four?"

However much it was, it's going to put a dent in Perez's business and may give him something else to focus on besides Avery long enough for me to kill the motherfucker.

8

CHAOS

The silent ride back from the rubble that is now *South of the Border* gives me far too much time to think about what I must face when I get home.

I used to relish returning from a mission to Avery waiting for me, used to fantasize about what I would do to her when I finally had her in my arms again. I would wipe away all the turmoil in my soul by driving into her welcoming body and accepting her loving touch.

But that's not what will be waiting for me tonight.

Avery is a broken woman with a target on her back who needed my help.

Nothing more.

She isn't my wife.

She isn't my anything.

We pull into the driveway of the repair shop, and Reaper reaches out and grabs my arm, stopping me from climbing from the car.

"Tonight was a good start. We got this."

I incline my head in agreement to him and Mouth, then head toward the side of the building and the stairs leading to my apartment a little slower than I normally might, a part of me dreading what might happen when I walk inside again.

The door to my apartment opens before I even make it halfway up the steps, and if we hadn't already called ahead and told Vik we were on our way back, I might have pulled my weapon, concerned about who might be coming out. As it stands, I'm glad someone was able to stay with Avery and watch her while I was otherwise occupied. Vik and I may butt heads at times, but without her here, we would have had to call in Flash or Cutter or one of the other guys who are in the country to assist, and we don't have the time to wait for anyone else to get here to act. Not with Avery's life on the line.

Viktoria slips out and gently eases the door closed behind her with a tiny wince at the noise it makes. I stop on the small landing just outside my place, and she leans back against the door, blocking my path, and gives me a look that could kill.

It isn't anything new from Vik, but concern for Avery trumps my raised hackles at Reaper's woman's attitude toward me.

"What? Is she okay?"

"Really?" Vik rolls her eyes and motions behind her. "She's scared out of her fucking mind. She's confused being this close to you again. And she barely ate—"

"I'll get her to eat."

She snorts and shakes her head with a humorless sigh. "Good luck with that, Chaos. I don't know why men always think they can get women to do whatever they tell them to."

"Because we usually know what's best."

"Wow." Her jaw falls open. "Is *that* why you destroyed that girl? Because you thought that was what was best?"

Her words knock me back a step, but I do my best to hide my reaction from the woman who loves to needle me about everything like she's one of the guys.

Destroyed her?

"Is that what Avery said I did?"

Did I destroy the woman who was my everything?

Viktoria looks over the railing down at the car where Reaper sits waiting for her. "Not in those words, but it's obvious, Chaos. She's a mess, and not just because of what she saw or because she's in danger. That girl is worried about her heart as much as she is her life." She releases a heavy sigh and returns her focus to me, her normally hard gaze softening for a moment. "I finally forced her to go lie down and get some sleep."

"I'll be quiet when I go in."

I take a step to move around her to the door, and she places her hand against my chest firmly.

"Don't mess around with that woman's heart. I don't think she can take it."

Me either.

She releases me, hustles down the steps, and climbs into the car with Reaper. They pull away, and I wait until their tail lights disappear down the tree-lined street before I open the door quietly and secure the deadbolt and chain behind me. Leaning back against the closed door, I inhale a long, deep breath.

Big mistake.

It smells like her.

Even though she's only been here a day, her light, flowery scent permeates everything. I'll probably have to move once this is over and get rid of anything she touched, like the chair I trudge over to with plans to settle in it for the night.

I kick off my boots and start to lower myself down into it, but something draws me back to my feet and toward the bedroom. The door stands slightly ajar, and I nudge it open and step inside.

A bright trail of moonlight filters through the partially raised blinds and falls onto the mattress, where Avery lies, her back to me. Her fragile form makes my heart squeeze in my chest. It's the same one I looked forward to coming home to after every mission. Clinging to every night. The one that fits perfectly with mine. Like she completed me and made me whole.

My feet carry me to the far wall where my footlocker sits, and I lower myself down next to it and lean back against the chipping-off white paint with a low sigh.

Tonight might feel like a victory—and in a way, it was. We learned something useful, and we hurt him by destroying all that cash and one of his places of business. But it doesn't solve the bigger problem, doesn't eliminate the threat to Avery.

The only way that will happen is if Ricardo Perez is gone.

This was only the tip of the iceberg. We have a lot of work ahead of us. A lot of death and destruction will have to happen before Avery is safe.

I scrub my hands over my face, rubbing at my tired eyes.

When was the last time I even slept?

Two days ago?

Three?

It doesn't really matter.

I've gone a lot longer on a lot less sleep, but never when anything so important was at stake. Not when my very heart is at risk. And I'd be kidding myself if I said this woman doesn't still hold it.

Sitting here, watching her sleep, so peaceful even with everything going on, my T-shirt wrapped around her, her beautiful face calm and serene, it makes my cock swell against the zipper of my jeans.

No other woman has done that to me since Avery, and none ever could. I belong to her mind, body, and soul and always will, even when we can't be together. Even when it's impossible.

Avery staying here like this will be torture, but it's the best place for her. Perhaps the only safe place she can go now.

She was once my safe place. I came home to her and felt her arms wrap around me, her body welcoming me, and I was able to forget everything that had happened during my missions. All the horrible actions I witnessed, the evil people I saw, and the things I had to do vanished. She was *safe.* Until suddenly, she wasn't. Until she became part of the greater nightmare.

AVERY

I STEP through the unlocked door near the loading docks into the warehouse, searching for Ricardo. Rushed, frustrated voices fill the air, making me tense and pause. I've never been here this late, but no one should be.

Something's wrong.

Inching around the large truck onto the main floor, Ricardo and several men finally come into view doing something near one of the freezers toward the back.

Loading a truck at this hour?

My gut churns immediately, knowing something isn't right. They shouldn't be here. This truck shouldn't be here. The information on the drive I left on my desk shouldn't exist.

This is wrong. All wrong.

Sweat beads across my forehead, and my hands start to shake at my sides as I step farther into the warehouse slowly.

Somehow, I know what's coming...but I still pull out my phone and record them.

I *know* what's coming...but I can't look away.

They pull open the walk-in freezer and drag out Amelia's bloodied body. Her open, dead, glazed-over eyes that once held so much life and joy stare at me. Her lips parted, begging me for help in a silent scream only I can hear.

My own cry wrenches from my throat and breaks through the air around me, piercing and frantic. The sound jolts me upright on the mattress, my heart thundering against my ribcage and blood rushing in my ears.

A sob falls from my lips, and tears pour down my cheeks like a tidal wave I can't stop.

"Avery..." Kalen's firm voice floats to me.

Probably just another dream...

Like what I just saw...

A dream that's also a memory...

One horrible...

One all I ever wanted...

"Avery, it's okay. I'm here." His voice gets louder. "You're safe."

The mattress dips, and familiar, strong arms wrap around me and pull me against a solid chest I know so well. I bawl, clutching at the material that smells so much like him, feeling the steady beat of his heart under my palm.

"It was just a dream." His large hand rubs up and down my back slowly, the touch so soothing, it almost makes me forget for one minute why I'm here, and he buries his face in my hair, holding me tightly to him. "You're safe, babe. No one can get to you here. I promise."

Here.

Kalen's place.

The apartment above the garage.

I suck in a deep, shaky breath.

I'm not at the warehouse.

I'm not seeing her again.

I cling to him like he's my lifeline, like he's the only thing keeping me present, in the here and now. And he is. If not for him, I'd be dead by now. Perez's men would have caught up with me at the diner and finished what they tried to start when they were chasing me in the car.

Not so long ago, I thought Kalen's leaving had ended my life—at least, any form of it where I was happy and content—but now, he's the one keeping me alive, keeping me secure. In the worst moment of my life, he's the one *here.*

Kalen pulls me away slightly and stares down at me in the moonlight, brushing away my tears with his thumbs. "Are you okay?"

I try to take another deep breath, but it gets caught on another sob, no matter how hard I work to keep from falling apart. "No…" I shake my head, sniffling. "I don't know. I saw her again, Kalen. I saw what they did to her…"

He drags me back against him, settling me on his lap and squeezing me tightly again, cocooning me in his strength. "I'm so sorry you had to see that. No one should ever have to see anyone like that, let alone their friends."

His words slash at my heart like a knife, the true meaning behind them lying just beneath the surface. Kalen has watched so many of his friends get hurt, get killed. He might be one of the only people on Earth who understands how this feels.

And he's here.

He's back.

"What time is?"

Fingers trail up and down my spine soothingly. "Late, early, actually."

"What were you doing in here?"

He stiffens under me for a moment before his hands resume their movement and he tips his head toward the wall beside his footlocker. "Sitting."

"And…watching me sleep?"

"Thinking. Making sure you were okay." He shifts to take my face between his palms, forcing me to meet his gaze. "Are you, really? It's okay to say no. I would understand if you did."

I don't know how to respond or what to say. For the first time in days, sitting here with him, enveloped in his arms, his strength, so close, I actually do feel all right for a second.

There's a flicker of hope that all this will go away, that I'll wake from it being a bad dream and go back to the days when he was my Kalen and not Chaos.

"No, I'm not okay." I manage to take a cleansing breath. "But I feel a lot better now that you're here."

He seems to consider my words for a moment before answering, like he's searching for some hidden meaning in them. "Viktoria can protect you. For me to do what I have to, I'm not going to be able to be here all the time. I wouldn't leave you with her if I wasn't confident that she will eliminate any threat."

"I know. I just…" I let my words trail off—unsure whether I should or maybe unwilling to say them.

"You just what?"

I press my hands against his strong chest and curl my fingers into the soft material. "It's just…having you here makes me feel safe. It always did."

His jaw hardens as he looks at me. "Don't, Avery." He shakes his head. "Please don't."

"Don't what?"

He shifts back slightly, then pulls me off his lap and sets me back onto the mattress before pushing to his feet, running his hands through his hair. "Don't put me in this position."

"What position?"

Instead of answering, he moves toward the open door, his body stiff.

"Kalen, please don't go."

He pauses with his back to me, shoulders rising and falling with his hard breaths.

"Stay with me."

The words hang in the air between us—heavy with so many things we never said to each other.

He stands frozen for a few minutes—minutes that seem like they'll never end, his hands opening and closing into fists at his sides. Finally, he slowly turns toward me, his jaw still clenched, body tense. "Avery…"

This time, my name comes out like a benediction, a prayer, something holy and unworthy for him to be speaking.

So much has happened between us. There are so many things we should be discussing, conversations he wouldn't have with me before that need to happen. But in this moment, all I want is to be in his arms again, for it to be the way it was before, to find a way to forget what's happening around us.

All I want is for him to give me *that*.

9

CHAOS

Avery looks at me like I'm the only person in the world who can give her what she needs right now, and I've never been able to deny her anything. Even when our relationship was falling apart, when *I* was falling apart, I couldn't stay away from her. I couldn't stop myself from touching her and loving her, giving her what she needed—at least physically. And now, she's asking for me to be there again, for me to be the one who gets her through this.

I don't know that I have the willpower to say no.

"Please, Kalen…" She stares at me with big green eyes, her bottom lip quivering, wrapped in my shirt, her hair rumpled, and looking so fucking broken and beautiful that my chest hurts.

"This isn't a good idea, Avery." I swallow thickly, trying to find the right words to explain to her what she's really asking. "In fact, it's a very bad one."

Avery slowly climbs off the bed and approaches me, her

long, bare legs glowing almost white in the moonlight coming from the window. "I don't care right now."

She stops in front of me and slowly presses her palm over my chest, unshed tears shimmering in her eyes from the dream she just had and maybe because she's afraid I'll say no.

My stomach twists, a jumbled mess of desire and restraint. "You're sure this is what you want, Avery? Really sure? Because if I don't walk out of here right now, it's going to happen."

It's the only warning I can give her. I've stayed away for years because I knew even just being in a room with her would be enough for me to lose control. Enough for me to snap and give in to how much I need her. How much I've always needed her even though I can't have her.

She leans closer to me, her lips only an inch from mine. "Yes, Kalen, I'm sure." Her fingers curl into my chest like she's grasping me to find some semblance of control over her life that seems to be spiraling. "Please…"

I can't have her. It's not good for either of us. Not safe for her.

But maybe for one night…

For *one night*, I can feel her in my arms again. Feel her underneath me. Feel her kiss and touch and give her what she needs.

And then everything can go back to the way it was. The way it *has* to be.

I can do this for her. I can give her this and live with the consequences of knowing what it feels like to be inside her again so she can find some peace in all this lunacy.

It doesn't matter how much it will hurt me tomorrow. She needs this.

I wrap my arms around her and drag her to me, crashing my lips to hers. A tiny mewl slips from her mouth, and she molds her body to mine, my cock hardening between us and pressing against her familiar, luscious curves.

She clings to me like she can't get close enough. Like she needs it and me more than anything else in this moment. Her lips move desperately against mine, seeking something, anything to take away her pain.

And selfishly, I'm going to give it to her.

Even though I should back away, even though I should walk out of this room and lock her in it for her own good, even though it's going to hurt later...

Despite all of it, I reach for the hem of my shirt hanging near her hips, tugging it up and hovering with it just below her breasts. "You know what it does to me to see you in this, don't you, Avery?"

My voice comes out gravelly, the heavy weight of what we're about to do making it hard to speak.

She ghosts her lips over mine. "I know."

The history between us doesn't stop me from pulling the shirt over her head, exposing her bare breasts, taut stomach, and the tiny scrap of fabric barely covering her pussy.

"Jesus, Avery, you had Viktoria buy you thongs?"

A low growl rumbles in my chest as I drag her naked body up against mine and press my lips to hers again, devouring the woman I know so well and have spent so much time thinking about, dreaming about, worrying about, who is tangled in every good memory I have of my entire life since I met her at sixteen.

She wraps her arms around my neck and scratches her fingers across the skin just below my hair as I walk her backward until her calves hit the mattress. I stop kissing her long enough to get my shirt up and over my head, then toss it to the floor with the one she just wore.

Her warm palms find my bare chest. The familiar touch sends an inferno coursing through my veins. This is Avery, the woman who knows me better than anyone in the world but who can never know the truth of why I left, why I did what I did to her.

She slowly trails her fingers down over my chest and abdomen, stopping briefly at each one of the scars she's intimately acquainted with, brushing her fingers reverently over them before she finally reaches for the waistband of my jeans. Capturing her lips again, I tangle my tongue with hers while she frees my hard cock and takes it into her small hand.

I groan into her mouth at the pleasure surging through my body, and when she glides her thumb across the head, spreading the pre-cum already seeping out, I have to grit my teeth to keep from coming all over her stomach and fingers.

This is what I've dreamt about. The kiss and touch of the woman who haunts me and curses me. The one I never thought I could live without yet have somehow managed to keep breathing away from over the last four years.

There's one other thing I've lived without, something my mouth waters for and my cock yearns for.

I drop to my knees in front of her and drag her right leg over my shoulder so I can dip my head and glide my tongue through her sweet cunt. She gasps and arches into me, her entire body bending back, head dropping. I wrap my arm around her hips, holding her steady, and she claws at me, her nails scoring my forearms as I continue to devour her and take in the only meal that ever satiated me.

This is dangerous, far more dangerous than even the men after her. To let myself experience this again. To let myself touch her and taste her and feel her hips rolling against my face. To hear her tiny little gasps of pleasure every time my tongue flicks across her clit.

All of it is catastrophically dangerous to both of us.

Still, my fingers itch to feel her, and I glide a hand up her inner thigh and slip two fingers into her heat while my tongue laves at her clit. She moans and squeezes around me, burying her hands in my hair as her legs begin to shake. I tighten my grip on her thighs, holding her steady as I eat her like a starved man. Because that's what I am—starved for her. For four fucking years…starved of this.

"Oh, God, Kalen…"

Her pussy starts to ripple around my fingers, and I suck her clit between my lips and pulse it in time with curling into that spot inside her that always drove her fucking mad.

She comes, throwing back her head, her mouth falling open. Her entire body spasms, twisting in my arm, her warm sheath clenching and grasping for what it really wants.

I draw out her orgasm as long as I dare until she's gasping and pushing on my head to get me away from her overly sensitive clit. She gazes down at me with glazed-over green eyes that burn with a raging conflagration of need and questions we both know she won't voice right now. I stare up at her, licking her release off my lips, and slowly withdraw my fingers from inside her.

It should end here. Like this. It doesn't matter that my cock aches and screams to get into her wet heat.

I've given her what she needed—a release of her tension, her pain.

That should be it.

I should walk away.

If I were a stronger man, I might, but any strength I had vanished the moment she signed those divorce papers, the moment *this* ended. Instead of leaving like we both know I should, I slowly lower her leg off my shoulder and push to my feet, still gripping her hips.

She watches me in a way that tells me she knows exactly what I'm thinking. For the longest time, she always did. She always knew—what I needed, what I wanted, how to make everything better. That's all I want to do for her now. It's the only thing I can offer.

I brush my lips over hers gently twice, then press my forehead to hers. Her heavy breaths draw me even closer to her quivering body.

Leave now.

Before this goes any further.

Somehow, I find a way to speak. "I should go."

She pulls her head back and runs her hand down to grasp my rigid cock. Her fingers squeeze around it, then she slowly drags her hands along the length, telling me without words that she needs me to stay.

Fuck.

Avery steps backward toward the mattress and sinks down, dragging me with her. I catch myself on my elbow, my body spread out across hers. The warm, familiar feel of her under me has more pre-cum seeping from the head of my cock.

She uses her feet to push my jeans down my thighs to my knees, allowing me to kick them off. Then she reaches between us, spreads her legs, and aligns me with her slick opening.

"Please, Kalen…"

The breathy way she begs for it and says my name makes me push aside all the reasons I shouldn't be doing this and plunge into her. Her pussy contracts around me, welcoming me into the place that's always felt like home. She drops her head back again and gasps, clinging to me, her nails scoring along my shoulders.

"God, Kalen…"

Her words reignite the fire in me, the one that's always blazed for her no matter how hard I've tried to extinguish it over the years—for the good of both of us.

She wraps her legs around my hips, pressing her heels

against my lower back to urge me a fraction of an inch deeper. I clench my jaw against the burning coil of release threatening at the base of my spine already. It's been far too fucking long, and this woman means far too much for me to control this. She tightens around my cock—another desperate plea to get me to move, and I take her face between my palms and force her to look at me.

"If you keep doing that, this isn't going to last very long."

Avery swallows thickly and turns her head to tug my ear lobe between her teeth. "Then, we'll just have to do it again."

Jesus fuck.

She is *trying to kill me.*

This woman is trying to pay me back for what I did to her all those years ago, for how I blew up everything and walked away. It's the only explanation for why she would look at me like this, touch me like this, *need* me like this.

But I don't even fucking care.

I issue a low groan, drag back my hips, and plunge into her again, driving her body down into the shitty, cheap mattress. She groans and gouges my back, rolling her hips to meet each one of my thrusts that I try to keep slow and steady.

If I go any harder, I'll come on the spot, and she needs more than that. She *deserves* more than that.

She's always deserved more than I could give her.

More than I *ever* could.

AVERY

KALEN HAS ALWAYS GIVEN me everything I've ever wanted or at least tried to, and he continues to as he drives into me, grinding his hips and adding a sharp upward thrust at the end that he knows will always catch me in exactly the right spot.

The fact that he has remembered after all these years shouldn't make tears well in my eyes, yet they do. I always knew I could never forget, but I always imagined that when he walked away, he did everything in his power to replace his memories with me with other ones, tried to forget everything we ever were or ever had in any way he could.

I could never do that. Could never let another man touch me. Could never bring myself to even consider it. Maybe because I've been waiting for this moment, for him to come back to me, for us to find a way to get back to *this*.

This is the way it's supposed to be.

Us…

Together…

Our bodies moving in unison.

Completing each other.

Filling all the places that have felt so empty for so long.

Kalen lowers his head and presses his lips to mine. A familiar kiss, the one I've longed to feel again, just like I've craved everything this man does to me when we're in the same room.

The heat that spreads through my body from a single look.

The way his hands know exactly where to touch me, *how* to touch me, to make the entire world disappear.

The way his cock fills me perfectly, making me feel whole for the first time in four years.

I know what asking him for this means, what it might do to him and me, but it's all I want, the only thing that will satiate my hunger and calm the turmoil boiling inside me.

He maintains slow, languid strokes, despite how pent up he appears to be, wound tight like a fucking spring about to snap. His tension builds with my own, and he eases in and out of me, ensuring maximum contact against all the places he knows I need it to send me over the edge again for another mind-numbing orgasm.

The years apart haven't changed how well he knows me. Kalen was my best friend, the only person I could rely on unquestionably, and he *still* knows me better than anyone.

He knew I would head up to the cabin, even though I haven't been able to go since we split because of the memories it held of the good times we had there. They overshadowed those I had with Gramps, made it too painful to go to the place that once held so much peace. But it was the first place I thought to go because deep down, I knew he would find me there. I *knew* he would understand I needed somewhere safe.

And he found me.

His strong arms have held me so much over the years, and they're doing it now—protecting me and making me forget all the reasons I should be afraid.

In this moment, all the fear is gone. All that exists is this feeling—his touch and his kiss.

He *knows* me and what I need right now.

Just like I know him and what he needs...

I catch his mouth with mine and pull his bottom lip between my teeth, biting down sharply.

His hips jerk wildly. "Fuck!" His entire body tenses even more, and I suck on his lip to ease the sharp sting before releasing it with a pop. "Fucking hell, Avery."

A strong hand tightens at my hip as the other cradles my face. I roll my hips up to meet his, spurring him to increase the pace, to get us both to what we're chasing—freedom. From our past. From the unsettled future. From all the dangers and uncertainty.

Those little bites of pain, the slight aggression, the scratches and the screams, it always pushed him over the edge. Always drove him mad. Always made him become what I knew he wanted to be when we were locked together physically like this, especially at the end. By then, I wasn't having sex with Kalen; I was having sex with Chaos. But this...this is some strange mixture of the two. Like he can't decide which one he's supposed to be in this moment.

Maybe he doesn't know.

God knows I don't.

The two are so entwined that they can't be separated anymore.

This is all I'll ever get of Kalen. All that's left is tainted and twisted by what Chaos has done. But he's still beautiful, still the strong, reliable, loving man I've always loved, deep down at his core. I know that; I'm just not sure he does anymore.

I squeeze around him, tightening with each retreat of his hips to keep the head of his cock dragging along that perfect spot, and his pace increases, every thrust building another orgasm deep inside me, in that place only *he* could ever reach.

Tears trickle down my cheeks—of pain, of hope, of regret.

There's so much he doesn't know, so much he never gave me the chance to explain, so much we could have been if he hadn't shut me out and given me no choice. The truth would destroy him, though, exactly as it has me since that day four years ago when I put ink on those papers that officially ended it all. So as much as I want to come clean, want to tell him everything, I'll keep it bottled up inside me the same way he does all his pain.

The pain that propels him on now, even when this feels so incredible. I can see it in the way he looks at me, the darkness in his eyes that never used to be there. Whatever it was that drove him away from me back then is driving him to do this now, to try to fix what's been broken in me by this entire situation.

And it's working.

Pleasure ripples across my heated skin and floods my veins. My body winds impossibly tighter, part of me not wanting to let go because it will mean an end to *this* moment with Kalen. I don't want to lose it, don't want to lose *him* again. I fight it with everything I have until my limbs are shaking violently and my chest is heaving with my effort. He presses his mouth to mine and twists our tongues, more frantic than the earlier kisses.

He's losing his restraint, his ability to control Chaos. There was a time not that long ago when that might have scared me, when I might have wondered where he was in his head if not here with me, but I know he's with me now. His blue eyes meet mine, holding the same heat and passion I've always felt from him, the same love, the same turmoil remain, just like the last few times we were together before our lives imploded.

His jaw clenches so hard that it almost looks painful, and he reaches between us to find my clit. He's close to coming and needs me to come first. I'm right there, and this man understands me well enough to know it.

He rolls his thumb over my most sensitive spot, and lights flicker in my vision, the orgasm just on the edge of the horizon. His lips crash against mine, catching my gasps and moans, and I kiss him like it's our last time, like I would have if I had known back then.

The heat building in my abdomen becomes almost unbearable with my effort to prolong this, but he adjusts his position and drives even harder, feeling the difference in my body, knowing what I need. He pinches my clit and rolls his hips, grinding his pelvis into his hand, adding more friction as the head of his cock drags against my G-spot until I finally blow.

My pussy clenches around him tightly, and he buries his

face against my neck and issues a deep groan, emptying himself inside me. My hips buck wildly, seeking more even as the pleasure threatens to drown me.

Waves of ecstasy crash over me, relentlessly stealing my breath, while all the pain floats away on a cloud made of this perfect moment in time. It drags on for what feels like forever, my body reveling in the release of everything that's been weighing me down, fragmenting the worries and agonies of the past and letting them go.

Kalen's heart hammers against mine, its rhythm an old song my heart knows well, as his body continues to move with mine.

Finally, as my orgasm starts to wane, he freezes and then sags against me, rolling slightly to one side to keep his weight off me, his cock still hard and buried inside where I need him most.

His hurried, warm breaths flutter against my cheek, and he sweeps his lips over my heated skin softly, barely there, featherlight and holding so many unspoken truths. This might be it, our final time together, our last chance to hold one another and experience what it's like to be with someone who completes you fully.

Tomorrow is uncertain.

Nothing is guaranteed, especially not with the nightmare we face.

But we have tonight.

We have *now.*

I let my eyes drift closed. His strong arm wrapped around my chest holds the incredibly blissful feeling overtaking me in place, keeps me from falling away, back to the dark place I was in when I woke. He grounds me in a way nothing else ever could.

Having Kalen at my side and watching my back is the only way I'll ever survive this. He holds my life and my heart in his capable hands that lightly brush over my skin as we lie here together.

The feel of his body pressed to mine and the post-orgasmic exhaustion finally start to drag me under with a sense of calm and rightness I didn't know I could find again.

Too bad it won't be there when I wake up.

10

CHAOS

I release a frustrated sigh, pinching the bridge of my nose. "Tell me you got something, Preacher…"

Reaper, Mouth, Viktoria, and I all stare at my phone on the counter, waiting with bated breath for Preacher to start talking.

"Oh, I have plenty." He offers a light chuckle. "I just don't know you're going to want to hear it."

Fucking hell.

"Shit." I scrub my hand over my face. That wasn't exactly what I hoped to hear from the man when he finally called with information on Perez. "That bad?"

The sound of his fingers flying over the keyboard floats through the line. "That bad."

Reaper releases an annoyed sigh. "*Well*, get on with it!"

None of us have any patience this morning, not after what we saw and did at *South of the Border* last night.

Preacher offers a huff at Reaper's tone. "Using the information Avery gave us the other night, I've been able to do a deep dive into this guy, and none of it is good."

Shit.

"I don't know how this fucker has stayed under the radar of the DEA and FBI because he is one bad motherfucker, or is at least *tied* to some. I traced the holding company listed as the owner of all of his businesses back to another holding company, and another, and another, and after about fifteen layers or shit, eventually to a trucking company in Merida, Mexico."

"Fuck." My eyes meet Reaper's. "Cartel?"

Preacher issues a humorless laugh. "It certainly looks that way. In that area, the number and type of trucks, the money being spent...this guy is either trafficking and selling it, or he is laundering the money. Likely both."

I nod even though he can't see me and exchange a knowing look with Reaper and Mouth. "That's exactly what I thought last night after what we found."

More clicking sounds come through the line as Preacher pulls up whatever he's looking for. "I checked DEA and FBI databases. This guy isn't even anywhere on their radar. So, he must be pretty good at what he does, or at least he's good at hiding it."

"Yeah, the restaurant seemed like a decent front, but after last night, he's gonna have some eyes on him." I lean back against the wall and cross my arms over my chest. "That amount of cash, if any of it survived that fire, the cops are going to want to know what the fuck was going on in that back room."

"I'm assuming that was intentional to draw his focus away from Avery?"

"Definitely, but I don't know if it did any good or not. I just wanted that fucker to suffer for what he has already done to her."

What I might have made worse last night.

It made sense at the time. Seemed like the right thing in that heat of the moment, when she was so terrified, so desperate to feel safe, but as soon as the fuzzy haze of my orgasm fully dissolved, I knew what I had done, how badly I'd complicated things by giving in to her.

Preacher's low chuckle crackles through the line. "Well, if you really want to make this guy pay, I've been able to locate a few more businesses in the area that Avery wasn't aware of that could potentially be drop houses and warehouses for storage of cash or drugs. I'll text you the updated list."

I nod slowly. "Good…"

The more places we can hit him, the more he will hurt until I can finally get my hands on the man himself.

Reaper raises an eyebrow at me. "What's our next play, Chaos? What do you want to do?"

This typically would be all Reaper's call. He's the one who put this crew together, technically the leader of our ragtag group. The one who always calls the shots on our missions, but he's looking to me because Avery is *my* responsibility.

Thank fuck, none of them know what happened last night.

If anyone suspected I ended up in bed with her, it would make things a whole lot more complicated than it already is, and I'd never hear the fucking end of it. Especially from Viktoria—who already eyes me like she suspects something even though I've given her no reason to.

I was out here within five minutes of Avery falling asleep, so there's no way anyone can know what went down in that bedroom. But I can't think about it. This is precisely why it was such a horrible idea because I need to be concentrating on our plan of attack, not how good her cunt felt wrapped around my cock or how her kiss made me feel alive again for the first time in years.

Tapping my foot against the wall, I consider our options.

We don't know enough about Perez's connection to the cartel or his current operations. That makes unease tighten my gut. "Taking out this guy locally won't be an issue. Reaper, Mouth, and I can handle it easily. But if he is someone the cartel relies on, if he's a big player in their organization, hell, even a medium-sized one, they're not going to look too kindly upon us destroying their network here."

Preacher types some more. "He has places in Baltimore, DC, and almost every city between there and Philly. He's likely controlling an entire region."

Reaper scowls. "Fuck, that definitely isn't good."

Mouth nods in agreement from where he stands near the door, hip propped against the wall, brow furrowed, and lips pressed in a hard line.

"No." I shake my head. "It's not. Going after the cartel would be a suicide mission, so we concentrate on this guy. If his accountant was onto him and he had to take her out, then he fucked up bad enough to let Avery see what they had done, he's not going to want to let his higher-ups in the cartel know that. If he reveals his own fuck-up, that puts his neck out there."

Vik finally speaks up, shifting where she sits on the counter. "So you think if we eliminate him, we remove any threat against her?"

Acid churns in my stomach at the thought that I could be wrong. "I sure as fuck hope so. I think it's our only play right now."

Reaper glances at me. "But where do we start?"

The sound of Preacher's fingers flying across the keyboard come through the line again. "He has a warehouse not far from the restaurant you toasted last night. From what I was able to get from hacking into some cameras at some surrounding businesses, he's there almost daily. But he keeps it locked up pretty tight. About a dozen men at any given time."

Reaper grins. "It's never stopped us before."

I chuckle and shake my head at the clear reference to what we did in New York to the Russian human trafficking ring. The Yankovich assholes never saw us coming and didn't stand a chance against Vik and the three of us. Still, Vik and Reaper both ended up with holes in them.

This time, let's hope everybody stays out of the path of gunfire.

Tilting my head side to side, I try to release the tension suddenly building at the top of my spine. "If we're truly going to take out this guy, we can't just hit one or two places. We need to eliminate his entire operation—every single one—and we need to do it fast so he doesn't have time to figure out what's happening and set up better protection."

Reaper nods his agreement. "Preach, how many businesses total that you can find within a hundred miles of here?"

"Thirteen."

"Fuck…" I rub at my neck, a throbbing starting to work up into my head. "That's a lot for the three of us to hit—"

"Four of us!" Viktoria's annoyed comment comes sharp and direct, pointed squarely at me.

"*Three*. You need to stay here with Avery."

Vik scowls. "You said it yourself—no one's going to find her here."

A low growl starts in my throat. "I'm not going to leave her alone."

She huffs an annoyed sigh and continues to glare at me. With her skill-set, she doesn't like to be sidelined from the action, but keeping Avery safe is the entire point of all this. Leaving her alone, even somewhere I know can't be traced back to her, isn't going to happen.

Reaper gives his woman a pointed look before returning

his attention to me. "What happens if we take out all these places and attract the attention of the cartel? What if it turns out he is important enough for them to come looking for whoever took him out?"

It's the last thing we want, but we can't ignore the possibility.

"We deal with it when that time comes."

Preacher clears his throat, reminding us he's still on the line. "You really want to fight an entire cartel?"

That's a fair question, but it still raises my hackles coming from Preacher. He, of all people, should know the lengths any of us would go to in order to protect the people we care about.

"If it means Avery will be safe, I'll go to Mexico myself, find the head of the snake, and fucking bite it off."

AVERY

"You're going to Mexico?" My question comes out soft, barely a whisper, more like it's said to myself than meant for the room, but all eyes turn toward me where I stand just outside the bedroom door.

Kalen's gaze locks with mine, and his shoulders tense and jaw tightens. He shifts against the wall and shakes his head. "No. Just talking."

"Is that Avery?" A voice comes from a phone set on the counter.

I glance at it with a raised brow. "Um…yeah?"

"Hey, Avery. I'm doing everything I can to help you stay clear of this fucker."

Kalen inclines his head toward the phone. "Preacher."

"Oh, thanks, Preacher."

Despite how long he's been friends with the guys, I never got to meet the man in person. I could never have imagined I'd one day be needing his kind of help. Then again, there are a lot of things I never thought would happen.

I never thought Kalen and I would grow so far apart that we could never find our way back to each other. I never thought I'd see someone so close to me killed in such a brutal way. I never thought I would end up back in Kalen's arms the way I did last night after everything that happened between us. And for some reason, despite all the evidence pointing to exactly what would happen, I never expected to wake up alone this morning.

You're a fucking idiot, Avery.

He never slept in the same bed a single night with me after he came home from the hospital. We would fuck and kiss and be frantic for each other, but as soon as it was done, he would slip out of the bed we once shared and sleep on the recliner alone.

Why did I think last night would be any different?

Just because I needed him. Just because I wanted him in that moment of weakness. That doesn't *change* anything.

He gave me all he could and then left, and now, he's standing here, acting like nothing even happened, looking at me with the same wall between us as he's had for the last four years.

Last night was a single desperate act between two people seeking something—me comfort, him a release. Maybe he was right when he said he shouldn't stay, when he tried to walk out before anything happened. It might have been smarter to ignore the desire, the pulsating, living, breathing attraction that always seemed to exist between us. But now it's too late to go back.

If it was a mistake, we've made it and have to deal with

the fallout. Which for Kalen apparently means pretending it didn't happen.

I tear my gaze from his and scan the room, taking in the concerned looks of everyone else. From what little I heard when I made it to the door, the level of danger we're all facing has skyrocketed with the information Preacher sent. "So...what are you guys going to do?"

The boys exchange a look, and Viktoria smiles at me.

She offers a slight shrug. "We have a plan. Sort of. I'll stay here as your babysitter, and the boys go do what they do best."

I lock eyes with Kalen again, unease creeping up my spine, a cold sweat breaking out across my skin. "Are-are you going to kill him?"

They all exchange glances again, and Viktoria finally offers me a sympathetic look, but the guys certainly don't. I wouldn't expect them to. When it comes right down to it, these men are all highly skilled killers, and just because they're "retired" doesn't mean they've stopped. The security company they've formed does a hell of a lot more than serve rich and powerful men and women who need protection from violent lovers. They're mercenaries for hire, and I didn't even have to pay them to want to kill Ricardo.

The thought of more blood being spilled makes bile climb my throat.

Kalen steps off the wall, his hands fisting at his sides. "This dude is bad news, Avery. Last night, at *South of the Border*, we found millions of dollars in cash stacked in a back room, and Preacher has linked him and his business to one of the cartels in Merida."

"What?"

Millions of dollars?

A cartel?

I shake my head. "No. No. That's not possible. He's so nice…"

Kalen's jaw hardens again. "Remember what he did to your friend, Avery. What he would have done to do you, too."

I flinch at the comment and regret instantly flashes in Kalen's blue eyes.

"I'm sorry, that was harsh." He lets out a frustrated sigh and shakes his head. "You just have to understand that men like this put on a good façade. They know how to make people around them feel comfortable and safe. Their goal is to ensure no one ever suspects they could possibly be involved in anything like this. That's the entire point. The cartel uses people who will never be suspected." He watches me for my reaction, but his words are only slowly sinking in. "This guy is in *deep*, Avery. And with the kind of people he's tied up with, he isn't going to stop coming for you until he's physically prevented from doing it anymore."

Any icy shiver rolls through my spine. I wrap my arms around myself and rub at the goosebumps on my bare skin. Visions of Amelia's dead, staring eyes flash through my mind again.

"I'm sorry. I just—"

I can't seem to get out the words, can't seem to swallow whatever is choking me. Four hard sets of eyes watch me, trying to figure out what's going on. I stumble backward toward the bedroom, close the door, and throw the lock before the tears start to flow again.

They're killing people. They have to. More than just Ricardo. They're going to kill anyone who gets in their way.

And it's all my fault…

A sharp knock at the door jerks me away from it, and I swipe at the tears on my cheeks.

"Avery…" Kalen's deep voice rumbles through the piece of wood separating us. The knob turns, and he tries to push it open. It doesn't budge, and he mutters something under his breath that makes my chest tighten. "Avery, unlock the fucking door, or I'll break it down."

He will.

That's not a threat.

It's a promise.

I unlock the door with a shaking hand, and the second it clicks, he shoves it open and stalks in, slamming it closed behind him.

Anger flashes in his gaze, and for the first time I can remember in all the years I've known him, it's actually directed at me. "Don't ever lock that fucking door again. What if I needed to get to you quickly?" His eyes widen as he takes me in, and his expression softens, his shoulders releasing a bit of the tension there. "Why did you run away? Why are you crying?"

"I-I…"

How do I explain this to a man who has no qualms about killing someone if he believes there's a reason?

"You're going to kill him, Kalen. You're going to kill Ricardo and anyone else who gets in the way."

He takes a step toward me, his lips curling into a sneer. "Damn fucking right I am. The man is trying to *kill* you, Avery, and he won't stop until he succeeds or until something stops him. That something is *me*."

"I know." I swallow back the emotion clogging my throat. "And I know I came to you for help, but he has a wife…kids. Couldn't you talk to him?"

"*Talk* to him?" Kalen throws up his hands. "Jesus, Avery, I know you're not this naïve. You don't really believe that would work."

"No…" I shake my head. "You're right. I'm not—"

"We aren't touching his wife and kids. They more than likely have no idea what's going on or how he's making his money, but Avery, listen to me." He steps forward and captures my face in his palms. "He and his organization cannot continue like this. If they do, not only are you in danger but so is anyone else who gets in their way. The only way I can protect you is—"

"To be Chaos," I finish the sentence for him, and his eyes harden again.

"Yes."

"Is that why you left last night?"

"Shit." He drops his hand from my face and scrubs it over his own. When his eyes meet mine again, a recognizable pain lives deep in them. "Last night was a mistake, Avery. I can't... we can't make it again." He takes a step back and reaches for the door. "My focus needs to be on protecting you and ending this threat. I can't be worried about your safety when you're in the one place you shouldn't have to."

He yanks open the door, steps out, and slams it closed behind him.

Worry about my safety in the one place I shouldn't have to?

His words ring in my ears.

What the hell is he talking about?

11

CHAOS

Sometimes, the things that seem the most innocuous can hold the worst danger, pose the greatest threat. The cinderblock warehouse in the rundown industrial area should be housing produce and restaurant supplies—as it advertises on the outside—but I know what's really hidden behind its walls.

A madman lurks inside, intent on destroying Avery for no other reason but that she stumbled upon something she shouldn't have and could get in his way.

According to what Preacher sent us this morning, this is his primary place of operation. The warehouse and offices where Avery worked were the face of the business only. This is where the real shit goes down.

Vehicles come and go constantly, at least two or three an hour. Even if Perez's business is flourishing, there is no way there would be this kind of heavy traffic with just deliveries for the restaurants. The trucks with Mexican plates tie directly to and confirm the information Preacher got us, and watching frantic men pulling up in expensive rides and rushing in proves what we did last night sent them into disarray.

Which means my plan worked.

Perez won't be concentrating on his search for Avery when he is trying to figure out who blew up his fucking restaurant and burned his millions.

We're in the right place to take out this fucker.

This guy has been getting away with it for far too long, manipulating people like Avery, who believe in the genuine goodness of people and are trusting and loyal. She had no idea who she was working for, and it's gotten her stuck in this quagmire.

But hopefully, it will end tonight.

Perez's car has been parked out front since before we even got here. He likely came here right after the explosion at *South of the Border* to do some damage control and to try to protect whatever it is he keeps in this warehouse.

The plans Preacher got for us showed four loading docks and multiple entrances, which makes it more difficult for Reaper, Mouth, and me to cover alone. But we don't have much of a choice. We can't wait for backup after what we did last night.

Perez might not know who was behind it, likely suspects it's a rival here in town, but our anonymity can only last so long. In a world with so many cameras, if we happen to get caught on one and he manages to ID us, Avery will be the one who pays the price for our actions.

I'll never allow that to happen.

I glance at Reaper and Mouth. "You guys ready?"

They both nod.

With Mouth's rifle aimed at the warehouse, no one is getting out of here alive.

"If you see that fucker come out, you put a fucking bullet through his heart."

The corners of Mouth's lips curl up. This is what he lives for, and knowing he's able to contribute to our very worthy mission will do wonders for him.

My count is still at ten inside the warehouse, but that doesn't mean more aren't there who haven't shown themselves yet. I would say this should be a simple in and out, but nothing is ever that easy, and thinking it will be is what gets people killed...or worse.

No one is getting hurt tonight except these cartel assholes who deserve it.

We get in. Take out everyone. Gather as much information as we can to help us shut down the rest of the operation. Make sure no one else is coming for Avery.

It's a simple plan. One we've executed a hundred times together over our years in service. It's one we could do in our sleep. But we won't be sleeping tonight. We'll be wiping out a part of what keeps Perez's business running, including anyone who tries to flee. It's hard to escape Mouth's shot, and he's raring to go.

Equipped with our night vision goggles, Reaper and I take off in the direction of the loading docks. If this place is what we think it is, the security here will be a lot better than at the restaurant. But the fucker wasn't smart enough to hook up this facility to a generator.

I check my watch.

11:53...

Two more minutes until show time.

Reaper and I wait until exactly 11:55, and the entire twenty-block radius goes dark.

Right on time, Preach.

That man can hack anything, and the dark brought by his

shutting down this area of the grid gives us the advantage even on their home turf. Perez's men will be scrambling.

Reaper and I don't waste any time making our move to the rear door near the docks. I set a charge on the handle, we step back, and I blow it instantly. The small blast does the job, the door easily swinging open, granting us access.

Confused shouts in Spanish fill the air, and men scurry away from the blast down the hall, illuminated only by a single-bulb emergency lamp. Reaper quickly shoots the two men and then the light, plunging us into complete darkness.

These fuckers thought they could go after an innocent woman who had no way to protect herself. They have no idea what they've just brought down upon themselves.

A tidal wave of pain is about to engulf them.

I reach into the bag slung over my shoulder, grab the first charge, and set it at one of the main load-bearing walls. According to the blueprints, I can bring down this entire place easily.

We hustle down the hallway toward the next target location. Voices approach, and Reaper takes the three men out with quick shots. Perez may have armed his employees, but they're wholly unprepared for someone coming in guns blazing.

Continued shouts and talking alert us to precisely where they are the deeper we get into the complex. We easily put them down—one by one.

The hallway intersects with another, and we pause and listen for the sound of anyone approaching, but all that greets us is an eerie quiet.

I signal to Reaper. He nods, and we go on three, turning the corner and instantly meeting gunfire. Bullets slam into the wall to my left, but our return fusillade of shots takes them down and allows us to pass to the next location for a charge.

With the second one set in place, we continue through the maze of hallways, clearing each room as we go.

Two down. Two to go.

Once I'm done, all that will be left of this place is a pile of smoking rubble and ash, but it isn't my primary mission tonight. Finding the fucker, Perez, is.

Where the hell is he?

We move deeper into the warehouse complex, but there isn't any sign of the man after Avery, only his minions, who we easily pick off.

The radio in my ear crackles with three taps, the signal from Mouth that he took out three men who either tried to flee or were coming in to assist. He would have given us a different signal if he thought any of them were Perez, which means we still need to find the asshole—and fast.

Though this area's mostly industrial, that doesn't mean there isn't somebody inside one of the nearby buildings this time of night who might hear the gunfire and alert the authorities. The last thing we need is to get caught here like this. Then not only would Avery be a sitting duck, but we'd likely go to prison for the rest of our lives.

Using the skills Uncle Sam gives you to become a mercenary vigilante is frowned upon in certain circles, mainly the ones frequented by people who put you in cuffs.

We need to get Perez and get out quickly, and now, we've finally reached the main massive warehouse area. It's the only place we haven't searched yet.

I pause for a moment to take stock. Mouth took out three outside, and we've hit four in here. That means probably three more, plus Perez, are somewhere in the building.

The warehouse itself is vast, with any number of hiding spots. This is where things get dicey, and I'd kill to have a full team here. Having Cutter and Flash with us would have made me feel a lot better about this, but there wasn't any time to wait for them to get to town. The immediate threat calls for immediate action.

Something rustles in the corner behind a large stack of pallets, and I signal Reaper. We approach cautiously, so quietly, there's no way whoever's back there will know we're coming.

We turn the corner and unleash into the two men with their backs propped up against a pallet. Their weapons tumble to the ground before they have a chance to fire, and I step over them and pump a few more rounds into each one to ensure they're not getting back up.

Reaper continues to scan the warehouse for any signs of movement, but it's far too quiet. If anyone else is still in here, they're laying low, doing their best to conceal themselves from us until they think the coast is clear.

They underestimate our ability to sniff out a rat.

Row by row.

Pallet after pallet.

Box after box.

We make our way through the warehouse, checking every nook and cranny possible.

There's nowhere to hide from us when we're on a mission.

A man tries to rush at us from between two massive crates, but his reaction time is so slow. Reaper ends him before he can pull the trigger.

"Where the fuck is Perez?"

Reaper inclines his head toward a small office off to one side of the warehouse, and I place the final two charges along the far wall as we make our way toward it, one of us always watching our backs.

But as soon as we step in, it's clear Perez isn't here anymore.

Open desk drawers.

Empty file cabinets.

Folders and papers strewn across the floor.

It definitely looks like this was Perez's office while he was doing business here, but whatever was in here is long gone.

Reaper and I sift through some of the discarded items on the floor. "He must have come in his car and left in the back of one of the trucks where we couldn't see him."

"Fuck!"

We missed him.

He holds up a paper to me. I tear it out of his hand and scan it in the moonlight coming in from a single window. The same address Preacher gave us for the company in Mexico draws my eye.

"You think he went there?"

Reaper offers a half-shrug. "It's possible. He may be going to smooth things over after his losses last night, or he may have gone to hide out."

"Shit."

I storm out of the office and back into the warehouse, over to one of the pallets, pulling out my knife. It easily slices through the plastic wrapped around the boxes, and I pull out one and hold it up.

"Boxes of dried fruit?"

No fucking way.

Reaper takes it from me and tears it open, pouring the contents onto the concrete floor. Dried apple chips come first, followed by tightly packaged stacks of cash. "Well, damn."

He drops the box and approaches a different stack. I join him and cut it open, grabbing one of the boxes and tearing into it.

"I think we have the answer about what they're doing." I hold up a large brick wrapped in duct tape.

Reaper grabs it and cuts it open, bringing up white powder on his knife.

"Cocaine?"

"Sure looks like it."

"So, he's dealing and laundering money. How the fuck did Avery get herself into this?"

"I don't know, man, but it seems Perez went south of the border—pun intended. You know what that means…"

I shove my knife back into my boot and follow him toward the door. "I sure as hell do."

The only way to end this is to go after him.

We'll check his house and all the other locations Preacher gave us before we head back to my place, but if we don't find him, then we're going south, too.

AVERY

THE CHINESE TAKEOUT Viktoria basically forced me to eat earlier sits like a lead weight in my stomach, heavier the longer the guys are gone. Any attempt at sleep would be useless—my mind and body far too restless to relax.

Between what happened last night with Kalen, the information Preacher provided this morning, and what I know the guys are doing right now, I'm back to being as big of a mess as I was when I fell into bed with Kalen.

With nothing else to do inside the apartment besides sit and wait, I pace along the already-worn ancient wood floors.

Back and forth.

Back and forth.

Back and forth between the recliner and the TV that plays some stupid rom-com movie I am in no mood to watch.

Viktoria glances up from her phone from her usual spot

sitting on top of the counter. "Please stop that. You're making me nervous."

Shoving my hands back through my hair, I shake my head. "I'm sorry. I can't help it." I glance at the clock on the microwave for what feels like the millionth time. Only eight minutes have passed since I last checked it. "They've been gone a long time."

"They'll be gone a while. They're heading to what Preacher thinks is the primary location for Perez's operations here. They have to do recon before they can go in, and they might face some resistance."

Resistance.

"You mean get shot."

"Don't be a pessimist." Vik releases a heavy sigh and slides off the counter to walk over to the fridge and pull it open. Holding up a bottle of red wine, she jiggles it from side to side. "You need some of this."

"Where did that come from?"

It's certainly not something Kalen would willingly keep stocked.

A grin plays on her lips. "I thought you might need a little something to calm you down, so I brought it with me. You were too busy obsessing over your ex-husband, so you didn't even notice it when I got here."

I wince at her easy observation, then do my best to brush it off. "I was not obsessing."

Vik barks out a laugh as she twists the top off the bottle. "Honey, you should have seen the look on your face when he walked out that door." She shakes her head and makes a little *tsking* sound as she opens a cabinet and pulls out two glasses. "The tension between you two. Seriously." She fans herself, then fills a glass for each of us and pushes one toward me. "Drink that."

I scowl at her but take a sip anyway. Alcohol is likely not

the best way to deal with the current stressful situation, but I'm not about to turn it down right now. With my nerves this frayed and no sign of the guys coming back anytime soon, anything that might help relieve a little of the tension is welcome.

The sharp tannins hit my tongue, and I almost release a little sigh at the sweet, fruity flavor. Even though it's far too soon to be feeling any of the effects of the alcohol in my system, some of the pain in my shoulders releases.

Vik watches me over the top of her glass. "You slept with him, didn't you?"

I jerk my head up, my body immediately tightening and going stock straight. "What?"

A grin tilts Viktoria's lips. "I *said*, you slept with him, *didn't* you? Last night…"

Fucking hell…

I stare into my drink and contemplate denying it for a moment, but Viktoria was a decorated NYPD detective before she left the force to be with Reaper, and she's not going to let me get away with it. She'll interrogate me until I break, wear me down until I can't hold it in any longer, and I don't have the energy to fight her.

"Yes."

She slaps her hand on the counter, making me jump. "I knew it. I fucking *knew* it." Her grins spreads wider, eyes alight with humor and interest. "The minute I walked in here and saw Chaos' face, I knew it."

"Please don't make a big deal about this."

She gapes at me. "Don't make a big deal about this? After the conversation we had the other night…really?"

I sigh and pinch the bridge of my nose against the threatening headache. Another drink of my wine gives me an excuse to consider my response and offers a bit of liquid courage to open this avenue of discussion. "It doesn't mean anything. He said it was a mistake."

She snorts and takes a sip of her wine. "Of course he did."

Ouch.

"What's that supposed to mean?"

"God love ya, Avery. For such a smart woman, you sure are blind when it comes to that man. Whatever happened between you two, it isn't over, and"—she holds up a hand to stop me from interrupting—"don't say it's just sex. Don't say he was just comforting you because you were upset."

I press my lips together to stop myself from interjecting and saying just that because that's what it *was*. Kalen made that very clear to me this morning. It was great while it lasted, but he won't let it happen again.

Viktoria locks her gaze with mine, suddenly serious. "Because it's more than that. You two have unfinished business. Things to say to each other that, for some reason, neither of you are saying, and it's about time you did and stop dancing around each other—for both your sakes."

For both your sakes.

That was why we got divorced, why we ended this in the first place. To save both of us the pain we were causing each other. He couldn't stand to be in the same room with me unless we were having sex, and I couldn't handle knowing he didn't love me anymore.

We were at a painful crossroads and going different ways, and that's the way it would have stayed had I not stumbled upon what Perez was doing. More than likely, we never would have seen each other again, each living with the memories of our mistakes.

I squeeze my eyes closed and shake my head. "It's not that easy. When this is over, we'll just go our separate ways again."

She raises a dark eyebrow. "You really believe that? That

both of you are just going to walk away and go back to how things were before this mess with Perez?"

I nod and take a sip of wine.

Viktoria barks out another laugh and shakes her head, a smile curling her lips. "Let me clue you in on a little something I've learned during my many years interrogating suspects—"

"What? I'm a suspect now?"

She grins at me. "I'm going to tell you something I think is obvious, at least to someone like me who watches body language and knows how to find someone's *tell*. I'm sure whatever happened between you and Kalen hurt both of you in ways I can never fathom. I've seen Reaper struggling. So, I can imagine what it was like when they came back from that mission where Kalen and Mouth got hurt. That would have been right around the time you're talking about." She shakes her head. "These are not the type of men who are going to want to openly talk about their feelings or who will admit they've made mistakes, who are going to ask for forgiveness. That's something I knew the moment I met Reaper, and I'm sure you knew it.

"So, if you're waiting for him to tell you he's sorry and somehow make amends, it will never happen. You need to be the one to bridge the gap. You need to be the one to tell him how you feel."

"What if I don't know how I feel?"

Her green eyes roll, and she smirks. "Then you're lying. You know *exactly* how you feel. You just don't want to admit it to yourself or me."

I tighten my hand around the glass, staring down into the red liquid. Harsh memories assault me from every side, ones I've tried so hard to keep buried. "There are things Kalen doesn't know…"

She raises an eyebrow. "Things like what?"

Things I promised myself I would never voice, never tell anyone. Saying it out loud makes it real, forces me to face the pain and guilt, but at the same time, Viktoria feels like more of a friend than I've had in a long time. And she's spent far more time with Kalen than I have recently. She might be able to provide some insight.

"If I tell you, you have to promise *never* to tell Kalen. If he ever found out, it would destroy him."

She slowly lowers her glass from her lips and sets it on the counter. "This sounds serious."

"It is. So, please, don't say anything. You can't."

I'm not even sure I can say this.

"I promise. I won't."

I inhale slowly, closing my eyes for a moment to try to center myself and keep from crying before I even get out the words that I've kept bottled up for so long.

A car door slams outside, and Viktoria rushes toward the window and peeks out between the blinds. "It's them." She turns back to me. "You have about thirty seconds before they get up here. So, if you want to get this off your chest, do it quickly."

Thirty seconds to drop this bomb.

But the words are already there, sitting on the tip of my tongue, waiting and ready. I let them rush out as fast as I can before the knob turns and the door pushes open.

Viktoria stares at me, mouth hung open slightly as Kalen, Reaper, and Mouth enter.

Kalen's gaze darts between the two of us, brow furrowed. "What's wrong?"

Everything.

And now, I don't even have time to explain anything to her.

Vik shakes her head and forces a smile. "Nothing. Everything's fine. Avery was just getting worried about you guys."

She turns to me. "I told you there was nothing to worry about."

I swallow thickly, trying to prevent the tears from falling. "I know."

It's a lie.

There are so many things to worry about—too many to count.

12

AVERY

As soon as the door closes behind Reaper, Viktoria, and Mouth, Kalen throws the lock and turns to me, arms crossed over his chest. "Tell me what's wrong."

I take a sip of my wine and turn back toward the kitchen so he can't see my face and read me like an open book the way he always has. "I told you...nothing. I was just worried." I offer a little half-smile over my shoulder as I put the cap back on the wine bottle and return it to the fridge. "But you're back now, so—"

"You're lying."

Shit.

I jerk upright at his voice so close to me, my heart hammering in my chest. The damn man moves like a ghost. I hadn't even noticed he came up behind me. Slowly, I turn around to find him only inches from my face. His tall, powerful body dwarfs mine, his anger evident in his stance and the set of his shoulders.

"Do you think I'm stupid, Avery? You think I don't know

you well enough to know when you're lying? When you're keeping something from me?" He shakes his head, offering a sardonic grin. "Plus, Viktoria did a shit job hiding her face when we walked in. What were you two talking about? What's wrong?"

I shake my head, looking at the cracked linoleum floor rather than at him. "Please, Kalen. Just drop it. It was nothing."

He uses his calloused hand to lift my chin until my eyes meet his. "Don't lie to me, Avery. I have *never* lied to you."

Bullshit.

I could call him out on *that* lie. I could tell him he lied when he told me he would love me forever. When he told me he would never leave. When he told me I would never be alone again. But that would just start a massive fight we don't need to have right now, not with everything else going on.

It doesn't matter anymore. What does is that he and the guys are safe while trying to keep *me* safe.

They remained suspiciously silent about what happened tonight and the plan going forward when they got back, and Kalen ushered them out before anything was said about it, leaving me in the dark with the confession I had just made to Viktoria.

One I wish I could take back now that it's out in the world, and one I can't reveal to Kalen. His demand that I come clean will only end in more pain.

"Please tell me what happened tonight, Kalen. Did you find Perez?"

He studies me for a moment, hand still clutching my chin, almost like he's debating whether or not to let his line of questioning go and my aversion slide. "We didn't get Perez. But we will. We're leaving tomorrow. We'll be gone for a few days this time. You don't need to worry about what happens next."

The wine churns in my stomach, suddenly harsh and acidic when it had been so fruity and delicious only moments ago. "A few days?" That can only mean one thing. "Are you going to Mexico?"

His jaw hardens, and he slowly releases my chin, almost reluctantly pulling his hand away. "That's where he went. So, that's where we're going."

"But you *can't*. If he's connected to a cartel, there's no way you can go up against them." I shake my head. "Just no. You can't go!"

He takes a step toward me, and I instinctively back away until my shoulders hit the refrigerator behind me—not because I fear he will hurt me, but because I fear what I will do if I let the man get close to me again.

"I told you I was going to protect you, that I would make this guy pay for what he did. If that means going to Mexico and taking out fifty of his fucking men, I'll do it. I'll do anything to keep you safe."

"But there are only three of you."

"We're calling in some help, babe. I promise—everything's gonna be okay."

Everything's gonna be okay...

He has said those words to me so many times over the years, made that promise, yet I have a hard time believing anything he says. Not when he returned full of holes and acting like a totally different person. Not when he's looking me in the eyes with an intensity that can only be Chaos when what I want to see is Kalen.

"Do you believe me, Avery? Do you trust that I'll fix this?"

"I know you'll try, but if you got hurt or—"

His hand circles my bicep and tightens. "Listen to me... that's not going to happen. We're going to go down there. We're going to remove the threat, and we're going to come the fuck home."

I close my eyes and take a shaky breath to keep from releasing a sob or calling him out on the truth. He and I both know there's a chance he won't come back. There's a chance none of them will, but he needs to hear me say I believe it. He needs the confidence that I'll be okay while he's gone and won't worry myself sick over something I can't control.

He needs me to lie.

I open my eyes and meet his hard sapphire gaze again. "Okay. I believe you'll take care of things, come back, and everything will be fine."

"Exactly."

We stand, staring at each other for what feels like forever. Familiar tension twists at my core the longer he keeps his blue eyes on me. They gleam with a hunger for something, but not for anything in the goddamn fridge behind me.

He might not return, and we both need what one more night together can give us—even *if* it's another mistake, even if both of us know it.

His lips crash against mine, heated and frantic, needy and desperate, as one hand cups my cheek and angles my head, and the other slides from my arm down across my hip to grip me there. He molds his body to mine, pressing me harder against the refrigerator, his tongue probing and seeking what both of us are looking for.

I wrap my arms around his neck, holding him to me, refusing to let him retreat even a fraction of an inch. Because if he does, it feels like I'll lose him forever. And even though I might not have any choice about that happening tomorrow, I'm not going to let it happen tonight.

Not when I can have this one more time with him.

His hand drops from my hip to between my legs, cupping me and sending a jolt of pleasure through me. I groan into his mouth and pull him impossibly closer, grinding down on his palm, ravenous for what my body needs.

This won't be slow and sweet; this will be how it always was after that deployment. It will be hard and fast. It will be all Chaos, but even if that's all I can get from him, I'll take it greedily.

I drop my hands from his neck to undo his jeans and shove them down his hips as he continues to work me up. My arousal seeps through my thong and pants, almost embarrassingly wet for the man who always knew just how to touch me to make me fly on a cloud of bliss.

He pulls his hand away long enough to shove the material covering me down to my ankles, and I haphazardly try to kick them off while stroking his cock between us.

A low, rumbling groan falls from his lips against mine, and he rolls his hips, driving his length into my firm grip. He fucks my hand, his body seeking that which I'm more than willing to give.

His hands move to my hips, and he lifts me easily to wrap my legs around his waist and align him with my slick core. He drives up into me in one long, hard thrust, fulling impaling me on his dick and slamming me to the unyielding fridge behind me.

I cling to his neck, digging my nails into his nape and tightening my pussy around him. He moans and plunges into me again, hitting that spot that makes my mouth fall open on a gasp.

"Yes! God, Kalen…Please, just like that. Don't ever stop."

CHAOS

Don't ever stop…

If we lived in a perfect world, I never would. I would fuck this woman to endless orgasms until we both die—content and in each other's arms, my dick still buried inside her for eternity.

But this isn't a perfect world.

It's a harsh reality.

One where we can never be together, where it isn't safe, where what we want must be ignored for what is *right*.

Christ, this feels right, though.

It always has with Avery.

From the moment she smiled at me in algebra, I knew I was a fucking goner for this woman. I got lost in her green eyes then, the same way I do now, like I'm surrounded by a forest full of towering pines engulfing me and preventing the outside world from invading.

All the threats, all the pain, all the lies and silent truths melt away.

Every drive of my hips cements me further inside her, secures the connection that's always been there even more. That can never be broken—not by time, not by distance, not by our best efforts to shatter it. Her cunt ripples around my cock, sucking me in deeper, begging me to stay inside her forever the same way her words did.

I would if I could.

Nothing has ever felt as good as her body cocooning mine. No sound as beautiful as our shared breaths and moans. No taste as addictive as her mouth or as divine as her cunt and release on my tongue.

Avery is *everything*, and I'll do anything for her—even die if that's what it takes to ensure she's safe. But in this moment, I can't think about what will happen in the next few days or what *might* happen after that. All that matters is her nails scoring the back of my neck, my name tumbling from her lips, the rolling of her hips to meet my thrusts, and the way she looks at me—the endless sea of green clouded with lust.

Her heels dig into my lower back, urging me forward,

demanding I move faster and harder. She chases her release the same way I do the dregs of society, the people who think they have no one to answer to and do whatever they want regardless of the consequences or who gets hurt. I always succeed at my missions, and I refuse to fail when it comes to Avery.

The harder I ram into her, the more frantic she becomes, her nails biting into my neck, chest heaving against mine, breaths short and hot, her skin ablaze with the heat of our connection.

How did I ever walk away from this woman?

It's a stupid question, but one I can't stop from running endlessly through my head with every drive of my hips.

A beautiful, loyal, giving woman who never asked me for anything but to love her...

And I destroyed it because I had to.

Because I had no choice.

And I'll walk away again when all this is over. But I'll leave with the memory of *this.* Of being inside her again, of her cunt clasping me, drawing me inside her, of needing me the same way I do her.

Her mouth falls open, head dropped back against the fridge, tossing side to side. "Kalen, please, I can't..."

She can't get there.

The explosive releases we both seek are so close, within sight and reach, but she's holding back again, just as she did last night. She's fighting it, allowing something else to interfere.

Whether that be her fear of what will happen when we leave tomorrow, her knowledge that this will be the last time we're together, or whatever she and Viktoria were talking about that she refuses to tell me, it's keeping her from finding the bliss she seeks.

Moving my hand from her hip, I bring it to her face and

grip her chin, holding it in place as I still inside her. "Open your eyes, Avery. Look at me."

Her lids flutter, and her lips part slightly on a frustrating groan. "Why did you stop?"

"Because you need to let go."

She shakes her head, tears shimmering in her eyes. "No, I can't. I—"

I drag my hips back slowly and then drive into her hard, ramming her against the fridge door. "Let. Go." I plunge into her again, using long, slow strokes. "Whatever it is. It isn't important. Not right now. Let." I thrust again. "It." Once more. "Go."

A tiny mewl falls from her lips, and a tear slowly descends on her pale cheek. "I can't. There's something you need to know. I should have—"

I silence her with a kiss, ending whatever confession she feels compelled to give me. There isn't anything she could say that would change the past or what has to happen in the future.

I'm leaving tomorrow, and I'm going to do whatever it takes to protect her. And right now, I'm going to do whatever it takes to make her come. So I can see that weight lift off her shoulders on a cloud of ecstasy and feel her pussy clenching on my cock.

I ghost my lips across hers softly, rolling and grinding my hips to hers, building the rhythm with languid strokes at just the right angle. "Just let it go, baby. For me. I want you to come for me."

"Oh, God…" Her lips tremble against mine, her hips moving faster, her hands clinging to my neck. "I can't, Kalen. I can't let you go. Not ever…"

Her words slice at my heart, making my strokes falter.

She doesn't mean it.

Not after all this time. Not after all the pain I've caused

her. It's the adrenaline flooding her system, the combination of her trauma and her body being primed and ready to explode that made those words come from her lips.

Letting go is the only option.

For both of us.

So, I redouble my efforts, kissing her like she's my oxygen while I pound into her relentlessly, pinning her in place with my body and my desire to give her one moment of freedom from whatever haunts her.

I know all too well what living with ghosts is like.

She doesn't need to ever know that pain.

Someone as perfect as she is inside and out should only ever know hope and beauty.

And with one final thrust, she finally gasps and gives herself over to her release, her pussy rippling and clenching at my cock, pulling my own orgasm from deep inside.

I empty myself into her, spilling not only my cum but also all the things I wish I could tell her, all the agony I've lived with every day since we've been apart, the truths that can never be spoken. She jerks in my arms, her body spasming and her head dropping back as she rides out the wave of pleasure coursing through her.

She finally sags against me, burying her face into my neck, her warm breath tickling my already-heated skin. I wrap my arms around her, clutching her to me, holding her like I never will again.

Because there's a good chance I won't.

We're leaving for an almost-impossible mission tomorrow, and if I don't come back, I want to remember this moment as I take my final breath.

CHAOS

For the first time since I became a professional soldier, my hand shakes. I switch my gun to my left hand for a moment to flex the right one, trying to stop the annoying quaking.

Reaper looks over at me, concern raising his brows. "You okay?"

No fucking way.

It would be impossible to be okay with everything that's going on.

I nod anyway. "Yeah."

He narrows his eyes on me but doesn't say anything else. And he doesn't have to. He sees right through my bullshit, just like he always could. Just like Avery always could.

She's the reason for all of this.

The reason we had to call in Cutter and Flash to help. The reason we had to hop on that shitty little plane and sneak across the border armed to the fucking teeth. The reason my hand is shaking now.

Every mission I ever went on was important, essential, crucial for one reason or another. A move against a serious threat. Rescuing someone innocent. Protecting everyone back home. There was always a compelling reason for what we were doing. One that allowed me to pull the trigger without a second thought. But none of those reasons were ever so personal.

My action, my success or failure, never meant life or death to anyone I care about as much as I do Avery, which is why, for the first time in my life, my nerves feel fucking frayed, destroyed, utterly shot.

It has nothing to do with the fact that we're about to take on one of the nastiest cartels in Mexico or that we're doing it outnumbered. Over the last few days, Preacher and Cutter have been able to uncover more information about the men who control Merida, the ones connected to Perez, and all of it is wicked. These men don't play around, and they're armed to the teeth.

But none of that ever really mattered with any mission we went on. When it came down to getting the job done, we did it—short on supplies, short on men, somehow, we always managed. And we have to again—Avery's life depends on it.

"Does anyone have a visual on Perez?" I scan the open courtyard below me that's crawling with cartel men armed with ARs and looking ready for a fight.

The only things going for us are our superior training and the fact that they will likely never anticipate that anyone will be stupid enough to attack them on their home turf, to come to their compound and try to stand against them.

"Negative."

"Negative."

Nothing from Cutter or Flash, and Mouth signals no through the com, from their watch points, but it doesn't mean the fucker isn't here. If he isn't outside, then he has to be inside the main house or one of the out buildings of the compound.

Preacher was able to use some of his sources to confirm Perez returned to Merida in the last few days and was seen heading out this way. Though the people here don't want to talk about what goes on here. The fear the cartel has instilled is very real. Taking them out won't just help Avery; it will help the entire area.

All we have to do is get him in our crosshairs and eliminate anyone else connected to this group who sets foot on the compound.

The sun finally sinks below the horizon, casting the entire valley into darkness. Spotlights blink to life around the compound, illuminating the perimeter so the cartel members can keep an eye on any potential threats.

Two men at the massive, iron front gates stand together, smoking a cigarette and chatting about something that has them both tossing their heads back and laughing.

You won't be laughing much longer, fuckers.

From what we've been able to piece together from our recon over the last two days, as many as twenty-two men occupy and control the compound at any given time.

We've had worse odds.

I glance at my watch anxiously. The sooner this is over, the sooner we can get back and return to our normal lives— helping people by doing the only thing we're good at—this.

We may not be heroes, but we're all some people have, including Avery. I was all she ever had after her grandfather died. Between a non-existent father and drug-addicted mother, she didn't have anyone she could rely on, except me. I told her I would never leave, yet that's what I did. She may have been the one who filed those papers, but I was the one who forced her hand.

I didn't leave her a choice.

But it's a decision I'd make again and again to protect her because that's always going to be my job. Even if we're not married, even if we're not together. Even if we live on opposite sides of the country. I'll always watch out for her in any way I can, even if seeing her and not having her kills me slowly every day.

My watch clicks over to the designated time, and the shots ring out in perfect unison. All the floodlights shatter and go black, and the men guarding the exterior succumb to bullets themselves. Between Mouth and Flash both taking aim, those men didn't stand a chance, and now, we have the benefit of darkness.

It's where we live, where we thrive, where I become Chaos.

Reaper, Cutter, Flash, and I descend toward the canyon, eyes locked on the various buildings, waiting for the resistance to emerge because these aren't the type of men who are going to go down without resistance.

That's okay. We enjoy the fight. It gets our blood pumping and makes us feel alive. We're ready to bring it to them. Any thoughts of Avery have been replaced by Chaos' absolute focus and need to destroy any threats.

I hustle with Reaper toward the main house, the most likely place Perez will be hiding, while Cutter and Flash clear the outbuildings and the rest of the compound with Mouth providing cover.

The house looms in front of us, a grand, opulent villa fit for a king, but according to Preacher, whoever is running this cartel has gone to great lengths to keep their identity hidden. Unusual considering most cartel heads flaunt their wealth and power publicly to keep people living in constant fear.

Whoever this guy is, he's now harboring our primary

target, and no amount of firepower is going to keep us from bringing him to justice.

Reaper and I pause just outside the back kitchen door we've chosen as our entry point and wait. Humans are predictable, especially dumb ones, and most of the men in this cartel are just muscle, only here to intimidate and blindly pull the trigger when told. They'll come running straight to us now that they've heard the shots.

Heavy footsteps just inside the door confirm I'm right, and it flies open without any concern for what's on the other side. The second the first man steps through, I put a bullet through his temple while Reaper fires into his friend directly behind him.

They both drop to the ground, and we grab their weapons and move immediately past them, sweeping through the back hallway and toward the main portion of the house.

Gunfire sounds somewhere outside, likely Cutter and Flash in one of the other buildings.

Kitchen…clear.

Office…clear.

Living room…clear.

We head down the hallway toward the bedrooms, but something on the wall catches my eye, and I freeze. I signal for Reaper to stop and motion toward the photo of Perez with his arm around a familiar face.

Holy shit.

I clench my jaw and tighten my grip on my weapon.

We thought Perez wouldn't want his mistake known to the cartel because it would make him a target, but he doesn't have to worry about that. Because this is all in the family…

The cartel.

The house.

The land.

It all belongs to Perez and the man standing next to him who looks so much like him that they're certainly brothers and potentially even twins.

Now we've got two of them to worry about.

Fuck.

We make our way down the hall, clearing each empty bedroom until we finally reach a massive set of double doors that must lead to the master suite.

If he's here, that's the only place he can still be. I reach out to open the heavy wood separating us from our target, and gunfire tears through it. Reaper and I dive to the side, pressing our backs flat to the wall, but I'm not quick enough, and pain sears through my arm, the bullet embedding deep in the flesh.

Fuck.

Gritting my teeth, I check Reaper, who appears fine.

He nods toward my arm. "You okay?"

I nod.

Not really.

The pain spreads up my arm and through my shoulder, blood immediately flowing, but I push it to the back of my mind to focus on the threat on the other side of the now-destroyed door.

Reaper signals what he wants me to do, and we wait for the tell-tale sound of an empty magazine. Whoever is shooting has to reload, which gives us an opening.

We both turn toward the wood that now looks like Swiss cheese, and Reaper kicks it open in one hard motion. It shatters easily, and we fire without hesitation, Reaper taking the left side of the room, me the right.

I unleash a torrent of bullets at whoever might be in here. One man cries out and crumples to the floor. Two more drop, taking cover from our assault behind a massive bed in the center of the room, but now that they've had time to reload, Reaper and I advance and peg them off before they can fire again.

Three down.

I scan the space quickly for any other threats, but it's silent and empty save for the regal furnishings.

Where the hell is Perez?

Reaper follows me down a small hallway that must lead to the ensuite. A brief flash of movement to my left is the only warning I get before another bullet slams into me, hitting me square in the chest.

I stagger, the blow thankfully striking my vest. It knocks all the air from my lungs, but I return fire as I stumble back, my shoulders hitting the wall behind me. Reaper returns a single shot from my right and hits my assailant.

The man lands on the carpet inside the closet where he was hiding, and I struggle to suck in a breath, agony engulfing my chest and arm. Reaper enters the closet and stands over the guy, and I push my feet, still unable to breathe, and struggle over to them on shaking legs.

I'm not about to let a bullet stop me from getting to this fucker. Pushing Reaper out of the way, I brace myself against the doorjamb and stare down at the man on the floor.

He rolls over toward us, a bloody, sinister smile on his face. It could be Perez, or it could be his brother. Either way, it doesn't matter. Both need to go for this world to be rid of the true threats.

"You think you've won?" He shakes his head as blood bubbles from his lips, the gaping wound in his chest a definite death shot. "You haven't done anything."

I press my foot down onto his chest, directly over the wound, ensuring the most pain possible. "Who are you?"

He tries to laugh, but all that comes out is a strangled, gurgling sound. "The question is…who are *you?*" He coughs up more blood and shifts uncomfortably under my foot. "You're too late, Kalen Riggs."

My name coming from his lips makes Reaper and me freeze.

"How the hell do you know my name?"

A slow grin spreads across his crimson lips. "You aren't the only one with powerful friends, Mr. Riggs. Friends who can find anyone, anywhere. Even your ex-wife."

"Fuck."

AVERY

VIKTORIA PEEKS out the window again, staring at the quiet street, chewing on her lip, her foot bouncing up and down. "Something's wrong."

Pulling my knees to my chest on the recliner, I hug them close and rest my head on them, watching the woman who is usually so calm slowly start to unravel. "I thought I was the one who was supposed to be unnecessarily nervous."

She looks at me with a furrowed brow and shakes her head. "This isn't unnecessarily." Her eyes dart to her watch, her lips twisting into a frown. "We should have heard from them by now."

The last two days have been pure agony waiting for a word from Reaper and Kalen—nothing but pacing and worrying and imagining every horrific scenario possible. It's hard not knowing what they're walking into and going up against.

I've done my best to try not to overthink it, to remain calm and trust that Kalen will make it back like he promised.

He said it would take a few days for them to do their recon and go in, so we really don't have any reason to be worried yet—at least, that's what I keep telling myself. "Maybe they don't have anything to update us with?"

Vik shakes her head. "No. Reaper has been texting me updates every few hours, and he said they were going in tonight and would get in touch with me before they got on the plane to head back."

I check the clock on the microwave. "It's only midnight. Maybe they got held up?"

She chews on her cheek, letting the blinds fall closed and wandering back toward me. "You know I'm not one to over-react, but after what happened with them when we were in New York, I'm a little leery about this whole *going up against an entire cartel* thing."

"What happened in New York?"

For all I know about Kalen, his life over the last four years is a complete mystery to me, and I haven't had the guts to ask him about it. Whatever Vik is referencing seems important, though, and God knows Kalen will likely never tell me a word of it.

Vik paces the room, continually glancing at her phone on the counter. "Reaper, Mouth, Chaos, and I took down a Russian human trafficking ring."

"You *what?*"

She offers a humorless smile. "Yeah, it's a long story, but needless to say, I witnessed first-hand what the guys are capable of, but I also saw Reaper almost die. He barely made it out of that mission alive, and these aren't some local thugs they're up against." Vik pauses, offering a half-smile. "I'm really trying to stop myself from having a total meltdown."

"You don't think something happened, do you?"

Her lips pressed together in a firm line, she shakes her head. "I don't know." She sucks in a deep breath. "No. They're fine. They're professionals. They know what to do and how to do it. I just have to trust they're okay and there's some valid reason Reaper hasn't gotten in touch yet."

"Yes, do that." I give her what I hope is a reassuring smile. "I know it's hard when you're worrying about someone you love."

Vik nods slowly. "Reaper and I are…complicated." She laughs lightly. "Though, not nearly as complicated as you and Chaos."

"Isn't that the truth?" I sigh and lean back in the chair, letting my eyes drift closed. Barely sleeping for days is taking its toll, but I know I won't be able to until I'm confident they're all safe.

"Have you given any more thought to talking to Chaos when he gets back?"

She doesn't need to clarify *what* I should be talking to him about. The last few days have given me time to completely come clean to Viktoria about what I've been keeping from Kalen…and to explain why.

"It's all I've been able to think about. It gives me something else to obsess over other than my worry."

Her humorless laugh fills the small apartment. "Oh, God, aren't we a pair?"

"You know why I can't ever tell him…"

It's the same debate I've been having in circles—both with myself and with Vik since the guys left. If Kalen comes out of this alive, I can't destroy him with the truth. It would be too painful for him to overcome.

"I think you need to give him some credit and trust he can handle it."

"Like you need to trust that they're okay and will call when they can?"

A grin tugs at her lips. "Touché."

Almost as if in answer to my comment, her phone rings

and vibrates across the counter. She rushes the last few steps and grabs it while I hold my breath.

"Reaper…what's the status?"

She turns back to me, her eyes wide.

I shift upright, my entire body tensing, seeing the panic in her gaze. "What's wrong?"

Holding up a hand to silence me, she shakes her head. "Okay." She hustles toward the window and peeks out the blinds again. "I understand." She ends the call, slides her phone into her pocket, and stares at the street in front of the repair shop. "Get your shoes on."

"What?" A chill spreads over my skin, instantly eliminating the confidence I tried to hold so tightly only moments ago. "What do you mean?"

"Get your shoes on." Her words come out sharp, like an order from a cop, not a request from a friend. "Now!"

I shake my head, trying to figure out what's happening as she pulls her gun from the holster at her hip. "What's going on?"

She snaps her head toward me. "Get your fucking shoes on. We have to *go*."

"Go?" I push up from the chair, my legs shaking. My heart stops as I try to process what's happening. "Go where? What the hell is going on?"

Viktoria flicks off the safety on her gun and checks the window. "They guys are on their way to the plane right now, but they think Perez knows where you are."

"What? How is that possible?"

I was supposed to be *safe* here. Kalen said there was no way this place could be traced to him, even if anyone ever connected us.

How could Ricardo have found me here?

Viktoria shakes her head. "I don't know. They just said to

get the fuck out. So, that's what we're doing. We'll figure it out later."

"Oh, God…" I press my hand over my mouth to keep myself from vomiting. "Are they okay? Are they meeting us somewhere?"

She rushes toward the kitchen, grabs her keys off the counter, and heads back toward the window. "Shoes. *Now!*"

Shoes.

Get shoes.

I stumble on unsteady feet toward the bedroom, grab my shoes from the floor just inside the door, and slip them on as I approach her near the window. It hasn't gone unnoticed that she didn't respond to my question. "Answer me, Viktoria. Are they okay?"

Her hard gaze meets mine for a second. "Kalen has been shot."

It's the second time I've heard those words. The first time was the beginning of the end of our marriage, and now, it feels like I'm about to lose him completely.

The room tunnels around me, my vision going black around the edges, and I stumble forward and press my hand to the wall to stop from falling over. "Oh, my God…is he…"

She shakes her head. "I don't know. We can't worry about that right now. It's out of our control. I have to get you out of here. You're my primary concern."

"But—"

Her hand tightens around my arm. "No *buts*. Move." She motions for me to head toward the door but then freezes. "Shit."

"What is it?"

Viktoria's body stiffens, her laser focus down at the street. "We're about to have company that doesn't look too friendly."

Bullets tear through the front of the window, shattering the glass and throwing fragments at us. Viktoria lunges toward me, knocking me to the floor and covering me with her body.

Another volley of bullets punches through the wall and soar through the now-open window, slamming into the opposite side of the room, tearing into Kalen's chair and the kitchen counter.

My heart thunders against my ribs, my ears ringing from the shots.

Vik pushes on my back. "Stay down."

"Wh-what do we do?"

She crawls back toward the window and reaches up to fire out. "Go into the bedroom. See if you can get out the window."

"What? I can't leave you!"

"Yes, you can!" She glares at me, then turns and fires off a few more rounds toward whoever is outside. "If you can't get out, you *hide* like your damn life depends on it."

Pushing aside the fear threatening to paralyze me, I scramble across the worn wooden floor, staying as low as I can, tears streaming down my face, blurring my vision. My hand hits the bedroom door. I nudge it open and crawl inside, slamming the door behind me before I reach up with a shaking hand and flip the lock.

Don't ever lock that fucking door again.

Kalen's voice rings in my ears, and a sob climbs up my throat. I clamp my hand over my mouth and scan the room. The window is far too small for me to fit out of, and the mattress rests on the floor—no bed to hide under.

My eyes land on Kalen's footlocker. Without even thinking, I race over to it, throw it open, and freeze. A photo of us sits atop his clothes, our much-younger, smiling faces staring back at me as if to taunt me with the time when we were so naïve and hopeful.

He has to be okay.

He has to come back to me.

I shove the stack of clothes to the side to make room, then climb in and curl up inside the tight space, resting my head on the shirts that used to bring me so much comfort, heavy with his scent. This has held Kalen's personal possessions since the day he enlisted, the only place he keeps the things most important to him. And now, it's my only hope to save my own life.

My fingers curl around the picture frame, and I clutch it to my chest, slapping my other hand over my mouth to stop myself from crying out in a way that might give away where I'm hiding.

The gunfire stops—the only sounds, my own breathing and the blood rushing in my ears. I strain to hear anything else through the closed box, any clues about what might be happening to Vik in the living room.

Sharp cracks…gunshots.

Closer this time.

Vik!

I bite back the sob and squeeze my eyes closed, willing myself to remain silent. Holding my breath, I wait in the pitch-black confines of what might become my coffin.

Heavy footsteps…

A loud bang, the bedroom door being broken down…

Indistinguishable words in Spanish…

I continue to hold my breath, clinging to the photo like I am my hope that Kalen is all right.

Please, God, let them just go…

The lid jerks opens, and I lash out with the picture frame, the only weapon I have, but strong hands reach down to grab me and jerk me to my feet.

A split second later, the world goes dark again.

14

AVERY

The world around me slowly comes back into focus. Hazy light breaking through the darkness, but with it comes pain. A constant throbbing in my right temple unlike anything I've ever felt before. Wincing, I try to reach up for it, but the sharp bite of something binding my hands behind me digs into my wrists.

"What the hell?" My voice comes out rough and tortured, like I've been drinking gravel or screaming endlessly.

I open my eyes slowly, my vision fuzzy and the room around me tilting as if on a ship riding vicious waves on an unsettled ocean. Flashes of beige carpet. An unfamiliar dark wooden bed. Brown drapes over a tall window.

Where the hell am I?

"Good morning, Avery." Ricardo's familiar voice jerks me fully awake and back to the present. "You've been out for quite a while."

The memories of what happened last night come flooding

back, threatening to overwhelm me at once, and I twist my neck, scanning the unfamiliar room and trying to find him.

He leans against a doorframe to my right, watching me with a smug tilt of his lips, arms crossed over his chest, in his usual pristine white dress shirt and perfectly pressed black slacks.

It's the same thing he wore every day—always well-dressed, always poised, always *perfect.*

How did I not see it?

How did I not know what he was doing?

I swallow through my dry, scratchy throat. "What do you want? Where's Vik?"

He raises a dark eyebrow. "Is that the other woman at your husband's place? I'm pretty sure she's bled out by now."

No!

The nonchalance with which he says the words twist a knife into my gut, and I gasp against the physical pain. New tears fall on my cheeks, and I shake my head, squeezing my eyes shut, refusing to accept what he says as true. "No, she's can't be. She can't…"

Ricardo pushes off the doorjamb and slowly walks toward me, casually, like he didn't just admit to having Viktoria killed on top of everything else I know he's done.

This man is a monster, one disguised as a caring, upstanding family man with a thriving business that helps immigrants and those struggling to make their American dreams come true.

I never knew what evil looked like until today, until I saw the man I used to eat lunch across from, used to laugh with, used to *trust*, look back at me with such blank disinterest. Ricardo doesn't care what happens to me. I'm nothing more than an obstacle to him—one to be removed by any means necessary.

He stops in front of me and offers me the same smile he

has for years. His hard eyes soften slightly, and he shakes his head and *tsks.* "It really is too bad you and Amelia stumbled upon what you did. You always did a very good job for me."

"What do you want? Why haven't you just killed me? You've already tried."

He nods slowly. "I'm impressed you got away from Manuel. He's very good at his job, but you outsmarted him." A grin spreads across his lips. "Impressive. Did you learn that from your husband?"

"Ex-husband."

"Right." He grins again. "I saw the divorce decree when I was digging into your background, trying to figure out where you might have run off to after you saw what you did." He paces in front of me, hands crossed behind his back. "You have cost me a lot of good men."

"Why did you kill Amelia?"

"Come now, Avery." Ricardo shakes his head. "I couldn't let her keep digging into where the money was coming from. You and I both know that."

I release a sob and drop my head. "You didn't have to kill her."

He squats in front of me and lifts my chin with a firm finger. "I did. But as soon as I get some answers from you, you'll see her again."

His words slowly click in my head.

"That's why you haven't killed me...you *need* something from me."

He smiles again. "Your ex-husband and his friends have caused me a lot of trouble over the last few days. I need all their names. Ways to find them. Because I'm certain they're smart enough not to go back to his place now that we discovered it—which wasn't easy, by the way. It took days of analyzing red light camera footage to figure out what vehicles were in the area of *South of the Border* before it was destroyed, then following them around town via other cameras to narrow down a location."

That's how they found Kalen's place.

We underestimated Ricardo and his resources. Preacher is our computer wizard, but it seems Ricardo has at least one of his own helping him in this sinister endeavor.

I refuse to give him anything that will assist him, no matter *what* he threatens to do to me. "I'm not telling you anything."

Ricardo chuckles and shakes his head. "They all say that, but let me tell you something, Avery. Everyone, and I mean *everyone,* talks, even the most well-trained men from some of the most violent families." A softness overtakes his gaze, and for a split second, I see the man I have known all these years. "I don't want to have to do it, Avery, but I will do what I must to get you to talk."

I have no doubt he means it and will inflict serious pain to get what he wants, but I'm willing to endure anything to protect the guys. "I don't know anything. Honestly. He always kept me in the dark to protect me."

He nods slowly. "Smart man, but you probably know more than you think you do, and once I'm confident I have all the information you can offer me, I'll end your suffering."

"They'll come for me, you know."

A low, dark laugh rumbles in his chest. "They'll never find you here."

Footsteps sound in the hallway just outside the bedroom, and a man enters the room, stoic, holding a phone. "Sir, something's happened at the compound."

Perez stands, looks at me without saying a word, and moves to the hall, putting his back to me. He speaks with someone on the phone, his body stiffening. When he turns back to me, he's a completely different man.

Eyes now cold and emotionless.

Body tense.

Fists at his sides.

This is the *true* Ricardo Perez. The part of himself he managed to conceal from me, from Amelia, from his own wife and children.

"Your ex-husband and his friends killed my brother in Mexico. Someone was just able to get word to me." His words vibrate with his anger. "I was just there, meeting with him to coordinate a response to the trouble you've caused. They only missed me by hours."

"Shitty luck."

His fist lashes out and slams into my jaw, snapping my head back and stealing my breath. I gasp, trying to suck in a breath through the agony, and he squats in front of me, jaw tight, flexing out the hand he just struck me with.

"Now, you are going to tell me everything you know. No more games. No more pleasantries. The time for all that has long passed."

CHAOS

THE CAR HITS A POTHOLE, jerking me violently across the back seat, and I grimace and grit my teeth against the pain threatening to make me black out. "Watch how you fucking drive, asshole. We barely got out of Mexico alive, and now, you're trying to kill me on the fucking way home."

Reaper glances at me in the rearview mirror, his jaw hard. "Shut up. If I *could* go any faster, I *would*, even if it fucking killed you."

He barrels through a red light, and a car lays on its horn, slamming its brakes to avoid T-boning us in the intersection.

"She's still not answering?"

Slipping in and out of consciousness since Reaper called Viktoria hours ago from Mexico has left me at a bit of a disadvantage in terms of knowing what the fuck is going on. I don't even know how long it's been since we landed.

He shakes his head. "She's not picking up."

The agony I feel matches what his words hold.

That fucker in Mexico said my name. He knew who I was and who Avery was to me, which means she and Viktoria are in danger. Not being able to get in touch with them during the agonizingly slow flight back has ratcheted up the tension on top of the fact that I seem intent on bleeding to death before we ever find them.

I push myself into a sitting position, and everything spins around me. Blood trickles down my arm despite the tourniquet and temporary patch we did on our way to the shitty airstrip we used to enter and leave Mexico.

Mouth turns back to look at me from the front passenger seat, a single eyebrow raised.

"I'm alive. That's all I got right now."

He nods and returns his focus to Reaper's phone in his hand, redialing Viktoria every few minutes as we try to make it back to my place.

The light in front of us turns red, and the cross-traffic speeds through the intersection in front of us. Reaper slams on the brakes, unable to make it across the sea of vehicles without killing all of us.

He punches his fist into the dashboard. "Why the fuck isn't she answering?"

"Maybe they're somewhere she can't. Hiding."

It's wishful thinking, but it's the only thing preventing me from either letting myself float off into the darkness threatening to encroach from all sides or to push Reaper out of that driver's seat and gun it straight through that traffic to try to find Avery.

If I didn't believe Viktoria would die before letting anything happen to Avery, I never would have left her. The fact that we can't reach them makes me heave again in the backseat.

The ring of Reaper's phone in Mouth's hand makes me jerk my head back up, and Mouth hands it to Reaper.

Reaper brings the phone to his ear, free hand tightening on the wheel. "Vik?" He listens for a moment, then his eyes widen. "What? Where is she? Is she okay?" He glances at both of us, panic in his gaze. "Okay, I'll be right there."

He ends the call, handing the phone back to Mouth. "That was Johns Hopkins. Viktoria was brought in with three gunshot wounds."

I shift forward slightly. "Fuck…"

"She's alive, but…"

"Avery?"

He shakes his head. "They brought her in alone. The woman at the hospital made the call from Vik's phone. She said she just dialed back the number she saw had been calling repeatedly. She doesn't know anything other than Viktoria was brought in and is being treated."

A vise tightens around my chest, making it impossible to breathe.

Reaper's knuckles whiten on the wheel. "We have to get to the hospital."

"No." I shake my head, trying to clear the panic and haze from blood loss. "I have to know what happened to Avery. She's…"

I can't even say the words.

She's everything to me…

If anything happens to her, it will spell the end for me. There wouldn't be anything left, no reason to keep going, to keep fighting for what's right.

The light turns green, and Reaper floors it. "We drive past

your place to see what's going on, then go straight to the hospital."

I hold my breath the rest of the drive there, unable to think, unable to feel, unable to do anything but picture Avery's lifeless body lying on the floor of my shitty apartment.

Reaper remains stoic and silent, and the closer we get to my street, the more tense I become, which only makes my arm hurt more and my heart threaten to stop beating with every passing block. Squad cars line the road ahead, preventing anyone from turning down toward my place.

I lean forward slightly, resting my good arm on the edge of Mouth's seat. "I need to know what happened up there."

Reaper pulls to the curb well short of the roadblock. "I need to get to Viktoria."

Mouth glances between us, and I nod at him.

"Get out. See what information you can get. Text us as soon as you know anything."

He nods and jumps from the car, jogging up to the road-block and then slowing down to walk casually toward the officers as Reaper makes a right-hand turn.

I relax back into my seat and dig into my bag on the floor for my gun. "I'm not going to the hospital with you."

Reaper glances at me in the rearview. "What?"

"I'm going after him."

He scowls at me. "You can barely sit up straight. You're not going after anyone."

I cinch the tourniquet around my arm even tighter. "I've got a few more hours before this gets lethal. I can't walk into the hospital with you like this, anyway."

"Shit." Reaper rubs at his nape with one hand and locks his gaze with mine in the mirror. "You don't want to wait for backup?"

"Go take care of your woman, and I'll go find mine."

My phone vibrates in my pocket, and I wince, shifting to my side to pull it out. "It's Mouth."

No coroner van.

A tiny bit of the weight threatening to crush my chest lifts. "He says there isn't a coroner van."

Reaper releases a relieved sigh. "So, she's not…"

"No."

At least, not yet.

If Perez's men went into my place intent on killing her, she would be dead. Which means, he wants something from her; he has some reason for keeping her alive—probably temporarily.

Police will only say it was a shooting. Single victim.

"Cops are saying single victim shooting."

Reaper nods. "So, Avery was gone before the cops got there. Do you think she got away?"

I shake my head. "I'd love to believe that, but I don't think so. She would have tried to find a way to get in touch with us, would have left us a message somehow. I think Perez's guys took her."

"Where?"

"Fuck if I know, but I do know where I can start. Give me the list."

Reaper peeks at me over his shoulder. "The list?"

I nod, and he leans over and pops the glove compartment, pulling out the list Preacher gave us of every property connected to Perez. *South of the Border* is already up in smoke, as is the warehouse where Perez did most of his dirty work. That scratches two addresses off the list, but it leaves almost a dozen others.

"I'll start with places he's most likely to take her, the businesses that aren't open or buildings that are remote, then work my way down the list." I squeeze Reaper's shoulder. "Text me with any updates once you see Vik."

He nods. "Drop me at the hospital and have Mouth come meet you."

I shake my head. "No, you need Mouth there watching the hospital in case they come for Viktoria again."

Reaper snarls at me, anger flashing in his eyes. "You can't go after them alone."

"I can, and I will. I'm getting Avery back, no matter what."

15

CHAOS

L*a Cantina* doesn't look any different than any of the other restaurants or buildings I've already visited and lit up tonight, trying to find Avery.

Trying…and failing.

Where the fuck are they?

Perez must have her *somewhere*, and this is the final building on the list from Preacher. If she isn't here…

No.

I can't even think that. If I start considering that possibility, my focus will be shot, and the belief that I will find her is the only thing keeping me from dropping to the fucking ground right now.

My body threatens to betray me, to give out when I'm determined to keep going. It's only happened one other time, and that was when my whole world went to shit. When I destroyed my life with Avery, when I blew up her world.

That won't happen again.

I refuse to fail tonight, refuse to fail *her*. Even if I have to crawl into this damn building and fight Perez with my one good arm, I'll fucking do it.

There isn't any other option *but* to succeed.

I climb from the car, wincing at the agony now engulfing the entire left side of my body, my arm essentially useless, hanging at my side. Physical pain, I can live with, but the thought of losing her, of *anything* happening to her, is far too much to bear.

Reaper must be completely losing his shit right now, waiting for word on Viktoria. Sitting at the hospital, helpless, while surgeons try to save her life. Perez will pay for what he did to her, just like he will for everything he's put Avery through. And if he's harmed one fucking hair on her head, I will rip his balls off and shove them down his throat until he chokes on them.

But I have to find the fucker first.

The building remains dark, the only lights small green dots on the cameras outside, facing the parking lot and street. They'll know I'm here, but it doesn't matter at this point. After what I've already done to all the other locations on the list, they have to know I'm coming.

It's been closed for hours, the employees long gone. Either Perez has her in there, or his men will be waiting to ambush me.

I make my way around the back, carrying my bag over my good shoulder, and disconnect the power to the building. Each step across the parking lot toward the rear entrance takes every ounce of strength I have left, but I manage to set the charge on the door and blow it, gaining entry.

Smoke still fills the air as I enter, gun ready, and scan the rear hallway and kitchen as I set the charges necessary to bring this place down.

Empty.

Storage room.

Empty.

Bathrooms.

Empty.

The entire fucking building...

Empty.

Just like my heart is knowing Avery's being held by that asshole and I can't find them. I've literally burned down his world, looking for her, destroyed everything, even killed his brother, and still, the thing that's most important to me is in his sick, twisted hands.

The room starts to spin, my vision blurring around the edges—no sleep and exertion over the last several days, combined with the blood loss and likely infection, create sheer havoc on my body.

I slowly lower myself to the tile floor of the kitchen and rest my head back against the fridge, releasing a long groan. Perez and his men may not have been waiting for me, but by now, they know I've taken out the rest of the restaurants and why.

All I have to do is wait, and soon rather than later, they'll come.

My phone buzzes in my pocket, and I lean to the side and pull it out to read the text from Reaper.

She's still in surgery. Might be a few more hours. Anya is on her way here.

Hell.

At least she's alive, though.

There's a chance.

Hope.

All I have is blind faith that Avery's alive and I can get to her in time.

I open my bag and ensure everything's ready for when Perez's men finally show up, and I fight the desire of my heavy eyelids to drift closed, instead focusing on the last few days with Avery.

It took her falling into something this bad to finally reach out to me because I hurt her so badly. She felt like she couldn't, *shouldn't* contact me, no matter how bad things may have been over the last four years. I had no idea how much she's been suffering. With all the harsh realities staring me in the face at that time, I thought what I did was right for her.

And I still do.

Once she's safe, I'll make sure she's far away from any form of danger again, even me. I'll get her set up somewhere new. Peaceful. Quiet. Somewhere she can restart her life without the pain I cause, where there isn't any chance she'll run afoul of anyone like Perez again.

Then, maybe, I can sleep, knowing she's safe.

The sound of an engine in the parking lot jerks me from my thoughts, and I tighten my grip on the weapon, waiting for whatever will be walking through that door.

Three car doors open and close outside, followed by hurried footsteps across the asphalt. As soon as the men round the corner of the building and step into the open doorway, I fire, taking out two with shots to the chest.

Where's the third?

I struggle to my feet and creep over to the door, checking to ensure they're not getting up. Kicking their weapons away, I press my back against the wall immediately to the side of the threshold and wait. Another minute passes, then another, before light footsteps finally move toward me.

Come on, fucker.

The man pauses just outside, looking down at his friends. He cautiously steps over their bodies to enter, gun held out in front of him. I fire one shot into his hand, and the weapon immediately tumbles on top of the bodies.

He cries out, and I wrap my good arm around his neck,

transferring my weapon to the other while ignoring the pain the movement causes. I drag him back, applying pressure on his windpipe and airway. He claws at me with his one good hand, the other hanging at his side, half of it blown off, blood dripping onto the tile.

I press my back against the wall and crank on his neck harder, fighting my desire to end him immediately. That will get me nowhere.

"Where is she?"

The man gasps for air, twisting his head to try to relieve the tension on his airway. "Don't...know..."

I crank my arm tighter. "Where. Is. She?"

His legs start to give out, and I ease up slightly before he passes out and is of no use to me. "I-I don't know who you're talking about."

Fucking liar.

"I can make this very painful for you"—I retighten my hold, pressing on his airway and artery—"until I get the information I want."

He tries to scream, attempts to plead for his life, but all that comes out are gasps and indistinguishable words.

"Tell me where your boss is."

His body stiffens slightly. He *might* not know who Avery is or where she is, but he knows where the man himself is, and if I find Perez, I'll find her.

"Tell me."

"A house." He swallows thickly against my arm. "Down on Umbra..."

"That's all I needed to know."

I force my almost dead arm up, press the barrel to his temple, and pull the trigger. He immediately goes limp in my arms, and I drop it unceremoniously like a rag doll, step over it, and grab my bag. Without a second look at the corpses, I step over them and walk away from *La Cantina* with renewed energy and hope.

That and adrenaline are the only things keeping me going at this point.

I hustle to the SUV, start it, and press the detonator switch for the charges I set inside. The place erupts, flames leaping into the dark sky, the bodies of Perez's men engulfed along with the last vestiges of his business here in the area.

Now all that's left is him.

***

AVERY

MY ENTIRE BODY SHAKES, my teeth rattling together as I fight passing out again. The coppery tang of blood fills my mouth from my split lip. I gag on it and spit it onto the carpet under the chair where the madman I once trusted implicitly has me restrained.

Ricardo looms over me, his hands fisted at his sides, ready to strike again. I squeeze my eyes shut, trying to get the room to stop spinning. He's hit me so many times already that I've lost count, and I can't watch it coming at me again.

But instead of another blow, he tilts my face up to him with an almost gentle hand at my chin. "You know I don't like having to do this, Avery. Just tell me what I need to know, and it can all be over."

I struggle to form words, my breath coming short and sharp. "I only have one thing to tell you." I swallow and lock eyes with him. "Fuck you."

His strike comes swift and without warning, his heavy fist slamming into my cheek and sending my head snapping back. I gasp at the pain searing through my face and swallow the bile rising in my throat.

"I don't think you appreciate your situation, Avery."

"I told you...I don't know anything about any of Kalen's friends, about what their plans are, or where to find them."

It feels like we've been at this for hours. He keeps asking, and I keep giving him the same answer while my body only gets more bruised and battered.

He grips my chin tightly in his fingers. "I don't like having to hit a woman, Avery. This can all be over if you just come clean."

"I don't know anything." I keep repeating the same words, over and over, but he doesn't believe me. "I don't know *anything*."

Probably because I'm lying.

Kalen worked with those guys for a long time, and over the years we were together, I learned lots of information about them. Plenty of things that would be useful for someone like Ricardo, someone trying to get to them, but I'll be damned if I give any of it to him.

I'm not going to put them in the line of fire any more than I already have. They've already risked their lives for me multiple times and are already facing jail time or worse if they get caught. I won't put them in any more danger than they're already in by having this madman know anything personal about any of them. But maybe there's something I *can* tell him that will buy some time, keep me alive long enough for the guys to find me.

"I-I don't know anything about them. I swear. But I'll give you something else, something even more dangerous to you."

One of his thick, dark brows rises. "What's that?"

"The zip drive Amelia made with everything she found."

His jaw tightens. "She saved everything?"

I nod slowly. "Yes, and I'll tell you where it is. Just...can I have some water, please?"

It isn't the first time I've asked for it, but an almost-kind smile spreads across his lips, as if he's actually considering giving it to me this time to ease my dry, cracked lips and bruised body instead of keeping me miserable, thirsty, and at his will.

A hint of softness touches his dark eyes, and he turns back and inclines his head to his men who have been standing near the door, watching him torture me for who knows how long. One of them disappears down the hall, and Ricardo releases my face, letting my head drop and hang since I no longer have the power to hold it up.

Ricardo paces in front of me, body tense and only growing more so the longer we're in here, almost like he's waiting for something to happen, anticipating some news.

His man returns with a bottle of water. Ricardo twists off the cap, lifts my chin, and holds it to my lips. I drink at it greedily, the cold water pouring down my neck and chest, the icy coolness welcome even though it stings against my injured mouth.

He pulls the bottle away, recaps it, and sets it on the floor near his feet. "Now, let's chat, like we used to back at the office."

I snort at the absurdity of the statement. "Like we used to? Before I knew you? You want to pretend I don't know what kind of a monster you really are now? That I haven't figured out what you've done? How many lives you've ruined."

His already-dark eyes go almost obsidian, his jaw hardening. "You have no idea what I've done or what I'm capable of."

The chill that spreads through me has nothing to do with the shock my body is going into and everything to do with the threat implicit in his words.

"What about your wife, your kids? How can you do this when you have a family?"

It's what I always wanted, what I always thought I would

have eventually with Kalen, and Ricardo is lying to them, putting them at risk by playing this dangerous game.

He sneers at me. "I'm doing this *for* them. I built this empire with my brother to provide for both of our families, to ensure we could give them everything we never had as children."

"By selling drugs? By laundering money? By killing people with poison they put in their veins?"

"Their choice."

"Is that how you sleep at night? By telling yourself that?"

His expression hardens, and a sly smile overtakes his lips. "I sleep on a very expensive bed, in very expensive sheets, sometimes next to my beautiful wife who trusts me and loves me, sometimes next to an expensive whore who does the things my wife never would, and I never have trouble sleeping."

"You're a monster."

"And what does that make your ex-husband, hmm? After what *he's* done over the last few days?"

His question makes me bite back my continued tirade, not because I think Kalen or the guys are monsters, but rather because I don't want to defend them and unwittingly give away any information Ricardo could use to hurt them.

He shakes his head, rising to pace in front of me. "You know, I looked into both of you after you saw us in the warehouse and got away from Manuel, and it's incredible how little there is to find. Given what he's demonstrated the last few days, I'd wager a guess he's former military, likely a SEAL, maybe a Ranger or Delta Force."

I steel my expression so I don't give away how close he is to the truth.

"His skills have certainly served him well, but if he continues this war against me, he's going to see the true power of my organization. Hopefully, he already has."

What the hell does that mean?

A grin plays at his lips, like he knows something I don't. Whatever it is, he finds it excessively amusing, and that threatens to make me gag on my own fear again.

"You see, your ex-husband and his friends have been playing a dangerous game, making their way across town tonight and destroying all my properties, but it means we know where they're going. And eventually, my men are going to catch up with them. When they do, they're not going to be as kind to them as I have been to you." Ricardo squats in front of me again, taking the bottle of water back into his hands. "Now, why don't you tell me about the zip drive."

Over my dead fucking body.

A phone rings in the hallway, and one of Ricardo's men pulls it from his pocket and answers. He glances back at Ricardo with wide eyes.

Ricardo rises to his feet. "What? Did they get them?"

His man shakes his head. "*La Cantina* just exploded, and we haven't heard from Erik, Jorge, or Miguel."

"Fucking how?" Ricardo chucks the water bottle against the wall, his face reddening, hands fisting at his sides. "Fucking *how* does he keep doing this?"

Before I can stop it, a laugh slips between my split lips and fills the room.

Ricardo whirls around and glares at me. "You think this is funny? What he's doing?"

I shake my head, unable to drop the smile. "No, I think it's funny that he's coming for you and you think you can escape him. When he finds you, I can't wait to see what he does to you."

In one smooth motion, he pulls out a gun and points it against my forehead, pressing the barrel into my skin. "Will he think it's funny when he finds you with a bullet through your fucking head?"

Knowing Kalen and the guys have outsmarted Ricardo's plans thus far gives me a strange sense of power. "You're the one who's going to end up with a bullet in his head."

Ricardo acts so fast that I don't even realize he's moving his hand until the gun strikes me in the temple and pain sears through my vision, blinding me. I try to take a breath, but the pain robs me of it, and vomit finally makes its way up my throat that I barely manage to swallow back before he hits me again.

Everything goes dark.

16

CHAOS

The quaint bungalow sits quietly, just like all the others on the street. It should house some happy family, asleep in their beds, dreaming of school plays and what they need to accomplish at work tomorrow, but instead, the man I'm here to destroy and the woman I still love wait inside.

Unlike his places of business, no cameras film the outside of the house. Either this is a new purchase, or he never expected anyone to ever find it. Even Preacher didn't with his extensive ability to locate information on just about anything.

That's good—it means they'll never see me coming.

I'd love to have more time to properly recon the place, but neither Avery nor I have that luxury. I've been bleeding for more than twelve hours, and the sun is coming up far too soon, which means the neighborhood will be coming to life.

There's only one way to go in, and that's full fucking tilt. I'm not about to give anyone in there any warning or long enough to prepare themselves for what's coming.

I grab the grenade from my bag—its familiar weight in my hand almost like finding an old friend—and my lips curl slightly despite the situation. Perez and his men have greatly underestimated the lengths I will go to protect Avery, and I will use that to my every advantage.

With my bag of tricks slung over my good shoulder, I'm ready for these fuckers. Ready for anything they could ever throw at me.

I ready my weapon. Pull the pin, release the spoon, and toss the grenade at the front door.

4...3...2...1...

It blows it wide open, and I storm in through the smoke, firing three shots into the man on the floor immediately inside while he's still stunned by the blast.

I sweep in through the front hallway, past the stairs leading up, and into the kitchen. Empty takeout containers and remnants of what must have been dinner last night still litter the table. Enough for at least three people—Perez, this fucker, and probably one more.

And they know I'm here now.

I've lost the element of surprise, which makes this even more dangerous for Avery. I have to take out those fuckers without hurting her, and she could be anywhere in this damn house.

Standing still, I listen for any signs of movement. Floorboards creak above me, but that doesn't mean someone isn't waiting to ambush me on this level. I make my way down the short hall to the two small bedrooms before returning to the stairs.

An ominous silence falls over the house, and the hairs on the back of my neck stand on end, a shiver rolling through me.

This isn't good.

I pause with my back to the wall just at the bottom of the

stairwell, where I'm protected from exposure to anyone at the top of the flight. He'll be ready to fire the moment he hears me coming up, but that's just a risk I have to take if I want any chance of getting out of here with Avery.

Failure isn't an option in this mission.

If I don't push and do everything in my power to get her back, that man *will* kill her.

That means shoving aside the exhaustion, the pain, the desire of my body to just fall to the floor right now. I square my shoulders and move for the stairwell again.

Bullets tear into the floor and the wall immediately next to me, and I slide back and take cover again. He has the high ground, which is going to make this a lot more difficult.

I would kill to be able to have Mouth and Reaper here now, but at least I know they're keeping Viktoria protected. The update Reaper texted me on my way over here said she was out of surgery and had lost a lot of blood, so it was touch and go, but she was fighting. The best news I could have hoped for in that regard and one less thing to worry about when I need to concentrate on getting Avery out of here.

The gunfire from upstairs stops as quickly as it started. "Hello, Mr. Riggs. I've been expecting you."

Christ. Perez sounds just like his brother.

"I would say I'm sorry about your brother, but I'm not. You'll be going to join him soon enough."

Perez issues a long, dark chuckle. "Many have tried to take us out in the past, and many have failed."

"I got your brother, didn't I? I decimated every one of your businesses. You have nothing left."

He releases a cold, sinister laugh. "Nothing left? You underestimate me. You have no idea the kind of reach our organization truly has. With my brother running our businesses in the West and in the South, that left me with our East Coast expansion, which had been going quite well until

Avery and Amelia stumbled upon our little accounting error."

"You get off on hurting innocent women, Perez? Is that your thing?"

"You have me all wrong, Mr. Riggs. I am actually rather fond of Avery and hate having to do this to her, but she's left me no choice."

My hand tightens on my weapon, eager to put a bullet through this guy's head. "What about your wife or children, Perez? How would you feel if I told you I stopped by your house before I came here and did to them exactly what you did to Amelia?"

Silence greets me, but then a chuckle fills the stairwell. "I would tell you you're full of shit. I moved them out of town the moment *South of the Border* went up in flames. I saw another attack coming. I just never anticipated it would be from someone like you—"

"I'm not going to stop until I have Avery."

"Then come and try to get her."

I can almost see the smile in his statement. He thinks he has the upper hand, and while he does have the high ground, he doesn't have what I do—skills that make me lethal and an unbreakable will.

Nothing he can do will stop me from getting to Avery.

My heart thunders against my ribs as I toss a flash-bang up the steps. It goes off; the sound is almost deafening, smoke filling the air. I move instantly, taking advantage of his disorientation.

His cough leads me straight to him, and I fire two shots in the direction of the sound as I race up through the smoke. I hit the top step, and something solid slams into me from the side, knocking me to the hallway floor.

Perez falls on top of me, his heavy weight keeping me prone, and he presses the barrel of his gun to my temple. He sneers at me, his eyes watering from the smoke. "I'm going to enjoy doing this up close and personal."

"So am I."

I pull the trigger on my pistol pinned between us. The bullet goes up into his chest, and his eyes widen, his body going limp almost instantly, gun tumbling from his hand next to my ear.

It was a calculated risk. Shooting him could have caused him to fire right into my head, but it wouldn't have mattered if I had died. As long as he's gone, Avery would be safe.

Avery...

She must be up here somewhere.

So close.

I grunt, struggling to push him off me with one fully functioning arm, and manage to roll him to one side. Blood pools from his chest and under him into beige carpeting. I grab the wall for support and push to my feet, kicking away his weapon even though he's never touching it again.

"Avery?"

Her name echoes through the hall, and I pause for a moment, both to listen for a response and to try to stop the world from tilting sideways.

I try to blink away the fuzziness from my vision and stumble down the hall toward the first bedroom.

Empty.

"Avery?"

One by one, I clear each room without any sign of her. My chest tightens with the possibility that she isn't here, or if she is, that I'm too late...

The master bedroom stands at the end of the hall, and a muffled noise from behind the closed door steals my breath. Weapon ready, I approach cautiously and turn the knob, pushing the door open.

Oh, God...

"Avery!"

AVERY

A FAMILIAR VOICE cuts through the gloom, something pulling at me, trying to drag me from the horrific place I've been.

Kalen?

I try to cry out to him, try to answer, but all that comes escapes is a muffled groan through my split lips. Pain drives at my temple where Ricardo struck me, relentless and agonizing.

Tears drop onto my legs, my head hanging limp from a neck that can't support it anymore. I manage to blink my eyes open, but I can't lift my head to see what's going on around me.

The door creaks open, and I squeeze my eyes closed and turn as much away as I can in case it's Ricardo again.

"Avery!"

Kalen's voice pulls me back toward the door, and familiar hands lift my face. Blood trickles from my split lip down my chin, and the blue eyes I've longed to swim in forever meet mine, dark with concern. I try to focus on his face, on the fact that he's right here, but everything is blurred, distant.

"That motherfucker! If he wasn't already dead, I would fucking kill him." He kneels in front of me, still holding my face between his hands, keeping my head up. "Are you okay?"

I attempt to move my arms and wince against the restraints still securing them behind my back. "I...he..."

"Fuck." Kalen gently releases my face and shifts behind me, pulling a knife from his boot. "I'm getting you out of here."

He cuts me free, and my hands fall limp at my sides. One

of his strong arms wraps around me and pulls me toward the edge of the chair. "We have to get out of here before the cops show up."

"Cops?" I scan the room, trying to process his words. "What's going on?"

Kalen glances toward the hallway. "It's over. Perez is dead, and so are his men. But I've made a hell of a lot of noise doing it. We don't have much time."

I shake my head against the fog enveloping it, narrowing my eyes on the open doorway. "Okay, let's go."

Only my absolute will allows me to try to push up onto my feet, but my legs collapse under me.

Kalen's hold keeps me from face-planting the bloody floor. "I got you."

He grimaces and scoops me up into his arms, jaw locked. His skin pales, sweat beading on his forehead, and he wavers slightly on his feet. Viktoria's words float through my head…

Kalen's been shot.

"Kalen, are you okay?"

"I'm fine." He barely gets the words out between gritted teeth. "We have to move."

My eyes drift down to the bandage and tourniquet wrapped around his left bicep. "You can't carry me."

He shakes his head and locks eyes with me, the look he offers telling me the discussion is finished. "I'm fine. I got you."

The corner of my eye catches a flash of movement in the doorway, and a man steps forward.

"Kalen, watch out!"

Kalen whirls faster than I've ever seen anyone move, transferring me to my feet, blocking me with his body, and pulling the trigger on the gun in his right hand all at the same time.

Glass shatters across the room, and multiple bullets hit

the man in the doorway square in the chest and right between the eyes. He collapses in a pile on the floor, and Kalen and I both whip our heads toward the broken window pane.

Without the benefit of any sunlight, I can't see anything beyond that. "Where did that come from?"

The tiniest smile graces Kalen's lips. "Mouth...I told him where I was heading, but I never expected him to come." He holds out his hand to me. "Can you walk?"

Even if I couldn't, I wouldn't tell him that now that the fog is finally starting to clear and I can see how bad he truly is—pale, shaking, barely staying vertical.

Kalen takes a few steps toward the hallway, then stumbles, leaning against the wall for a second, sweat trickling down his almost-white skin. He slowly sags to his knees, using his shoulder to keep himself upright.

"Oh, God." I clamber over to him and slide my arm under his. "I got you, Kalen. Come on."

He tries to get his feet under him, putting almost all his weight on me, but even using all the energy left in my body, I can't get him upright. His body falls limply onto the floor, and I release a sob as tears stream down my face again.

I take his face in my hands and shake gently. "Kalen, wake up!" My tears fall onto him, but even that doesn't get him to budge. "Kalen, wake *up*. Please! We have to go!"

The thought of what will happen to him if the police show up makes me heave and stagger to my feet.

I have to get him out of here.

Pressing my hand against the wall to keep from falling over, my vision blurs from the tears and what is likely a wicked concussion. I make it a few steps down the hall before my foot hits something.

I look down into the open, dead eyes of Ricardo—a

gaping wound in his chest, blood soaking the carpet under him.

All this death.

Because of *him.*

I turn my head to the side and empty the acid from my stomach as I force myself to keep moving.

Have to get help...

The throbbing in my head makes it almost impossible to focus, and I stumble again, the world spinning. I stare down the steps, and everything twists sideways, a wicked case of vertigo threatening to make me heave again.

I lower my foot to the first step, then stumble and slide down two or three more. A dark, hulking shadow appears at the bottom of the stairs, I blink rapidly to try to focus while I scramble up backward, but he's on me in two quick steps, dragging me upward with impossibly strong hands.

"No, please don't—"

A large, calloused palm cups my cheek and shakes my face gently, and I open my eyes to familiar ones.

"Mouth?" I throw my arms around his neck and hold him tightly, a cry slipping from my lips. "Kalen's up there. He won't wake up."

Mouth nods his understanding, then rushes down the steps and carries me onto the front lawn. A black SUV sits running at the curb, and he opens the back door and lowers me into it.

Before I can ask him anything, he double-times it back into the house. Waiting for him to return with Kalen is sheer agony, like more knives being shoved into my heart with each passing second.

Seeing his massive frame in the door with Kalen over his shoulder finally allows me to release a heavy, relieved breath. He runs across the yard, dumps Kalen into the backseat with me, and slams the door.

"Kalen?" I scramble across the backseat to him, running my hands over his face. "Mouth, how long ago was he shot?"

Mouth glances at me in the rearview mirror as we peel away from the curb but doesn't say anything; he just drives like a bat out of hell away from the quiet, suburban neighborhood that's now been wracked by more gunshots than they've probably ever heard before.

We barrel toward the highway, but rather than feeling relieved to be free of Perez's threat, a new fear grips me, staring down at Kalen and his blood-soaked arm.

"Is Kalen going to be okay?"

The big, silent man offers me a hard stare in the rearview mirror but doesn't answer, either because he doesn't know or because he doesn't want me to know the truth.

17

CHAOS

The door to the bedroom of Reaper's guest room where I've been laid up opens slowly, and Avery slips inside, turning to try to quietly ease it shut without waking me.

"I'm up."

She jumps and whirls toward me, her hand pressed over her chest. "Jesus, you scared the crap out of me."

Shit.

"I'm sorry. I didn't mean to."

The last few days haven't helped ease her constant fear. Even knowing Perez is gone and most of his organization decimated, she's always on edge, always anticipating the worst and reacting to even the smallest things with a racing heart, tears, or a full-blown meltdown.

Who can blame her?

She's been to Hell and back, but she came out alive. I keep trying to remind her of that while also reminding myself that she doesn't have the benefit of having seen as much as I have. It doesn't affect me the way it does her but being so close to losing her has left me nervous every time she leaves the room, which is why I didn't sleep a wink while she was visiting Viktoria with Reaper.

We have eyes on Perez's henchman still operating in other regions of the country, but they won't be a problem. With as many friends as we have, they'll be taken out one by one before they can stir up any shit.

She examines me with a keen eye, looking for signs of how I'm feeling because she knows I'll never complain or admit how weak or in pain I really am. "Did you talk to Preacher?"

I nod. "Yep, he's confident he scrubbed any traces of what we did from any security cameras, and he's continuing to monitor Baltimore PD for anything that spells trouble for us. We'll still need to come up with a solid story for you to give the cops since we know they're looking for you to talk about what happened at the diner. But right now, it appears they're focused on rival cartels as the perpetrators, especially due to the almost simultaneous attack on their compound in Mexico. We just need to wait until all your bruises heal for you to go get things tied up with them and with Bernice."

"So, you and the guys are in the clear?"

"We're in the clear." I push myself up with my good arm, struggling to bite back a groan at the ache still overtaking my body. Waiting to get my wound properly treated left me fighting both blood loss and a nasty infection and knocked me the fuck out for days. Other than lying in bed and having Mouth and Avery take care of me, I haven't been able to do much else. "How's Viktoria today?"

Avery makes her way across the room to me and lowers herself to the mattress next to me as I wince and sit up with my back against the headboard. She watches me try to hide my pain but bites back her usual comment about it. "Better. Ready to get out of the damn hospital and being very vocal about it, but the doctor said probably another week before she can go home."

I snort and shake my head. "That doesn't surprise me at all. Vik isn't the type who enjoys being laid up."

Her green eyes flash with humor, and the corner of her almost-healed lips twitches. "Reminds me of someone else I know."

"Let's not argue about that again." I brush my fingers along her exposed arm. "I'm tired of that conversation."

She narrows her gaze on me. "You think that was arguing?"

"Wasn't it?"

I'm not sure I can take another disagreement over how I should be staying in bed or how I'm overdoing it after almost dying from blood loss and shock only a few days ago just by showering or using the damn bathroom.

Avery grins at me. "You've been single for too long. You don't remember what an argument really is."

I grin at her. "We never argued."

Something flashes deep in her eyes, a pain I hadn't expected to see while we're just joking around, and she throws her head. "No, we didn't. We just fucked like you hated me once you stopped loving me."

Her words make me stiffen, and I shift uncomfortably against the headboard, though not from the pain still lingering in my arm but because of how insane her words truly are. "That's what you think? That I didn't love you? That *that* was why I was acting the way I was...because I was attracted to you but didn't *love* you?"

Even saying the words is enough to make me fist my hands at my sides to fight the desire to destroy something.

Avery examines me, her mouth opening and closing a few times. "I-I guess. What else was I supposed to think? All you ever did was fuck me, and then you would leave as if you couldn't bear to be around me."

"Jesus, Avery…" I drag her to me, clutching her against my chest and pulling her face between my palms firmly, ensuring she's looking me in the eyes and can see my sincerity as I say these words to her. "How could you possibly believe that?" I swallow back the emotion threatening to choke me. "I didn't leave you because I didn't love you, Avery. I left *because* I loved you more than anything. Because I was trying to protect you. I was trying to keep you safe, just like I am now."

Her lips quiver, and tears pool in her eyes. "Protect me from what?"

"From *me*. From what I might have done to you."

"What you might have done to me? I don't…" She shakes her head again, tears streaming down her cheeks. "I don't understand what you're saying."

This is a conversation I never wanted to have with her, one I've avoided for half a damn decade, but after everything that's happened between us, I owe her an explanation. She needs to understand why it's not safe for us to be together, why we *can't* go back to how it was before.

I take a deep breath, fighting with the words I've kept buried deep inside me for so long. "After I came back from that mission, when I was in the hospital, I started having nightmares. Horrifying and violent ones about some of the things that happened. That's why I never wanted you around, never wanted you to spend the night there. Every time I fell asleep, it would happen, and it was always worse at night."

The memories of those nights, of the terror and panic that seized me, tighten my gut, but I have to tell her. I have to get this out, so she'll truly understand why it isn't safe to be with me.

"One night...when one of the nurses came in to check on me...I almost killed her."

Avery's eyes widen. "What?"

"I woke up with two nurses trying to get my hands off the neck of this woman. I was choking her, Avery. I was literally strangling the life out of that woman because I couldn't see her. I couldn't understand what was happening around me. I was so lost in my own head, in my dream and my memories, that I didn't know what I was doing. And I almost killed her. If she hadn't been able to reach over and hit the emergency button next to the bed, I don't..." I shake my head and squeeze my eyes closed. "I can't even think about what might have happened."

"Oh, my God, Kalen." A soft hand brushes my cheek. "Why didn't they tell me? Why didn't *you* tell me?"

I tighten my grip on her face, needing her to understand. "Because I didn't want you to see me like that. I didn't want you to be afraid of me. Someone higher up ran interference with the woman I hurt and the hospital to ensure I wasn't going to get charged or punished for what happened. At that point in time, they were concerned about getting me back in the unit. They didn't want anything to interfere with that. Not you. Not some lawsuit from the nurse I fucked up while *I* was fucked up."

I pull my hands off her face, talking about what I did suddenly making me fear touching her right now.

You can't hurt her any more than you already have.

"I couldn't trust myself with you anymore, Avery. I couldn't trust what I would do if I slept next to you, if I held you in my arms, even when that's the only thing that ever felt right. The only time I ever felt normal after what happened."

"Kalen..." Her lips tremble, and she swipes at her tears. "You could have told me. You *should* have told me. I thought—"

"I thought I knew what I was doing. I thought I was protecting you, but I was also too selfish to fully give you up. Because I loved you. I *still* love you. And the only time I felt *okay* was when we were together, even if it was just for sex." I struggle to come up with words to explain everything that happened back then, for the way I suffer every day. "When I deployed again, I had hoped being there with the guys, getting back to work, would...I don't know, maybe snap me out of it and I could come back, and I could be everything I used to be for you. But—"

"But instead, you came back...and I had already moved out of the house and served you divorce papers."

The worst fucking day of my life.

Being given those papers felt like holding my entire life in my hand and watching it burn. That day I signed them, it felt like I had died, and I haven't really been living since then.

I nod slowly. "Yeah. And I couldn't blame you. Not really. After how I acted, after what I did to you. You had every right to divorce me and to believe what you did. I'm just so sorry it made you feel like you weren't enough for me."

"No." She shakes her head, reaching out to clutch at my chest. "*I* am. I should have pushed you harder to talk to me. I should have forced you to tell me what was going on. Maybe if I had—"

"No." I lean forward and silence her with a finger over her lips. "You can't blame yourself for any of this. I won't let you. This is one hundred percent on me. *I'm* the only one who made mistakes here."

Avery squeezes her eyes closed, refusing to look at me. "That's not true."

"What do you mean?"

"I made so many mistakes, Kalen. So many damn mistakes."

"What are you talking about?"

"No matter what you say, I should have tried harder. I should have pushed. I should have known that you loved me and that whatever was happening to us was something else. But I was an emotional mess, especially toward the end when I talked to the attorney and got the divorce papers."

She opens her eyes. The pain there is so deep, so real that I can physically feel it weighing down on top of my own.

"I was pregnant."

I freeze, ice flooding through my veins. "You were what?"

"It must have happened right before you left again. You were gone for about two months, and we left things on such bad terms that I didn't want to tell you while you were over there. We barely spoke as it was, and I didn't want you to have that weighing on you on top of everything else for your first mission back." Her tears fall in earnest now, mixing with the sobs she can't fight back. "I was going to tell you the next time we saw each other, when we had to sign the papers, but…"

"But what?"

"I had a miscarriage before we had the meeting. The baby was just…gone. I felt like maybe it was a sign that we were doing the right thing. It erased any doubts I still had lingering about signing those papers."

"And you never told me…"

She chokes on a sob, pressing her hand over her mouth. "And I never told you that you were going to be a father. Instead, I went into that meeting angry and took it out on you with the horrible things I said. I'm so sorry. I should have told you the truth."

Fear lives in her gaze as she stares back at me—for how I'm going to react to this news, for how I might lash out. She's expecting me to be mad at her, to be furious about the fact that she kept something so important from me.

But she couldn't be more wrong.

My heart shatters, thinking about what she went through, what she had to endure completely on her own. I was all she had, and I pushed her away, isolated myself from her, therefore isolating *her* from the only person she could ever rely on it.

"You went through that all by yourself..." Guilt cuts at me, more painful than any time I've been shot. "I'm so sorry. I should have been here with you. We should have been together, supporting each other. We wouldn't be sitting here like this if I had been."

"But we *are* here." Avery offers a sad smile, one I've seen far too much in the last few days since I rescued her from Perez. "This is our reality now, where we are."

I pull her hand into mine and squeeze it. "The truth is, I still have those nightmares. I wake up in a cold sweat and can't always come back to reality right away. It's why I don't sleep. I try to avoid it."

"That's why you left the bedroom the other night, why you wouldn't sleep with me while I was here."

I nod slowly. "I knew it would be safer for you if I didn't stay." The words I don't want to say sit on my tongue like lead weights. "Nothing has changed, Avery. I love you more than anything, which is why I'll never let you be in danger around me."

AVERY

I LOVE you more than anything...but we can't be together.

That's what he's saying without *really* saying it. He can't even form the words because he knows it's wrong.

We finally came clean with each other. After *everything* that happened, we're finally in a position to make things right, to have a second chance at what we failed so miserably at once before. But he's pushing me away, trying to send me back to that lonely, horrible life I had without him.

I lean in, lowering my forehead against his. Our breaths mingle, my body coming awake again this close to him after so many days, avoiding touching him for fear I would hurt him. But he seems stronger today, strong enough to finally tell me the truth, to open the door for me to tell him what I've kept locked away for so long.

And he loves me

Hearing those words from him almost made everything I've suffered worth it. It was the one thing I thought I had lost and could never get back, but really, I had it all along. Viktoria was right about that—about a lot of things, actually. And now Kalen is trying to destroy what we've finally found again because he's scared.

I'm scared, too. Absolutely terrified that this is all some dream I'll wake up from to find him gone again. But I won't let him run away again. He won't shut me out.

I ghost my lips over his softly. "It's not the same as before, Kalen. Everything has changed now. I know the truth, and I'm not going to let you push me away this time. I refuse to give up on you and me."

His heart thunders under my palm, and I curl my fingers into his warm flesh, needing to feel him, all of him, so he can't find a way to put up another wall between us again.

"This, you and me, Kalen, it was always meant to be forever. We just got in the fucking way."

We're older now—battered and bruised and scarred by life and the horrible things in it. But also wiser. We know better. We're stronger. We're finally being honest with each other for the first time, and that means *everything*.

He considers me for a minute, our bodies pressed

together, my hand pinned between us. "Do you really believe that?"

"I always have." I shake my head, running my free hand back through his unruly hair. "We both have been miserable for years. Neither one of us getting what we wanted out of this divorce. So why? Why do we keep doing this to ourselves? Whatever is going on with you...we can figure it out. *Together*."

"That's what you want?"

I nod and kiss him again. "That's what I want. That's what I need. You. Us together like this."

He inhales deeply and swallows slowly. "You know what the guys and I do, right? What our business is?" Concern furrows his brow. "Do you really understand who I am?"

Who he is?

That question pulls at something deep inside me, something I've known since I met him. I stare into his blue eyes, the ones I've loved since I was sixteen. "I have always known *exactly* who you are, Kalen Riggs. I've always known there was something chaotic deep inside you. It's what drew me to you in the first place. You are always so fearless. It was exciting, addictive. And I always knew what you did. Maybe not the details. But I knew enough. I knew who you had to become to do that job and then come back to me and pretend like you didn't. I know you tried to separate yourself from Chaos. But I always knew who he was. And I've loved Kalen *and* Chaos the entire time."

Tears roll from his eyes, and it isn't because the pain medication is likely wearing off. He didn't even cry when we got married, so to see this now both gives me hope and makes me fear that he may do exactly what he's so used to doing—push me away.

If I lose Kalen again, I don't know that I'd survive it.

Murder. Kidnapping. Beatings. All of *that* would be

nothing compared to what I would suffer knowing he walked away again.

"You really mean that, Avery?"

"I don't care what other people might think about what you're doing. I know you, and I know those boys out there. None of you would do it if you didn't think the people you were doing it to deserve it one hundred percent. I believe in what you guys are trying to accomplish, and I don't need to know the specifics." I lower my forehead to his again, tangling my fingers in the hair at his nape. "I trust you. I trust Reaper and Mouth and Viktoria, and I trust Chaos."

Kalen's stillness and silence makes a vise tighten around my chest, and I pull back slightly. He raises his hand and drags me back to him, brushing his lips over mine.

"I never thought I'd hear you say that. I never thought I would have another chance with you again." He kisses me deeply, dragging me fully on top of him. "Christ, I love you, woman."

I try to back off from his prone body. "Stop, Kalen. You're going to hurt yourself."

He grins at me, the light I haven't seen in years finally touching his eyes again like it used to. "I don't care."

Maybe I don't, either.

My body heats at his touch, seeking what I always have from him—comfort, passion, acceptance, love.

He pulls me back down onto him, gliding his tongue along mine, his hands finding my ass and positioning me across his lap to grind me against his hardening cock. "I'm so sorry it took us this long to figure it out, babe."

"But we did. We figured it the fuck out, and we'll figure out anything else we need to in the future."

The future.

Something I thought we could never have, something I thought *I* might not have when I made that call to Kalen, seeking help. There were so many times it was almost snatched away from us, almost stolen not only by evil men with evil intent but also by ourselves being stupid and stubborn.

Never again.

"Together. We'll figure it out together."

He grins at me. "Right."

This man has always known exactly how to take care of me, how to make me feel everything exactly as I should. This moment is no different. He groans into my mouth, dragging me impossibly closer against him, demanding what we both want.

The fingers of his left hand tighten on my hip as his right slips over my thigh and between my legs to rub in exactly the right spot. I moan against his lips, grinding against him, even though I should probably climb off and let him rest.

The last thing we should be doing is *this* right now, but after almost dying, after watching him fight for his life after saving mine, we both need something life-affirming, something that *feels* good, something that is for *us*.

"Kalen…"

He answers my plea by taking my mouth in a desperate kiss, rolling his hips to mine. Any pain or exhaustion that has kept him down the last few days disappears in a single second, both of us needing this more than we need to acknowledge any potential restrictions.

I push down his boxers, freeing his cock, which strains toward me. Taking it in my hand, I stroke him slowly, brushing the pad of my thumb across the head. He groans and thrusts into my grip, and my pussy clenches, seeking what's so close.

His frantic hands shove at the waistband of my yoga pants, pushing them and my thong down my thighs, and I release him long enough to slide them off and toss them onto the floor.

Kalen's heated gaze rakes over me, and he takes his cock in his hand and strokes it languidly, watching as I pull my shirt up and off. His eyes drop to my breasts, and I climb across the mattress and straddle him again.

He reaches out and captures my breasts in his rough palms, flicking his thumb across the nipples and sending tiny jolts of pleasure straight to my clit. I groan and grasp his cock, gliding it through the wetness already pooling between my legs. His mouth finds mine again, hungry and determined, and I align him with my pussy and sink down onto his cock, his flesh spreading me wide open, filling me and the place that's always belonged to him.

My mouth falls open on a gasp that he swallows down, stroking my tongue with his as his hands find my hips and squeeze, urging me to move. I lean back and raise myself up, locking my gaze with his so I can watch his blue eyes darken as I slowly engulf his cock again and again.

His fingers dig into my skin, hard enough to leave bruises, but I don't care how he marks me. He already owns me, all of me. It doesn't matter whether he's Kalen or Chaos; he will always have me and my heart.

Whether he likes it or not.

He can fight me, fight this, try to push me away again, but I won't let him. Whatever happens in our future, we'll face it together.

I roll my hips and set a slow rhythm that he matches with his thrusts up. We move together fluidly, like waves crashing against the shore, like we were always meant to be like this. Because we were. We *are.*

We were just too wrapped up in our own pain to see it and accept it.

It may have taken both of us almost dying to finally find

each other, but now that we have, I'll do anything to ensure I never lose him again.

I squeeze his cock, watching the muscles in his neck and jaw tighten, and he slides a hand down until his thumb finds my clit. My hips jerk at the contact, and he sits up to take one of my nipples into his mouth, sucking and flicking it with his tongue while I grind on him, feeding the slow warmth building between my legs.

He moves to my other breast, giving it the same treatment. I gasp and drop my head down to bite into the flesh of his shoulder, my pace increasing as he braces his feet on the mattress and thrusts up, driving himself even deeper.

"Fucking hell." Kalen issues a low growl as I sweep my tongue across the mark I just made on his body. "Come for me, Avery. Come for me and then marry me again."

"Wait…what?" I return my focus to him, blinking away what must be enough lust to completely fog my brain. "What did you just—"

"Marry me. Again." He captures my face in his hand and grips me tightly, bringing my lips to his. "The biggest mistake I ever made in my life was walking away from you. I got so off course that I never thought I could get back on it. But now that we are, I don't ever want to lose you again. So, marry me."

It was the last thing I expected him to say, but there is only one possible answer.

"*Yes.*"

Mrs. Kalen "Chaos" Riggs…

It has a nice ring to it.

Keep reading for *Clean Slate*, Mouth's story and the third book in the Scarred Heroes Series.

CLEAN SLATE

THE SCARRED HEROES SERIES BOOK 3

PROLOGUE

MOUTH

The crosshairs at the center of my scope remain frustratingly empty, our target either not there or not presenting himself.

Yet.

Though it's been almost twelve hours of sitting, watching, waiting for the prime opportunity to take out my mark, I continue to remain vigilant because he *will* make an appearance.

They always do, eventually.

Even the most well-trained adversary on the battlefield makes a mistake. And the current target is far from that.

He's nothing more than a selfish, entitled prick who thinks he can get away with doing whatever he wants to women by virtue of his wealth and power over the politicians who control making him pay for his crimes.

And John Blaire is definitely someone who needs to pay.

Even if that means waiting here 'til the sun comes up and coming back again and again until the right moment presents itself to find final justice for his victim…or victims —because there's no way a guy like this only does *that* once.

Joanie was just the first one who had the guts and determination to come forward to try to press charges. The system may have failed her, but we won't.

I won't.

Reaper nudges me with his knee from where he sits beside me, with his back to the high roof wall of the building a few streets over from our mark's condo I use as a perch. "Anything?"

I shake my head. He releases a long sigh and glances at his watch, which seems to be moving agonizingly slowly this evening. We won't have much more time dawn. Once it does, we'll need to hightail it out of here.

Fewer prying eyes at night. Fewer chances someone sees something that can get us caught. If I can't seal the deal before the sun comes up, I'll come back tomorrow and do this all over again.

Reaper peeks over the wall toward Blaine's building and huffs back into his spot. "Either this fucker somehow slipped out of his condo without us knowing, or he's been in his bedroom with that redhead for close to twelve hours." He shakes his head and laughs. "I wish I had that kind of stamina."

I snort and chuckle.

Don't we all…

The government may have trained us to be machines in the game of war, but those skills don't automatically equate to being machines in the bedroom.

Reaper grins and waggles his dark eyebrows. "Though, Vik isn't complaining."

I roll my eyes at him, then return my focus to the dark condo lined up in my scope. After the way Chaos and I saw Reaper going at Vik in the shower when they were holed up in the safehouse in New York, I wouldn't imagine she *would* have anything to complain about. Reaper is good at everything he does—including his woman. Apparently, a lot.

If only I could say the same.

It's been so long for me that I likely forgot how to do it altogether.

Just like I forgot everything else important.

A low buzzing draws my attention away from the scope for a moment, and Reaper reaches into his pocket, pulls out his phone, and checks the screen, wincing slightly before bringing it to his ear. "Parrish, didn't think I'd be hearing from you anytime soon."

Me, either.

The last time our paths crossed in New York, it was a bloodbath that almost ended very badly, and a call from Parrish out of the blue can't be a good sign. Getting involved with the Satan's Knights MC again isn't high on my to-do list, but the former club president wouldn't be reaching out to Reaper if it weren't important. That doesn't bode well for us.

Reaper listens to the other end of the line for a moment, his jaw tightening. "You're fucking kidding me."

That doesn't sound good.

I return my focus to the quiet, dark condo several streets away while Reaper deals with whatever clusterfuck Parrish has gotten into this time.

"Where is he now?…Uh, huh…Fuck…We'll take care of it…Yes, I'm sure. Obviously, time is of the essence."

Definitely not good.

He releases an annoyed groan, shifting positions beside me. "I'm tied up on a job here, and Chaos has some personal shit going on at the moment and won't be available for a few days, but I'll send Mouth."

I jerk my head toward him, furrowing my brow and mouthing, *"What the fuck, man?"*

Is he fucking kidding?

The last thing I want to be doing is heading back to NYC alone to handle something Parrish needs help with. The Knights may have been allies in our mission to take down the Yankovich organization and stop the human trafficking ring they were running, but they aren't people I want to start doing regular favors for.

Reaper gives me an *"I'll explain later"* look. "Yeah, no problem. It'll be done by the end of the week." He ends the call and shoves his hand through his hair, tipping back his head to stare at the sky above him, the stars barely visible with the light pollution D.C. produces. "Those fuckers in New York…"

I raise an eyebrow.

He drops his head to the side, meeting my gaze, and nods. "Yeah, *those* fuckers…the Russians who were selling women off a fucking menu like rare wines…turns out we didn't do as good of a job cleaning away that stain on humanity as we thought. One of the Yankovich cousins stepped in and picked up right where they left off."

Fucking hell.

That family is full of evil douchebags. They seem to just keep coming out of the damn woodwork.

I scowl at Reaper's information, then return my full attention to our mark. After sitting here for so long, I don't want to miss the moment when it presents itself.

"That was Parrish. He said this asshole, Maksim Yankovich, came over from Russia shortly after the warehouse raid to help clean up the mess we left, and they've been keeping an eye on him. They already started getting wind of a new auction taking place next month. Those fuckers…just when you thought you wiped some major scum off the face of the planet, more of it pops up."

He shifts to face me fully, and I peek at him out of the corner of my eye, tension building at the base of my skull, waiting for what he's about to say.

"I know you're worried about going alone, Mouth, but I need to finish this job for Joanie. After we take care of Blaine, we still have two more to take out, and as soon as Chaos is back, I'm going to need him on that with me." He pauses for a moment, and even though I keep my focus on the still, dark condo in the scope, I can feel his eyes on me, boring into me and assessing me the way only Reaper can. "You can handle this."

Easy for him to say.

He isn't the one living in this head, this body, dealing with what I do, day in and day out. I'm not the person I was when we were in Delta. And he seems to keep either forgetting or ignoring that. He has more confidence in me than I have in myself.

What we did in New York was a good step in the right direction. It proved there are still *some* things my brain hasn't forgotten, those ingrained reflexes and habitual movements that still make me lethal. Working with the guys since then has kept me busy, kept me moving, and kept me from dwelling on all the things I lost, but to try to pretend it will ever be the same as it was before *that* day would be lying to myself. This is just the way it is now, the way it will always be. And Reaper needs to accept that I'm not the same man I was.

I keep looking through the scope, so he won't see the way his comment affected me. His hand falls on my shoulder. Despite trying not to, I flinch at the contact.

He squeezes firmly, the move somehow familiar, bringing

bits of a hazy, distant memory. "You can do this, Mouth. Maybe it's exactly what you need to get back in the game."

I haven't been in the game for so long that I don't even know if I remember how to play.

At least, it sure feels that way.

An op on my own.

No one watching my back.

Chaos and Reaper have both done it—gone out on their own and completed missions for clients and friends. But they don't have the *complications* I have to deal with. They have their shit together. They've both moved on from everything that happened, despite the scars they'll always carry. Somehow, they've found a way to live with the constant reminders of what we all lost in order to concentrate on something real that's right now.

Maybe it's time I try to do the same.

If that's even possible.

Reaper shifts next to me, wincing slightly, his body likely stiff from sitting on this hard roof against a brick wall for the entire night. "It should be a relatively easy in and out. The guy has settled in Brighton Beach, in one of the other warehouses owned by Nikolai Yankovich, and after what happened to his cousin, he's tightened security. It would be a problem for anyone else, but not you.

"Parrish is going to have his crew stake him out until you can get there to help figure out when and where's the best place to hit him. All you have to do is pull the trigger and get back here." He pauses for a moment, like he's considering his words. "No matter how you may *feel*, you're still the best shot of anyone I've ever met, Mouth. I trust you to have my back. Always. And I trust you with this."

I trust you to have my back...

A lot of people have. Some regretted that decision.

I close my eyes, trying to picture their faces, but all I get are brief flashes that I can't connect with any names or places. It's all one big jumble, a complicated mess of memories, dreams, and nightmares that will never straighten out.

Going to New York alone is a risk. But it's one I have to take. If I don't, a lot of innocent people are going to get hurt.

That auction next month needs stock for the menu, and that means they'll be collecting them soon. The faster I can get to Brighton Beach and take out the fucker running things now, the greater chance we'll have at stopping the trafficking business before they are at full speed and it's too late for a group of girls.

I glance at Reaper and give a quick nod, letting him know I'm in.

A slow grin spreads across his face, and he squeezes my shoulder again. "Good. Now, let's hope this fucker comes up for air soon so we can get this over with and go home."

A-fucking-men.

After two weeks of stalking these three fuckers, following them and watching, determining the best time and place to take out each of them, neither of us expected to have to sit this long, waiting for the opportunity at Blaine at his own place.

He really does have stamina.

Lying in this position for this long used to be nothing for me. I could go an entire day, even longer, without moving a fucking muscle, but now, a dull ache starts to form at my temples and the base of my skull. I clench my teeth, trying to will away the migraine before it starts to get bad.

Not now.

Not tonight.

I can't afford to have that interfere with my job. Joanie deserves this relief, this form of justice.

A light flickers on in the window of Blaine's condo, and I

ready myself, shaking off the pain to concentrate on the here and now and what's important.

Reaper glances up and over the roofline. "Thank God he came up for air."

I chuckle and wait, but the condo remains quiet. No movement. Whatever Blaine is doing with that redhead we saw him bring home earlier, it's certainly keeping him occupied.

She finally appears, her breasts scarcely contained in a tiny tank top, booty hanging out of barely-there shorts. The girl wanders into the kitchen and opens the fridge, leaning into it, giving me an excellent view of her tight ass.

There was a time I would have made a smartass quip about it, and the guys would have all laughed. At least, I *think* that's what used to happen. Chaos and Reaper say it was, and I have no reason to distrust them after everything that's happened since that fateful night. Occasionally, one of those comments even still pops up in my head, sitting right on the tip of my tongue, but now, I bite it back.

I have to.

The redhead pulls out a bottle of orange juice from the fridge and drinks straight from the carton.

Fucking gross.

Her hotness level just dropped by about five points, but then again, she's with Blaine—apparently voluntarily—so that brings her down to a one. The girl needs to be more careful and selective about who she gets involved with.

She places the juice back inside and reaches for something else.

Come on, Blaine. Get your ass out of that bed.

The man we've been waiting for appears stark naked from the bedroom to the left, seemingly unconcerned with the entire wall of floor-to-ceiling windows that share everything with the world—or at least anyone bothering to look.

Like me.

He makes his way over to her as I dial in the scope, perfectly lining up the shot.

Dead calm.

No wind.

Five hundred ten meters.

Not that long ago, this shot would have been a given. One I could do in my sleep, with one hand tied behind my back. But now, even after the years I've spent rekindling the ingrained training, trying to awaken those instincts and natural reflexes, I have to take a deep, calming breath to get my heart to steady and prevent my hands from shaking.

You got this.

One shot.

Clean.

Blaine approaches the redhead, wraps his arms around her, then presses his lips to the side of her neck. She backs into him, rubbing her ass against his crotch.

Oh, God.

If I have to watch these two fuck before I can take him out, this is going to be a really long night.

Blaine reaches around her, grabs a container of strawberries and a bottle of what looks like champagne, and turns toward the bedroom.

So, he is a rapist and a romantic...

I snort to myself.

This lowlife thought he got away with what he and his buddies did that night. He believed he could walk away from the horror they enacted against Joanie and pretend it never happened. And maybe he could have, if not for one fatal mistake—they left her alive.

The criminal justice system may have failed her by not being able to convict these guys—but that's where we come in. And after all the evidence we've seen against them, no amount of money or connections will save them from our brand of justice.

He releases the redhead, laughing, and turns back toward the bedroom. One. Two. Three. He finally steps far enough away from the woman for me to pull the trigger.

The shot hits him square in the chest. He drops instantly, the champagne bottle shattering on the floor, bubbling up across the smooth surface.

I can't hear the girl scream from here, but she jerks around, her hands over her mouth. Blaine doesn't move as blood pools under him.

A heart shot.

He was dead before he even hit the floor.

Content that he's not getting back up, I sit back and turn to disassemble the rifle and police my brass.

Reaper grabs the casing before I can and holds it up. "That was quite a shot. Now, go do the same fucking thing in Brighton Beach."

I'll certainly try.

1

FINLEY

The buzz of conversations around me mixes with the steady bass of the 80s classic rock song, filling the trendiest new speakeasy-themed bar in New York, Keys and Heels, with an upbeat, welcoming atmosphere—at least for most of the patrons.

I take a sip of my gin and tonic and watch the blond supermodel in the booth across the bar with Schwartz. Whatever he just said to her shifted her entire body language toward him. This isn't going to end well for him, and I'm just waiting to enjoy the fireworks.

Whenever David Schwartz is involved, there always seems to be some.

Sometimes—like tonight—I have to remind myself that he's a brilliant lawyer who can teach me a lot; otherwise, I might quit and walk out the door to hang up my own shingle when his bullshit hits the fan. Which it looks like will be any second now…

A large body steps in front of me, blocking my view of the free entertainment. "Hey, is this seat taken?"

I let my gaze drift up the man, over his dark jeans, black polo shirt, and to his striking green eyes and dark, ruffled hair. He motions to the open spot beside me on the couch.

"Looks like it's not."

He grins at me and slides onto the cushion, intentionally pushing his thigh against my bare one. I roll my eyes and shift away from him an inch. I was willing to give him an opportunity to take his shot, but he isn't exactly starting off on a good foot.

The chances of my bringing him home for some fun tonight just went down significantly with that suave move.

"So"—he leans in closer to me—"what's your name?"

For a split second, I consider giving him a fake one, but the entire reason I came out tonight was to blow off some steam and maybe find someone to help me release a little tension. So, I shouldn't brush him off completely without giving him a second chance.

"Finley," I answer without looking at him, instead focusing on the full-on argument now happening between Schwartz and the model. "Finley Banks."

I take a sip of my drink as the model throws hers in Schwartz's face. That almost makes me choke, and I chuckle against the rim of my glass.

The man next to me follows my line of sight. "What's so funny?"

"See that guy over there?" I motion toward the booth near the bar. "The one with what looks like an entire drink dripping down his face…"

"Yeah?"

"Well, that's my boss. Kind of."

I may have to listen to Schwartz day-to-day on certain aspects of my practice since he signs my paychecks, but it's easier not to think of him as my boss when I made the mistake of sleeping with him while I was a law student.

"Damn, looks like he's not having a very good night." The man on the couch with me shifts closer, brushing my leg again with his, and his palm comes down on my thigh. "But *you* can."

Oh, hell no.

I slowly turn my head toward him and lock our gazes. "I highly suggest you remove your hand from my thigh before I break it."

His eyes widen slightly, only instead of removing the offending appendage, the asshole grins and squeezes my flesh. "Oh, you like to play rough. I can get into that."

"The only thing you'll be getting *into* is a police car or an ambulance if you don't take your hand off me right now."

"Whoa, lady." He jerks his grubby mitt off me and opens his mouth to argue. "You—"

I push to my feet, not missing the way his eyes zero in on my exposed legs and heels, even after my warning. "Let me give you a piece of unsolicited, free legal advice. Not only do women *not* want to be treated like pieces of meat but touching one like that is third-degree sexual abuse under the laws of the State of New York."

He gapes at me. "What are you, an attorney or something?"

I snort and down the rest of my drink in one gulp. "Or something."

Apparently, my doctorate doesn't prevent me from being nothing more than a potential lay for a perv like this asshole. It shouldn't be surprising, but I had hoped tonight I could meet a nice guy and enjoy myself without being smashed in the face by misogyny.

I turn away from him without another word and make my way over to the booth where Schwartz sits, wiping the drink from his face with tiny bar napkins, the model nowhere in sight.

Fighting back a grin, I slide into the side of the booth she just vacated, setting my empty glass in front of me. He looks over at me and releases an exasperated sigh. I can't stop the laugh this time, shaking my head and pointing at his empty tumbler on the table that likely once held a single malt scotch —his usual drink.

"Looks like you could use another."

He glowers at me. "It's not very becoming to revel in the misery of others."

"Not reveling." I motion for the waiter and point to our empty glasses while Schwartz tosses the dirty napkins onto the table. I lean forward, returning my attention to him, fighting back a smile. "Swear, I'm not reveling."

"Yes, you are." He bites the inside of his cheek, the tiniest of grins playing at his lips. "You're taking pleasure in my misery. It's all over your pretty little face."

Pretty little face...

It's crap like that from Schwartz that makes working with him so frustrating sometimes. He respects the hell out of what I do in a courtroom for our clients, but he just can't seem to rein in the inappropriate comments that cross the line more often than not. That's partly my fault for ever letting him get in my pants. But when you're a young law student and a handsome, successful attorney flirts with you —especially when you've had a few strong drinks—you don't think about the fact that you may end up working with or *for* the man later in your career and have to look him in the eye with the knowledge of what his junk looks like.

As per usual, I ignore the sexist remark he likely thinks is world-class flirting. Inappropriate shit from men is just part of the job when working as a trial lawyer, and David Schwartz is no different. I understood it before I ever went to law school, and nothing has changed despite years of building up my reputation.

"What did you say to her that pissed her off so much?"

He offers a shrug. "Nothing too offensive."

I tip back my head and laugh, the sound eaten up by the din of the patrons filling the almost-impossible-to-get-into bar. "I know you well enough to know that isn't true."

He scowls at me and reclines against the booth seat, stretching his arms across the back of it. "Okay, so maybe I pissed her off, but that's only because she has a problem with honesty. Throwing her drink at me—that was a bit extreme."

Cocking my head to the side, I dart my tongue across my lower lip, considering how great it would feel to do the same to him sometimes. "I might have thrown a drink at you for some of the things you've said to me if I had one handy."

That grin of his makes another appearance, and he lowers his arms and leans in too close for professional comfort. "Yet you still went to bed with me."

The waiter has perfect timing, appearing with our drinks and setting them in front of us.

"Thanks." I immediately take a sip of mine, and as soon as the waiter retreats, I point at Schwartz. "That was once—a long time ago. I was very young. Very drunk. And very horny. It's not going to happen again."

He shrugs and grins at me mischievously. "I can try to wear you down."

"I would advise against it."

One of his dark eyebrows rises. "Offering your boss legal advice, are you? That's cute."

"Seems like you need it."

He chuckles and reaches for his drink, but as his fingers close around the glass, the shrill ring of his phone cuts through the tension between us. A quick glance at the name on the screen brings a litany of curses from his mouth. He swipes his finger across the screen and brings it to his ear.

I sip my drink and watch him, waiting for him to flip out on whoever seems to be annoying him so much.

"You've got the worst fucking timing, Parrish, and for that, my rate just doubled." Schwartz practically hisses his words into the line, and given who is on the other end, I can't blame him.

His relationship with Parrish and the Satan's Knights has always been complicated, to say the least. After being saddled with representing the club when his father moved to California to run the West Coast office of their firm, it's a weight I'm sure he'd love to have off his shoulders. They always seem to be getting into some kind of trouble Schwartz doesn't want to be dealing with.

Schwartz's hand tightens on the phone. "An associate? I don't run for your pals, Parrish." He listens to whatever the former president of the ruthless MC says on the other end and snarls. "Where are you?" He pulls the phone away from his ear and swipes the screen before bringing the phone back to his ear. "I'll be right there."

He slides out of the booth with an annoyed groan.

"Where are you rushing off to?"

He slips his phone into his pocket and pulls out his wallet. "That was Parrish." He drops some bills onto the table. "One of his associates got locked up." He points toward his untouched drink. "Help yourself to that when you're finished with yours."

I smile at him, despite the annoyance I still harbor toward the man. This is just how it is with David Schwartz and how it likely always will be. "I just might. See you tomorrow."

Schwartz makes his way out of the bar, and I lean back in the booth with a sigh, scanning the room for anyone else interesting even though I'll more than likely just head home alone.

It's been a long fucking day already, and dealing with douche canoe over on the couch just made it feel even longer. But at least I'm not stuck going to one of the jails tonight like Schwartz.

That really would put a damper on the evening.

MOUTH

REAPER WAS RIGHT. After what we did to Yankovich's organization the last time we were in New York, they're ready for us—or whoever else they might think could be coming for them. They've closed ranks and increased their security tenfold over what they had at their various locations only months ago.

More men.

More cameras.

Less risk for them.

They think that will keep them safe, but they've underestimated me and what I'm capable of—or at least, what I *was* capable of and *hopefully* still am.

The ache at my temples starts up again, and I lower myself to the roof and roll onto my back, squeezing my eyes closed against the pain that has become almost a constant over the last few years, especially in stressful situations.

It will dissipate with time.

It will get better.

The empty promises made to me over and over again ring in my head, slamming against my skull in a beat that only seems to be racing toward an agonizing crescendo.

Better. Yeah, fucking right.

I was stupid to believe the doctors when I knew in my heart it never would get better, and I was stupid to think I could somehow come to New York and take care of this mission without it interfering. But Reaper is counting on me to get this job done, and the women these fuckers are dragging into their web of sex and violence need to be protected.

There isn't any time for weakness. Over the years, I've pushed through worse, kept working, kept firing, kept others alive even when I was bleeding, exhausted, and on my last fucking leg.

I can do it again. I have to.

It seems like I've gotten here in time to stop another auction from happening since the girls don't appear to be here yet, but I need to act quickly. The longer this guy has to make plans and try to get the organization back up and running at full speed again, the greater the chance innocent women are going to get hurt.

Get in the game, Mouth.

I shake off the cloudiness fogging my brain, push away the pain, and flip back onto my stomach to return to my perch and watch my prey. With so many other things I can't remember clearly, this—stalking and waiting—feels more natural than anything else I do daily.

This was my life. This is what I did—hunted and protected my men. Yet so much of it is lost. The good and the bad. Some of the memories are better left in the past, though. Too much pain lies there, too many mistakes and consequences. Those are the ones I dread, the ones I hope never do come back fully. The flashes I get of them are enough for me to know I don't want them to ever become crystal clear.

And I won't make a mistake tonight.

I can't.

The weapon in my hand has always been my best friend, the tool I relied on over and over again to do its job as long as I did mine. It's a part of me. Still, tonight, I'd much rather be handling this guy up close and personal.

A nice knife to the gut and genitals. A little water-boarding to really send a message. Maybe even some sleep deprivation. There are just so many things I'd love to do to him to make him really pay for his actions. But New York City has too many eyes. There's always somebody watching or a camera recording. Always someone with the potential to see something you don't want them to, and I definitely don't want any witnesses for this.

The moment that fucker makes a mistake, he's mine. No amount of security will protect him from the bullet with his name on it. Justice will be served, one way or another.

He's been good, though. Meticulous. Not even stepping outside to get into the car, only entering through a covered, protected garage at his place or inside the warehouse.

This is a man who's aware that what he's doing has made him a target. He's paranoid for a reason. Likely after he discovered what happened to his cousin here, he knew he would be up against an opponent he couldn't eliminate first.

All this careful planning and protection will be for naught, though.

Everybody fucks up, eventually. Everybody gets complacent. It's what people in my position count on to get the job done, and I will get the job done—hopefully, tonight.

Not that I don't enjoy a nice evening in Brighton Beach, but it would be a lot better without this migraine and *with* a little bloodshed.

And my opportunity may be finally presenting itself.

The rear door to the warehouse he's been operating out of swings open, and one of his men steps out, an unlit cigarette dangling from his mouth. It's his routine. Every thirty minutes, almost to the second. And each time, he props open the door, giving me brief glances of movement inside.

All I need is for the right man to take the wrong step.

Maksim Yankovich's goon pulls a Zippo from his pocket and lights his cigarette, sucking on it like it's oxygen. The irony almost makes me chuckle, but I hold it in and keep my eyes on him and the open door.

Several sets of feet walk past, but nothing else is visible. Nothing that will give me certainty of my target.

It's a waiting game—and *this* game, I can play.

Almost like the big man upstairs is giving me a giant *fuck you*, the migraine roars back, stronger than before, a piercing pain that makes me wince and grit my teeth.

Not now.

Not now.

Not now.

The smoker glances over his shoulder at someone and yells something I can't make out from here. I wait a moment for something, anything, to happen. The flash of movement behind him might have been missed by someone else, someone without my keen eye and experience, but all it takes is that split second for Maksim to step toward the door to respond.

Crack.

Crack.

I fire off two rounds, taking out him and his man standing outside almost instantaneously. They both crumble to the ground, dead before they even hit it.

Mission accomplished.

But there isn't any time to enjoy my success.

Even out here, surrounded by dilapidated buildings and warehouses, there are eyes and ears. Someone will have heard those shots even if it takes a few minutes from Yankovich's men to process what happened, and I need to be long gone before anyone starts searching for where it came from.

I pack up my rifle, grab the shell casings, and start to push to my feet. By the time anyone can come looking for the source of the shots, I'll be blocks away, strolling down the street toward where I parked my getaway car like nothing even happened.

In theory.

As soon as I get halfway vertical, the world spins around me like I'm stuck on some sadistic merry-go-round. I clamp my eyes closed against the agony assaulting my head. My stomach turns, vertigo and pain making acid crawl up my throat.

Fuck.

This one is bad—perhaps the worst I've had in months. And history tells me it's only going to get worse—fast. There isn't any way I'm going to make my exit plan.

Time for plan B.

All I have to do is keep my shit together long enough to get to the basement of this shithole.

I stagger over to the door on the roof that leads to the stairwell and step through it, kicking away the rock I had holding it open to let the door slam closed behind me. Staring down at the four flights of stairs, the world tilts, and I have to swallow back the bile, my vertigo kicking in even stronger.

There's no time for weakness, Mouth.

Complete the mission.

Do what must be done.

I stumble down the steps as fast as my unsteady feet will carry me, but the wail of police sirens hits my ears, and I freeze.

Fuck.

A squad must have been in the vicinity and heard the

shots. There's no way those assholes called this in. The last thing Yankovich's men want are the cops crawling around that warehouse.

I double-time it the rest of the way into the dark, dank, dilapidated basement; the only thing keeping me vertical is my iron grip on the handrail. A quick scan of the dark space ensures I'm still alone. Even though this warehouse has been empty and condemned for years, vagrants still use it as a flop house at times. It's currently visitor free.

Thank fuck.

The last thing I need is a witness. Getting out of here without being caught will be hard enough as it is when I'm like this.

I make my way to the far corner to the spot I found during my first surveillance of this place, pull my rifle out of the soft case, and break it down quickly with trembling hands.

My vision shifts in and out of focus, and I reach up to the foot-wide hole near the top of the brick wall and drop each piece into the gap between the ancient foundation and the earth behind it, one by one.

Each part clanks ominously, and I fold the rifle case and shove it as deep down into the hole as I can.

No one will find anything here. Once the smoke clears, one of the Knights or I can come back to get everything. It will require pulling down more of the wall to access it, but so be it. That's a problem for later. Right now, I need to focus on getting the fuck out of here.

The sirens grow louder as I stagger toward the stairwell, head twisted in an invisible vise.

Feet thud against the concrete above me.

Fuck.

I scan the basement, knowing what I'm going to find. The only window is far too small for me to get through. There's only one way out, and that's back up the stairs and through the main warehouse, without whoever is up there seeing me.

Unlikely to be a problem if I were at the top of my game, but I'm far from that at the moment. My stomach roils, and I hustle up the steps, gritting my teeth against the stabbing in my head, then pause at the top and listen for signs of anyone else.

It's quiet. A little too quiet since I know someone just came in. Maybe I'm lucky and it's a vagrant and not a fucking cop or one of Maksim's men who somehow followed the shot.

Easing my way out and along the wall, I keep to the darkest of the shadows, away from the faint moonlight coming in through the broken windows on the opposing wall.

One of the exits is only a few feet ahead.

So close, I can almost smell freedom.

Get there, Mouth.

A blinding light hits my eyes. "You there, freeze! Police!"

Fuck.

I throw up my hands against the harsh beam made ten times worse by the light sensitivity I always suffer during one of these attacks.

My night just turned into a clusterfuck, and it's about to get worse.

I can't fight the nausea anymore, the flashlight in my eyes and the hurried movements finally getting the better of me. Despite my best efforts to choke it back, I turn to the side and wretch, the contents of my stomach splattering against the cracked concrete at my feet as the officer advances with his gun drawn on me.

Fuck.

2

FINLEY

The shrill ring of my cell phone wakes me from what was about to be a fabulous dream. Strong muscles. Warm skin. Expert hands. All of it was about to culminate in something I had hoped to find earlier tonight.

Instead of the payoff, I groan and roll onto my side, fumbling on my nightstand until my hand finally wraps around the offending device.

I pull the screen toward my face, squinting against the brightness. "Fucking Schwartz…"

There are only two reasons he'd be calling at two a.m. Neither of them is good.

I accept the call and bring the phone to my ear. "I told you at the bar that it's not happening again. Go to bed, Schwartz."

"Not a booty call, Fin. I wish I was calling for that, but you need to wake up."

His tone makes my brain fully snap awake. I push myself into a seated position and scrub my hand over my face. "Why? What's going on?"

"I need you to head out to Brighton Beach. 60th precinct."

"What? Now?" I double-check the time on my clock. "It's two o'clock."

"I know, but I'm still dealing with the issue Parrish called me about earlier tonight over on Staten Island, and now, two more of his associates got picked up in Brighton Beach."

"Fuck…doing what?"

"I'm not entirely sure. You need to go see both of them and make sure neither of them talks. Figure out what you can before they get in front of the judge."

"This can't wait a few more hours?"

If these guys are Parrish's "associates," they should know not to talk, and I can grab a bit more sleep before I have to drag my ass all the way out to Brighton Beach.

"No. One of them is Wolf's son."

"Shit…" I scrub my hand over my face, trying to wake myself up. "I'm on my way. Text me the info."

I throw off the covers, end the call, quickly grab appropriate jail clothes from my closet, and toss them onto the bed.

It's far too late—or too early—to be doing this, but when the son of the president of the Knights gets popped, going immediately isn't even a question. Wolf isn't the kind of man you mess with, and you don't keep his son waiting in lock up.

I step out into the kitchen and punch the start button on the Keurig to get a cup going while I change and haphazardly pull my disheveled hair back into a ponytail, so it doesn't look like I just rolled out of bed—even though I did.

Typically, I'd never let a client see me with bags under my eyes and looking haggard as hell, but I'm too tired to care and Schwartz will kill me if I make Wolf's son—and whoever this other client is—wait any longer than necessary.

Only the blackest of coffee will help me right now. I grab the travel mug, pop on the top, and head out the door with my briefcase in hand. Between the drive out there and these meetings, by the time I'm done, I'll have to come straight home and shower before heading to court for my morning calendar.

What the hell is going on tonight?

Three of Parrish's guys all picked up at almost the same time?

I unlock and open my car door, glancing up at the full moon.

That explains it.

That and the fact that anyone associated with Parrish always ends up with at least one foot in shit at some point.

The only thing that keeps me awake during the half-hour drive from Staten Island to Brighton Beach is chugging the black coffee and wincing at how bitter it is. I'd much rather have a triple latte, and God knows I'll be getting one as soon as I leave the damn police station. But at two in the damn morning, I can't be picky about where I get my caffeine.

It's just the glamorous life of a criminal defense attorney working for Schwartz.

I pull up in front of the 60th precinct building, park, and make my way inside, feeling slightly more awake than I did forty minutes ago. Locating my identification, I approach the front desk sergeant.

He glances up at me over the top of his wire-rimmed glasses. "Can I help you?"

"Yes, I'm attorney Finley Banks, and I need to see two people you have in custody."

The bored-looking man glances at his watch. "It's two thirty in the morning, ma'am."

"A fact of which I'm intimately aware, sir, but that doesn't change my needing to see my clients immediately."

He releases a deep sigh and flips through a stack of papers on a clipboard in front of him. "Their names?"

I scan the text Schwartz sent me after we hung up. "Vincenzo Scotto and...Jude Lawson."

Another annoyed sigh slips from his lips. "I don't have a Jude Lawson."

"Then, he's likely listed as John Doe."

The man stares at me for a moment, his hard eyes narrowing, then scans his paperwork again. "First-degree murder. Two counts. Nice."

I fight a wince.

Of course, it has to be a murder case in the middle of the fucking night.

"Which one would you like to see first, ma'am?"

"That depends. Are either of them currently in questioning with detectives?"

The corner of his mouth quirks up into a little half grin. "I'm not sure, ma'am. Likely not Mr. Lawson since he hasn't said a single word since they brought him in. Wouldn't even give us his name."

Not a single *word?*

Smart criminals know to keep their mouths shut, but most at least ask for their lawyer or a phone call. Hell, a *bathroom.* Something.

"Let's start with Mr. Scotto, then."

"Ah, a first-degree assault charge. Starting out light."

I scowl at him. At this hour, I could do without the sarcasm. "Buzz me through. I know the way to the meeting room."

He shoves a clipboard at me to sign in, gives my ID a cursory glance, and presses the button under his desk to unlock the door that will get me into the precinct. I make my way down the hall toward the meeting rooms and slide into the first one with an open door.

Pulling out my legal pad and pen, I cover a massive yawn with my hand.

So much for the black coffee.

Hopefully, these meetings will be quick, and I can get home for at least a nap before I have to make myself presentable for court.

Heavy footsteps make their way down the hallway toward me, and a uniformed officer leads in my first client. Dark eyes meet mine from beneath tousled brown hair. The scruff covering his jaw can't hide the way he clenches it as he glances back at the officer escorting him, who pushes him down into the chair facing me.

"Thank you, Officer." I look down at the cuffs on his hands. "Please uncuff him."

The officer gives me an exasperated look. "Ma'am, that's against policy."

"I don't care. Uncuff him. I need him to be able to write."

"He can write just fine with cuffs on." He turns and closes the door behind him, effectively ending that debate.

The young man stares at me from across the table, his knuckles swollen and bloody.

"Vincenzo Scotto?"

He nods. "Call me Enzo."

"I'm Finley Banks. I'm an attorney, and I work with David Schwartz. Parrish and your father asked for me to come to see you to figure out what's going on."

He relaxes slightly.

"They arrested you on first-degree assault charges, and from the looks of your hands and the spot of blood on your shirt, it seems to me they might have a case. So, tell me what happened."

Enzo lowers his head, taking in the speck of blood, then looks back at me. "My stepbrother owns a boxing gym, and I nicked myself shaving."

Smartass.

But he's just trying to protect himself. I can't really blame him for that.

"Whatever you tell me must remain strictly confidential. Protected by attorney-client privilege. You're going to go before the judge in the next forty-eight hours. We're going to face whatever these charges are, and it's helpful to know what we're up against so we can get in front of it."

He reaches up and rubs his eyes with his palms, a task made all the more difficult by the fact that they're still cuffed together. "Brent Matthews donates to my father's charity, Frankie's House. He was holding a fundraiser tonight in Staten Island. I thought I'd show my support."

I quirk an eyebrow at his casual clothes. Jeans and a T-shirt are hardly appropriate attire for a fundraiser. "Dressed like that?"

He shrugs. "I wasn't aware of a dress code until I arrived at the place. That's why I didn't go in. I was about to leave when I saw Danica, Brent's ex-wife, step outside. She and I are...well, we're acquainted."

I purse my lips. "Acquainted?"

He shakes his head. "It's not like that between us. Look, when she walked outside, she was with Matthews. They were arguing, and when they left, I suspected something bad might happen. I followed her to make sure she was safe. They came out here to Brighton Beach. She confronted him; they started yelling at each other, then he grabbed her. I got out of my car and intervened."

"Badly enough to charge you with a first-degree assault." Which means Mr. Scotto did some serious damage to the man who is currently running for office.

"You and I both know Brent Matthews is a powerful guy. He's running for Congress. But everyone has skeletons in their closet. They put on a good front, but their marriage didn't end simply because they grew apart. He's been treating her like shit for a long time. Now, I witnessed a heated argument between a divorced couple, and the second he raised his hands to her, I separated them. He took a swing at me, and I defended myself."

"Are there any witnesses? Anyone who might be able to back up your story?"

Convincing the DA that a prospective congressman is an abusive asshole is an uphill battle. We'll need to dig deep and find some evidence to support Mr. Scotto's allegations if we have any chance at defending this.

Enzo stares at me for a moment, contemplating his response before he nods. "Brent's ex-wife will back me."

"Are you sure she'll tell the same story?"

"Yes."

"All right. Well, that's good." I jot down a few notes. "You'll go in front of the judge tomorrow or the next day. The charges will be read, and they're going to set a bond. I'm sure your father will get it posted as soon as possible. They'll set a preliminary hearing date, but given that you were arrested on the scene, have a couple of busted-up knuckles, and have blood on your clothes, we will likely want to waive that hearing and gain access to the police reports and any other evidence quicker. This will come down to what his ex-wife says and whether the DA believes you and her or the alleged victim." Not a slam dunk by any means when the man is in a position like Brent Matthews. "Do you have any questions right now?"

"No. I'm good."

"Okay. Then, sit tight. Keep your mouth shut and head down." Things I'm sure his father and the Knights have taught him over the years. "I'll see you at court."

I push up from the table, make my way to the door, and open it. The officer stands just outside and glances over at me with an annoyed look. He doesn't want to be doing this at three in the morning any more than I do.

"Finished with Mr. Scotto. Can you please bring in my next client?"

His jaw hardens. "Ma'am, he's here on a double murder charge."

I raise my eyebrows at him. "Your point?"

"We typically wouldn't allow anyone to meet with him without additional security measures."

"*Anyone?*" I cross my arms over my chest. "Or a woman?"

He freezes for a second, then opens his mouth and closes it again, likely second-guessing what his response would have been when he sees the glare I'm giving him.

"Go get him."

Muttering something about blood-sucking lawyers, he steps in and grabs Mr. Scotto, jerking him to his feet a little too forcefully. I offer him a parting smile, and they make their way down the hallway toward the holding cells again.

Misogynist asshole.

I return to my seat to jot down a few more notes about what Enzo just told me. If it's true—that he witnessed an assault and was intervening—this may be, at worst, a defense-of-others claim. The complication is the victim's position—something we'll definitely have to address once we get the written statements and other evidence.

Footsteps sound down the hallway again, and I wait for John Doe, aka Jude Lawson, who apparently, has been arrested for two murders, to be brought in.

Lovely.

The officer appears in the open door with my new client, dressed head to toe in jail garb.

I don't know what I was expecting, but it sure as hell wasn't this.

Icy-blue eyes cold enough to freeze anything they look at assess me with an intelligence I rarely see in my clients.

No fear.

No panic.

No sense of unease.

Despite sitting in here on these very serious charges.

Instead, a heat simmers beneath their surface. A danger contained only through sheer will and confidence.

My misogynist friend leads him in and seats Mr. Lawson across from me, holding up a hand. "Don't even bother asking about the cuffs." He stares at Lawson for a moment, then turns his focus to me. "Good luck. This guy hasn't said a single word since he was picked up."

"Then how did my firm find out he was in custody?"

The officer smirks. "He had a notebook in his back pocket. We pulled it out while we were stripping him. He pointed to it, and the detective gave it to him. He wrote 'phone call' and a number on it. The detective dialed it, and this guy wrote, 'Tell him where I am,' and that was the end of that. Whoever was on the other end hung up and then, I assume...called *you.*" He narrows his eyes and shakes his head. "All very strange."

Indeed. Maybe Mr. Lawson is deaf or mute?

He moves to the door and pauses before closing it behind him. "Thanks for giving us his name, though. Helpful since his prints haven't brought up anything."

No record?

That's definitely unusual for one of Parrish's guys. Most of them have a rap sheet a mile long and the attitudes to match it. But this guy...

Broad shoulders. Lean, hard muscles visible under the jail clothing given to him. Eyes that seem to see right through me while they also strip me bare. A calm that makes me more uneasy than anything any client has ever said to me before.

Jude Lawson stares back without reaction to me or anything the uniformed officer said.

The door clicks closed, and I take that as my cue to jump right in.

"I'm Finley Banks. I'm an attorney. I was sent here by Parrish to represent you." I pause to try to gauge his reaction and to attempt to determine if he can even hear me. "I'm happy to hear you haven't said anything potentially incriminating." I offer him a half-grin, but all that earns me is more continued staring. "They have you here on some pretty serious charges."

He doesn't react, just continues to analyze me with the cool gaze that somehow heats my body all the same, his large, muscular body immobile.

I shift on my hard, plastic chair to try to dispel some of the strange sensations of having him look at me like that sends through me. "I already know you didn't say anything to the arresting officers or detectives. I need to make sure you can hear me and understand what's happening, Mr. Lawson."

MOUTH

Ms. Banks' frustration rolls off her like a tidal wave set on destroying whatever she thinks it is that keeps me from answering her.

Stupid. Stubborn. Arrogant. This woman likely believes all of these things about me.

And why shouldn't she?

To her, I'm just another criminal who got busted, who forced her to roll out of bed in the middle of the night to come down here and hold his hand. Another in a long line of clients who don't respect her or what she does and only see her for what she is on the outside—a stunning woman who could just as easily be on the cover of a magazine as in a courtroom.

No doubt, she's used to having chauvinistic men—like the officer who just led me in here and even her own clients—give her shit because she's a beautiful woman doing a job they despise and think should be left only to men. Her days are likely spent dealing with that type of asshole, the kind who make her prove over and over again that she belongs and that she can win her cases in heels bigger than their dicks.

I don't envy her at all.

Every man I ever served with had to prove they belonged there—me included. Each one of us was put through the wringer. We were the best of the best. And something tells me Ms. Banks is one fucking fantastic attorney.

Parrish wouldn't trust her to represent someone if she weren't, and her entire energy has filled the room since the moment I was brought in. It bounces off the tight walls, a "don't try me" vibe emanating from her in a way that can't be denied.

She may be tiny, but she doesn't back down. And all she wants is my cooperation. The least I can do is confirm I understand what's happening.

I offer the tiniest shift in my head, just enough to let her know I'm listening.

"Good, I'm glad you're with me, but I need to know what they said to you and what, if any, physical evidence they may have before we go into the arraignment so I can start developing our plan of attack."

I remain still, assessing the woman sent by the Knights to help me.

Frustration tightens her grip on her pen. "Mr. Lawson, I don't think you're quite grasping the seriousness of this situation here. I understand not speaking to the police, but not speaking with your lawyer is going to cause a lot of problems. I can't do anything for you if you won't talk to me. I'm here to *help* you, but you need to help *me* first."

She keeps her clenched hand around the pen poised on an empty sheet of paper that she likely had anticipated being filled with notes by now.

Her green eyes bore into me, not looking away for even a second.

Impressive.

She's the first person in a long time who has been able to stare me down and not be intimidated. This tiny, five-foot-nothing woman who can't weigh more than a buck-twenty has more balls than some of the men I've served with.

Ms. Banks must be an absolute shark in the courtroom.

Thank fuck she's on my side rather than at the prosecutor's table.

I'm going to need someone like her. Someone who doesn't back down from anything. The cops may not have found the weapon, but they have enough to hold me and charge me.

Not only was I caught trespassing in a condemned building, but they also have a vagrant who heard the shot while on the street below only minutes before. Seeing them speaking with him outside when they perp walked me made me want to puke again.

The only thing saving me from assured conviction is this woman and the fact that New York's finest don't have the resources to tear apart a three-story dilapidated building to conduct an in-depth search for the rifle. They'll do a cursory search, at best, perhaps assume I had someone else with me who got away with it, and hopefully, they'll leave it at that.

But even if they may not be able to convict me in the end, they can make my life hell while the charges are pending. Ms.

Banks will surely do her best to ensure that doesn't happen, but she'll have to do it without my help.

"Mr. Lawson?" She raises a thin brow at me, tapping her pen against the legal pad.

The tick, tick, tick might be annoying to someone else. Not me. It's almost…therapeutic. Like a metronome clicking back and forth, setting a steady tempo. All the tension in my head eases for a brief moment concentrating on the sound.

A brief flash of a memory flutters through my mind.

Broken images…

A woman at a piano.

The ticking of a metronome.

Music filling the room.

Warmth and comfort.

A feeling of being home.

Secure.

Safe.

"Mr. Lawson, please." Her tension seems to have ratcheted even tighter while I've been lost in the shattered memory. "Help *me* help *you.*"

Despite the continued pain in my head, I fight the twitch of my lips wanting to smirk at that phrase. So many people have said it to me over the last few years—my team, my doctors, the government, others who claimed to care. Yet they all disappeared when it was clear I wasn't getting better and would never remember why I should care about them and that I would never be who I was before that night.

Help me help you…

People say the words in an effort to get you to let down your guard. But some guards are in place for a very good reason. Those words rang in my ears, said too many times to count by too many people who should have been able to make it better.

A lot of good it did.

I'm not any better now than I was when I woke up after the explosion four years ago. If anything, the migraines are only getting worse, the memories fuzzier as time passes rather than coalescing and coming back the way I was promised.

The longer it goes on, the more confusing they become until I can barely tell what's real and what's a dream or nightmare anymore. That, coupled with the almost daily pain, becomes unbearable at times—like earlier tonight. The only thing pushing me forward is my mission, the jobs Reaper, Chaos, and I do. The justice we seek for people who can't get it anywhere else.

I just need to keep reminding myself of that when I feel like I do now.

At least I haven't puked again.

Doing that in front of a beautiful woman like this would be…embarrassing. It's bad enough having to sit here across from her in jail garb while she's in a form-fitting suit that accentuates her curves. Even the slight bags under her eyes she didn't bother to try to hide can't mar her true beauty.

It shines in her eyes—along with her determination and irritation.

She's a good person, just trying to do her job. And while I'd like to help her, the headache throbs behind my eyes, radiating out through my whole head. The only thing that will end it is a day of sleep or my meds, which I'm not getting to anytime soon, apparently.

Ms. Banks sighs and sits back in her chair, flipping the pen between her fingers and staring at me for what feels like an hour, waiting for me to break.

She has no idea who she's dealing with. Men far stronger and—maybe—more determined than her have done far worse things to get me to talk…and failed.

I cross my arms over my chest and wait, my eyes locked

on her green ones. Something flashes deep inside them, something that, for a moment, almost makes me open my mouth to answer her questions. But I know what that brings, so I bite back the words like I do every day of my life.

Finally, she throws up her hands and shakes her head. "All right, Mr. Lawson. I guess I'll do the talking, then. If you have something to say, you let me know. If you don't want to talk, I'll give you my notepad and pen."

She sighs. "In the next forty-eight hours, you'll be led out of here to the courtroom. You'll appear in front of the judge, who's going to look at a criminal complaint the district attorney's office is drafting right now. That complaint is going to charge you, more than likely, with two counts of first-degree murder and any other charges they can throw at you because I can tell you right now, Mr. Lawson, they'll do everything they can to keep you in custody. And the more charges they can pile up, the less likely you are to be able to meet the bond that gets set. If you're stuck here, that puts them at an incredible advantage preparing for trial."

She taps her pen against the table, letting her words sink in.

"It makes it very hard for me to argue on your behalf when you won't talk to me, when I have no idea who you are, why you were there, what you were doing, or have any explanation I can offer the court that would give the judge a reason to release you on a reasonable bond while we try to figure this thing out." She leans forward slightly, the top of her breasts just barely visible in the V-neck blouse she wears under her suit jacket. "I'm on your side, Mr. Lawson. It would behoove you to start acting like it."

Her words are meant to terrify me, and with her typical clients, her tough attitude and no-nonsense approach probably scares them into complying with her requests. It probably makes her job easier when clients know they can't walk all over her just because of her appearance. In her profession, looking like a cover model probably makes it harder for her to get people to take her seriously. She's fixed that by becoming an unbreakable pillar of strength and determination.

If they let women on Delta Force, she'd have been a real badass operative.

Exasperation finally getting the better of her, she shoves to her feet and practically throws her notepad and pen into her bag, her eyes still on me. "I'll see you in court soon, Mr. Lawson. And I seriously want you to consider your attitude toward me. This type of behavior isn't going to get you anywhere."

She stalks past me, her thigh lightly brushing my shoulder. Despite layers of clothing between us, a little buzz of electricity courses through my arm and radiates into my entire body. I swallow thickly, listening to the click of her heels on the linoleum until I hear the doorknob twist in her small hand.

Something burns in my chest, something I haven't felt in so long. I don't even recognize it. And it has nothing to do with the permanent brain damage that has ruined my life. It's because I haven't experienced it before, at least, not that I can remember.

For some reason, for the first time I *can* remember, I actually *care* what someone thinks about me. I actually care what *she* thinks about me. I don't want her believing I'm a total asshole who's being difficult and uncooperative just because I can be. I want her to know I appreciate her being here, coming down in the middle of the night to ensure I'm taken care of and protected. I want her to understand this has nothing to do with *her.*

I want her to know the *truth.*

No matter how painful it may be to admit it to her.

Slowly, I turn my head to the side, swallowing to give myself a moment to get my tongue and mouth working when I haven't used them to speak for so damn long. "Th-th-thank y-y-you, M-M-Ms. Banks."

Out of the corner of my eye, I watch her freeze, her hand still on the half-open door. The fingers wrapped around her briefcase ease their grip slightly, and she looks over her shoulder at me, her green eyes meeting mine without blinking.

There it is...

The familiar look of pity.

The thing I've been avoiding during this entire conversation.

The look I knew would come as soon as I opened my mouth.

No one sees me the same after they know. Even those who know who I am and what I'm capable of no longer see me as an elite military operative. All they see is someone to feel sorry for, someone who needs their sympathy. They see a weak mind when really, it's just this stupid fucking body that betrays me.

But unlike most people I deal with, the look of pity vanishes from her warm gaze just as quickly as it appeared, and her perfect pink lips curl into a kind smile.

She inclines her head to me, acknowledging my statement, then walks out and leaves me sitting in the room by myself to consider what just happened with my new attorney.

Well, that went well.

It certainly wasn't what I was expecting when they told me my attorney was here. *She* wasn't what I was expecting. I never could have anticipated the way she would make me feel, the need to have her understand the thing I've kept hidden from so many for so long.

It definitely complicates things.

FINLEY

The judge steps out from his chambers and takes his seat, glancing at some paperwork on the bench before nodding to his clerk. Enzo shifts nervously beside me, and I reach out and squeeze his shoulder.

This isn't routine for him, and he has every reason to be nervous. Now that I've seen the damage he did to the alleged victim, I can see why the State is pushing these charges. You can't cause that kind of damage to someone as high profile as this and expect them to let it go.

The clerk pulls out a file from a stack on her desk and calls the case.

Judge Forest acknowledges us with a nod and accepts the file from her. "Appearances, please."

At the table next to me, the prosecutor clears his throat. "The State of New York is represented by Jonathan Waters."

I smile at the judge. "Attorney Finley Banks appears on behalf of Mr. Scotto, who appears in person and in custody. Good morning, Your Honor."

"Good morning, Counselors. We're here for an arraignment. Mr. Waters?"

Waters flips open his file to read from it. "Your Honor, the defendant is charged with one count of assault in the first degree, in violation of New York Penal Code section 120.10." He rattles off the penalties and other required items for the arraignment before moving to the bond. "The state is asking for a $10,000 cash bond, Your Honor. Mr. Scotto assaulted a congressional candidate and beat him so severely that he may have to have reconstructive surgery on a shattered orbital socket. He was still present at the scene when the police arrived. This is a very violent crime, Your Honor. Mr. Scotto poses a danger to the community, and therefore, a substantive cash bond is warranted."

"Thank you, Mr. Waters." The judge raises a brow at me. "Ms. Banks?"

"Thank you, Your Honor. Mr. Scotto is twenty-eight years old, has lived in the greater New York City area for his entire life, and has not had any police contacts prior to this incident. He has not exhibited any sort of violent behavior or in any way demonstrated that he poses a threat to the community. The state paints a very rosy picture of the alleged victim in this case and the facts surrounding it that they believe support their version of events, but I can assure this court that Mr. Scotto in no way poses a danger to anyone. As the court is aware, the purpose of bond is to ensure compliance and appearance in court and to protect the public. Mr. Scotto has a full-time job, numerous connections to the community, and there is no reason to believe he won't make all court appearances and cooperate with his defense. Therefore, we are asking for a $5,000 cash bond."

The judge examines Enzo for a moment. "Mr. Scotto, these are very serious charges. You understand that?"

Enzo straightens his shoulders even more and nods. "I do, Your Honor."

"You understand that if you're released on bond, you must make all your court appearances and will not have any contact with the alleged victim or any of the witnesses in this case. If you do, that could result in additional felony charges?"

"Yes, Your Honor."

The judge hands the file to the clerk. "Given Mr. Scotto's ties to the community, his lack of prior record, and the statement of his attorney regarding his cooperation with her, I'm going to set a $5,000 cash bond. Standard conditions including no contact with victims or witnesses."

I nod at the judge. "Thank you, Your Honor."

The clerk quickly gets us a date for the next hearing, and I scribble it onto my calendar and start pulling out Mr. Lawson's file.

Enzo looks over at me, and I lean in. "You can go with the officers. They'll have the paperwork. Your dad will have you bonded out quickly. Call me tomorrow."

He nods his understanding. "Thank you, Ms. Banks."

The courtroom officers approach and lead him back to the holding cell. No doubt the Knights will have him bonded out within an hour. My other client, I'm not so sure. I have no idea how this will go at all, especially given the information I've been able to gather since my meeting with the enigmatic Mr. Lawson.

They bring him into the courtroom, and he carries the same stoic look he did when I saw him in the meeting room in Brighton Beach, not giving away anything. But his eyes still rake over me with a heat that makes me shift uneasily.

There's just something about Jude Lawson that's impossible to pinpoint, and now that I know his history, it sheds a completely different light on our entire first meeting.

I offer him a tight smile as he takes the chair next to me, unwilling to do anything that might reveal how unsettled he makes me. As expected, Jude doesn't do or say anything to acknowledge me, where we are, or why we're here.

"The State of New York versus Jude Lawson…" I tune out the calling of the case, pulling out the criminal complaint and my notes for the bond argument.

The judge accepts the next file. "Appearances."

"The State of New York appears by Jonathan Waters."

"Attorney Finley Banks appearing on behalf of Mr. Lawson, who appears in person and in custody."

"Your Honor, the State has charged Mr. Lawson with two counts of murder in the first degree in violation of New York Penal Code section 125.27 with the anticipation that additional charges may be forthcoming as we continue to investigate. This was a brutal double homicide that took place in a populated area with what appears to have been a high-powered rifle. Mr. Lawson is the most dangerous threat to the community I can imagine, and therefore, we're asking for a $2 million cash bond."

Two million?

I glare at the prosecutor, hoping he'll feel my disdain for his request even if I can't voice it.

The judge raises an eyebrow. "Ms. Banks?"

"Thank you, Your Honor. Mr. Lawson is thirty-two years old, was born in Canton, Ohio, to a father who was career army and a mother who was a homemaker. Both are sadly now deceased. He has two younger sisters and served honorably in the US Armed Forces, enlisting when he was only eighteen years old and remaining on active duty until he was medically discharged about four years ago. Mr. Lawson has not had a *single* contact with law enforcement in his entire life."

I pause to let my words sink in, glancing between the

judge and prosecutor but intentionally avoiding looking at Jude. Not when I can feel his eyes locked on me instead of where they should be—the judge.

He's wondering where I got all this information since he didn't give me anything the other night. I thought I was going to have to go into this without any ammunition to argue for bail, but thankfully, Parrish came through with what I needed. Though, something tells me that having this knowledge is only going to make things more tense with Jude.

If he had wanted me to know any of it, he would have told me—or at least written it down.

The man wanted me in the dark about his background and medical situation. I won't speculate on why, but now that I know, his tension rolls off him palpably.

"Let me repeat that, Your Honor. I'm not talking about an arrest or conviction. I'm talking about not a *single* police *contact*, not a *parking ticket*, not a *speeding ticket*. Nothing. Mr. Lawson served his country and has respected the laws of this country his entire life. Mr. Lawson is exactly the type of law-abiding citizen we expect everyone to be. Whatever the State thinks happened here, Mr. Lawson is not a threat to this community. He's a protector of this community, which he showed in his exemplary military service. There is no reason to believe he will not be cooperative with me or make his appearances in court. I would ask the court to set a reasonable $10,000 cash bond."

Judge Forest directs his attention to the prosecution table. "Mr. Waters, any response?"

"Your Honor, Mr. Lawson does not have any contacts we could find in the city of New York or the state of New York. As far as I can tell, his employer is in Baltimore, Maryland, where he resides, and given his military training, the state has serious concerns about Mr. Lawson disappearing should he be released on bond."

I shake my head. "Your Honor, may I respond?"

"Yes, Counsel."

Here goes nothing.

If Jude was uncomfortable with what I told the court before, he's really not going to like this.

"Your Honor, Mr. Lawson suffered a major traumatic brain injury in an incident overseas four years ago. Due to this injury, he now deals with debilitating migraines, memory loss, as well as a speech impediment caused by the brain damage."

Jude's hand tenses into a fist on his thigh under the table, and I reach and lay mine over his to keep him from doing something stupid in court. He tenses slightly at my touch, but I squeeze gently and brush my thumb over his, trying to comfort him somehow when he clearly doesn't want this information out in the world—or for me to know it at all.

"He's dependent on multiple medications to treat this brain injury, none of which were available to him during his time in holding. Mr. Lawson is not in any position to be fleeing the country, nor does he have any reason not to appear before this court, given the weak nature of the probable cause in this case. The State has no weapon. Their evidence is loose and circumstantial, at best."

I pull my hand away from his, returning it to the top of the table, but still feeling his skin under mine. Swallowing thickly, I glance at the prosecutor before focusing on the judge again, trying to ignore the heat still radiating through my body at the innocent contact.

"Mr. Lawson's employer *is* in Baltimore, but if the court should require it, Mr. Lawson can and does have a place to reside within the state of New York while the charges are pending. And he would be more than happy to do so."

MOUTH

I LOOK OVER AT HER, watching her mouth move and hearing the words coming out of it but not really understanding or processing them, still feeling her touch lingering on my hand and through my chest.

How the hell does she know all this?

And what the hell is she talking about, a place to live in New York?

That migraine that hit me the night I took out that Russian scum was a brutal one, but I think I would have remembered telling her all that background information… and having a damn place in the city. Which I most *certainly* don't.

While the judge considers his notes, she glances over at me and offers me a half-smile, not giving away anything. If her little squeeze of my hand affected her the way it did me, she's doing a damn good job of concealing it.

Finally, the judge sighs and leans back in his chair, looking at me with a shrewd gaze. "Here's what I'm going to do, Counsel. While I appreciate your client's service to this country and understand your position concerning his medical status, these are very serious charges with very serious consequences. And while I agree that probable cause may be light in this matter"—he tosses a look to the prosecutor—"it *is* there, nonetheless. If it weren't, I'd be entertaining a motion to dismiss. Which means, I have to take into consideration the protection of the public from Mr. Lawson and what he's charged with. Therefore, I'm going to order a $500,000 cash bond along with electronic ankle monitoring. And I'm going to require that he turn over his passport and remain in the state of New York while these charges are pending."

Ms. Banks nods, trying to bite back a smile at her victory. "Understood, Your Honor."

She climbs to her feet while I'm still working on trying to figure out where she got all this information, what the hell she was talking about, and the feeling her touch sent through me.

An officer steps behind me and uses my cuffed hands to pull me up, gripping me a little too tightly. I don't even acknowledge him, just wait for directions either from him or Ms. Banks.

I could have him on his back and end his life in ten seconds, even with my hands cuffed, but it doesn't do me any good to fight with this guy in the courtroom, even if he's clearly looking for one.

My determined and apparently sneaky-as-hell lawyer leans over to me. "I spoke with Reaper last night. Your bond will be paid—most likely today. I'll pick you up and get you set up at an apartment Reaper rented for you."

Well, hell...

I haven't given her nearly enough credit. She must have put the screws to Parrish and insisted he connect her with someone who could give her some information on me. Either she got Reaper's number, or he called her. She wasn't going to let my silence prevent her from doing her job and representing me the best she could.

Fucking brilliant.

It shouldn't surprise me at all that she managed to pull this off, given the way she stood up to me the other night and failed to be fazed by my silence.

I incline my head toward her, acknowledging her work and thanking her in the only way I can, and she smiles and reaches out to squeeze my shoulder. Her hand remains there a second longer than it should, and something passes between us that makes a shiver run through me despite the heat in the courtroom.

Her pupils dilate slightly. She shakes her head and jerks her hand back like she's been burned, then grabs her briefcase and hustles out of the courtroom while I get led in the opposite direction, still feeling her touch on my arm.

Even three hours later, when I push open the door from the jail and walk out onto the dark New York City street to find her leaning against a BMW, scrolling through her phone, I can still feel that heat.

The rush.

The energy that passed in that simple action.

This woman is dangerous.

And not just in the courtroom.

The jail door slams shut behind me, and her head jerks up, her green eyes finding me quickly.

She pushes off the car, wearing skin-tight jeans and a loose top that hangs off one shoulder, exposing her collarbone. "Oh, hi." Shoving her phone into her pocket, she scans the street on either side of us, avoiding looking at me as her cheeks redden. "Sorry that took so long. When you're dealing with that much money, the clerk's office sometimes takes forever crossing their *T*s and dotting their *I*s."

So confident in our meeting and the courtroom earlier today, now she seems frazzled.

By what?

Having to leave me there for the rest of the day before I got bailed out?

I offer her a shrug to let her know it's no skin off my back. Really, I could have stayed in there forever and not given much of a shit as long as they could get my meds. I can sleep just about anywhere and block out the noise under normal circumstances. This migraine is finally tapering off naturally after a few days, but who knows what the next one could bring. Being unprepared never ends well.

As I've just proven.

Not that I didn't plan this mission. I did, down to the fucking last second from the moment I left Baltimore to what was supposed to be my return trip home. But I can't predict when my body will betray me anymore. Which is why I had plan B—the damn hole in the basement wall. At least being caught without the weapon makes their case almost impossible to prove beyond a reasonable doubt.

But my weakness is what got me caught.

It was exactly why I didn't want to come to do this alone and why I didn't want to talk to Ms. Banks when she was trying so damn hard to help me the other night.

Now, she knows it all, and it's going to change everything, the entire way she sees me and this case.

She shifts awkwardly on her feet, now clad in Chucks instead of the four-inch stilettos she sported during our jail visit and court this morning, and motions toward her car. "Um, I'll take you to your new apartment. The Knights got it set up for you with some basics—clothes, food, etcetera."

How kind of them...

She steps around the front of the car and slides into the driver's seat while I open my door and take the passenger seat. Almost instantly, her scent invades my lungs—crisp, minty, citrusy—and my cock stirs.

Fucking hell.

The stank of the jail and the musty smell of the court-house masked this before. I shift awkwardly in the seat while reaching for the belt to relieve some of the tension building below mine. She glances over at me furtively, starts the car, and pulls away from the curb into the light evening traffic.

I rest one hand on my thigh and massage my temple with the other, an almost constant motion for the last few days.

The longer we're in the small car together, heading away from the jail and toward wherever I've been set up to stay, the more her scent permeates my every breath, making it harder and harder to sit still. I turn away slightly, staring out the window, watching the dark streets blur by, cracking the window in a vain attempt to get some fresh air instead of smelling *her*.

Normally, during a migraine, watching this would make me lose my stomach again, but...

But it's completely gone.

At some point during this awkward, tense car ride, my migraine completely disappeared.

Impossible.

That never happens. It slowly dissipates on its own most of the time, but without medication, it could take a whole damn week, and there are times I have to go to the neurologist for emergency treatment when it gets really bad.

Yet, somehow, in a matter of minutes, all traces of the headache that has been plaguing me for days have vanished.

I sit up straight, letting my hand fall away from my temple, and glance over at her, but she keeps her eyes on the road in front of her, seemingly unaware of my confusion—or maybe intentionally ignoring it the way I've been trying to ignore the pull I have toward this woman.

We reach a red light, and she finally feels my gaze on her and looks my way.

One of her eyebrows wings up. "Are you okay? You look...confused."

Shit.

The last thing I need is her knowing how she affects me. She has one job—get me off.

Of the charges.

The charges ONLY.

She narrows her eyes on me, concern furrowing her soft

brow. "Do you need something? Something I can get for you on our way to your place?"

Nothing you can buy at a store.

The light changes to green, and she sighs and relaxes back in her seat, her focus returned to the road. Her hands tighten and twist on the wheel, the tension building in her body.

Finally, she glances my way again. "Look, I understand we don't know each other and why you might not want to have a friendly chat, but I'm trying to—"

"H-h-help me. I kn-know."

She flinches, and I instantly regret my words. I didn't mean them to come out sounding so...angry and annoyed. But tone is definitely hard to convey when you can't get words out without stuttering.

Shit.

I scrub my hands over my face and sigh. "S-s-sorry."

She shakes her head, forcing a half-smile. "You don't have to apologize, Mr. Lawson. You've had a rough few days. Your friend, Reaper, he sent some medications he said you need. Said you likely left them somewhere you can't get back to them right now."

Like the damn glove compartment of the car that has long since been towed by now and is sitting in some impound lot.

It isn't her fault I fucked it all up, and I'm going to need her to get out of this mess. If that's even possible. So, the last thing I want to do is have her pissed off at me or thinking I'm mad at her for just trying to help.

"Th-th-thanks. I really d-do appreciate it."

She swallows thickly, something clearly running through her head that she's struggling with voicing. "I'll do whatever I can to help you, Mr. Lawson. Please, just trust me."

That's easier said than done, but I sure as hell don't have anyone else here I can.

"P-p-please, call me Mouth."

Her head jerks in my direction, her lips twisted. "Mouth?"

"It's a l-l-long story…"

One I am in absolutely no position to tell—nor would I want to even if I were capable of it, especially to a woman who stirs up so many things inside me.

Lust.

Need.

Hate.

Concern.

Rage.

I didn't know one person could bring them all, yet somehow, she has.

And that's a very dangerous thing for a man in my position.

4

FINLEY

N o matter how hard I try to concentrate on the stacks of discovery spread out across my desk, my eyes keep drifting to my computer screen and the headline in bold spread out across the e-version of the *New York Post*.

PURPORTED RUSSIAN MOB LEADER KILLED

Shit.

The last thing Mouth or I need is the local news latching onto his case and turning it into some sort of exposé on organized crime violence in the city. While I can't say I shed a tear over Yankovich or his man's deaths, that doesn't mean I want a spotlight on the fact that my client *may* or may *not* have been the one to take them out of commission.

I certainly don't want to be spending my time fielding calls from reporters when I have a trial coming up in a month on the Bergman case, motion hearings on three others next week, and need to get Rick on investigating both

Mouth and Enzo's cases and securing statements from anyone and everyone who can help in either.

A sharp knock on the door jerks me from my trance, and Terri grins at me.

"Sorry, didn't mean to scare you." She holds up a big, brown paper bag. "Ho Wop just delivered your lunch."

Thank God.

It's an excuse to get away from this file and the newspaper article I can't seem to stop reading about the case I can't stop thinking about.

Or the client I can't stop thinking about.

I push away from my desk and smooth out my skirt. "Awesome. I'm starved. Did you get that medical record release Jude Lawson signed over to Charlotte so she can make the request?"

Terri nods. "Yes, she's on it."

"Good." Making my way over to her, I glance across the hall to Schwartz's closed door. "He in with anyone?"

Terri shakes her head. "No. He's been holed up in there a while."

"He can probably use lunch, then." I hustle to his office, raise my hand, and rap my knuckles against the door, then open it without waiting for an answer. I stick in my head and dangle the bag. "Have you had lunch yet? I got your favorite from Ho Wop."

Schwartz sits up straighter in his leather chair, loosening the tie around his neck, and motions for me to enter. He glances at the desk drawer where I know he keeps a bottle of Johnny Walker Black as if he's considering that for lunch rather than the delicious Chinese food I brought him.

"What? No inappropriate comments or snide remarks? Are you sick?"

His usually bright eyes wear dark circles under them, and the way he was slumped in his chair when I first stuck my head in certainly didn't scream *I'm loving life and my job right now.*

I close the door behind me and make my way toward the sofa situated in the far-right corner of his office, depositing the bag full of takeout on the glass coffee table as I lower myself onto the couch. The firm, expensive leather dips with my weight, and I glance over at Schwartz, who still has barely acknowledged me.

Hell, I was just messing with him with my last comment, but maybe something really is wrong.

"You won't even answer me?"

He gives me an exasperated look.

"That doesn't bode well. Did someone die?"

"Sorry." He mutters the apology, swiping a hand over his face. "I've got a case that's haunting the fuck out of me."

Been there. Done that.

This area of law is always complicated. Everyone deserves the protections the Constitution grants, and it's up to us to ensure that the cops, the district attorneys, and everyone else on *that* side plays by the rules and gives our clients a fair shake, but that doesn't mean there aren't some cases—or clients—that get under your skin, from time to time.

Typically, it's the really violent fuckers who have no remorse, but sometimes, it's the really *human* ones who latch onto your soul. The people who are good deep down and simply made a mistake or got themselves into a situation they saw no way out of except to commit a crime.

It's not usual to see Schwartz struggle like this, though. Whatever the case is, it's bad. And despite my not-always-pleasant feelings toward the man, my heart aches for him and his discomfort.

He lumbers out of his chair and rounds the desk to join me on the sofa, walking with far less bravado than he normally does, almost looking defeated.

I study him for a moment as I remove the takeaway cartons from the bag and place them on the table in front of us. "Want to talk about it?"

"Not particularly." Schwartz hands me a pair of chop-sticks from the bag, then browses the containers, ultimately reaching for the dumplings. "I've got Parrish's guy coming in soon to discuss his case."

That definitely isn't what his current mood is about, but I'll let the change in topic slide to avoid digging him deeper into whatever is bothering him. "How's that going?"

With both of our calendars stacked with cases, we haven't had a chance to see each other since Monday at the bar, and aside from a few texts with brief updates for him to pass along to Parrish about Enzo and Jude, we haven't even spoken.

Schwartz seems to consider the question like it doesn't have a simple answer like it should. In this office, "like shit" or "good" are the typical responses thrown around to that inquiry.

Ultimately, he shrugs. "They released him, for now. They're waiting on forensics. They got some DNA from the victim's nails and fingerprints from the hotel room, but the lab is so backed up, who knows how long it will be before they get any results."

"What about the hotel's security footage?" I pop a piece of General Tso's into my mouth.

"From what I could gather from my conversation with the ADA, they have him entering the hotel; that's it. The cameras on the floor of the victim's room weren't working."

"And yet, they still picked him up?"

Schwartz offers me an annoyed look. "They acted on an anonymous tip."

Of course they did...

There's a reason the Supreme Court of the United States

has said that information provided anonymously must first be verified independently before it can be used as probable cause to arrest someone—because it's inherently unreliable.

I finish chewing the bite in my mouth and swallow. "Sounds like what they have so far is a total bullshit case."

"No argument there, and the ADA knows it, too."

The same thing that's been rattling around in my head since I learned the identity of the victims in our respective cases races to the forefront of my brain again.

"Though you have to admit, it's a little suspicious that your guy is a suspect in a case against my victim's business partner. I don't think it's a coincidence. Do you?"

Coincidences don't exist where Parrish and the Knights are involved. Two men attacked on the same night by assailants both tied to the Knights, and the victims are business partners...there's absolutely no way this wasn't part of some larger plan with a goal we aren't privy to or just can't see.

Something flashes across Schwartz's face for a second that makes it seem like maybe I'm the only one in the dark before he dips his head and takes a bite of a dumpling, shaking his head.

"I don't know what to make of it." He lowers the carton back to the table and turns to face me. "What's going on with the other two cases? I saw Brent Matthews' mug on the news this morning, something about him going in for surgery."

I dig inside the container with my chopsticks and pull out another piece of chicken. "Enzo swore to me that Matthews' ex-wife would corroborate his story about only acting in her defense after Matthews got rough with her. That's good for Enzo since it's an uphill battle when the victim is a damn congressional candidate.

"I'm hoping the negative light the statement from the ex will cast on Matthews will be enough for the case to go away so they can keep him squeaky clean for the election. Enzo seems like a clean-cut guy with no record, which is crazy considering who his father is.

"The only potential hiccup is that I did get the impression there is something going on between him and the ex-wife, or at the very least, there *was*. If it's true and it comes out, that would obviously raise a question about the veracity of any statement she makes to support his defense."

I toss the bite of chicken into my mouth and chew, thinking about all the potential ways Enzo's case could come back to bite me in the ass, the least of which is him actually going to prison and Wolf and the Knights showing up at my place to make me pay for my failure as counsel.

Schwartz leans back against the arm of the couch, considering what I just told him, apparently not as concerned for my life as I am. "And the other guy?"

Shit.

I pause the chopsticks at my mouth, then slowly lower them back into the container, releasing a heavy sigh. "The other guy is a pain in my ass."

One of Schwartz's dark eyebrows quirks. "Aren't they all?"

Chuckling humorlessly, I shake my head. "Oh, they definitely all are, but this one is a whole other level of complicated."

"How so?"

I lean back on the couch and release another exasperated sigh, thinking about Jude Lawson. "Well, for starters, he doesn't talk."

Schwartz chuckles this time. "Isn't that a dream client?"

A smirk pulls at my lips. "Ha ha. Yes, clearly, not speaking with the cops is a good thing, but the man literally doesn't talk to *anyone*. He had some major brain trauma when he was special ops, and it's apparently caused not only debilitating migraines but also a stutter so bad that rather than talk, he writes everything in a notebook."

"Seriously?"

I nod slowly. "I got him to talk to me briefly when I dropped him at his place, but he wasn't exactly chatty or forthcoming with anything. It's like pulling teeth, and I don't anticipate him cooperating or offering me anything that's going to really help me present a defense."

"Is there one?"

"I hope so." Leaning forward, I shrug. "Right now, all they have is two dead bodies and a homeless witness who heard shots from the roof of a building they caught my client coming out of."

"That isn't much."

"No." I shake my head. "It isn't, but ballistics on the bullets will narrow down the weapon type, and if it's something that comes from a sniper rifle, it's going to look very bad for the trained sniper. You know as well as I do that circumstantial evidence can still get someone convicted."

"Sounds like you've got a lot to keep you busy."

Understatement of the fucking year.

"Yeah, thanks for that." I elbow him playfully.

He just laughs and shakes his head.

It's nothing I can't handle, and he knows it. I thrive on the rush I get from deadlines and court and having people's lives in my hands. Some people crack under the pressure, but for me, it's my own brand of drug, one I can literally feel surging through my veins when I'm in "lawyer mode" and in my element.

But Jude Lawson is another thing altogether.

In all my years as an intern and then an attorney, I can't remember ever feeling this pull to a client, this *personal* desire to ensure he's protected.

Yeah, right, Finley. Tell yourself that's why you care so much.

The intercom sounds, and Charlotte's voice fills the air. "Your client is here."

That's my cue to leave.

Schwartz rises from the sofa and makes his way to his desk. "Send him in." He glances back to watch me pack up the barely-eaten Chinese.

"I'll get out of your hair."

"Thanks for lunch."

I wink at him. "No, thank you. I paid for it with the company card."

With that, I grab the bag and start for the door, but Charlotte opens it and ushers in Schwartz's client, allowing me to slip out and avoid being pulled into a meeting I want no part of.

There is enough going on with Enzo and Mouth, not to mention the rest of my calendar. I don't need to be dragged into another Parrish case, one that's likely connected to Enzo's in some way I'm just not seeing yet.

At least one client doesn't appear to be tangled up in whatever it is.

Mouth may be *somehow* connected to Parrish—enough that the former president of the Satan's Knights sent me over there to help him—but there is no way there's a connection between the two men reportedly tied to the Russian mob who Mouth allegedly took out the other night and Brent Matthews or his partner, Guthrie.

That would just be *far* too "convenient"…and make my job a *lot* harder.

MOUTH

MY KNEE BOUNCES wildly on the rusted grate of the fire escape, and I take a deep inhale off my cigarette and hold the smoke in my lungs, allowing the nicotine to seep into my blood and spread through my body.

It's a nasty habit I've tried to kick at least a dozen times over the years, especially after my discharge, but unlike Chaos, who has his ex-wife-turned-current-wife to keep him on the straight and narrow, being here alone, cooped up in this apartment with nothing to do but surf the internet or binge watch shows I have little interest in, smoking again kind of became a given.

Over the years, my body just got too used to it as a way to relieve tension and relax. We all smoked like chimneys on deployments. It's an easy habit to fall back on at times like this. And being stuck here, the cravings were too much to ignore.

Thank fuck for Reaper.

It's almost like he knew exactly what I would need.

The man certainly knows how to take care of his people. Just like he always led us and watched over us when we were on Delta, he's still ensuring we have anything and everything we need now.

He rented the furnished apartment, ordered and shipped a computer, and ensured the Knights had stocked the place with necessities—including food and smokes—before I had even been released from jail.

All the things I would need to feel at home as much as possible while this fucking case plays out.

I should be able to relax, enjoy the time *off* with nothing to do, but this uneasiness isn't just about being caged up in here, like some dangerous animal threatening to bite. It's the entire situation—the whole reason I'm here—that has my mind running a mile a minute.

The fucking Russians...

I may have cut the head off the snake by taking out the newest Yankovich to grace New York with his smarmy presence, but there were other men at that warehouse. People I never got a shot at or *couldn't* take out before I hit the head man because it would alert him to the threat and might have made it possible for him to avoid my kind of retribution.

At least *some* of Maksim Yankovich's minions are still out there. Even if they're just hatchet men for the bratva, not the decision-makers pulling the strings, they can still be dangerous. They may figure out a way to revive the trafficking ring under new leadership or even resort to snatching women locally to satisfy the needs of their particular customers—the sick fucks who believe women are objects to be owned and traded and used like cattle.

Had things gone differently that night, had my body not betrayed me, I would have tracked them down elsewhere and taken them out by now. I'd be back in Baltimore helping Reaper and Chaos take out the remaining two men responsible for the assault on our client, Joanie.

Instead, I'm stuck here with this court-ordered hunk of jewelry strapped to my goddamn leg. I take another drag off my cigarette and let my eyes drift down to the green light, but it soon morphs into another shade surrounded by long, dark lashes and set on a beautiful face with flawless alabaster skin and lips I keep picturing wrapped around my cock.

Fuck.

Finley Banks.

That woman is pure fire.

The kind of roaring flame that lures you in close only to burn you.

It's a great quality to have in an attorney, but it wasn't her legal skills that kept me awake last night.

I can't stop thinking about how the remnants of my migraine evaporated being in that car with her; just simply sharing that space somehow eased the pain that had been plaguing me for days.

Nothing like that has ever happened before. Nothing but a lot of medication and time has ever offered me that kind of relief. Yet, half an hour in that enclosed space, breathing in her scent, allowing it to wash over me like a soothing balm, was all it took.

And by the time we pulled up outside this place, I practically leaped from the car to get away from her because of it.

If she hadn't called me back to sign that damn paper she said she needed to get my records, I wouldn't have even looked at her again before going into the building.

But I did go back, and she stood just outside her car, her brunette locks flowing in the breeze, looking every bit the beautiful girl next door every guy always has a crush on and not an attorney fighting for my life.

Fuck.

She's your lawyer, Mouth.

A fact I keep trying to remind myself of every time the parts of my brain that still work start to flash fantasies of her in very non-lawyerly positions in my head.

I take a final drag from my cigarette and stomp it out under my boot, then rise from my seat on the fire escape to climb back through the window and into the apartment—intent on finding *something* to do to occupy the brain I haven't been able to control for years.

My phone vibrates with an incoming message, and I pull it out and glance at the screen.

REAPER

Getting anxious yet?

I snort and shake my head as I type a reply.

What do you think?

I think you're feeling like a caged animal.

> Then you'd be right. There are still more vodka drinkers out there, and I left something someone needs to go recover.

That rifle must still be safely tucked behind the basement wall; otherwise, Finley would be alerting me to a major change in the status of the evidence in my case. But I won't risk leaving it there any longer than it needs to be, and with this damn monitor on my leg, I can't go back to dispose of it personally.

> I knew you'd be concerned about both those things. I have Preacher looking into the first issue. He's checking for other names and locations. And I asked Parrish to send one of his guys to take care of the other problem.

Knowing the rifle will disappear relieves a little of the tension from my shoulders, but I still roll them, trying to dispel more of it before it brings on another migraine.

> Is Chaos back from his second honeymoon yet?

> A couple more days. They decided to stay a little longer.

Lucky bastard...

I'm happy for the fucker that he finally got back together with Avery after everything they've been through and found a slice of the happiness we all look for, but this second honeymoon is really bad fucking timing. Not only could Reaper use his help in finishing our job back in Baltimore, but having them here to assist with wrapping up the Russian problem would put a nice cap on something that should have ended when we were here a year ago.

> If you're looking for something to occupy yourself with, I have another potential job from Parrish.

>> Fucking hell. What is it with this guy? The Knights can't handle their own shit anymore?

> Apparently, some politician up there named Brent Matthews stole some money from one of their charities.

>> A man with a death wish.

> No doubt. Only the guy they hired to do it fucked it up and got the dude's partner instead...and didn't finish the job.

That's what happens when you farm out your dirty work to cheap labor or unproven operators. You end up with some asshole who has no clue what he's doing and causes the kind of mistakes that can end up blowing back on a lot of people. The Knights are probably worried about this getting back to them.

>> What does Parrish want?

> The partner, Guthrie, is in a coma, and they're looking for anything they can use to keep him quiet in case he wakes up.

>> That really isn't my department, and besides, I'm stuck here as long as I have this new anklet.

> While Preacher does the deep dive on our Russian friends and this Guthrie guy for Parrish, he's also looking for a way to get you free of your new jewelry.

> Is that possible?

We'll know soon enough. I'll keep you updated. Sit tight.

> Like I have a fucking choice.

I shove my phone back into my pocket and work my way into the kitchen to pull a beer from the fridge. My bond conditions might say no consumption of alcohol, but if I'm going to be stuck here, I'm at least going to have a few beers.

Or more than a few.

Maybe if I drink enough of them, I'll stop remembering the way Finley looked at me before I climbed out of her car. And the way her hand felt on mine in that damn courtroom.

I pop off the cap and take three long, cool gulps of the hoppy liquid as I lean against the counter. My gaze drifts over the open floorplan of the loft apartment.

There are worse places to be stuck. Still, my skin itches and feels too tight, like it's suffocating me while I stand here. Like everything is closing in around me and will crush me under its weight.

I grab a second beer, pop the cap, and carry them back out through the window and onto the fire escape, the one place I can actually breathe the "fresh" New York air and, for just a second, close my eyes and pretend I'm somewhere else.

Out here, I have a good line of sight and the freedom to run if and when I need to. It's something that was ingrained in me at some point in my life I can't remember, a time I've only been told about by the few friends who still remained after the man they knew didn't come back.

With my eyes closed, the light breeze blowing against my face, flashes of memories come again.

Trees...

So many trees...

Woods...

A rifle in my hand...

My small hand...

This memory is older.

Childhood.

Maybe hunting with Dad and Grandpa.

A dull ache starts to form at the base of my skull, just like it typically does when I try to dig too much, try to drag up one of the old, fractured memories, and I reach back and massage it slowly, trying not to think about what I know would stop another migraine from coming.

The best thing I can do for myself and for Finley Banks is stay away from her as much as possible while this case is pending.

My phone vibrates again, but instead of Reaper's name, an unknown number flashes on the screen.

Only a handful of people on this planet have this number, and all of them would know not to call me and just to text. Unease slithers up my spine, and I slide my finger across the screen to answer the call, bringing the phone to my ear.

"Jude? Sorry, Mouth? It's Finley. Finley Banks, your attorney?"

Her unsteady voice rolls over me like a fog, enveloping me and clouding my brain instantly with that scent I can't forget and the tingle of her touch.

"You don't have to say anything. I just wanted to let you know that I should have the discovery in about a week—the police reports and photos of any other physical evidence they think they have. When I receive it, I'll want you to come into my office to review it with me. I have my paralegal trying to get those records you signed the release for."

She pauses for a moment, almost like she's expecting me to say something even though she explicitly told me it was fine not to.

"Um, in the meantime, if you need anything, just call or… I'm sorry, just text this number. It's my cell phone." Silence lingers on the line before she takes a sharp inhale. "Please call at any time, Mr. Lawson. Really. I'm worried about you."

The call ends, and I pull my phone away from my ear and stare at it, trying to process what just happened and what she just said. It takes a moment for her final words to click.

She's worried about me?

What the fuck does that mean?

My hand shakes, bringing the beer bottle to my lips, and I down the rest of the first one and set it down to immediately grab the second and drink half of it, too.

Finley Banks seems determined to get under my skin with her passion and compassion. I just have to make sure she doesn't succeed.

5

MOUTH

*I*t's like these assholes want to die.

The heat of my anger blurs my vision and makes my hand tighten around the empty beer bottle as I take in the information on my computer screen that Preacher just sent over

I shove up from my seat on the couch and chuck it across the loft. It smashes against the exposed brick wall, glass shards exploding out across the worn wood floor with a satisfying sound.

Fucking hell.

I flex my fists at my sides, wanting so badly to escape this cage and go after these fuckers to see they get what they deserve.

And what they deserve is a fucking hole blown through them.

These guys are definitively tied to the Yankovich crew, and they're definitely dangerous.

Three came over from Russia with the cousin. Three more who were low-ranking associates here, under the previous Yankovich, and who managed to escape the retribution we enacted against them last year. Six too many terrible people still alive and out on the streets, still potential threats to the innocent people of New York and beyond. Because these fuckers don't keep things within the city limits.

They're bringing in girls from all around the world. Their dirty hands touch people everywhere, and no matter what we do, it seems like it may be never-ending.

We thought we had taken care of it before, believed we had eliminated their entire operation here in a way that not only ensured it would never be resurrected but that also sent a message to anyone stupid enough to try.

Yet now, these fuckers are rearing their ugly, sinister heads again. All while Chaos is out on his goddamn second honeymoon and Reaper needs to stay in Baltimore to continue to keep an eye on Joanie and Viktoria, who is still not back to one hundred percent after what happened when Avery ran back into Chaos' life so unexpectedly.

That means these fuckers are *my* responsibility, and there's not a damn thing I can currently do about it.

I glance down at the green light flashing on my ankle. It continues to taunt me, a constant reminder of how badly I fucked up that night. A reminder of how badly my body betrayed me and left me vulnerable to mistakes.

It keeps me tied here, stuck with my regret, my broken memories, and the constant flow of information from Preacher that only confirms my worst fears—these guys are unlikely to disappear just because I took out Maksim Yankovich.

Since Preacher hasn't had any luck so far in hacking the system that controls the GPS monitor and anti-tampering portion of this plastic manacle, it means all I can do is pace and take out my frustrations on unsuspecting beer bottles and myself.

My phone buzzes with a text from Preacher.

Check out what I just emailed you.

A part of me dreads what it might be, what other horrific things he's dredged up, but I need all the information if I'm ever going to be able to move against them.

Even if it makes my head throb and my entire body so rigid that it's about to snap in half.

I lower myself back to the couch and click on the attachment on Preacher's email.

Bank records pop up—huge cash transactions of fifty up to three hundred thousand dollars at a time. Many of them happening on the same dates over a number of years.

What am I looking at?

I tracked down some bank accounts on some of the fuckers you guys took out last year while I was trying to look for anybody alive who is still connected to them. This one stood out. It's an offshore account in the Bahamas. Look at the dates on page two.

I scroll down past a blur of numbers, and my blood runs cold.

Holy shit.

I grab my phone and fire off a text.

That was the date of the last auction. The one that happened before we came to New York.

Exactly. This is where all the money from the auctions was going.

> Holy shit. Can you trace the deposits to who made the purchases?

Purchases...

What we're talking about are women. Some mere girls. Innocents stolen from their lives and families and sold into sexual slavery to wealthy, evil, and entitled men.

> Working on it. And I have a friend helping me with your little jewelry situation.

I snort and shake my head, rolling out my ankle under the coffee table.

> Good. It isn't really my style.

> Didn't think so, buddy. I'll have more for you soon.

It better be a message saying he figured out how to get this damn monitor off because I don't know how much longer I can stay in here. I set down my phone and click back over to the original information Preacher sent me on the remaining Russians.

Six is doable, even without Reaper and Chaos or anyone else here—as long as I can get out of this place without the court knowing I'm violating my bond.

My gaze drifts over to the crate in the corner of the room that was delivered only a few hours ago. With the necessities the guys just sent me, I'll have everything I need to continue my original mission here. The one that was so rudely interrupted by that fucking migraine that ruined everything.

I push up from the couch and stretch my back and neck, cracking and popping audibly the same way they have every single day since the explosion that knocked me off the roof of the building and destroyed my life as I knew it. And now, the new life I've created with Reaper and Chaos, protecting innocent people, helping them find peace through justice they can't get any other way, could all be over.

Reaper put so much faith in me to do this job, and I fucked it up.

If I get put away for this...

I shake my head, trying to clear that thought from my mind, but the one that immediately replaces it isn't much better—the stunning attorney fighting to make sure that doesn't happen.

The way her light, reassuring touch simultaneously sends shivers and heat racing through my body. The way my cock stirred to life for the first time in years.

Christ, like it's doing right now just thinking about it.

I reach down and adjust my cock away from behind my zipper as I make my way toward the window to stare out at the street below. Staten Island is quiet this time of night, especially in this area.

Reaper definitely picked a good place to have me stay until this is resolved. I'd much rather be at the safe house we usually use when we're in New York, but we need to keep that place hidden and available whenever we need it—not listed on record with the damn court.

This is only temporary.

Hopefully.

If the fiery brunette with the kind smile and soft touch has anything to say about it, I'll be back in Baltimore and returning to my life there soon.

I reach up and grab the lintel, leaning forward to watch the occasional car or pedestrian move along down the street or sidewalk. People just living their lives. People with families and memories.

Things I'll never have. Things I never *can* have. Things everyone else takes for granted.

Like Abigail and Michaela.

Even my own sisters are strangers to me, which is why I pushed them away when I woke up and didn't recognize them. No number of stories from growing up together would jog my fractured memory. No amount of "unconditional love" would return to me what was stolen by that RPG. So, I fought them and their efforts. I kept them at arm's length, and that length grew and grew until they were no longer coming to see me. Until I made it clear I didn't want them to. Until the only people left in my life were the ones I did have fleeting memories of—Reaper and Chaos. The people who helped explain to me who I was, even if I never truly remember it. What they said, what they told me about *that* life was the only thing that ever seemed right, that ever seemed real.

I can't lose it to get locked away in a real cage somewhere. I won't let that happen.

And I won't let these feelings raging inside me about my damn attorney get in the way of letting her do her job.

A familiar car pulls up to the curb in front of the building, and my chest tightens immediately, my heart beating rapidly against my ribcage.

What the hell is she doing here?

***

FINLEY

I STARE up at the building and the window of the apartment where Mouth is staying. I don't want to call it his because it really isn't.

It's just temporary.

Like this feeling I get around him that is sure to dissipate.

Just a place Reaper rented for him to ensure the court was

going to let him out on bond, but even just looking at the darkened window, I can almost feel his presence sizzling across my skin. That blue assessing gaze that seems to see everything even though he says nothing.

And I can't blame him for wanting to remain silent. With everything he has been through, all that he has suffered, why would he want to engage in a conversation with someone when he doesn't have to?

But it makes it impossible to gauge his state of mind or know how he's doing—alone, injured, facing something that could send him away for the rest of his life.

I glance at the paper bag on the passenger seat.

This is stupid, Finley. What the fuck are you doing?

It's the same question I've been asking myself for the last half an hour ever since I walked out of Malicious Meatballs with two subs, two fries, and a plan to come to see my most intriguing and frustrating client.

Turn around.

Go home.

Forget about Jude Lawson until you have to talk to him about the case.

Despite knowing how wrong it is, I still turn off the ignition. I still grab the bag and step from the car. What I should do is drive over to Charlotte's and make sure she's okay after the Braxton Hicks excitement earlier today.

I almost wish I had been there just to see Schwartz freaking out and having to drive our pregnant paralegal to the hospital when she thought she was in labor. She would likely appreciate what I have in this bag since it's been one of her pregnancy cravings, but something tells me the man in that apartment needs it more.

Or maybe I do and I'm just making excuses for my reckless actions.

I scan the street with some ridiculous fear there might be

someone out here who would know I have no business being at my client's residence at eight o'clock on a Friday fucking night.

Of course, no one's watching me.

The only other person on the street, a single pedestrian with a dog, walks in the opposite direction, likely heading home to settle in for the evening. Still, I feel eyes on me from somewhere. I peer back up at the window.

No, it can't be.

There wouldn't be any reason for him to be watching me. It's just my own self-consciousness making me crazy.

I shake off the feeling, lock the car, and make my way into the lobby. Staring at the buzzer for his apartment number, I shift nervously from foot to foot. This is my last chance to turn around. To walk back to my car, drive to Charlotte's to share this or home, and gorge on this entire bag of food. I'd surely regret it tomorrow, but maybe not as much as reaching up and pressing the buzzer button.

Instead of a greeting, just the soft crackle that tells you someone picked up comes through the line.

"Jude…Mouth. Sorry, it's me." *Shit.* "It's Finley. I brought you something. I know it's a Friday night, but—"

The buzzer sounds on the door to my left, and I quickly grab the handle and pull it open to gain access to the main lobby. Each step I take should be one in the opposite direction, but the elevator dings, and the doors slide open, almost as if in welcome.

A woman carrying a small white dog steps out and offers me a smile. "Good evening."

"Hi. Have a nice night." I slip into the elevator and punch the button for the fourth floor, then lean back against the metal interior and squeeze my eyes shut. The crinkle of my hand tightening around the paper bag fills the tight space, adding to the rushing of my blood in my ears.

What the hell are you doing, Finley?

My knee bounces.

This is a professional visit.

I'm checking on a client who has no other connections here.

No one to rely on and who has a serious medical condition.

That's it.

I nod sharply to no one, almost as if it will convince me that's true.

The elevator pings, and the doors slide open. I suck in a deep breath and push off the wall, stepping out into the hallway and up to his apartment.

Shit. Shit. Shit.

I raise my hand and lightly knock. The door opens immediately, and Mouth stands there as if he has been waiting for me the whole time. His icy-blue gaze meets mine, and he raises an eyebrow.

His way of questioning my sudden appearance at his place without having to actually voice it.

Hell. I wish I had an answer.

I offer an awkward smile and hold up the bag. "Hi. I worried you might not know the good local places to eat." When he doesn't offer a response, I shrug. "I thought I'd introduce you to one of my favorite spots."

His gaze drops to the bag in my hand and the words "Malicious Meatballs" written on the front of the brown paper.

"Meatball subs and fries…"

Silence spreads between us, and he slowly lifts his head until he's piercing me with those Caribbean blues again. He takes a half step back and opens the door, making room for me to enter.

Shit. Shit. Shit.

I force each step forward, and the door clicks closed behind me, making me jump and look over my shoulder at him as he approaches to my left. He walks past me without a word and over to the kitchen counter with four high stools. I follow him cautiously, scanning the loft space.

Nice but not extravagant.

He'll be comfortable here until his case gets resolved.

And hopefully, he's not heading off to a new place with bars after this.

If I do my job well and if things pan out the way I hope they will, he won't be.

I set the bag on the counter and slide on to one of the stools, unsure what I'm supposed to be doing as he moves to the refrigerator and tugs it open. The hard muscles of his back punch and flex under the tight T-shirt stretched over wide shoulder blades, and my tongue darts out across my lips, imagining what he must look like under all of that.

He turns back toward me, holding two beers, his biceps bulging, and knocks the fridge shut with his foot. Holding up one of the bottles, he raises a brow.

Alcohol sounds good right now. Though, lowering my inhibitions around this man is probably the last thing I should be doing. Still, I nod because I can't seem to think rationally when I'm around my client.

Client. Client. Client.

If I think the word enough, it might remind me why I'm here and what he is.

He pops the caps off with a bottle opener and tosses it back into the drawer, then moves around the counter to slide on to the stool next to me. Almost instantly, my body becomes aware of how close he is, the heat radiating off him mixing with a heavy, masculine scent—like leather and gunpowder.

I don't realize I'm staring until his eyes connect with mine, and he quirks a brow again.

"Oh." I turn back to the bag in front of me and pull it

open, the heat of a flush over my cheeks assuring me they're already bright red. "So, like I said"—I point toward the name on the bag—"Malicious Meatballs has the best meatballs on Staten Island. To be honest, I probably shouldn't eat them as much as I do. I don't need that many calories in my life. But they're addictive."

And I'm rambling.

He narrows his eyes on me, his reproach about the calorie comment evident without him saying a word.

Damn this man.

I swallow thickly, pull out the sandwiches and fries, and arrange them in front of us. He unwraps his while I glug three long drinks from my beer. The smell of the delicious meatballs, sauce, and freshly baked bread hits me, and my mouth begins to water more than I already did at the scent emanating from the man next to me.

Mouth digs in and takes a bite, and a little appreciative groan comes from deep in his throat.

Sweet Mother of God. That sound...

My pussy clenches, imagining him making that sound for other reasons, and I shift on the stool to relieve the pressure building there.

I take a way-too-big bite of my sandwich to fill my mouth and prevent myself from saying something stupid. Chewing, I chance a glance at him, and it's my turn to raise an eyebrow at his assessing gaze locked on me. "Good?"

He mouths *"very"* to me, and I can't fight the grin, knowing he's enjoying it.

This is the most relaxed I've seen the man, and he offers a half-smile that tilts his perfect lips.

Mouth.

That name can mean so many things. And now, I can't stop thinking about what they could be—one in particular.

He takes another bite and chews slowly, his strong jaw

working under several days of stubble. I shove a French fry into my mouth, and his tongue snakes out across his lips to catch the sauce there.

I practically choke and start coughing violently, pounding on my chest and grabbing my beer to wash down my embarrassment.

Good God, I'm in trouble.

6

FINLEY

"**A**re you freaking insane?" Laura's eyes practically bug out of her head, and she almost spills her coffee. "You brought a client food and went into his apartment alone? Were you high or something?"

I groan and shake my head, her reproach almost as bad as what I've been doing to myself since I left his place last night. "No. I definitely feel like I was possessed by something, though."

Some sort of supernatural power that draws me to a dangerous man who very likely just murdered two people and has killed countless more in his life.

"You must have been because you're not dumb, Finley. You're probably the smartest person I know. But that is just fucking *stupid*. That's how you cross a line. That's how you get your license suspended or worse—end up disbarred or dead."

I slam my palm against the table. "You think I don't fucking know that?"

She recoils slightly, her jaw dropping incredulously, while a couple at the table next to us in the small coffee shop gives me a dirty look.

"I'm sorry." I shake my head and groan, reaching across the table to squeeze her hand. "I didn't mean to snap at you. This guy...just...I don't know. He just *unnerves* me."

Her bourbon eyes widen. "That's saying a lot considering the type of people you work with on a daily basis."

I nod slowly, take a sip of my double latte, and casually pick at the half-eaten doughnut on my plate. The one I *should* be enjoying considering it's our Saturday tradition once we finish pilates class, but I can't even bring myself to eat it when all I can think about is what happened last night.

"Well"—she raises a blond eyebrow at me—"what happened?"

Nothing and everything.

Somehow, it was both, and I don't even know how to explain it to her.

I glance around us to make sure no one's eavesdropping and lean forward slightly closer so I don't have to talk so loudly. "I showed up with some Malicious Meatball subs."

Her eyes roll back in her head, and she licks her lips. "God, they're good."

"I know, which is why I brought it to him. He doesn't have anyone here, Laura. He has no friends, no family. He can't leave the apartment because he's on electronic monitoring from the court."

"That's why they invented grocery and food delivery, Finley. It's called Uber Eats."

I twist my lips at her jibe. "I know. But I've been worrying about him being alone in there with his medical issues and this case hanging over his head."

"What type of a case is it?"

Crap.

I brace myself for her reaction. With as busy as she's been at the hospital all week, I'm sure she didn't see anything on the news about it even though the death of the current head of the Russian bratva definitely drew a lot of attention and had Mouth's name splashed all over the newspaper due to his arrest. I close my eyes and force the words out. "Double homicide."

"Are you fucking *nuts*, woman?"

The same couple next to us glares again.

Laura turns to them. "Oh, you two—stop eavesdropping." She returns her attention to me. "You went into the apartment of a man accused of double homicide—by yourself—to bring him a fucking sandwich because you were *worried*. Girl, you need to get checked out by a mental health professional —stat."

"I know how it looks, how it sounds, but I swear he's—"

"He's what?" Her eyebrows rise. "A killer?"

"Not sure yet." I drum my fingers on the table and take another sip of my drink. "At this point, it's *allegedly*."

She snorts. "Your favorite word."

"That's because everyone is entitled to the benefit of the doubt. Innocent until proven guilty."

"Sure, of course, but if they charged him with *homicide*, they must have some evidence suggesting he did it."

"He was found at the location they *think* the shooter set up at, and he was military special ops. One of those people you're not supposed to know about unless you have some sort of top-secret security clearance."

"Are you fucking kidding me?"

I shake my head. "And he's charged with killing two Russian mobsters."

"Holy shit."

When you hear it out loud, it *does* sound bad. Really bad. About as bad as any case I've worked on. But Mouth isn't like any client I've ever had. His silence forces me to actually *see* him, and what I see isn't what others think he is.

"I don't know what it is about this guy, Laura. He just doesn't seem like someone who would commit cold-blooded murder."

She shifts forward slightly and glances at the eavesdropping couple. "Well, they have enough to charge him…"

"Yeah, but not enough to convict—at least based on what I've seen so far. I'll get the discovery next week sometime and be able to review all the police reports. All I have right now is the criminal complaint which is really a bare-bones summary of their case."

"So, the guy *maybe* killed two Russian mobsters, could kill *you* and anyone else with a fucking toothpick, and you felt inclined to bring him a meatball sub? Sure, that seems totally sane to me."

She takes a sip of her tea and gives me a look I know all too well.

"I could do without the sarcasm, Laura."

I'm already dealing with two major cases that are going to be a pain in my ass on top of the caseload I was already weighed down with before that two a.m. call from Schwartz that sent me down this fucked-up avenue in the first place.

How do I describe this to her without sounding more like a lunatic than I already do?

"He's…he's complicated." I glance up and meet her concerned gaze. "He doesn't talk."

Her brow furrows. "What do you mean *he doesn't talk?*"

"He has a traumatic brain injury from when he served. That's why he was discharged, and it causes him to stutter badly, badly enough that he doesn't want to talk."

"Hell"—her shoulders sag, and she frowns—"that's kind of sad."

"It is." I shake my head and drop my focus to my donut

again. "But it's not that I feel bad for him. Because I don't. This isn't a sympathy thing. I'm just drawn to him in some way that makes me want to help him and ensure he's okay."

"You mean as an attorney to her client?"

I finally let my gaze meet hers. "I don't know. That's the problem."

"Shit." She releases a mirthless laugh. "You have yourself in some deep fucking water. Does Schwartz know anything about this?"

I shake my head. "God, no. If he knew, he'd probably pull me off the fucking case. But he's tied up with an attempted homicide of his own and several other big cases. It's not like he could step in, anyway."

"So, what are you going to do?"

I shrug and take a sip of my now-cold drink. "I guess just try to keep things professional."

She scowls at me. "*Try* to keep things professional. That does not instill a lot of confidence."

Then this won't, either.

But now that I've opened the floodgates of discussing Jude Lawson, I can't seem to stop. Laura is the only person I ever discuss my personal life with, and she's the only one I can count on to remain absolutely brutally honest with me when I come to her for advice.

"The thing is…I don't totally trust him."

"Nor should you, Fin. He is likely a murderer."

I flick my gaze to hers. "But what if the people he killed deserved it?"

Her eyes widen. "Did I really just hear those words come out of your mouth?"

"I know, I know how crazy it sounds."

"I don't think you do, Finley. This guy is potentially a double murderer who certainly has the background and training to have done it. There's enough evidence to charge him, yet you're showing up to bring him dinner on a Friday night. You need to get a grip, or you're gonna end up drowning in that deep water."

What if I already am?

MOUTH

I NEVER TRULY APPRECIATED WHAT freedom meant until I lost it.

All the years I served, everything I saw, all the horrors and mistreatments, I thought it had given me a deep understanding of it—of its cost, of what it means to those who never had it, of how lucky I was to never have to worry about my own. But it only took two days of being restricted in the condo to drive me absolutely mad as if it had been two decades.

By the time Preacher texted me earlier tonight to tell me he had hacked the monitor and could set me free, I was practically crawling out of my own skin.

I roll out my ankle, relishing the feeling of having that stupid thing off. Now that it's safely back at the condo, green lights still active so they think I'm there, it allows me to get out *here* and do what I do best.

Work on taking out these nasty motherfuckers.

Our vodka-drinking friends don't suspect anything. They sit in the restaurant across the street, laughing, joking, stuffing their guts with food and booze, not a care in the world. Completely unaware they're already in my crosshairs and will soon be dead.

Other patrons move in and out of the building, either oblivious to the fact that these horrible men sit right out in the open or ignoring it to ensure their own personal safety—

likely the latter. In this neighborhood, there isn't anyone who doesn't know who these guys are and what they're capable of.

A couple holding hands exits and makes their way to their car in the parking lot next door, but they aren't the ones I'm waiting for.

Two of the men who escaped me the other night emerge a few moments later, chatting as they share a cigarette near the front door. Neither of them seems to have a care in the world, even though their boss was just taken out less than a week ago.

Probably because they know I was arrested. Had I remained in custody, had Finley not been able to get me on bond, they would have undoubtedly sent someone after me on the inside to try to take me out. One of their guys or a cop on their payroll. It wouldn't have worked, but these guys weren't smart enough to move fast, and they certainly aren't smart enough to be afraid now.

The taller of the two leans against the brick of the building and takes a long drag from his cigarette. He releases the smoke in a ring that floats over his head into the night sky.

After hours of being up here and doing recon on the place, it's clear the restaurant is a front for the bratva and likely laundering money from the account we found. And while I would love to pull the trigger right now so there would be two fewer scumbags out on the street, that's not what tonight is about.

It's about watching, waiting, and planning to ensure what happened when I took out their boss doesn't happen again.

This will be an easy place to eliminate them. At least four of the men on that list have come and gone tonight. All I have to do is wait until they're all here at the same time to give myself the opportunity to hit as many as possible.

I climb to my feet and step away from the low wall around the roof that I used to conceal myself, scanning my phone for messages. Secretly hoping there will be one from a certain woman who left my head spinning last night with her impromptu visit and quick, awkward exit.

Preacher: Call me. You're not going to believe what I found.
Shit.

If Preacher wants me to call him, it's far too detailed or important for him to tell me in a text message.

Hopefully good news.

I slowly wander back toward where I parked the car I rented under one of my aliases. Nothing more than an average Brighton Beach resident out for a lovely stroll on a summer night. I dial as I walk, bringing the phone to my ear as I approach my ride.

Preacher answers on the first ring. "I found something you're absolutely going to love or hate, depending on how you look at it."

I snort and slide into the car, closing the door behind me.

"So, you know how Reaper called me to have me look into this Guthrie guy for Parrish? Well, those accounts I was tracking down that made the deposits at the same time as the auction…guess who one of them belongs to?"

I freeze with my hand at the ignition. "Holy s-s-shit."

"Yeah, my reaction, too. The guy was one of the original buyers in the auction the month before you guys came in and tore the place apart."

This fucker Parrish wants dirt on was buying women. And his business partner was apparently embezzling money from a charity. It can't be a coincidence. Perhaps it's the reason Matthews stole from the Knights in the first place. Undoubtedly, all sorts of sketchy things were going on with both of these guys in order to support what must be a very expensive and nasty habit.

"I already relayed this all to Reaper, and he says he's likely going to have you meet with Parrish in person to explain it because he's about to go dark for a while doing recon on something else you have going on in Baltimore."

Likely final planning for taking out those last two fuckers for Joanie as soon as Chaos gets back.

"I wanted to let you know right away because now that you're a somewhat free man, I thought it might not be a bad idea to have you look to see if you can find out what happened to the girl while you're there in town."

My heart climbs into my throat, considering the possibilities.

That was such a long time ago when it comes to this world. So much could have happened to her. Chances are, she isn't with Guthrie or even in the city anymore. She might not even be alive.

The men who frequent those types of auctions often trade women based on their changing whims and preferences, letting others use them for their own pleasure while destroying them bit by bit until they finally can't take it anymore and do what they must to escape permanently—one way or another.

"I'm seeing what I can find from my end, but I'm texting you all the addresses I have for Guthrie. With him in the hospital, I would imagine it should be pretty easy to get in and out of these places."

There goes my plan to head back to the condo.

But I couldn't go sit on that damn couch or try to sleep knowing what I do now—that there might be an innocent woman somewhere in the city who has been abused by Guthrie—and God only knows who else—for the better part of a year. Though, even if Preacher hadn't just shaken me with this news, it would be better that I don't go back to my place now that it smells like Finley.

That light, citrusy-mint fragrance has lingered since she left last night. After I had to watch her eat that goddamn sandwich.

Her lips closing around it…

Her tiny little noises of pleasure…

All while I pictured her doing the same with my cock.

Fuck.

Knock it off, Mouth.

She's your attorney…

Who brought you dinner on a Friday night…

I fire up the ignition and pull away from the curb, heading toward the first address on the list of Guthrie's properties from Preacher.

She's just worried about you.

She told you exactly that the other day.

Someone calling or texting to check in because they're worried is one thing…bringing them dinner and sitting and eating with them is another. And that's exactly what she did, just inhaled that whole foot-long like she was a deep-throating champ while interjecting one-sided small talk without expecting me to respond, seemingly unfazed by my silence.

It felt too natural, too real, too easy.

This woman literally holds my life in her hands, but I feel her touching other parts of me. Parts I thought died in that explosion. Parts I can't give her.

If this mission fails, a lot of very bad people are going to continue to do a lot of very bad things.

Finley is one distraction I can't afford.

7

MOUTH

The buzzer sounds, and I make my way over and thumb the button to unlock the lobby door without even checking who it is. Only a handful of people know I'm here, so it's either Parrish, one of his guys, or Finley again.

That last possibility suddenly tenses every muscle in my body. Maybe I should have looked so I could have at least prepared myself to see her, to have her in this space with me, steel myself against what I know being near her will do to me.

Too fucking late now.

A bang sounds on the door. "Knock, knock, motherfucker."

I release a tiny breath of relief at the sound of Parrish's voice through the wood. I'd rather deal with that asshole than Finley right now.

God, that's fucked up.

I flip the lock and open the door, stepping back to allow him to amble in.

He scans the apartment and nods approvingly. "Nice place. What are you going to do with it when you're done?"

I shrug and pull out the notebook from my back pocket that I already wrote in to prepare for this meeting. It would have been a lot easier for Reaper to just call Parrish with this information, but he needs to concentrate on our client back home. This is my mess, and after Parrish got me an attorney, the obligation to assist with this Guthrie issue weighs heavily on my shoulders, as much as I hate owing this man anything.

Plus, while I trust that everything I say to Preacher and the guys is secure, we don't know shit about Parrish's phone or who might be listening in or watching him. In-person assures there aren't any listening ears or prying eyes.

I flip open the first page and turn it to him.

He scans it and lifts a brow, pulling the toothpick from his mouth. "You have something on Guthrie?"

Nodding, I motion for him to follow me into the kitchen, where that same minty scent still lingers even two days later. That fucking woman is messing with my head, and I haven't even touched her yet.

No, not YET.

You're not GOING to touch her—ever.

A fact I have been reminding myself of continuously since I watched her car drive away after our meal the other night.

I grab two beers, pop them open, and slide one across the counter to Parrish. He takes a sip as I flip to the next page in my book and turn it toward him.

Our guy dug up some financial information on the Russians we never had before. And guess who he found on the original buyers list from the auctions before we shut them down!

Parrish's jaw drops. "You're fucking kidding me."
I shake my head and motion for him to turn the page.

> *He wired $250,000 to the Yankovich bank account the same night we know an auction happened.*

"Holy shit. Maybe that's why Matthews was embezzling the money from Frankie's House? Were they both involved?"

I shrug and pull the notebook away from him, flip to a blank page, and scribble in it.

> *I don't know anything about that. Just that Guthrie bought a girl. Our guy, Preacher, is trying to find her, and I have been scoping out a few of the remaining Russians and also swung by Guthrie's place to see if there was any sign of her there.*

Taking a drink, I slide the note over to him and wait for him to read it. I could probably just tell him all this. It would make it a lot faster and a lot easier, but the thought of exposing my weakness to a guy like Parrish, who likely has none, makes my blood run cold.

Not that he doesn't likely know by now after Finley exposed me in court but knowing and actually experiencing and seeing it are two different things.

"How the fuck did you get out of here"—he scans the apartment and glances at my leg where the lights still flashes green—"with that still on?"

I grin at him and mouth the word *"magic."*

He barks out a laugh, shakes his head, and takes a sip of his beer. "Man, you guys are something else. I respect the creativity."

I grab the notebook and scribble, twisting it back to him.

I'll take that as a compliment.

"You should."

As much as I enjoy having the company and the distraction from constantly fantasizing about my damn attorney, I'm ready to get things moving in the direction of some sort of resolution.

What's the plan?

Parrish's lip curls into a sneer, and he takes a drink of his beer, letting the bottle dangle from his fingertips. "I don't run the show over there anymore, unfortunately. Frankie's House is near and dear to the Knights, so the fact that this asshole was likely involved with Matthews stealing from us put a target on his back already. Now with this new information about the auctions…" He pauses for a second, drumming his fingers on the counter. "You know, Matthews was out in Brighton Beach the other night. Supposedly, he was visiting his girlfriend, but that could be a cover."

Not everyone in Brighton Beach is connected to Russian bratva.

"But it's definitely an interesting coincidence."

I nod and consider what I found last night while

snooping around Guthrie's house. There was certainly a lot of indication that he and Matthews were tight, practically attached at the hip. I doubt one did anything without the other knowing about it. So even if they weren't both actively involved with each other's crimes, they certainly had knowledge and did nothing to stop them.

That puts targets on *both* their backs, as far as I'm concerned.

I write down as much and flip it over to Parrish.

He nods. "That's what I thought as well. Thanks again for doing this."

I turn to the last page I already wrote before he even came.

I'm working on cleaning out the rest of our Russian problem.

Parrish smiles and sticks that damn toothpick back into his mouth. "Good. Don't want these fuckers starting shit up here again. Twice was enough."

I snort and nod.

It sure was.

"As far as I know, Guthrie is still in a coma, and they're not sure if he is going to wake up. If he does, you may need to go in there and work your magic so it doesn't land back on us."

I make the slitting throat motion, but he shakes his head.

"No, just a threat to keep him quiet. The cops already have their eye on the guy who fucked up the whole thing. If Guthrie dies, it's a murder charge that could come back to the Knights. If he lives but doesn't reveal anything about who did it, the prick can walk and we'll be in the clear."

My hand tightens on the bottle. Going in to take out a

scumbag like Guthrie is the kind of thing I live for. Not being able to end him will certainly put a damper on that, but at least I can fuck with the man and make him live the rest of his days in constant fear.

I flip to an open page and write, grinning at Parrish.

It would be my fucking pleasure. Just tell me when and where.

FINLEY

THE COUPLE on the TV embrace and kiss, the hero swinging the heroine around in her white wedding dress while the sun sets behind them and dramatic music designed to make you cry and question your own life plays in the background.

And it's working.

I don't usually fall into the "watches sappy romance movies" category, but flipping through channels aimlessly tonight, something about the story on the screen drew me in.

Maybe because it's about as far from how I've pictured my future for so long that it's completely foreign. Work is my life, and I never even considered what putting off relationships would mean for me ten or twenty years down the line.

I didn't think I cared, but the tears pooling in my eyes seem to suggest otherwise.

Don't be a fucking sap, Finley.

My phone vibrates with an incoming text, and I swipe at my eyes and hold my breath before I flip the screen to face me, a huge part of me hoping to see Mouth's number there.

RICK

Talked to Matthews' ex-wife. You got a
minute to talk about it?

My stomach tightens.

That doesn't sound good.

Rick knows better than to call me on a Sunday unless it's urgent, and urgent usually means *bad* news—the kind that will keep me up all night and make my job a lot harder. As a former cop and private investigator for the firm, Rick has seen it all over the years and knows how to judge a witness, and he almost *never* calls me with information he can easily provide to me tomorrow in the office.

I turn off the TV and type a response to him.

Yeah, I'm around.

My phone rings almost immediately, and I slide my finger across it to answer the call. "Hey, what's going on?"

"I know how much you hate to work on the weekend if you can avoid it, but I talked to Danica Matthews, and I just got done typing up my report. I thought you might want to know the results quickly on this one, considering who your victim is."

I release a tiny breath of relief. "So, it isn't bad news, then?"

"No, quite the contrary. Danica Matthews is going to be a very good witness for you and make the State's case against Enzo a lot harder."

"Why?" I shift up into a sitting position. "What did she say?"

"Basically, the exact same thing Enzo did. She confirmed that she attended the fundraiser with her ex-husband and that she's continued to appear with him at these events—not because she still has feelings for him or anything like that, but because she didn't want to tank his campaign. Now, here's where I think she was holding a little something back."

"Okay."

I figured there had to be *something*. Nothing is ever clear-cut in these situations.

"She says they got into an argument at the event and that he tried to leave before they had finished their conversation."

"What were they arguing about?"

"She wouldn't say—said it was a personal, private matter."

I wince. "That doesn't sound good."

"Might not be, but she says she followed him because the conversation needed to happen that night. He pulled up outside the house out in Brighton Beach, and she confronted him again. That's when he attacked her."

"She used the word *attacked*?"

"Most certainly did."

"Excellent."

"He lunged at her and grabbed her by the throat."

"Damn, some potential congressman, huh?

Rick snorts. "Exactly the thought I had. Anyway, she says, suddenly, somebody was pulling Matthews off her, and when she managed to break away from the scuffle for a moment, she realized it was Enzo."

"And how does she know Enzo?"

That's the ultimate question, one I never got a satisfactory answer to from my client at the jail.

"She claims they know each other because Matthews hired him to do some repair work on a boat they shared when they were still married."

"That's it? That's all she said?"

"That's all she said. But you know me too well and know I have some extra thoughts."

I chuckle at him, dropping my head back against the couch. "I know. Lay it on me, Detective."

He chuckles. "I *do* think she was holding something back, either about the reason for the argument or about Enzo."

"I agree with you." Thinking back to Enzo's reaction when I made the suggestion, there was definitely something off about his reaction. "There may be something going on between the two of them, if not currently, then in the past. Do you think she had an affair with him while she was married to Matthews?"

"Can't say and she didn't want to expand on her relationship with Enzo, just brushed it off as being acquaintances because he did the repair work on the boat."

"But she's willing to testify that a US congressional candidate attacked her and tried to strangle her?"

"Yep, everything else is all just a feeling and supposition on our part."

Exactly.

Which means the State won't be able to prove it, either. If there were something out there to find about Danica and Enzo, then Rick would find it. The man is relentless, like a bloodhound sniffing out the truth. He goes far beyond what the State does when looking into these witnesses and their backgrounds, so if he hasn't located anything damning, it might not exist. And if it does, it's so well-buried that it's unlikely to surface.

"Okay. Email me your report tonight so I can read over exactly what she said. Call her tomorrow and have her come in and sign an affidavit to that effect. Can you type it up for her, or should I have Charlotte do it based on your report?"

"I can do it tonight."

"Right, get it to Charlotte. Tell Danica to come into the office and sign it whenever it's convenient for her."

"Will do, Fin, but I didn't even get to tell you the best part."

That perks me up. "What's that?"

"We're not just going to have this statement."

"What do you mean? Was there another witness?"

"Not that I know of, but Danica says the night it happened, she had to leave the scene. I don't know what she meant by 'had to leave.' But my guess is Enzo told her to before the cops arrived. When she realized they had arrested Enzo even though he was only protecting her, she apparently went down to the station."

"Really? I didn't see her there that night."

Then again, it was three in morning by the time I left, and even if I had walked past her, I wouldn't have recognized the woman. I've done my best to avoid politicians and their campaigns.

"It may have been after you already left. I don't know the exact time, but she says she met with one of the detectives on the case and gave them the same statement she just gave me."

A glimmer of hope lights in my belly. "So, her story has stayed the same, and she was a good citizen and went to the police to give a report as soon as she was able to."

"Exactly."

"Then, the only real problem arises if there is a relationship between Danica and Enzo and the State were to find out about it?"

"Pretty much."

"Then we have to pray there isn't one or that they're both smart enough to keep it under wraps."

We end the call, and I drop back down onto the couch with a sigh.

It's good news.

I should be thrilled.

But it's impossible to celebrate this small victory when, as of now, I have nothing to help the client who is occupying my every waking thought and has made an appearance in a very hot dream after I left his place.

If I can't help him, I'm certain he'll haunt me forever, even worse than he already does.

8

FINLEY

The light knock on my office door pulls my attention away from the police reports I've buried myself in all afternoon to try to keep my mind from wandering to another client who seems impossible to forget. "Come in."

It swings open, and Charlotte steps in, carrying a large stack of papers in her right hand and a wadded-up tissue in her left. Her red, puffy, tear-soaked eyes meet mine, and my breath catches in my chest.

I shove to my feet and rush around the desk. "Oh, my God, are you okay? Is it the baby? More contractions?"

After all the excitement on Friday with her Braxton Hicks, Schwartz didn't even want her to come in today. But she insisted she needed to be here and be working to take her mind off how uncomfortable she is. Given how distressed she looks now, maybe it would have been better if she had agreed to take her maternity leave early.

Charlotte waves me off. "I'm fine. It's not that."

She waddles in and slowly lowers herself into one of the chairs facing my desk as I return to mine.

"What's wrong?"

Her gaze softens, and she holds up the stack of papers and waves them slightly in front of her. "Did you see what I emailed you a couple hours ago?"

I swallow thickly, averting my attention to unnecessarily shuffling the papers on my desk, and give a sharp nod. "Yes. Jude Lawson's medical records." I glance up at her. "I'm surprised you got them so fast. They usually take weeks to receive once we've made a request."

Charlotte nods. "Considering the circumstances of the case, I knew we had to get them quickly. So, I followed up on our emailed demand Friday morning and again this morn-ing, and they were able to email them right away."

She must have really been up their asses to get them so quickly, but she's right about needing them fast. The sooner I can convince ADA Waters that Jude's injuries prevent him from being able to have executed those two men, the sooner I'll have the charges dropped and that man out of my life for good.

Her eyes drop to the stack again. "I've been reviewing them. Have you had a chance to take a look?"

I shake my head. "No."

Because I've been intentionally avoiding it and instead burying myself in anything else I can—currently discovery on a drunk and disorderly—so I won't have to think about the man who has insisted on occupying my dreams. If that sweaty, hot one I woke up from in the middle of the night last night is any indication, they won't be going away anytime soon.

Charlotte dabs her eyes again with the tissue. "Well, make sure you have a box of tissues ready when you do."

My chest tightens. "That bad?"

She sighs and sets the stack on the edge of my desk. "Fucking awful, Finley. This guy…" She takes a deep breath and rests her hands on her belly. "He lost his entire life. The amnesia and aphasia appear to be permanent. They drilled into his head and took out an entire section of his skull to relieve the swelling caused by his brain smashing around. He was in the hospital for months, trying to rehab and retrain his mind, trying to get back who he was before he finally signed out AMA."

"He signed out AMA?"

She nods. "The doctor's notes said he became frustrated with his lack of progress and decided he would rehabilitate himself at home."

"Shit."

Although it doesn't surprise me at all based on what I do know about the man.

"Yeah. I really think you should look at these sooner rather than later." Charlotte shakes her head. "I can't imagine any juror would be able to hear testimony about this and not only feel for the guy but also think it's impossible for him to have been able to carry out an assassination like they're accusing him of. It just isn't something people with the kind of brain damage he has are capable of."

I press my lips together to keep myself from revealing anything I've learned about him that I shouldn't know as his attorney and instead hold my hand out for the papers. "Give me the printed ones. I'll take a look at them since you already have a hard copy instead of looking at them on my computer."

She shifts forward in her chair with a grunt, and I reach across to take them from her.

"You can see I've tabbed a couple places I thought were especially important things. I think if this goes to trial, we're going to need to have an expert come in to testify about all this medical stuff."

"Agreed. Start looking for some experts on TBI, amnesia, and aphasia. Make a list for me so I can start contacting people."

"Got it."

"Thank you. I appreciate it."

She releases a little sigh, grabs the edge of the desk, and uses it to help hoist herself up from the chair with her other hand on her lower back.

"Are you sure you should be here? I mean, if reading these is making you burst into tears…"

Charlotte glowers at me. "That has nothing to do with the fact that I'm a hormonal mess and about to pop and everything to do with what that man's been through. You read them, and I challenge you not to cry."

"You know Schwartz is going to try to get you to go on leave early again if he sees you like this."

She swipes under her eyes and sucks in a deep breath. "And I'll tell him exactly what I'm telling you. I'm fine. Really." Waddling to the door, she glances back at me. "Don't forget the tissues."

Fucking hell.

Mouth is even getting to my paralegal, and she's never even *met* the man.

The door clicks shut behind Charlotte. I lean back in my chair and stare at the stack of medical records. She's right, of course. I need to review them as soon as possible and get a copy to ADA Waters. This is the type of information that could get this case dismissed short of trial. Exactly what could get Jude Lawson out of New York and out of my orbit.

My gut twists. Even though it's better for everyone if he isn't here, the thought of him leaving is somehow worse.

I nudge the police reports I was working on to the side

and grab a pen to start taking notes on Jude Lawson's medical records. Within five minutes, my eyes begin to burn with unshed tears, and I clench my fist on the top of my desk, annoyed at how easily Charlotte knew what my reaction would be.

Dammit.

Charlotte was right; this is horrific.

No one should have to suffer through this. Losing who they are. The good memories with the bad. Their ability to interact with people on a basic level. No wonder he acts like he has a chip on his shoulder.

He's carrying around a massive one.

I've only seen him let down his guard once, for a few seconds while we were eating. He was calm, relaxed, carefree, just enjoying a meal with me while I kept talking to myself like he was responding.

He might have even been *happy* for those brief moments.

But it was gone just as fast.

Reading these, I wouldn't be surprised if I don't ever see it again.

MOUTH

THE HOSPITAL'S QUIET, dimly lit halls late at night carry the same smells and sounds that have haunted me for years.

Months in a place like this.

Being told things would get better.

People forcing me to try to remember things my mind had already lost.

Arguments with those who were supposed to be protecting me and helping me.

Anger and pain.

So much pain.

That antiseptic scent invades my lungs, and the longer I stand here, waiting for the signal, the stronger the migraine becomes—hammering at my skull like a sledgehammer intent on breaking it more than it already has been.

The soft squeaking of the nurses' shoes on the tile floors and the beeping and hissing of the various machines keeping people alive reach me through the pain.

But there's one person here who doesn't deserve to be breathing.

A spineless piece of shit...

When Parrish texted earlier tonight that Guthrie was awake and needed to be taken care of, an immense twisted conflict of anger and determination raced in my head.

This would have been a lot easier if he never woke up from the coma. If he had simply died and faded away into oblivion, the way he made the girl he bought disappear, but now, I get to do what I do best.

Well, second best.

Killing this asshole would be the ultimate vengeance for what he's done, but I understand Parrish's reasoning. If Guthrie dies, the guy they sent after him will be looking at murder charges—something they want to avoid in case it can ever be traced back to them. And since this guy sounds like a real moron, I wouldn't bet on that not happening.

I would have liked to avoid murder charges, too, but no such luck on my end.

Almost as a reminder of that fucked-up night, the migraine throbs again, brought on by all the reminders this place holds. Still young. Still new. But it's there, all the same, threatening to rush forward and knock me on my ass again.

Not tonight.

I just need to get this done and get back to the apartment.

If I can do that, if I can complete this, then I will at least have one thing I didn't fuck up on this mission.

The blonde Parrish said would get me into Guthrie's room turns the corner and approaches where I wait near the stairwell door. She motions for me to follow her down the quiet hallway.

She glances back at me a couple of times as we make our way past the other ICU rooms but doesn't say anything. We pause outside a closed door, and she leans into me. "You have ten minutes before one of the other nurses comes to check on him."

I give her a sharp nod and step into the dark room lit only by the tiny lights on the machines beside his bed.

It would be so easy to end this now. To kill him and say *fuck you* to whoever Parrish is trying to protect. So damn easy it makes my hands flex to do it, to feel the life draining from him as I tighten them around his neck.

I approach slowly, examining the monster and utter douchebag. He looks so peaceful lying on the white pillow, eyes closed, chest rising and falling with his soft, silent breaths.

So damn easy to end them.

So damn unfair that he gets to keep living his life when his heinous actions have harmed so many others.

I stop beside his bed, pull the stack of notebook sheets from my back pocket, and shove my free hand over his mouth. His eyes fly open, and he scrambles, flailing his arms and legs and clawing at my wrist.

It's going to take a lot more than that to get me to release my grip, but I need him to calm down and pay attention. Even in the dim lighting, fear and panic soak his gaze, and I force my hand down harder again to get him to stop, holding up the first piece of paper I pre-wrote.

STOP FIGHTING ME.

His eyes widen as he reads it, and he gives me a sharp nod, relaxing slightly under my hold. I flip to the next page.

Don't Talk!

Two words that speak volumes.

The tears that pool in his eyes make me want to move my hand down to his throat and tighten it there. But I can't. This man doesn't deserve to live, and everyone knows it, but the Knights are protecting whoever put him here, and it isn't my decision to make in this particular situation.

Any other time, he's exactly the kind of prick Reaper, Chaos, and I live to take down.

Perhaps another day.

Another place.

Preacher can easily keep tabs on this guy, and when the heat cools regarding whoever put him in here, I'll do what should be done now.

I show him the final page I wrote before I came up here.

You Talk = You Die!

This close to him, I can see the fear dilate his pupils. He gives me another sharp nod, and I pull my hand away from his mouth. If I can get to him here, I can get to him anywhere, and he knows it.

He won't fucking talk.

I make my way to the door and peek out the hallway to ensure the coast is clear. All remains quiet, and I slip out and casually move toward the stairwell, giving a sharp nod to the blonde where she sits at the charge desk at the end of the hall.

She doesn't acknowledge me but watches as I step through the door and hustle down the stairs. This time the swirl of vertigo only encroaches on the edges of my vision, but I grab the handrail anyway to ensure I'm not hit harder.

If this keeps happening every time I step out to handle a mission, I might as well go to prison because I'll be useless to Reaper and Chaos like this. Useless to all those people who come to us seeking justice and protection.

I crack my neck from side to side to clear the tension building there and pull out my phone to text Parrish. He'll want to know right away that it's done and off their plate.

> It's done. He's not talking.

The three little dots that indicate he's replying pop up almost immediately.

> FUCK YEAH! Thanks, man.

I slip the phone into my back pocket and push out into the warm summer night air, inhaling a deep breath of it, hoping it might clear the headache I've been trying to fight off since I stepped into the hospital, but only one thing seems to do that.

The one thing I can't have.

9

FINLEY

B rent Matthews' smarmy face fills the television screen, still bruised and bandaged from the surgery he had to repair the broken orbital socket Enzo caused. Now that I know what Matthews did to his ex-wife, what Enzo did to *him* doesn't seem like nearly enough.

"Thank you all for being here. The support you've shown over the last week and a half has truly touched me. As most of you know, I was brutally attacked after my last fundraiser, and the recovery has not been an easy one."

I fight my gag reflex and roll my eyes.

Dramatic much?

The man—no doubt—had aides running around like little lemmings, completely at his beck and call the entire time he was laid up in the hospital. And what does he do the moment he gets released—rush straight to the press to figure out a way to milk the situation for everything he can before the election.

Absolute douchebag.

I'd give anything to push him aside on that podium and tell everyone gathered in front of him that he abuses women. Instead, I have to sit here in my office and listen to this horseshit.

"But it is because of all your well wishes and my unbridled desire to serve this community that I will prevail. There's work to be done, and I will not let this unfortunate situation deter me from my quest to be District 11's next congressman."

The audience applauses, and Matthews pauses, slowly lifting a hand to his chest to appear moved by their claps.

Absolute total douchebag.

He holds up a hand to the crowd. *"Thank you!"* The clapping starts to die down. *"That being said, it is with a heavy heart that I announce I will be severing ties with Frankie's House. My hope is that the organization continues to help the community, especially our youth, but for personal reasons not attached to my campaign, I can no longer support the establishment."*

I snort and shake my head. Frankly, I expected Matthews to flat-out say the man who assaulted him is connected to the charity. It's public record that Enzo was charged, and it's already made the newspapers. The only reason I can come up with that Matthews *isn't* calling him out is his fear of the Knights retaliating if he does.

Which is a legit concern.

"I do not condone violence of any kind."

Except trying to strangle your ex-wife...

The pure hypocrisy of the statement makes me want to release Danica's statement to the press right now, but that won't do Enzo any good.

"I stand for law and order and the wholesome values the neighborhoods I serve were built on. We will rise from this. Justice will be served, and on Election Day, the great people of Staten Island and Brooklyn will send me to Capitol Hill, knowing I have

their best interests at heart. We will be a community that bands together. A community that lifts one another up. We will not knock each other down, and we will not turn a blind eye to violent crimes. The streets of our city have been filled with crime for too long. It's time to take a stand, and I hope you stand with me."

This entire dramatic show makes my stomach churn. It's a good thing I haven't had time to eat yet today, or my lunch might have ended up spewed across the files covering my desk.

Cheers and further applause pour from the crowd, reporters taking photos and calling out questions. Matthews doesn't respond to a single one. He stands at the podium, a plastered-on saccharine-sweet smile never moving from his lips, waving and eating it the fuck up.

Why wouldn't he?

The assault plays in his favor. It's a way to gain some sympathy votes while also beefing up his stance on violence and crime in the district.

You aren't getting my vote, fucker.

He wouldn't be getting any if people knew what Danica said happened. But as of right now, the police reports won't be released publicly. Unless the press manages to get someone to sneak them copies, they won't know Matthews' ex-wife said he assaulted her. And I'm banking on the fact that he will do anything to prevent those reports and the statement we have from ever going public.

Finally, his campaign manager steps to the podium. *"Mr. Matthews won't be taking any questions. Under his doctor's advisement, he will be heading home to take it easy for a couple of days. We'll see you next week on the campaign trail."*

I shift my focus back to the files on my desk, mostly tuning out the continued questions being thrown by the reporters since he doesn't seem inclined to answer any.

"Mr. Matthews, do you have any comment on your business partner's attack? Is there any correlation?"

"Mr. Matthews, what does this mean for your ex-wife? Will she still be involved with Frankie's House?"

"Does she still support your campaign?"

"What does she think about your girlfriend?"

That question draws my eyes back to the TV. Matthews' manager tries to usher him from the podium, but he brushes the hand away.

His shrewd, intent gaze lands on someone in the crowd, and he steps back and adjusts the microphone. *"Danica and I will always support one another. She may no longer be my wife, but she's always been my anchor, and that shall remain true until the end of time."*

Fucking hell.

My hand tightens to a fist around my pen, and I shake my head. "You're in for a surprise when you find out about her statements, asshole."

He won't be happy to learn she came forward with what really happened that night and that she has no intent on backing whatever his version of events is in court—or with the press.

This could get very messy.

The shrill ring of my cell makes me drop my pen and reach for it.

Enzo.

One guess why he's calling...

I pull the phone to my ear and lean back in my chair. "Hey, Enzo."

"Did you see that circus Matthews just held outside the hospital?"

"Sure did."

"Am I allowed to say he's a total asshole?"

I chuckle and spin my chair to stare out the window. "You

can say whatever you want as long as no one else is around to hear you. And, for the record, I agree—completely. He's going to milk this for all it's worth, even if everything he says is a fabrication."

"What about his little parting statement about Danica?"

"You have nothing to worry about. Not only did Danica go to the police the night of the incident and tell them exactly what you told me, but she also gave my private investigator a statement confirming it. She will testify that you were only protecting *her* and only *after* Matthews violently attacked her."

He clears his throat. "I knew she'd do the right thing, but…"

"But Brent Matthews holds a lot of power around here, and she might have felt pressured to back him despite what really happened?"

"Yeah."

"My investigator said she came across as very sincere and believable. That a jury will love her. That's *very* good for us. Matthews doesn't want this story getting out, so I'm going to have a little private conversation with the ADA handling your case and see if we can't make it go away without even having to go back to court again."

"You really think you can pull that off?"

I climb to my feet and walk over to the window, leaning my shoulder against it to look down at the bustling street. "You know I can't promise you anything, but if I were Matthews' attorney or campaign manager, I would want the statements from Danica buried so deeply that no one will ever get a whiff of it. I'll threaten to release her signed affidavit to the press and see where that gets us."

"Thank you, Ms. Banks. I appreciate it more than you could possibly know."

"Save your appreciation for when I get these charges dismissed."

"Deal."

He ends the call, and I slip my phone into my pocket and cross my arms over my chest. We have information that could destroy Matthews, but I still don't trust the Danica-Enzo situation. If he's hiding anything about their history or why he was there that night, it might come back to bite us in the ass in a way that we can never recover from.

I return to my desk, trying to forget about the press conference and the potential complications in Enzo's case, but my mind seems to only go in one direction—directly toward Jude Lawson.

What I read in his medical records keeps flashing in my head, reminding me constantly of what he's suffered and is currently going through. Being cooped up in that apartment can't help the situation, and he isn't the type to ever complain about being in pain.

Laura may not understand why I had to go check on him, but if she knew what I did, she would know why I have to go back.

MOUTH

THE MIGRAINE THAT started at the hospital hasn't abated, even with the litany of medications I've taken since last night. It's going to be a bad one, which means I need to take care of this before it fully settles in.

I can't have another incident like what happened with the Yankovich hit. I can't be caught in such a weak moment again or be so vulnerable, especially when, according to my ankle monitor, I'm sitting back at the apartment on the couch, watching television like a good little inmate.

But it's okay.

This won't take long.

The men sit at a table near the large front window of the restaurant, chatting, drinking, laughing, and groping the waitress each time she stops by to deliver their drinks and food.

Fucking assholes.

This late, the place is almost empty—free of innocent customers who could potentially get caught in the crossfire. It's the only reason I've waited this long to get rid of these fuckers tonight.

Fewer witnesses.

Fewer potential complications.

Otherwise, I would have smoked them hours ago when they arrived.

The waitress reappears with another tray of food, and the douchebag on the far right smacks her ass as she walks away. He laughs and waggles his dark eyebrows at his friends while the girl winces and casts an angry look back at him. No one at the table can see her reaction, but I don't miss it, watching through my scope.

A sharp pang in my chest briefly makes the migraine pain disappear, replacing it with something far worse. It's impossible not to feel for her, not to want to storm over there and beat those men to death and torture them the way they do these women. To let her see there are people out there who care about what happens to her and are willing to take action against those who think they're untouchable.

She deserves to know not all men are like these guys— something she likely hasn't ever experienced. Chances are good that she was brought over with their trafficking business. It certainly wouldn't surprise me if they kept a few for themselves and put them to work at their own establishments since these fuckers have no souls.

But what they do have are heads and chests—things I can hit with a fucking bullet. The ones loaded in my rifle right now have their names on them.

I've spent enough time watching them, waiting for the perfect opportunity. It's time to finally act. To end what I started when I came to New York, what Reaper entrusted me with.

All six of the men Preacher identified have gathered here tonight. They've worked together to ruin lives, and now, they'll die together.

Any of Yankovich's men who managed to live through what we did last year and somehow escape what I'm about to do tonight will be left without their organization. They'll scatter and hopefully disappear into oblivion. If they don't...I can always come back.

We'll never stop protecting the innocent any way we can, and if that means a thousand trips to hunt down these pieces of shit, so be it.

Now.

The waitress has safely walked away, and I'm in the clear. I fire off the shots in quick succession. They shatter the glass of the front window and impact each of the men so fast that no one knows what's happening.

All of them crumble in their seats, two of them tumbling to the floor.

A sense of accomplishment swells in my chest as I rise to my feet, police my brass, and tear down my rifle to put it into the case. Even though it's only been just over a week, it felt like this was a long time coming. And in a way, it was, since those men slipped through our grasp when we took out the bulk of the organization.

Mission accomplished.

I throw the rifle case over my shoulder and hustle down the steps from the third floor of the building across the street. Memories of the night I took out their boss come swirling back. Of the vertigo on the steps. My stomach revolting. The police snapping the cuffs on my wrists while I wretched.

Shaking my head, I take the final flight.

It's not happening tonight.

I'm getting home before it hits.

Through sheer willpower, I fight the pain and casually stroll to my car the next block over. I drive away slowly, going exactly two miles per hour over the speed limit. Nothing an officer would ever notice or pull me over for.

Getting caught outside the apartment when I'm supposed to be on house arrest would be bad enough, but with a rifle in the car and six bodies back at that restaurant, there wouldn't be any way to escape going to prison.

My vision starts to blur as the tension in my head mounts. I tighten my grip on the wheel and shake my head slightly, narrowing my eyes to try to ensure I keep a good view of the road in front of me.

Reaper was so confident I could handle this on my own, and I almost fucked it up tonight. Again. If I'd been out there another half an hour more, I might have found myself in the exact same position with the way the agony is building.

I pull my car up a block from the apartment, grab my rifle case, and slowly make my way toward the front door of my building, the sidewalk blurring under my feet.

"Ahem."

Someone clears their throat, and I lift my head, knowing exactly who it is without even having to look.

Finley leans next to the entrance to my building, a scowl on her perfect, pink, bow lips, eyes and jaw hard. She glowers at me and pushes off the wall. "Where the hell were you?"

Her eyes dart down to the case in my hand and widen. She whips her head side to side, ensuring no one is around us. "Is that what I fucking *think* it is?"

Fuck.

Instead of answering my very annoyed attorney, I step around her, put my key in the lock, twist it, and open the door.

She grabs my arm, tightening her hand as much as she can around my bicep. "Answer me, Mouth. You can't just walk away and pretend I didn't just see what I think I saw."

I can certainly try.

This is a conversation I would rather avoid entirely.

I continue to ignore her, press the button for the elevator, and squeeze my eyes closed against the threatening vertigo, inhaling deeply.

That crisp citrus-mint scent she always seems to have invades my breath, and the tiniest bit of tension releases from my head.

Fuck.

The elevator door dings and slides open, and I step inside, knowing she'll follow directly behind me. There's no shaking her tonight. There's no coming up with some excuse or explanation. She knows what I carry in my hand and what I was doing with it—there's no way around that.

Finley steps into the car, standing directly in front of me, chest almost touching mine. "*Answer* me, Mouth. None of this silent bullshit with me tonight." She glances down at my ankle as we move up. "Where the hell is your ankle monitor?"

I lock my eyes with hers, and the elevator jerks to a stop on my floor. The doors slide open, and I step around her and out to unlock my place. She rushes into the apartment behind me and slams the door.

The sound reverberates through the room and off the

high ceilings. I glance over my shoulder at her and find her standing with her hands propped on her hips, a wild, angry blush flooding her cheeks.

"I swear to fucking Christ, Mouth, if you don't answer me—"

It's better if I don't, so I point to the counter where the ankle monitor flashes green against the granite—exactly where it has sat every time I've left the condo to do recon on the Russians since Preacher figured it out.

She stalks over and grabs it. "You rigged your ankle monitor?"

I shake my head.

Her lips twist into a scowl, and she throws up her hands. "Well, maybe not *you* personally, but it seems you have resources who are pretty fucking smart." She sets it back on the counter with a scowl at me. "Unlike you, apparently."

True statement.

It was stupid to think I could ever be in the same room as this woman and control the way my body reacted to her. In the no more than one minute we were in that elevator together, my migraine already started to ease while the ache migrated to between my fucking legs.

I move over to the closet and hide the gun behind the few clothes I have hanging there before turning back to her.

Finley shakes her head, sending her long, silky brunette hair flying wildly around her face. "What the hell am I supposed to do with you, Mr. Lawson? I now have knowledge that you've violated your bond by tampering with your ankle monitor, leaving your residence, and..." She stops short of saying what's obvious, but her eyes dart toward the closet. "I know what you did that night with Yankovich. I can only presume it was the same thing you were doing tonight?"

That must be a rhetorical question. She can't possibly

want me to answer her and explain I just killed half a dozen men.

I raise an eyebrow but don't answer.

"Jesus, Mouth." She shoves her hands back through her hair and stalks toward me, stopping a few feet away. "Do you have any idea the position you've put me in? How much trouble this can cause for both of us?"

10

FINLEY

This man is infuriating.

He stands mere feet from me, staring into my eyes and watching me as if I haven't just confronted him about murdering people, about violating his bond, about the fact that he just walked in here carrying a goddamn rifle case.

"How long before I get a call from the DA's office saying that more members of Yankovich's crew were killed tonight?" I tap my foot and raise an eyebrow at him. "Tomorrow?"

He takes a step closer, his imposing form starting to loom over me.

This man just went out and killed someone. Maybe multiple someones. I have no doubt about that. Yet, here I am with him. In his goddamn apartment. Standing so close that I can smell the night air on him mingling with gunpowder and leather and a strong masculine scent that makes my entire body clench.

He offers a shrug to my question and inhales deeply, closing his eyes.

"What the hell are you doing?"

His lids slowly flutter open, his body relaxing slightly, but he still doesn't say anything.

"I'm not playing this game tonight, Mouth. I know you can talk, so *fucking talk*. I can't be your lawyer if you're going to do this. I can't be involved in this. I can't be involved with—"

The word "you" almost slips out of my mouth, but instead, I bite it back, unwilling to voice what's been rattling around in my head since the moment I met this man.

The corner of his lip twitches, almost like he knew what I was going to say. He takes another step closer—this time, close enough that the heat radiating off his body seeps into my skin.

"Please, Mouth. I need to know what we're looking at. I need to know what to say when I get a call from the DA about this because they're going to try to pin it to you if whatever you just did is in any way connected to the murders you're already charged with. They're going to know, and they're going to come for *you*."

He inclines his head toward the counter, where the piece of technology that's supposed to keep him here sits, almost taunting me with its uselessness. "B-b-but I was h-h-here the whole n-n-night."

I fist my hands at my sides. "What if someone saw you? A witness?"

Mouth shakes his head. "N-n-no one saw m-m-me."

"You have to be out of your ever-loving mind." I release a heavy sigh, my frustration making it difficult to even form words. "You know why I came here tonight?"

He smirks, and I practically growl at him.

"I was *worried* about you. About your being here alone,

with no support system, trapped inside an apartment that isn't even your home. And you go and do this, making me look like a total asshole for ever being concerned."

Mouth appears unmoved by my concern. His blue eyes spark with something that definitely isn't anger or worry. He offers a casual shrug again and finally steps so close that his chest brushes against mine. "There isn't a-a-anything to w-w-worry about. I'm g-g-good at my j-j-job, Ms. Banks."

"And what is your *job*?" I raise an eyebrow at him, refusing to back down or retreat even in his powerful presence.

He smirks again. "You kn-kn-know. I w-w-work for a p-p-private security c-c-company."

I scowl at him. "Which is a front for what? Seems to me like you're a fucking mercenary."

A killer.

Mouth offers a casual shrug as if accusing him of that doesn't mean anything.

As expected, he doesn't respond.

"What the hell am I supposed to do with you, Mr. Lawson? Just let you continue to run around killing people while you're supposed to be on bond for killing people?"

The continued silence claws at my patience, and I shake my head, throwing up my hands. "Fucking *talk* to me."

"W-w-what do you want me to s-s-say?"

"Anything? Nothing? Fuck. I don't know. I just want you to—"

My words get swallowed by his lips crashing against mine, and despite my surprise at the sudden kiss, I don't push him away.

I should.

He's my client.

He's dangerous.

He's a *killer.*

But I don't push him away. I don't run. I can't.

I issue a little moan as my body responds to his, molding myself to his hard, firm chest. His mouth moves against mine eagerly, as if all this arguing has built up some sort of soul-crushing need instead of making him want to throw me out of here like he should.

Mouth's cock hardens between us, pinned against my belly, and my pussy clenches at the thought of having that between my legs. So much strength. So much power. So much turmoil all wrapped up into one man.

His tongue sweeps against mine, seeking, longing, stroking, demanding, and I cling to his T-shirt to keep my shaking legs from giving out under me.

Fuck. What the hell am I doing?

I push away from him and stagger back, hand over my mouth, my heart thundering against my chest and heated blood rushing in my ears—my entire body hot and primed and ready for something that can never happen.

"What the hell am I doing?" I say it out loud this time like I'm going to get some sort of answer, as if Mouth is actually going to give me one.

He takes another step toward me and dips his head to meet my eyes, concern and heat lingering in his gaze.

I shake my head to try to dispel the fuzziness overtaking my brain. "We can't do this. We can't. I could lose my license for getting involved with a client. Fuck...even for just being here in a position like this. I...shit. I should know better."

Squeezing my eyes closed, I fist my hands at my sides to keep myself from reaching out for the hard, warm body directly in front of me.

His strong, calloused palm captures my cheek and tilts my face up to his. I let my eyes open to meet his, and all I want is to close the distance between us. To feel his lips on mine again.

No.

I back away, watching his hand fall to his side. "I can't."

This is wrong. On so many levels.

Wrong for me.

Wrong for him.

Just *wrong.*

I rush to the door, throw it open, and race to the stairwell, afraid that if I wait for the elevator, he'll come after me.

Fuck. Who am I kidding?

That man is likely faster and stronger than anyone I've ever met. If he really wanted to make me stay, he'd already be on me, forcing me to.

And as much as I don't want to admit it, a massive part of me wishes he would do just that.

MOUTH

"FUCK!"

I run my hands through my hair, stalk over to the open door Finley just ran out of, and slam it shut, the sound vibrating through my chest with my pent-up frustration.

Her minty scent that seems to alleviate the pain in my head and in my fucking soul still permeates the air, mocking me with what was just in my grasp but I can never truly have.

Fucking hell.

That woman masquerades as a law-abiding, upstanding attorney, but really, she's a fucking menace. An exasperating temptress sent to drive me insane and twist me up in ways I never could have imagined. To make me question everything I'm doing and everything I have done. To make me want something I *know* I can never have for too many reasons to count.

And she's right, of course.

She's my lawyer, and getting involved with her, kissing her, even *thinking* about it is as fucking inappropriate a position as I can put her in. It could destroy her career. Her life. End her ability to do the thing she loves and is so damn good at.

All because my dick decided to come to life after four years of snoozing and shriveling from disuse. With the taste of her still on my lips, that scent hanging in the air, my painfully hard cock twitches against the front of my pants.

Fuck. Fuck. Fuck.

This went too far.

I went too far.

It would be easy to blame it on being amped up after what I did tonight, or on the migraine, on both of those things combined, but it's so much more than that—and that's what makes it so dangerous.

Neither of us can afford the kind of complications this brings.

It can't happen.

My dick thinks otherwise, though, so I head to the bathroom, crank on the shower as hot as it'll go, strip, and step under the spray while it's still icy cold. Maybe the chill of the water will help cool my libido and convince my body it's not gonna fucking happen. That I won't feel her warm cunt wrapped around it tonight, that I won't come down her pretty throat or deep inside her.

Goddammit!

My cock doesn't go down, even with the icy water pelting it and my best efforts to enforce the reality of our situation. There's only one way this is going to fucking resolve.

I grit my teeth and take my length in my hand, a low groan rumbling in my chest at the relief the first stroke brings. The water begins to warm, hitting my already heated skin, and I grip myself tightly, remembering the way she plastered her body to mine.

Her breasts pushing against my chest.

Her hands clinging to my T-shirt.

That tiny little moan that came out of her throat when my lips hit hers.

Fucking Christ, that woman...

I can't remember what it was like to be with someone in that way.

To argue with her.

To hold her.

To kiss her.

To fuck her.

To completely lose myself in another person who wants to be with me.

All I ever see are flashes. Brief moments of the past that never linger long or give me any sense of context. The only thing I have to picture with my hard cock in my hand is that fiery brunette who holds my life in her small, soft ones.

Every stroke tightens my body more, and I move faster, slamming my free palm to the tile and letting my head fall forward, the now-scalding water hitting the back of my head and neck and flowing down over my shoulders. The tension that's been building since the moment my eyes first landed on Finley in that police station struggles to release, fighting against the part of me that knows how fucking *wrong* this is. How wrong I am for *her.*

All kinds of wrong.

I'm a killer, a man who operates on the wrong side of the law, and she's someone who has built a life and career on ensuring it's upheld. Her passion for her clients and job shines in everything she does. And it shows me how determined she will continue to be to keep a wall up between us, to protect herself from what it would mean for her career.

And it's for the best.

Even if no woman has ever affected me like that—at least, not one I can remember. She's the first one in almost five years who doesn't look at me with pity. Who doesn't look at me like something to be fixed or nursed back to health. She knows exactly what I am and what I do, saw evidence of it tonight. Yet, she still kissed me back. She still wanted it and needed it as much as I did in that moment.

One that can never be repeated.

I stroke harder and faster, imagining her lean but curvy frame spread out under me as I drive into her welcoming heat over and over again, desperately trying to find something I haven't been able to in so fucking long that I forgot what it even feels like.

My orgasm builds quickly. The tingling at the base of my spine surging through my body until my cock hardens even more in my grip.

Fuck.

My cum spurts out over my hand and onto the tile, the rush of water pounding around me, washing it down the drain at my feet. If only it were that easy to wash away my feelings for that woman, the way she affects my mind, body, and soul. It won't be that easy, though. Nothing in my life ever is or ever will be again.

It can't be. I don't deserve it to be, and the big man upstairs has made that abundantly clear.

My future is destined to be filled with more pain, more struggles, more unfulfilled dreams like being with Finley.

I stand motionless with my hand firmly wrapped around my still-hard cock, the release not enough to cure my desire for her.

How could I ever think it would be?

She's as addictive as she is fierce.

As controlled as she is passionate.

As beautiful as she is dangerous.

When Reaper sent me here, I thought this mission was going to be a problem because of my fucked-up head, but it turns out it's Finley Banks who is the problem. Because I don't know if there's any way I can stop myself from doing again what I did tonight, the next time I see her any more than I can stop my trigger finger when I see someone who deserves it.

11

MOUTH

The high afternoon sun beats down overhead as I light up my cigarette and settle into my usual spot on the balcony to wallow in my misery over what happened last night.

That wasn't fair to Finley, and I never should have put her in that position. I certainly shouldn't have jerked off, fantasizing about her after she left.

It only makes the reality of the impossibility of it worse. It's only going to make things harder going forward for us.

I take a long drag, and my phone lights up with an incoming text.

CHAOS

Open up, asshole.

What the hell?

A hard knock sounds at the door, and I snuff out my cigarette, climb inside, and make my way over to the door. I throw it open and barely have time to register Chaos' grin before Avery throws herself at me.

"Mouth!"

I catch her small frame and hug her tightly as Chaos chuckles and brushes past us into the apartment.

He glances back. "Our flight home came through LaGuardia, so we thought we'd stop and say hello before heading back home."

Avery pulls back from our embrace and smiles at me. "You look good. A lot better than I thought you would, considering the circumstances."

I smirk at her back-handed compliment and press a kiss to her forehead as she slides out of my arms.

Chaos scowls at me. "Hey, keep your lips off my wife."

I grin at him and mouth, "Your *wife*."

He just smiles back.

There was a time not that long ago when none of us thought this could ever happen. That Kalen and Avery would never find their way back to each other. Seeing them like this —happy and tan from lying in the sun in Mexico for their literal second honeymoon—I can't help but feel like I'm staring at a miracle.

Chaos claps me on the shoulder, and we walk deeper into the apartment as Avery scans it.

Her jaw drops. "Wow, this place is really nice. Are you going to keep it once your case is resolved?"

I glance at Chaos.

How much does she know?

Without having to voice the question, Chaos responds to her for me.

"I don't think anyone has any intention of keeping this place, Avery."

She laughs and spins around with her arms out wide.

"Why not? It's great. We could use it when we come to the city."

Chaos and I exchange a look. He shakes his head and pulls his wife into his arms. "There isn't any reason for any of us to be in New York once Mouth can come home."

Yet, I wish there were. I wish Finley could be that reason. But that's impossible. And after everything that went down since I arrived in New York, I don't have any desire to ever come back unless absolutely required to by a job. Even then, I'll do my best to send Reaper or Chaos without me. The Big Apple has turned sour for me—for a lot of reasons. The least of which is the beautiful woman I can never have.

Pushing away those thoughts, I lead Avery and Chaos into the kitchen and grab each of us a beer.

Chaos accepts his and motions toward the open window to the fire escape. "Hey, babe, Mouth and I need to talk about some stuff. You hang out in here, okay?"

She takes a sip of her beer, leaning against the counter, and offers a tight smile that tells me she knows we're going to be discussing something she probably wouldn't like.

After what went down only a few months ago, Avery knows there are some things she'll never be privy to. She isn't like Viktoria. She wasn't a cop or in any way a part of this life, and there isn't any reason to drag her into it by exposing her to information she shouldn't know.

Chaos follows me out the window and takes my seat on the step, leaving me to stand against the railing. He glances through the window to ensure she isn't looking or listening and takes a sip of his beer. "Avery wanted to stop to say hi and see how you're doing, but I wanted to make sure you don't need me to stay and help you with the Russians."

I shake my head and mouth, "*It's done.*"

His dark eyebrows rise. "Already?"

The genuine shock in his question slices at my heart more

than maybe anything else ever has. There was a time when he never would have questioned my ability to handle this on my own, a time when he and Reaper and the rest of the team relied on me to be unshakably accurate and lethal. The fact that he questions it now is just another reminder of no longer being that person.

Almost as if he can read my thoughts, he winces. "Shit, I didn't mean it like that. It's just that I talked to Reaper yesterday, and he said you were still working on it."

I set down my beer and pull out my notebook.

Got the six Preacher found last night.

He holds up his beer bottle. "Nice job." His eyes dart down to the monitor on my ankle. "How long are you going to be attached to that thing and stuck here?"

I release a heavy sigh and rub my neck before I write my response.

Don't know. However long it takes my attorney to resolve this. If we end up having to go to trial, it could be months or maybe even a year.

Chaos narrows his eyes on me. "Is your lawyer good? Does he know what he's doing?"

I stiffen at the question, and the memory of her lips moving with mine flashes to the front of my brain.

She. And she definitely knows what she's doing. She's a real pit bull.

He chuckles. "I guess she'd have to be if Parrish trusts her."

I nod and retrieve my beer to take another long drink. The last thing I want to be discussing with Chaos is Finley. He knows me too well, actually, better than I know myself since I can't remember any of the years we spent together before my injury.

Chaos can read me like an open book, and he narrows his gaze on me now. "Something going on with your attorney, Mouth?"

Shifting my stance, I avoid looking directly at him and shake my head.

He watches me for a minute, sipping his beer, then finally averts his gaze down to his feet. "I'm sorry I wasn't here to help you with all this. You wouldn't be in this position if I—"

"N-n-no."

He jerks his head up and looks at me, his brow furrowed. It's the first time he's heard my voice in four years, the only time I've wanted to say something badly enough that it compelled me to do it with actual spoken words instead of writing it to him. But I can't bear hearing myself anymore.

This isn't your fault. Just bad timing with one of my migraines.

His gaze softens as he examines me, searching for an answer to a question he hasn't even asked yet. "Are they getting any better?"

I clench my jaw and shake my head.

Not unless I'm with Finley

Chaos takes another drink, looking out at the part of the city we can see from the fire escape. "You're sure you're good here?"

We've waited things out in worse places, haven't we?

He barks out a laugh and rises to his feet, clapping his hand on my shoulder. "A lot fucking worse. But Reaper and I are both here for you, even if we're not here." He motions around us. "You know we're only a text away and we'll be here in two hours."

I nod my understanding, and he steps through the window. If we leave Avery alone in there any longer, she's going to get restless. I follow him in to find Avery looking in the fridge.

"I was checking to see if you had something I could make us if we stay for lunch, but you don't have much in here. What do you eat?"

I grin at her, set my beer on the counter, and grab my notebook.

Takeout.

She reads it and scowls. "That sounds healthy."

I know a great meatball place we can order from.

She raises an eyebrow. "Meatballs?"

Trust me. They'll leave you craving more.

Just like my damn attorney has.

FINLEY

STARING AT MY UNEATEN LUNCH, I drum my fingers on my desk and finally grab my phone to make the call I've been waiting to initiate until I had given my opponent some time to consider his position on my client—while I consider my own position as it relates to him in a whole other way.

ADA Waters picks up the phone on the third ring and with an annoyed sigh. "Ms. Banks, there can be only one reason you're calling me during my lunch hour when you know I'll be out of court and at my desk. You want to ruin my damn day."

I chuckle and lean back in my office chair, letting my head drop against the headrest, picturing Jon with his sack lunch spread out across his desk piled high with case files. "Well, I think it's time we had a discussion about Mr. Lawson's case, especially now that I've reviewed all the police reports and his medical records."

The deep dive I did on the medical records rattled me, but after seeing them *and* the police reports, they've firmly convinced me that no juror will ever convict Jude Lawson of these homicides. His injuries and apparent disability are too severe, and this crime was far too meticulous and perfectly executed to have been done by a man who was so ill when the police found him that he literally vomited.

"What is that you think we have to discuss, Ms. Banks?"

He wants to play hard to get, and I understand it. It's his job to put criminals away, and that's how he sees Mouth. That assessment might not be wrong, but it isn't about what the DA prosecuting the case thinks and sees; it's about what he can convince a jury of.

"Oh, come on now, Jon. You and I have both been doing

this for a long time, and you know as well as I do that there's no way you can prove this case to a jury."

"That's a pretty hard stance you're taking."

Which has absolutely nothing to do with my attraction to the client.

"You don't have anything, Jon, except the testimony of a drug-addicted homeless man with a rap sheet two miles long who you might not be able to find or who may be dead by the time we go to trial. And he didn't even see my client *do* anything, just heard what he *believed* to be gunshots before the cops *happened* to find my client at the building. That's weak, Jon, and you know it."

"And just what was Mr. Lawson doing in that building, let alone at that time of night, Ms. Banks?"

"That's irrelevant."

He barks out a laugh. "It is very relevant, and *you* know it. We have a strong circumstantial case here. Who else is going to be able to take two shots like that, Ms. Banks, except a former member of the military, one who, I'm sure if I dug deep enough, would turn out to be trained as a sniper? You cannot tell me that man didn't do this."

I can't, but that isn't the question that is making us do all this work. And there is no way I'm going to confirm that Jon's right about the sniper training. The information Reaper gave me on Mouth's background is safely locked away in my head until I can get some sort of confirmation in writing from the government. Given his service record and what he did, those written reports are sure to be very lean on details —which is ideal for us from a case standpoint.

"You have no evidence that he *did*. You have no weapon. You have no gunpowder residue on his hands. You have nothing but a speculation that because he was in that building around the time the kill shots were taken, he must have been the one who took those shots."

"No one else was in the building."

"According to the reports, it took the police three minutes to get there after the report of shots being heard. That's a lot of time for someone to flee a scene."

Unless they're suffering from a debilitating migraine that prevents them from getting away.

I let ADA Waters ponder my words for a few minutes before I finally release a long sigh. "Come on, Jon. Why are we wasting time and the State's money on this when we both know you can't prove this beyond a reasonable doubt?"

"I think we can."

Good God, this man doesn't want to see the writing on the wall.

It's time I stick his face in it.

"I sent you a copy of Mr. Lawson's medical records. Did you review them?"

He clears his throat uncomfortably. "I skimmed them."

"And you really want a jury hearing about how Mr. Lawson was so damaged by his service that he has almost no solid memories of his life? That he has moments of confusion and excruciating migraines? That he, in fact, had one that made him throw up that night in front of officers? That perhaps he was in one of these confused states and happened to just wander into the abandoned building at the wrong time? All I need is one juror for a mistrial, Jon. *One.* You need all twelve to unanimously agree that he did this beyond a reasonable doubt, and you're not going to get them because there is all kinds of doubt in this case."

He's silent for a moment, likely because steam is shooting out of his ears, knowing I'm right. "I can't just let this go, Ms. Banks. He murdered two people."

"Allegedly." At this point, it's still important to emphasize that fact. "Why are you pushing this so hard? It's not like the victims here were anyone society is going to miss."

"That's exactly my point, Finley. I can't have vigilantes

running around the city, killing whoever they feel like, acting as judge, jury, and executioner. We have a legal system for a reason. Did you know six other associates of Maksim Yankovich were hit two nights ago? It makes me wonder if your client has an accomplice."

His words sink in slowly.

Vigilantes.

Oh, my God.

That's what this is…

Jude Lawson never struck me as the cold-blooded killer type. Because he's not. I assumed he was acting on behalf of some rival of the Russians, some other group who hired him as a mercenary to remove the men standing in their way. But I had it all wrong. He took them out because they're *bad fucking men*. Men who likely would find a way to avoid ever having anything pinned on them. Men who would never go to prison or ever pay for their crimes.

He's a vigilante.

And that somehow makes things even worse.

"Review his records in detail, Jon, and really consider if you were a juror what you would think if you saw a decorated war hero with all sorts of physical and mental limitations because of his exemplary service, sitting there next to me, accused of committing a calculated crime that took precision he can't possibly execute anymore. Really think about whether you want to put your neck out there so publicly, to lose so badly, and then, call me so we can get this thing resolved and my client can go back to Baltimore."

As far away from me as possible. Before I do something stupid again with the man who is here for a purpose, one founded on the belief that he's doing the right thing.

He may be a killer, but he's one with a conscience.

And that changes everything.

12

MOUTH

Darkness starts to fall outside, and the door buzzer sounds in the apartment. Almost immediately, my heart climbs into my throat…

Finley.

I don't know how I know, but I do. Almost like I can sense her presence even from four stories down on the street.

What the hell is she doing back here after the way things ended the other night?

She should have stayed away. I thought she would revert to text messages and one-sided phone calls before she'd ever set foot in the same room alone with me again.

But I was wrong.

I could let it continue to buzz, let her believe I'm out again, doing something I shouldn't be—according to her—but instead, I make my way over and press the button to let her in.

I'm part masochist and part selfish bastard. It's fucking

torture being so close to her and not being able to have her, but it's also the most relief I get from the pain plaguing my body.

Something about her, about being around her, somehow releases the tension she also produces. It should make things worse, but that minty, crisp, fresh scent she carries everywhere with her somehow tames the raging damaged nerves in my head. She calms them as she simultaneously drives me insane.

I unlock the door and open it, leaning against the jamb to wait for her to come up in the elevator. Each second it takes seems to drag on, and I shift slightly, eyes locked on the metal contraption bringing her to me—the source of my turmoil and my potential salvation.

It dings, and I freeze, waiting for the doors to slide open. Her green eyes meet mine, and she steps out in the hallway and stops just in front of me.

"W-w-what are you doing here?"

A light blush spreads across her cheeks, but she doesn't look away. "I talked with the DA on your case today, and we need to have a little chat."

About the case or about what happened the other night?

I don't ask. I just follow her in and close the door behind us, throwing the deadbolt. This time, if she tries to run away, she'll have to really want to.

She stops in the middle of the open living room and turns to face me. "I sent the ADA handling your case a copy of your medical records."

My entire body stiffens, my jaw tightening. "D-d-did you r-r-read them?"

Confusion furrows her brow. "Yes, of course. I had to know what I was sending him, had to know what was in them that might help our case."

I fist my hands at my sides, anger tightening in my chest. "Y-y-you n-n-never told me y-y-you would r-r-read them."

She pauses for a moment, her eyes widening slightly. "I had to, Mouth. I have to know everything about you. If I'm going to defend this case, if this thing makes it to trial, we're going to have to get a jury to understand your situation."

"M-m-my *si-si-situation?*"

What the hell is that supposed to mean?

Finley winces slightly. "I'm sorry. That didn't come out right."

"Th-th-that's what I h-h-have? A *si-si-situation?*"

"Shit." She pushes her hand back through her hair, her exhaustion and frustration lining her face. "Really, that's not what I meant. You saw how the judge reacted during your arraignment when I told him your history and your medical condition. That's the type of information that's going to be invaluable with both the ADA and the jury." Her green eyes connect with mine, begging me to understand. "You're a goddamn war hero who is now permanently disabled."

I flinch at the word, and her gaze immediately softens.

"Mouth—"

"P-p-please d-d-don't. Just s-s-stop. I don't w-w-want your f-f-fucking pity."

Her lips twist. "That's what you think? That I *pity* you?" Finley steps closer to me—this time, the anger all hers. She scoffs and releases a sardonic laugh. "I don't *pity* you, Mouth. I'm in *awe* of you and what you've been able to accomplish. What you've done in your life. What you're still *capable* of doing."

"You're n-n-not afraid of m-m-me?"

I take another step closer to her even though my own fear of being rejected again screams for me to retreat. To give her space. To walk back to that door, unlock it, throw it open, and *ensure* she leaves. But I force myself to keep moving until

I'm standing in front of her, so close I could reach out and drag her up against me in a split second.

Finley stares up at me, her eyes clear of any fear. "I know what you can do. I know what you did the other night. I know what you're doing when you're supposed to be sitting here."

I fight a grin.

She finally figured it out.

"Whatever happened to you out on that deployment, whatever may be messed up in your head, it didn't change who you are. And I'm not afraid of you because, deep down, I believe you think you're doing the right thing."

The right thing right now would be for her to walk away. For her to run out of here as fast as her feet can carry her back to her place. Back to safety. Somewhere my tainted hands can't reach her. Somewhere she can find a man who will give her everything she deserves. Who isn't broken and damaged and on the verge of potentially going to prison for the rest of his life.

She takes a tentative half-step toward me. "If you think that what happened the other night was because I *pity* you, then you have it all wrong. I can't explain it, can't figure out why I'm so drawn to you. Why I can't stay away when I know I should." She shakes her head. "I don't know what it is, but I do know what it *isn't*. And it isn't pity. I could *never ever* pity you."

Those words reach deep inside me, to a part I thought had died along with the memories of the life I had before. The memories I fought so hard to get back but only return in painful flashes I can't understand.

Heat ripples across my skin, making it feel too tight, this condo suddenly too small to hold Finley and me and everything building between us.

"But you have to understand. This"—she motions

between us—"this is far more dangerous than anything you do."

"L-l-leave."

I barely manage to get the word out between gritted teeth that don't want me to say it.

Finley keeps her gaze locked with mine. "I already know I should leave."

She takes a slow step toward the door, almost like she's waiting for me to object to the move.

I reach out and grab her shoulder, stopping her in place. "B-b-but you're n-n-not g-g-going to."

Her shoulders sag, almost as if in resignation, and she slowly turns to face me.

"Y-y-you could h-have called m-m-me to tell me about t-t-the c-c-call with the DA. E-e-especially after wh-wh-what happened the other n-n-night. But you di-di-didn't."

Because despite what the consequences may be, Finley is as drawn to me as I am to her. A force so strong, neither of us can deny it.

I tug her toward me, and she sags into my arms as I sweep my lips over hers. A tiny moan climbs up her throat, and she molds herself to me like she can't get close enough.

Her arms tighten around my neck. "Jude, please."

No one calls me Jude—at least, not that I can remember. Maybe Mom and Dad and Abigail and Michaela when I was a kid, but they're long gone from my life, along with any friends I've forced away after I couldn't remember them and fought their efforts to try to jog my memory. The only ones left call me Mouth because that's what I always was to them —the mouthy sniper who cracked jokes at the most inappropriate times and never shut up.

Hearing it from her lips instead of the nickname sends an inferno of need blazing through my veins.

Finley doesn't know Mouth, doesn't know who I was

when I got that nickname or why it was so damn fitting. She only knows who and what I am now—the shattered man with no past and an uncertain future.

Yet, she wants to be here. She wants *this*. Wants *me*.

I grab her hips and lift her small frame easily. She wraps her legs around my waist, aligning her core against my hardening cock and rolling her body, grinding down against me.

Fuck.

It's been so long since anyone has touched me, since I've felt a warm body molded to mine, seeking and desperate the way I am. Her tongue glides along mine, and I groan into her mouth as I consume her, content to take everything she is willing to give me because I have nothing to offer her.

Anything I had and everything I was disappeared with my old memories. But all she seems to want is this moment.

The only thing I *can* give her.

I walk to the bed, kissing her, clutching to her tightly, afraid if I loosen my grip, she might run for the door again, but she clings to me in a way I'm not sure any woman ever has.

All of it is new and exhilarating. Almost like it's my first time because, for all intents and purposes, it is. I don't remember what it's like to be with a woman, to have her under me and be inside her. But my body seems to know what to do, what it and she wants.

My shins hit the mattress, and I slowly lower her down onto it, tearing my lips from hers to skim them across her cheek, down her neck, and to the exposed *V* of cleavage in her white blouse.

Her chest heaves with heavy breaths, and I slide my fingers under the buttons and rip sideways, sending them flying across the room. Finley issues a sharp gasp at the destruction of her shirt, but the heat intensifies in her gaze as

I tug down the cups of her pale-pink bra, exposing the mounds of flesh and hard nipples.

My mouth waters to taste them, to taste *her*, to devour every inch of her luscious body. She runs her fingers through my hair, scratching at my scalp and sending goosebumps over my skin. I duck my head and suck one taut peak between my lips. Her entire body arches off the bed against me, her legs tightening around my waist so she can rub her pussy against my cock.

"God, Jude…"

I lift my head and shift to the left to give the other nipple the same attention—this time, lightly grazing my teeth over it to gauge her reaction. She bucks hard into me, and a pleasured groan falls from her lips.

"Fuck, yes."

Finley moves like a wave under me, undulating and seeking something more than the teasing I'm doing now. She pulls her hands away from my head to push at the waistband of her skirt, shimmying it as far down her hips as she can with my body pinned between her legs.

Never taking my eyes off her, I release her nipple from between my lips, step back, and reach for the button on my jeans. Her gaze dips to my hands, and she watches me slowly lower the zipper and free my aching cock while she kicks off her skirt, leaving her in only the tiniest scrap of fabric and the bra below her breasts, forcing them up in an erotic offering.

I stroke my length, fighting back the desire to fuck her like a crazed animal. That isn't who Finley is, isn't what she wants. She doesn't want a man who can't control himself. And I don't want to be that man with her.

Instead, I drop to my knees at the side of the bed and drag her to the edge, spreading her legs wide and giving me access to her most sacred spot. She pants wildly as I drag my finger over the black strip covering her already-soaked pussy, and I push it to the side to slip a finger inside her.

Her head falls back on a gasp, and she clenches around me immediately. I grit my teeth and use my free hand to tear away the thong so I can lower my mouth to her cunt.

The first lick is the sweetest thing I've ever tasted in my life. Surrounded by that minty scent she always seems to hold, her flavor coats my tongue and makes my cock weep pre-cum while I stroke it with my other hand.

She whimpers and moves her hips against my face, wanting more, and as much as I would love to have her come down my throat, no matter how badly I want to see her fall apart that way, I'm going to come before the main attraction if I don't stop right now.

I rise to my feet, position myself at her slick opening, and plunge inside the welcoming heat I've been dreaming about and never thought I would ever get to experience.

Fucking hell.

FINLEY

Sweet mother of God...

Jude sinks into me, his thick cock spreading me open, filling me, finally giving me what I wanted for what feels like so long.

Has it really only been two weeks since I met this man? Since he walked into that tiny room in the jail and looked through me with the same blazing blue eyes he has locked on me now?

It can't possibly be, not with the way my heart thunders against my chest, my body craving everything from him and frantically trying to get it. His lips against my skin, tongue dragging through my pussy and gliding over my clit wound me up so tightly, it felt like I might explode, but now that I have him inside me, I can barely breathe.

He tugs his shirt off over his head, exposing his hard, lean body, marred with vicious scars visible even in the darkness of the apartment. I feather my fingers over them, and he stills inside me, buried so deep it feels like he's reached to the very core where I hide all the things I've longed for and didn't think I could find or have without sacrificing everything I worked so hard to obtain.

Blue eyes swimming with lust find mine, and he pulls my hand away from his chest and kisses my fingers lightly as he gradually withdraws. I groan and let my eyes drift closed at the almost agonizingly slow movement. He tugs my hand above my head and does the same with the other, pinning them there as he stares down at me with a barely contained wildness tightening his jaw.

He pulls out and pumps into me again. My hips bow up to meet his, and every time, I clench around him, letting the head of his cock drag along that spot deep inside me, sending ripples of pleasure across my skin and heat surging through my blood.

This is crazy and frantic, a combustion of two volatile forces thrown together in an impossible situation. We were doomed to fail, set on this collision course with each other the moment he set foot in New York. There was nothing we could have done to stop this once our eyes met, once we truly *saw* each other.

There was no turning back.

Fighting it was futile.

We shouldn't have even tried.

I knew what coming here tonight would mean.

After the realization I had about what Jude was doing—why he's here—it all became so crystal clear.

Why things felt different with him from day one. Why I

wasn't treating him like other clients. Why he never seemed like a criminal.

Because he doesn't hold that kind of selfish hostility toward the law. He's a good man, torn apart by a brutal injury, who just wants to do something good for the world.

He isn't a monster.

Far from it.

But buried inside me like this, I can see the animal lurking within him, the beast that drives him to act where so many won't. A man seeking justice where there is none and fighting himself at the same time.

Every muscle in his body tenses, each shove inside me coiling him tighter and tighter until it looks like he's going to snap. His grip on my hands loosens, and I wrap my hands around his neck and drag his mouth to mine, kissing him deeply, tasting myself there along with his own unique flavor born of strength, danger, aggression, and pride.

Jude Lawson is a man who has always fought—for his country, for his life, for people he thought needed protecting, and now, he's fighting with himself, holding back for fear of hurting me or maybe himself, keeping himself from letting loose everything he's bottled up inside for so long.

All his anguish.

All his pain.

All the reasons he keeps silent and builds up walls around himself.

Walls I want to disappear.

I want to see them shatter so the man who's hidden behind them can finally be free—at least for tonight.

We can deal with the fallout of this tomorrow.

I suck his lip into my mouth and bite down, and he releases a heavy groan that vibrates through his chest and into my body as he plunges deeper into me. Each stroke, his fingers tighten on my hips, and I capture his face between my hands. His neck strains, sweat beading across his forehead.

"Don't hold back, Jude." I clench around him, trying to enforce my words as much as the friction. "Don't hold *anything* back."

"F-f-fuck." He pulls out sharply and slaps the side of my thigh. "G-g-get on your kn-kn-knees."

His low, gravelly voice, heavy with need, forces me to roll over and up onto my knees, raising my ass into the air and toward him. He grips my hips and drives into me again, going so much deeper, feeling impossibly bigger this way.

"God, yes." My words tumble out on a gasp. "Like that."

A strong hand at the middle of my shoulder blades forces me down, and I lower my chest and face to the mattress, turning my head to the side to watch his raw power and beauty as he fucks me.

The new position makes him grit his teeth, his muscles straining so hard it looks like they'll burst. Every thrust of his hips forces him deeper into my body and soul.

He's not the kind of man you walk away from. Not the kind of man you can forget. Not the kind of man you can resist. Not even if it might cost you what you love more than anything.

Jude grips my side with his left hand while the other grasps my hair and tugs, jerking my head back and up.

Fuck.

It changes the angle slightly. His fingers dig into my flesh, his grip on my hair tightening, too. A few more long, hard strokes are all it takes for the blazing heat to spread and ripple across my skin and out through my limbs. He rolls his hips up with each thrust, giving another sharp tug on my hair until tiny pinpricks of pain flash across my scalp.

My orgasm comes quickly, a cataclysm of pleasure erupting from my core and out to every cell in my body. I gasp and jerk on his cock as he continues to plow into me relentlessly, his entire body shaking violently, seeking his own release.

He lets go of my hair and grips my other hip, tugging me toward him and tilting me up until he's ramming down, driving into me like a drill trying to get to the center of something, or maybe he's trying to cement himself inside me, prove something to both me and to the lingering questions in his mind about how I feel about him, about this.

With my body still twitching, ecstasy still coursing through my veins, he races toward his own orgasm, dragging mine out until I can't catch my breath and fully fall onto the bed.

If he only knew what we were risking, what *I* am.

Maybe that's what makes this so hot—the fact that we can both lose big.

He releases a strangled groan and pushes into me one final time, coming deep inside me before he feathers his lips to my neck and collapses on top of me.

His hard body pins me down, cocooning me in strength, sweat, and hot skin. Warm breath flutters against my ear, heavy and labored. His heart beats rapidly against my shoulder blade, matching the rhythm of my own.

It's one minute of peace.

A chance to linger in the ecstasy of the moment.

To forget the world outside and what it expects of us.

Because all too soon, reality is going to slap us in the face.

In the stark light of morning, we'll see what we've done. We'll have to acknowledge the problems it has caused. We'll see everything we risked for this moment. And we'll have to deal with the consequences.

I let myself sink into the strong arms of the man who is worth so much more than he knows, who has made me reconsider everything, who has made me see who and what he really is, who has let me into his fragile, shattered world even if only for one night.

His calloused fingertips brush along my spine, and I shudder as goosebumps break out across my skin. He skims his lips over my skin, letting them linger there, offering featherlight brushes that ignite that fire in my blood again as his cock hardens, still inside me.

He rolls his hips forward, jamming himself deeper, and I moan and arch toward him. One strong arm wraps around my waist, molding me to him, as he languidly draws his hips back before driving himself into me again.

Any rational thoughts flee on the wave of renewed ecstasy.

Jude's lips find the nape of my neck and kiss up to my ear. "F-f-fuck you f-f-feel good."

His words, the ones he never shares with anyone else, resound loudly in my head. He's giving me something he never gives anyone else.

This isn't Mouth. He's giving me Jude.

FINLEY

I finally push back from my desk, after what has been an absolute killer week full of complications I never could have seen coming, and release a deep groan.

My body still aches in all the best ways after my night with Jude, even while my mind can't stop running over the fact that I violated every moral and ethical code I've ever believed in to get those glorious results.

I can't get out of here fast enough. Spending some time at home, away from the office, away from Jude and what he does to me, will give me some time to seek some clarity.

Almost as if to say, "fuck you," my phone rings, and I wince and glance at the screen.

Enzo.

My stomach tightens right away. He knows I will call him if I have any news on his case, so if he's calling me, it can't be good. "Hey, Enzo. What's going on?"

"Um, I have something to tell you that you're not going to be happy about."

Fuck.

I rub at the headache suddenly forming at my temples. "What happened?"

"Well...I went to Danica's house—"

"You *what*?"

"I know. I know, but look, Matthews has been on her since before he got discharged, blowing up her phone and threatening her. You saw the press conference. He implied that he was never going to let her go. I don't trust him, so I went to check on her. But when I was leaving, I saw Matthews' Mercedes parked across the street from her place. I turned around and went right back in and told her she had to leave. She can't stay there anymore, Ms. Banks. Not alone. I took her to Big Nose Kate's and put her in the apartment above it so my dad and the guys can keep an eye on her."

Fucking hell.

Now the Satan's Knights are protecting the key witness in the case against their president's son. If that doesn't *scream* interference with a witness, nothing does.

"So, what you're telling me is that you completely ignored the no-contact order issued by the court as part of your conditions of release on bond, and now, you're going to bring into question the credibility of the only witness we have, and whom we need to potentially get your case dumped, by being personally involved with her?"

Enzo releases a little sigh. "I guess it does sound bad when you put it that way."

"You think?"

"I don't have a choice, Ms. Banks. She's in danger. Matthews is dangerous. And now that he knows she's on my side, it's only going to get worse."

Shit.

He isn't wrong about that. Matthews has to have learned about the statements by now since I sent the affidavit to

ADA Waters, and her ex is likely willing to do anything to protect his picture-perfect image for the campaign. Danica's statements could ruin everything for him, and he's already proven he's the kind of man willing to put his hands on a woman—even one he was once married to and supposedly loved.

That puts Enzo—and me—between a rock and a hard place.

Danica clearly needs protection from Matthews. I could call the detectives in charge of the case and tell them everything Enzo just revealed to me, ask them to put a car on Danica and watch to ensure Matthews isn't a problem, but then they'll know Enzo was violating his bond, exposing him to further charges.

"So, you're saying you won't stay away from her and just let her deal with Matthews on her own?"

"That's not an option. I won't abandon her."

That's what I thought.

Deep down, despite who his father is and the type of people he grew up around, he's a good guy and thinks he's doing the right thing.

"I want you to listen very carefully to me, Enzo. Having contact with Danica or Matthews is a violation of the terms of your release. If the district attorney's office finds out, they will issue additional felony charges against you, ones to which we have no defense like we do the original charge. My legal advice as your attorney is to abide by the terms of your bond and have no contact with either of them." I inhale deeply and release a sigh. "If you do, don't get caught, and I can't know about it. Do you understand?"

"Understood."

He better. If this goes sideways because he couldn't stay away from Danica and he ends up going to prison, the Knights will have my—and likely Schwartz's—head for it. It won't matter that his own choices and actions got him into the situation; I'm the one who is supposed to get him out.

The intercom on my desk phone buzzes just as I set down my cell phone, and Terri clears her throat. "Um, ma'am, there's a Mr. Lawson here to see you."

"What?" I jerk my head toward my closed door. "Um, okay, I'll be right out."

Shit. What the hell is he doing here?

I force myself to my feet and walk to the door, but I can't seem to make my hand twist the knob. Not when I know what is waiting for me out there. *Who* is waiting for me.

The man who utterly destroyed all the walls I had built around my heart, decimated my ethics and values, and made me come more times than I could count last night.

I stand, staring at my hand for a moment, trying to muster up the courage to walk out there and see him after I slipped out without a word this morning. It was a bid to avoid the awkwardness we're about to face right now, and in hindsight, the privacy of his condo seems like a much better place to do this than in my damn office.

Fuckity fuck fuck.

This isn't going to end well, and I need to maintain a professional composure in front of the office staff—and my client.

I pull open the door and walk out to the reception area, holding my breath. Jude stands against one wall, leaning his shoulder to the painted surface, ankles crossed over each other casually—like he isn't here to meet with the woman he just fucked last night.

His blue eyes find mine immediately, and the corner of his lip twitches. But otherwise, he doesn't offer any other reaction or say anything. Not that I would expect him to.

"Mr. Lawson"—I plaster on my most professional smile —"I wasn't expecting to see you today."

He smirks, pushes off the wall, and walks toward me, practically undressing me with his gaze.

I glance at my watch. "I have a few minutes before my next appointment, so we can talk about whatever's on your mind."

Jude pauses next to me and gives me a look that tells me it isn't going to be nearly enough time.

Oh, hell.

I clear my throat and offer a tight smile to Terri. Jude inclines his head toward her in passing and follows me back to my office. Pausing outside the open door, I motion for him to enter first. He strolls past casually, watching me over his shoulder as I step in and close the door behind me, leaning against it and letting out a whoosh of held breath.

"What are you doing here?"

He slowly meanders over to my desk and sits on the edge of it facing me, arms over his barrel chest. "Y-y-you disappeared this morning. T-t-that's usually my j-j-job."

"Ha, ha. Very funny." I step away from the door and take a step toward him. "Is there something wrong?"

A smirk spreads across his lips, and he shakes his head. "C-c-can't I v-v-visit my l-l-lawyer's office?"

I glance down at the monitor on his ankle and the green light flashing there. "Yes. If the meeting has been approved, but I didn't—"

"I c-c-called them this m-m-morning."

He called them and actually spoke to someone on the phone just so he could come down here and see me.

What the hell?

My chest tightens, and sweat breaks out over my skin as he continues to stare at me. "Really, Mouth. What are you doing here?"

MOUTH

FINLEY SHIFTS NERVOUSLY on her stilettoed feet, twisting her hands in front of her as she watches me with trepidation that definitely wasn't there twelve hours ago.

This isn't the Finley Banks I know.

She's always so sure of herself. So confident. So unwilling to back down. This version of her is so much more vulnerable—this is the one who spent the night with me, who let me touch her and kiss and take her all night long…and then slipped out while I pretended to still be asleep.

This may be what she's really like underneath all the bravado and armor she wears to do her job in a business that can be misogynistic and volatile. And it didn't slip my notice that she's back to calling me Mouth again, trying to distance herself from the name she called me while I was buried inside her.

I may have let her leave this morning without confronting her or stopping her, giving her the space she clearly needed to mentally sort through what went down between us, but I'm not about to let her pretend last night didn't happen.

It meant too much, even if she wasn't ready to accept that this morning. I've given her the day to think, to figure out how she's going to play this, and I'm done waiting to know how she feels about all this.

"I w-w-wanted to make s-s-sure you w-w-were okay."

Something flashes in her eyes for a second before she closes them and takes a deep breath, flattening her hand against her stomach like she's trying to quiet something fluttering there. "I don't know how to answer that, Mouth. What happened was…"

She trails off like she can't think of the word.

Incredible.

Fantastic.

Mind-blowing.

So many descriptive words come to mind to explain what happened between us, but looking at her, I know the word she's thinking of is *mistake*.

Last night wasn't a mistake, though.

She may be questioning her own actions; given her position, I'd be shocked if she weren't. But us coming together like that was what we both wanted. What we both *needed*. And I won't let her regret it.

Finley averts her gaze, keeping her focus on her feet or the window, anywhere but at me. "Things are very complicated right now, Mouth, and I found myself in a position I thought I would never be in professionally, where I'm having to not only question my ethics but also break the code I vowed when I was sworn in as an attorney in the state of New York." She glances over her shoulder toward the closed door, nervous we might be overheard or interrupted. "I always knew that working with Schwartz would mean I'd have to take cases I wouldn't like and represent people I wouldn't choose to. I accept that because I've always believed that the system only works when everyone is entitled to vigorous representation. But I also believe there are lines which shouldn't be crossed, and lately..." She shakes her head, her eyes shimmering with unshed tears. "Christ, Mouth, I've been crossing all of them."

I stand from the desk and walk over to her, taking her biceps in my hands and rubbing her arms gently. "Y-y-you didn't d-d-do anything wr-wr-wrong."

She releases a sigh. "Yes, I did, Mouth. I did. You're my *client,* and what happened never should have. On top of that, I have knowledge that you are tampering with your surveillance bracelet and willfully violating the bond of the court. And that's the least of your crimes."

You don't know the half of it.

Although, I'm sure she suspects that the bodies that have been turning up have been at my hand, no one will ever prove it, and that's all that matters.

Last night, she said she understood what I was doing, and that didn't make her run because deep down, she knows I'm not in the wrong. That what I'm doing is a form of justice the courts she serves can't give.

This internal war raging through her is going to destroy her.

"It isn't just about you, either. There are other things going on with other clients that just…"

Finley lets out a breath so heavy it actually makes my heart hurt for her. She's a good person who firmly believes that what she's doing is right, and I've helped put her in a situation where her ethics and morals are being smashed to pieces.

That can't continue.

I lift up her chin to force her to meet my gaze. "Y-y-you're f-f-fired."

Her green eyes widen, brows flying up. "What?"

"I-i-if th-th-that's the p-p-problem, t-t-then you're f-f-fired."

"No." She shakes her head, her hands finding the front of my shirt. "You can't. That's not what I—"

I brush my thumb across her lips, silencing her before she can argue with me about this. "I w-w-won't let you f-f-feel guilty about th-th-this."

"You're not firing me. Schwartz is too damn busy to handle your case, and I'm not going to pass this off to anyone else, especially not when I have already spoken with the ADA on the case and have things moving in the right direction." Her gaze locks with mine, determination hardening them, but the affection and fire still blaze in their depths. "What happened just can't happen again."

Just like she knew she should leave but wouldn't last night, I know she doesn't mean it. Not really. She's just still fighting the battle in her own head.

I smirk and lean in until my lips are just short of hers. "B-b-but it's g-g-going to."

No matter what she tries to tell herself, she can't walk away from this any more than I can. If either of us could, we never would have kissed, we never would have fucked each other into mindless bliss last night, and we wouldn't be standing here having this conversation while wanting to be back in my bed.

Finley sighs again and sags slightly, her fingers curling into the soft material over my chest. "I know."

Her green eyes hold mine for a moment, both of us resigned to the fact that this is happening and there isn't any hope of stopping it.

I press my lips against hers softly, then release her chin and step back from her. "I'll s-s-see you t-t-tonight."

Without waiting for her response, I step around her, open the door, and move out of her office and toward the reception area.

Finley Banks is one of a fucking kind, and as long as she's going to look past all the reasons I'm all kinds of wrong for her, I'm going do everything I can to make her happy.

Life may have stolen my memories, but my broken body still knew what Finley needed last night and gave it to her.

It may be all I ever *can* give her.

14

MOUTH

I'm going to fucking kill him.

The text from Parrish said to head to the marina for "boat washing" and to come quickly. I was just *about* to— inside Finley. This better be a fucking life-or-death style emergency, or I will put a bullet between his fucking eyes and throw him in the damn harbor.

Who the fuck does he think he is?

We teamed up *one* damn time with those Satan's Knights fuckers, and now Parrish acts like I'm his fucking lapdog at his beck and call.

We're going to come to an understanding about that tonight.

Whatever the hell is going on can't be more important than burying myself inside Finley. Nothing is.

I slam the car door and jog the block to the marina, where Parrish waits near the bait and tackle shop, standing next to his bike, toothpick dangling from his lips. He scans his surroundings carefully, vigilant like he's expecting someone he doesn't want to see to show up at any moment.

Hopefully, it isn't the fucking cops.

The last thing I need right now is to get caught out of the apartment—sans monitor—associating with a member of the fucking Knights and doing God only knows what.

He watches me approach him. "Hey, thanks for coming so quickly."

I grab the front of his shirt and shove him back against the building, his toothpick tumbling to the ground. "I am n-n-not your f-f-fucking dog to c-c-call whenever you n-n-need so-so-something d-d-done."

His eyes widen, and he sneers at me. "Ah, so you do fucking speak. What's the problem, motherfucker? Did I interrupt you fucking your girl?"

Motherfucking asshole.

No one knows about what's going on between Finley and me, and no one *can* know. It would ruin everything for her. Him even joking about me *having* a girl is way too close to the truth for comfort.

I press my face close to his. "N-n-never a-a-again."

Before the notoriously insane man can snap back, the crunch of footsteps approaching from behind me makes me spin toward the sound, gun already pulled, but Parrish grabs my arm.

"No. He's with us."

This douchebag is with us?

The guy approaches, his curly dark hair blowing slightly in the breeze, in dark jeans and a black shirt, staring at me with icy-blue eyes.

Parrish steps between us. "Mouth, this is Mayhem. Mayhem, this is Mouth." A low chuckle slips from his lips. "You two will get along great." He smacks Mayhem in the chest. "You never shut the fuck up, and he"—he glances at me —"well, he's fucking quiet."

Christ. Just what I need. Some asshole named Mayhem fucking up whatever it is Parrish needs me to do.

Mayhem scowls at him. "I don't need a babysitter."

"You need whatever the fuck I say you need." Parrish issues a growl. "If you hadn't fucked up the Matthews hit by going after Guthrie instead, we wouldn't even be in this situation."

I dart my gaze between the two men.

This *asshole is the reason I had to threaten Guthrie and couldn't just whack him? They're protecting* this *guy?*

Parrish answers my unspoken question with an exasperated sigh and nods toward Mayhem. "Listen up, fucker. You two have different skills, and this is extremely personal to me. Don't *fuck* this up. It has to look like a suicide."

Oh, hell.

Parrish glances around to ensure we're alone. "It's Brent Matthews. Apparently, he grabbed Enzo's girl, brought her to his boat, and argued with his partner, Guthrie. They fought, and Matthews killed him and threw him into the water. Enzo arrived in time to stop him from taking Danica anywhere else, but he had to use a tire iron to do it. We need it to look like he did this himself so there aren't any questions."

Fucking hell.

I incline my head, indicating I got it. No wonder Parrish wanted me here. This Mayhem guy is clearly a fucking moron who can't do a job properly. Parrish needs to ensure this is done right to protect the son of his president, and I'm the only one he knows can do it who isn't tied to the club.

Just my fucking luck.

But somehow, it almost seems fitting that I be the one to clean up this mess. Considering what I've learned about Guthrie and Matthews over the last couple of weeks, they would have met their end through my scope eventually anyway.

I turn away from Parrish and make my way toward the dock.

Mayhem hustles after me. "Okay, here's what we need to do—"

With a hard tug on his shirt, I swing him around to face me. His eyes meet mine, and I shake my head and point to myself.

He raises a confused brow. "What?"

Motherfucking fuck.

"Bro, we need to hustle here. You know, time is of the essence and shit."

Why the hell did Parrish saddle me with this guy?

This is something I could have handled alone in my sleep, but he had to bring in Chatty Cathy over here. I pull out my notebook and start to write while Mayhem shifts nervously.

"No time to journal, asshole. Let's fucking go!"

I rip out the page and slam it into his chest, knocking him back a few steps, almost into the damn water. He pulls the paper up and reads it.

I'm in charge!

"You needed that in print?" He stares at me for a moment like he's trying to figure something out. "Are you mute?"

Somehow, I stop my fist an inch from connecting with his face.

We don't have time for this bullshit.

I scribble in my notebook again, rip out the page, and hand it to him before making my way onto the boat.

NO! I'll tell you what to do!

"I do this very well. Thank you very fucking much."

Unfuckinglikely.

This guy is clearly a fucking amateur playing at being whatever the fuck it is he thinks he is. If I left him in charge, we'd be cuffed and in a jail cell before the damn sun comes up and the Knights would be fucked, their prez's son in the slammer for murder.

I growl at him and step onto the boat.

Matthews' body lies in the center of the cabin, a bloody gash on his left temple, a tire iron beside the body. I don't waste any time pulling on my gloves and wiping the weapon clean as I walk to the deck and toss it into the water.

Mayhem reaches into his waistband with a gloved hand and pulls out a Glock. "It's clean. Untraceable."

Huh. Maybe this guy isn't as fucking stupid as he looks.

I squat beside the body and lift his right hand to place the weapon and pull the trigger. The shot will blow out the other side of his temple and destroy any evidence of what Enzo did with the tire iron.

"No." Mayhem squats across from me and lifts the stiff's other hand. "He's a leftie." He wraps the fingers of Matthews' left hand around the gun. "I noticed at that press conference that he made a writing gesture with his left hand. See, he wears his watch on his right hand, too. When cleaning a scene, you have to notice those little details."

Fucking prick.

I would have noticed the watch when I went to put the gun in his hand, but I have to say, it's a nice catch. A half-nod is all the acknowledgment he gets for that as I rise to my feet and move out of the way of the spray about to come.

He grins at me. "Ah, see, we had a little bonding moment there, you and me, big guy. Maybe we'll go grab a beer after?"

I glower at him and shake my head.

"Hate to break up this little bromance, but..." Mayhem

pulls the trigger with Matthews' fingers, the congressional hopeful's brains blowing out across the cabin.

Job done.

And now, I'm done with Parrish, too.

The only good thing the guy ever did for me was introduce me to Finley, and now, I need to figure out what the fuck I'm going to do about that situation—besides get back home and back inside her as quickly as is humanly possible.

FINLEY

JUDE SLIPS in the apartment door, throws the lock behind him, and kicks off his boots before slowly making his way toward the bathroom.

Where were you?

The question sits on the tip of my tongue as I watch him stripping off his clothes and letting them fall to the wood floor. I want to know what was so important that it made him rush out of here in the middle of sex. I want to know what was more important than *me,* than *us* in that moment, but I won't ask because I also *don't* want to know.

His bare shoulders tense, he steps into the bathroom nude, flicks on the light, and nudges the door halfway shut. He cranks on the shower before he returns to stand in front of the mirror, entranced by something reflecting back at him.

What does he see?

My understanding of amnesia is limited, at best, and even though I've read his medical records, I still don't have a grasp on what it means to him on a day-to-day basis.

Does he even recognize himself?

Lately, it's seemed like I'm staring at a stranger when I

look in the mirror, so I can't imagine what it might be like for him. From where I still lie on the bed, in the same place he left me, I can't tell what he's doing, but the tension practically rolls off him, reaching me even over here.

Whatever he was just out doing, it rattled him for some reason. He's come back a different man than he was when he left only a few hours ago.

Steam starts to fill the bathroom and pour out into the main loft area, and Jude finally turns toward the shower and steps inside, sliding the glass door closed behind him.

I don't know Jude well enough to know if this is one of those times I should leave him alone, but something compels me to climb from the bed and pad into the bathroom.

He stands under the spray, his face raised to it, arms stiff at his side, hands fisted. I take a step closer, and he flinches, his head twitching slightly toward me.

There isn't any way to hide that I'm here now. I could turn around and go back to bed alone, wait for him to come out after he's decompressed from whatever happened, but something about that doesn't feel right.

This isn't the time to abandon him to his own head.

I slide the shower door open and step in behind him, wrapping my arms around his waist and resting my face against my back. "You weren't going to tell me you're back?"

He doesn't have a response, at least not one he's going to offer. Likely because he doesn't want to have to answer questions about where he was or what he was doing tonight.

We're on unsteady ground, and he won't risk shaking it by answering any more than I do by asking those questions.

I brush my lips to his spine, squeezing him gently. "Are you okay?"

That seems like a safe question to ask, one that leaves him plenty of room to give whatever answer he wants.

Jude glances over his shoulder at me, the water still

pounding his chest, and watches me for a moment before he nods.

I swim in his blue eyes, searching for the lie in the statement he didn't even make. "I'm not going to ask you what you were doing if that's what you're worried about."

He clenches his jaw and turns to face me.

I stare up at him, pressing my hands against his chest. "I won't ask. I don't want to know. I'll never ask if you don't want to tell me."

Our nakedness and proximity, or maybe my words, make his cock harden between us, and he grasps my hips and crushes me against him, crushing his lips to mine like I'm the only one who can provide the oxygen he needs to breathe in this moment.

Sometimes it feels like that for me, too, like everything that's going on in my head, all the cases, all the lives in my hands, are all so overwhelming that I can't focus on anything because I don't have the air to make my body work properly.

I score my nails down his chest, over his abs, and circle his cock. My first stroke drags a low groan from his lips against mine, and I work him tenderly, slowly, trying to show him that life doesn't always have to be so painful or fast.

His body tenses more, and I pull away from his kiss.

Wide blue eyes meet mine and watch me lower myself to my knees under the hot spray.

Jude has made me feel so good and done this for me so many times that I can't think of a better way to help him find his release from whatever is weighing so heavily on him.

I take his cock in my mouth and drag my tongue along the bottom of it.

"F-f-fuck, Finley."

His hands tangle in my wet hair as water beats against his back, sluicing over his shoulders and down over me. I let his cock pop free of my lips and grip at the base so I can lift it up to lick and suck all along the shaft, swirling my tongue around the head.

"Christ, is th-th-there anything you aren't g-g-good at?"

I grin against his flesh at the compliment and with the knowledge that this is driving him as insane as it is me. Suctioning my mouth around him fully, I reach down with my right hand and swirl my finger around my throbbing clit, needing the friction to dispel the pressure building there the longer I do this to Jude.

Watching him come undone, seeing him forget whatever was plaguing him while I suck his cock is the greatest feeling in the world, and I only want to do more.

I swallow him even deeper, so far down my throat that the head of his cock hits the soft fleshy part at the back that might make anyone else gag, but I just continue to swallow, desperate to taste him on my tongue.

His fingers tighten in my hair, and he shoves his hips forward, coming straight down my throat in hot bursts. I rub at my clit feverishly, wanting to get there with him, to feel the same release, but he jerks me from his length and glances down, eyes zeroing in on where my hand moves between my legs.

He reaches down and jerks me to my feet, molding his mouth to mine in a soul-searing kiss, his own cum still lingering on my tongue. It doesn't seem to bother him, though, his dick growing even harder where it presses against my stomach. He lifts me, turning us to slam me against the cool tile wall, and drives into me in one swift motion.

I gasp and drop my head back against the tile, my moan echoing off it and around in the bathroom as he pumps into me, driving me harder against the wall with each aggressive thrust.

It's like he doesn't know any other way to be with me. Each time is this frantic rush, as if he can't get inside me or make me come fast enough, like he's trying to meld us together permanently before the entire world might collapse around him.

And I love it.

My body craves it. Yearns for it. Reaches for it, for *him* every time he's near.

He pummels me, his strokes harsh and aggressive.

Exactly what he and I need.

"God, Jude. Fuck me harder. Harder."

I dig my nails into his shoulders, digging my feet into his lower back for leverage as he demolishes me, taking out his anger at life or whatever else it might be tonight through me. Then he suddenly stills, and I open my eyes to meet his concerned ones.

"I'm s-s-sorry."

"For what?"

Tears pool in his eyes as he struggles to find the answer. The pain is too much for me to bear, and I grip the back of his head and drag it to me to kiss away his agony.

I press my forehead to his, and he keeps pumping into me, slowing his pace, changing from frantic to long, languid strokes.

It's torture.

A form I can't survive.

I shake my head from side to side. "No, harder. I need it. I need you like this."

His brow furrows like he can't comprehend why I would want him like that—uncontrolled, wild, reckless. He doesn't see it, doesn't understand why it's what we both need. That we've both been waiting for someone who can give us that.

He renews his harder, faster strokes, and another orgasm starts to tingle at my core. Jude grinds his pelvis on my clit, giving me as much friction as he can while the water pours down over us. His mouth finds mine again, and we kiss and pant against each other's lips until my body stiffens, my pussy tightening and clasping at his cock to drag out his orgasm.

It doesn't take long before we're both finding that release.

Jude groans and collapses against me on the wall, still embedded deep inside me.

I skim my lips against his neck softly, kissing my way up to his ear. "Don't ever apologize for that, Jude. Never."

15

MOUTH

Neither the fresh air nor the nicotine flowing in my veins can stop the overwhelming anxiety coursing through me, making my foot bounce up and down on the metal grate of the fire escape.

I take another drag and hold the smoke in my lungs for a few seconds before I blow it out, watching it curl up to the steps and dissipate into the soft light of early morning.

The hours I've sat out here thinking haven't helped clarify any of the questions endlessly floating through my head since I returned last night. Lying next to Finley while she slept so peacefully only made it worse. Which is why I'm a quarter of a pack in and still don't feel any better about the situation I've created.

Less than twelve hours ago, I helped cover up a murder, and I didn't even feel bad about it. But as soon as I walked in and saw Finley in my bed, guilt ate away at my stomach, wondering what she would think about what I had done.

And then I took out my frustration on her in a way I never should have, even if she asked for it.

Don't ever apologize for that, Jude. Never.

Her words ring in my ears even now, but it's impossible not to contemplate how different our worlds are, how different *we* are, and how, in the end, that is what is going to pull us apart.

I sense her before I hear or see her—my skin heating under her careful assessment from inside the apartment. Finley climbs out the window and onto the fire escape in one of my T-shirts that hangs down to her mid-thigh.

She offers me a little half-smile as I take another drag. "I didn't know you smoke."

"S-s-sometimes." I drop it to my feet and grind it out with my boot. "I sh-sh-shouldn't."

Finley rests her arms against the metal railing in front of her and looks out across the city. "There's a lot I don't know about you. I don't even know what happened to you to cause your injuries." She glances over at me with pain in her eyes that makes my chest tighten. "I don't even know what your favorite food is."

It's the same realization that has occupied my thoughts the last few hours—how little we actually know about each other and the fact that I don't even know most of it about myself unless someone else tells me.

At least one of those is easy to answer.

I reach out and wrap my arm around her thighs, dragging her toward me to stand between my legs and press my face against her lower belly. "Y-y-you know exactly wh-wh-what my favorite thing to e-e-eat is."

A tiny laugh shakes her body, but when I pull back my head and look up at her, the pink blush on her cheeks doesn't hide the pain still etched on her face. "I barely know you. It's only been two fucking weeks, and I'm in bed with my client."

She runs her hands through my hair lazily. "What are we doing, Jude? What am *I* doing?"

It's a fair question.

Finley's been an open book for me about her reservations and her life, chattering on about growing up in a small town in Illinois before coming to New York for undergrad and then ultimately law school at Fordham, where she met David Schwartz, who she now works with. She's never afraid to just keep talking, to hold a one-sided conversation when she knows I can't or won't respond or interject.

Someone else might be annoyed by it, but her voice has become my favorite sound—especially when she's moaning my name while I'm inside her.

She's told me so much about herself, revealed everything, but I can't say the same. And it isn't just because all I remember are bits and pieces and the only things I really *know* are what's been told to me.

I don't *want* her to know me when I don't even know myself. I want to protect her from what I'm capable of, what I plan on continuing to do. The things she's come so close to being on the wrong side of since she met me.

She continues to thread her fingers through my hair, correctly assuming I don't want to answer her. "The only things I know about you are what I read in your medical records and the information Reaper gave me so I could get you out on bond."

I'd love to keep it that way.

The less she knows, the easier it will be to walk away when she realizes I'm completely wrong for her, that I have nothing to offer her except mind-bending sex, when she sees how *truly* broken I am—beyond what was written on those pages in my medical records.

She retreats a step from me, her distress at my reluctance to open up to her, making her not even want my touch. Her green eyes plead with me, though they hold no anger, just affection and confusion that I'm sure mine match.

Finley deserves an answer.

She deserves everything.

It's the least I can give her.

"I o-o-only remember b-b-bits and pieces. The r-r-rest, my fr-fr-friends t-t-old me. M-m-my parents b-b-both died over a d-d-decade ago—my d-d-dad from cancer and my m-m-mom a heart attack. I'm n-n-not in contact with my s-s-sisters anymore. M-m-mostly because I d-d-didn't know them when I w-w-woke up and w-w-wouldn't l-l-let them h-h-help me."

She waits patiently for me to continue, and I swallow through my dry throat. This might be the most I've spoken in almost five years—the most I've wanted to, but the subject matter is more painful than just about anything else.

"I h-h-have these little fl-fl-flashes of m-m-memories from growing up. G-g-going ice sk-sk-skating. Christmas t-t-trees and pr-pr-presents under them. But I ca-ca-can't piece them t-t-together into any o-o-one solid m-m-memory. It's all j-j-just jumbled. The only th-th-thing I don't seem to st-st-struggle with is d-d-doing th-th-this."

I spread my hands wide, knowing she will understand exactly what I'm talking about without saying the words.

"For s-s-some r-r-reason, even though my m-m-memories are sh-sh-shattered, my instincts are all st-st-still there. E-e-everything I was tr-tr-trained to d-d-do. If y-y-you hand me a r-r-rifle, I'll have it dis-dis-disassembled in under th-th-thirty seconds without e-e-even th-th-thinking about it. But a-a-ask me my b-b-birthday and I w-w-wouldn't know it unless s-s-someone else t-t-told me."

A single tear trickles down Finley's cheek, and she quickly swipes it away.

I let out a deep sigh and scrub my hand over the stubble

on my face. "I s-s-sometimes remember h-h-hunting with my d-d-dad when he w-w-wasn't deployed. T-t-turns out, I w-w-was very g-g-good at it."

Despite the heavy topic, a smile tilts her lips. "Somehow, that doesn't surprise me."

"I enlisted o-o-out of h-h-high school, and my p-p-particular skill w-w-was picked up on v-v-very early in my c-c-career. I w-w-was in t-t-the R-r-rangers first as a sn-sn-sniper, then m-m-moved to D-d-delta Force."

She nods slowly. "That sure explains a lot. I requested your military records, but I kept hitting a wall with getting them."

"I m-m-managed to make it th-th-through m-m-most of my c-c-career relatively unscathed u-u-until that f-f-final deployment wh-wh-when an RPG h-h-hit the b-b-building I w-w-was in."

Her brow furrows. "So, that's how it happened?"

I nod slowly, bits and pieces of the memory flashing in my head.

Scanning the village square.

Shots coming from another building.

Reaper's voice in my ear.

The world exploding around me.

Pain.

"I d-d-don't remember it. At l-l-least, not all of it. R-r-reaper p-p-pulled me from the ru-ru-rubble and got me o-o-out of there. I'd be d-d-dead if it w-w-weren't for him."

And so many days since then, I wished he would have just left me there. It would have been easier to go out that way than to live like this.

"And the headaches?"

I wince and rub at the back of my neck. "Th-th-they get especially b-b-bad when I'm st-st-stressed, b-b-but sometimes they c-c-come for no r-r-reason at all." I pause for a moment and look at her, considering not revealing the thing that's been on my mind since we first met. "E-e-ever s-s-since I m-m-met you, I've di-di-discovered something."

One of her eyebrows wings up. "What's that?"

"Wh-wh-when we're t-t-together, wh-wh-when you're w-w-with me, they s-s-seem to g-g-go away."

She considers me for a moment, then offers a humorless laugh, shaking her head. "That isn't me doing that, Jude; it's just my perfume."

"Wh-wh-what?"

A sad smile turns her lips. "It's my perfume. The main ingredients are citrus and peppermint, which have been used for hundreds of years to treat headaches. Feeling good around me has nothing to do with *me* and everything to do with *that*."

I reach out and grab her again, dragging her to me. "N-n-no, it d-d-doesn't. That m-m-may b-b-be a side effect. But it's y-y-you. I haven't f-f-felt alive. I haven't f-f-felt like I was w-w-worth anything f-f-for so l-l-long th-th-that I f-f-forgot what it f-f-felt l-l-like to w-w-want something and be w-w-wanted by someone."

She stares down at me with tears pooling in her eyes.

"Y-y-you g-g-gave me all th-th-that, and I d-d-don't kn-kn-know wh-wh-what to d-d-do with it. All I kn-kn-know is that I d-d-don't w-w-want to lose it. I d-d-don't want to l-l-lose y-y-you. But it already f-f-feels l-l-like I'm going to."

FINLEY

I STARE DOWN at the man I should have walked away from the moment I saw him because I knew there was something there. Something different. Something I hadn't felt before.

An attraction.

A desire.

A need and a pull toward something that was dangerous and wild yet controlled in a way I couldn't possibly fathom.

And the more I got to know Jude, the more he let me in, the easier it was to fall for him and the harder it becomes to walk away. Yet, the reality of who we are and where we're heading isn't something we can ignore anymore.

"You're going back to Baltimore. As soon as your case is resolved, you'll return to work with Reaper and your other friends. You're going to go do"—I wave a hand absently, not really ready to voice what it is he does—"whatever it is you do in other places, and I'm going to be here defending other criminals."

A smile twitches at the corners of his mouth. "Th-th-that's h-h-how you s-s-see me?"

His question holds no malice, and he doesn't seem offended—more hurt. Which is almost worse.

I shake my head and release a sigh. "I don't know what to think. The day I met you, I knew you were different than my other clients. I saw something, felt something, that told me whatever was going on, whatever the situation was that put you in that jail, was not what it appeared. And I was right."

When I look at him, I don't see a criminal. I don't see a bad man doing bad things. I see a good man doing what he believes is right. But those are often two sides of the same coin—one that has a very heavy weight.

"I don't think you're a criminal, but I don't know if I can just pretend it doesn't bother me to know what you're out doing at night."

He flinches but doesn't interrupt me.

"Yes, I represent criminals and defend them in court, but what you're doing is different, something that dances the line between good and bad. I believe in the justice system, believe everyone has the right to a defense and the protection of the law. If one of my clients has a case dismissed because the state did an illegal search or there wasn't enough evidence, am I going to find him dead in a few weeks, a bullet through his head or chest because you and your friends deemed it justice?"

I raise an eyebrow at him in question, but when he opens his mouth to answer, I shake my head. "I don't want to know. That was a rhetorical question. I just don't know how to navigate this, Jude. Don't know how to justify it in my head."

If that's even possible.

For the first time I can remember, I truly am at a loss for words. The more I say, the larger the rock in my throat becomes, the more I'm convincing myself that this has to end now before things get even more complicated between us, before I let things go any further.

Jude pushes to his feet and takes my face between his palms. "I kn-kn-know this is h-h-h-ard for y-y-you. Y-y-you may not agree w-w-with everything I d-d-do, but y-y-you kn-kn-know I would n-n-never h-h-hurt you, r-r-right?"

The pain in his eyes as he asks the question makes another tear trickle from my eye. "Jesus, Jude, of course, I know that. I know you could never hurt me. You would never hurt me." I shake my head, trying to collate my disjointed thoughts into something that makes sense. "I understand why you do what you do. Sometimes people slip through the cracks or walk away from crimes when they shouldn't. I've represented people I wish I hadn't, seen people walk out of court free, who I know will re-offend immediately, but it doesn't mean I agree with you and your friends being judge, jury, and executioner, and I don't know if I can ever be okay with it."

"I u-u-understand."

"No." Another tear drops down my face. "You don't,

because I should walk away right now, get your case resolved, and then watch you leave."

"B-b-but you w-w-won't?"

He watches me, waits for me to answer the ultimate question.

Can I just turn my back on Jude and whatever this is?

I wrap my arms around his neck and press my forehead against his. "I don't think I can, even if I tried. I've never felt like this before. Never needed or wanted anything as much as I do this. And that's absolutely terrifying for me."

Jude pulls back slightly. "Wh-wh-when I w-w-woke up in that h-h-hospital and r-r-realized I didn't kn-kn-know who I w-w-was, w-w-when the d-d-doctors t-t-told me my d-d-diagnosis, I th-th-thought my life w-w-was o-o-over, but n-n-now"—he brushes his lips over mine—"I s-s-see it d-d-differently. I've been g-g-given a c-c-clean slate. A ch-ch-chance to st-st-start over, but I'll n-n-never be n-n-normal, Finley. My b-b-brain will n-n-never work r-r-right. My w-w-words will n-n-never come out r-r-right."

The fact that he feels the need to apologize for that, to explain what a future with him would be like, makes my heart ache for him. "I just can't have you going silent on me, Jude."

"I c-c-can't guarantee th-th-that won't ha-ha-happen at t-t-times. I've sp-sp-spent f-f-four years being s-s-silent, wr-wr-writing my words rather than sp-sp-speaking them so n-n-no one kn-kn-knows how truly f-f-fucked up I am. I d-d-don't kn-kn-know how to retrain m-m-myself to get used to t-t-talking again."

I smile at him. "You're doing just fine."

He barks out a laugh that releases a tiny bit of the tension from the moment. "I'm n-n-not, but th-th-thank you."

Tangling my fingers in his hair, I feather my lips over his. "I'll help you figure it out. We'll figure it out—together. Your clean slate may be chipped and broken, but it's not an end. It's a new beginning, one that we have together."

He raises an eyebrow at me. "You're s-s-sure?"

"I'm sure. Now all I have to do is get your case dismissed so I don't lose my license because I fell in love with my client."

His body stiffens, and his eyes narrow slightly. "R-r-really?"

I hadn't even thought those words until they came out of my mouth. It's crazy. Impossible. People don't fall in love in two weeks. But the words feel right. *Saying* it does.

"Yes, really. I don't know how it happened, but I fell in love with you, Jude. Every fucked-up, broken piece of you."

He grins at me, tightening his hold. "Finley, I l-l-love you, too."

No one else has ever said that to me—at least, not someone I wasn't related to. Most people wouldn't believe it possible, wouldn't accept the words as true in this situation, but with Jude, I know every single thing he says is the absolute truth, or he wouldn't bother to speak it.

"We'll figure this out, Jude."

"A cl-cl-clean slate."

"A clean slate."

16

FINLEY

The phone on my desk buzzes. "I have ADA Waters calling for you."

I stare at it for a moment before I pick it up. If he's calling, it's either to talk about Enzo's case or Jude's. While I'd love to have both wrapped up quickly, resolving Jude's case would mean he's free to go back to Baltimore, and I'm not ready to think about what that will mean for the future we hope to have together.

My hand shakes, picking up the receiver. "This is Attorney Banks."

"Hi, Finley. It's Jon Waters." He gives a humorless laugh. "And apparently, today is your lucky day."

"Why's that?"

"Did you see the news this morning?"

What?

"No."

I was too busy talking to Jude out on the fire escape and then going back in to let him devour me again. It's a wonder

I even made it into the office at all today. If Jude had his way, I would still be wrapped up with him in bed.

"Well, Brent Matthews blew his brains out last night."

"*What?*"

"Yeah, on his boat. After apparently killing his business partner, Guthrie, and dumping him into the harbor. The bodies were discovered this morning."

"Holy shit."

He releases an annoyed sigh. "Which means...we no longer have a victim in Enzo Scotto's case and will be moving to dismiss it."

Oh, my God.

Jude got a text message and disappeared last night, and when he came back, he was tense, upset about something. Not himself at all.

Did he have anything to do with this?

I shake my head to dispel the question because I don't *want* to know the answer. Whatever happened, it resolved Enzo's case, and I need to concentrate on my client. "Well, that's good news for Mr. Scotto, then."

"It certainly is, and I would say awfully convenient, too, but he clearly had nothing to do with whatever went down between those two."

"I'm sure he will be happy to know he's no longer facing charges."

"Oh, I'm sure he will. Now, as far as Mr. Lawson is concerned, I have reviewed his medical records."

"Very interesting read, aren't they?"

More like depressing, painful, traumatizing.

He releases a heavy sigh—one that carries the weight of the job he has to do on a daily basis. "I have to tell you, Ms. Banks. It does me no pleasure prosecuting somebody with a history like this, but if I just dismiss these charges, everybody and their brother is going to think it's okay to run around killing people they believe deserve it."

"No, they won't, Jon, and you and I both know that. Mr. Lawson isn't a threat to the community."

Just my heart.

I glance at my copy of the records still stacked on the corner of my desk. "If he did this, and that's a big *if*, he's doing the community a *service*. Doing *you* a service and the *police* a service by taking these guys off the streets. It might be strictly outside the letter of the law. I can concede that. But it doesn't mean it's wrong."

ADA Waters probably isn't the person to be getting into this ethical debate with, especially when I myself have issues with Jude's nighttime activities, but sometimes, it takes being frank with the opposing side to get things done.

"What do you expect me to tell my boss, Ms. Banks?"

"The truth—that you can't prove your case."

He grumbles something under his breath about vigilantes and bloodsucking defense attorneys. "Okay, fine. I'll dismiss *without* prejudice, but if he steps out of line, or if the gun ever turns up and his fingerprints are on it, then I'm going to reissue the charges."

"That's not going to happen."

I never asked Jude what he did with the gun that night, but he's smart enough to have put it somewhere it will never be found, before he got arrested.

"Then, I guess it really *is* your lucky day, Ms. Banks. Double lucky."

"It appears it is."

Though, luck had nothing to do with it. I'm certain the Matthews situation resolving was more than what it appeared, and getting Jude's case resolved is more to do with who *he* is than luck.

"I'll see you next week at the status conferences on these cases, and we'll dismiss them then."

I end the call with a grin spread across my face until I glance up and see Schwartz leaning against my doorframe, looking more haggard and tired than I've ever seen him. "What's wrong?"

He inclines his head toward my phone. "You go first. You look pretty happy about something."

I shove my hands back through my hair, my stomach suddenly turning at the reality of what the news means. "Yeah, I guess you could say that. You can tell Parrish that both Enzo's and Jude Lawson's cases will be dismissed."

Schwartz's eyes widen slightly. "Really?"

I nod. "Apparently, Matthews killed his business partner and then himself last night."

His mouth opens and closes a few times before he finds his words. "Holy fuck."

"Exactly my thoughts."

"So that means Mayhem is likely in the clear, too, since there isn't a victim anymore."

I'm not going to let him in on my suspicions about what Mouth might have done last night because, ultimately, it's irrelevant, and I don't want to know the truth.

"Well, that's exactly what we wanted. All the cases Parrish saddled us with are resolved. Nice fucking work, Fin."

Reclining in my chair, I raise a brow at him. "Thanks. So, why don't you tell me why you look like someone pissed in your Cheerios?"

He rubs the back of his neck as he wanders in, shuts the door, and then makes his way to a chair facing me. "We need to have a talk."

"About what?"

"About something really fucking stupid I did that might change things around here for a while."

Shit.

Schwartz does a lot of stupid stuff, so that statement doesn't narrow it down.

"What happened?"

"Well, that night that you went to Brighton Beach to help Enzo and Mr. Lawson, and I went to Staten Island because I had to deal with the attempted murder."

"Right…"

"I got a flat tire and had to have an Uber bring me there."

"Okay. I'm not following where any of this is going."

"Well, I wound up knowing the Uber driver. She and I were close back in college." He pauses, biting the inside of his cheek. "Until we weren't, and she disappeared. But that's not the point. The point is, I slept with her."

"I'm still not seeing a problem. You sleep with a lot of women, Schwartz."

He smirks. "I do. But she's different, Finley. I knew it back then, but I was too much of a self-absorbed prick to act on it." I stop to point a finger at her. "Before you say anything, I know I'm still self-absorbed, but I'm working on it."

"Holy shit. Are you in love?"

He scowls at me. "Don't talk crazy. No one said anything about love, and it's a delicate situation. It's not just her; she comes with two little girls."

I let my jaw fall open at that revelation. Schwartz isn't exactly kid friendly.

"Don't look at me like that. I think the little one might actually like me." A faint smile wisps across his lips. "She decorated my Ferragamo loafers with stickers, and you *know* how I feel about those shoes."

"They're your babies."

He nods. "And I didn't even flinch. The problem is…" A moment passes where he considers what he's about to tell me. "She's the sister of the victim in one of my cases."

"You're shitting me."

His lips press together in a thin line, and he shakes his head. "I wish I were."

"Did you know?"

"Not when I took the case, but I also didn't have much time to go over the file before the status hearing. She was in the courtroom. I should've walked away, but I didn't. Instead, I took any opportunity to insert myself into her life that I could. And this morning, I told Judge Otto that I've been seeing her."

"Fuck, is he reporting it to the bar?"

"He has to, so there's a good chance I'm going to be looking at a suspension soon."

"Shit." I rub my hands over my face, push back from my desk, and wander over to the window to look out of it rather than at Schwartz while I confess my own indiscretion. "Well, there's something I should tell you, too."

"That doesn't sound good."

I glance over at him and sigh. "It isn't. Or, it wasn't. It might be okay now, I guess."

"What are you talking about?"

Tapping my foot, I cross my arms over my chest, like that might actually do something to protect me from the blow-back I'm about to receive. "That call about Mr. Lawson's case getting dropped came at a very good time because I've been sleeping with him."

"You *what?*"

I drop my face in my hands and groan. "I know."

"You are sleeping with a client…"

"Christ, I know how bad that sounds, how bad it is, but Schwartz"—I finally force myself to turn around and look at him again—"you don't understand this man. I tried to keep things professional, tried to act only as his lawyer, but when-ever I got near him, everything I was supposed to be doing slipped away, like I wasn't even in control of my own mind or body anymore."

"You could lose your license *permanently* for this, Finley. And I thought what *I* did was bad."

I offer him a humorless grin. "Yeah, I have to say, I'm glad you came in here and told me about your indiscretion. It makes me feel a lot better about my own and made telling you easier."

"Fuck." He drops his elbows to his knees and scrubs his hands over his face. "We really fucked up big time, didn't we?"

"Yep." I walk over to him and lower myself into the chair next to him. "But I think it will be okay. Waters is dismissing Jude's case at the status next week, and it's not like we had planned to go public with our relationship anyway. If anyone *does* find out, it would be after my representation of him is complete, and it wouldn't be an ethical violation anymore. No one but you knows anything happened before that point."

He lifts his head, his blue eyes meeting mine. "And you're okay with that? With having violated your ethics?"

I sigh and lean back. "Fuck if I know, Schwartz. Aren't we always doing that in some way in order to do this job?"

Nodding slowly, he sits up straight. "I guess so. I had to come clean with the judge in order to withdraw from the case, but I don't know what I would have done if I were in your situation."

"You think they'll suspend you?"

"Probably. You're going to have to pick up the slack on cases for however long I'm not allowed to practice."

I nod and smile at him. "I'll hold down the fort."

"I know you can."

"I have to ask...is she worth it?"

He doesn't hesitate before answering. "Fuck, yes. Is he?"

"Absofuckinglutely."

MOUTH

It's over.

I HIT SEND ON the text, and even though it's the middle of the night, almost immediately, Reaper starts his reply.

Shit.

The entire reason I waited to tell him was that I wasn't ready to have a conversation about it; I wasn't ready to admit what it meant for me and the woman asleep beside me.

REAPER

Does that mean you're coming home?

I groan and scrub my hand over my face, looking over at Finley sleeping so peacefully. She isn't tormented by her dreams, doesn't dread closing her eyes at night, afraid of what might come. I envy that but watching her sleep somehow makes the fact that I can't easier to accept.

Even if I *could* sleep under normal circumstances, I wouldn't be able to tonight. When she told me what should have been good news about the charges being dropped, it felt like the floor was falling out from under me rather than something to celebrate.

This stupid anklet will be gone in a few days when we finally go to court and get the charges dismissed. It means the end of my confinement and potentially going to prison, but it also means it's the end of this.

I ghost my fingers down Finley's exposed spine, and she shifts in her sleep, rolling toward me and wrapping her arm over my chest, letting her face rest above my heart.

She releases a little contented sigh, totally oblivious to the turmoil twisting me up inside. I run my fingers through her hair, the silky texture so different from the calluses on my fingers.

We couldn't be more different—her in her suits, arguing cases in front of a judge and jury, me using my hands and anything else at my disposal to destroy people. And we've been living in our own isolated world this entire time, wrapped up in each other and what we have together.

Going home.

It's what Finley has been fighting for, to allow me to go *home.* It's what I had planned to do after I took out Yankovich and his cronies, head back to Baltimore, back to the life I was living with the guys, doing these jobs. Go home. But now, the word doesn't seem so simple anymore.

I had one once, a home, with a mother and a father and sisters. A place full of laughter and affection. I felt safe, secure, loved. The memories may not all be there, but the *feelings* are. So, I know what it is; I know it can exist. And I know I haven't felt like that since the moment I woke up in that hospital.

Until now.

The woman in my arms feels more like a home than anywhere else has in the last four years, and the thought of walking away from that, away from her, to return to the kind of life I had back in Baltimore, makes my eyes burn.

We said we would figure it out, that this was a clean slate to start our lives together, but the very real fact is, the only things I know are there, and she is here—in the city that has caused me nothing but grief.

I squeeze her gently and type up a reply to Reaper.

> Not for a bit. Will go to court in a week or so to have the charges formally dismissed. Then Parrish wants to have a little celebratory party.

Not that I particularly want to see him or any of the Knights again, but it gives me an excuse to stay longer, to ensure I get more time with Finley before life puts hundreds of miles between us and what we have.

I hit send, knowing I haven't answered the ultimate question.

Where is home?

Reaper, Viktoria, Chaos, and Avery all flicker through my head. All the good times we've had together. The way we've all worked together to make it through seemingly impossible situations.

I can't walk away from them any more than I can the woman sleeping across my chest.

Finley stirs and finally pushes up on her elbow, blinking tired eyes at me in the dark. "Hey, you okay?"

I nod because even if I tried to speak, I'm not sure what words would come out.

She glances at the phone in my hand. "Who are you talking to?"

"R-r-reaper."

Her smile falters a little. "What does he want?"

"T-t-to kn-kn-know when I'm c-c-coming back."

She presses her hand over my heart, resting it there where the heat of her skin can sizzle against mine. "What did you tell him?"

I turn the phone so she can read the text messages, and any humor she had completely disappears with her frown.

"I guess we haven't really talked about that. Because I have been avoiding bringing it up. And I know better than to assume you will."

Despite how unsettled everything feels, I grin at her acknowledgment that she knows me so well and that she's willing to accept all the intricacies my fucked-up self comes with.

I set my phone on the nightstand and drag her up across my body, her breasts pressing to my chest. My cock reawakens between us, but I ignore the desire to drive into her again and instead address the elephant in the room we've both been dancing around. "I d-d-don't want to l-l-leave, but—"

Her green gaze softens. "But it's all you know how to do."

A tiny bit of relief floods through me. She really does understand without me having to explain it.

What I do with Chaos and Reaper *is* all I know. It's the only thing that has felt real, like I'm making a difference and am still useful even though so many parts of me feel useless at times.

"I can't ask you not to go back, Jude. Can't ask you not to keep doing what you're doing with your friends. I won't, but there's a good chance I have to stay here. If Schwartz gets suspended, someone's going to have to handle all the clients until he gets reinstated. And I can't just up and leave him in the lurch like that. Plus, I'd have to take the bar exam in Maryland and—"

I press my finger over her lips to silence her. "I kn-kn-know, and I wouldn't a-a-ask you to give up th-th-this, either."

Her career is her life as much as what I do is mine. She belongs in the courtroom, and taking her out of it would be selfish.

"So?" She presses her lips to my chest. "What do we do?"

"Wh-wh-whatever w-e-we have to."

She chews on the inside of her cheek, considering the logistics of a relationship where we're in two different cities. "One of us traveling back and forth every weekend?"

I shrug. "If th-th-that's what it t-t-takes."

My answer doesn't seem to appease her, though, her lips

twisting down. "And how long before that becomes too much? Before it gets too complicated?"

Complicated.

Now that's a word I'm familiar with. My life has been nothing *but* complications, but I could never, would never think of Finley as one.

I take her face between my hands and kiss her deeply, letting my lips say what my words never can. "N-n-never. Whatever it t-t-takes."

She tilts her head, leaning into my hand. "You really mean that?"

For years, I've withheld my words, relied on other people to know what I am trying to say without having to voice it, but with Finley, I don't want there to be any question about my intent.

"I n-n-never thought I had a ch-ch-chance at a life, at a fu-fu-future, at anything more th-th-than being a machine w-w-working on reflex and tr-tr-training."

Tears fall down her cheeks, and I wipe them away with my thumbs, hating to see her so distressed. "You're so much more than that, Jude."

"I kn-kn-know. Because of y-y-you. N-n-nothing and no one w-w-will get in the w-w-way of that. I pr-pr-promise."

17

TWO WEEKS LATER

MOUTH

B ig Nose Kate's is every bit the dive I thought it would be based on the description Reaper gave me after he was here. Being inside it for the little impromptu celebration organized by Parrish, sticking to the floor each time I try to lift my feet, I can't help but love the place—even if the men who operate out of here have complicated my life more than I can even fathom.

It's exactly the kind of bar I would hang out at if I had to choose one, and it fits the Knights perfectly. Skeezy, a little bit dirty, but also homey and welcoming, in a weird sort of way that makes you want to saddle up to the bar and order a cheap beer.

Various members sit at the long-worn piece of wood to my right, and I watch them all carefully, enjoying the dynamics of the group. They remind me so much of how Chaos, Reaper, and I are when we're together, and a knot forms in my stomach at not being able to remember all the years before my injury—my time with them and all the other men who were part of our unit who didn't make it back.

Finley's soft hand squeezes at the nape of my neck, bringing me back to the present.

Clean slate.

A fresh start.

I keep thinking about our conversation, about how I need to look at this differently than I have been. I got a raw deal. I'm damaged goods that can never be fixed, but if I weren't, none of this would have ever happened.

Reaper may not have sent me on this mission. I might not have ever met Finley. I might not have ever been given a chance to find what Reaper and Chaos have, with a woman who owns my heart, and even though it took getting arrested to get me to this moment, I can't say I would change anything.

Finley leans over from her seat next to me. "Are you okay? You look like you disappeared there for a second."

I nod at her and press a kiss to her cheek, brushing my lips over to her ear. "I'm f-f-fine."

Schwartz eyes us from across the table. The man who is technically Finley's boss still appears a little perturbed at discovering she is now shacking up with one of her former clients, but she keeps reminding him that "former" is the key word here—and what he did wasn't much better.

No one will ever be able to prove when Finley and I got personally involved. For that reason, "case dismissed" were the sweetest words I've ever heard—next to Finley telling me she loves me—because it meant we were free. Free from the confines of the attorney-client relationship. From everything else that held either of us back. Free to be together and not risk everything she worked so hard for her entire life.

The guilt still lingers over her actions, and she may always struggle with what the guys and I do, but for some reason, I'm not worried anymore. Because I see the way she looks at me, feel the way she clings to me when I'm inside her, hear it in her words when she begs for more and tells me she loves me.

We'll work it out.

We'll overcome any obstacle that tries to come between us.

She rests her head against my shoulder, nuzzling into me in a way that makes me want to drag her home immediately instead of hanging out at this "party" to celebrate the resolution of the flurry of cases. "What time are you leaving tomorrow?"

I run my fingers through her hair. "A-a-after I've made s-s-sure you're thoroughly f-f-fucked and have e-e-eaten my favorite b-b-breakfast."

Her head jerks back, and I grin at her and waggle my eyebrows. She bursts out laughing, a flush spreading over her cheeks as she glances around to make sure no one heard my lewd comment. "You can't talk like that in public."

I raise a brow and scan the room. "L-l-like any of these g-g-guys care and w-w-wouldn't say the same th-th-thing?"

Finley scowls at me, but there's no anger in it. "True." She releases a little sigh. "It's going to be weird—not seeing you every day."

I nod. "I kn-kn-know. B-b-but absence m-m-makes the heart g-g-grow fonder. Isn't th-th-that what they s-s-say?"

"I guess so." She flutters her lips against my ear, stirring my cock almost instantly. "You know, if we're going to do this long-distance thing, we're going to have to use the phone or Facetime or something and, you know, actually *talk*."

She pulls away and eyes me knowingly.

I scowl at her. "I s-s-see what you're d-d-doing."

"I would hope so since I'm being pretty blatant about it."

While it has gotten easier to talk to Finley without my

ego and anxiety silencing me, around other people, it's a completely different story. She loves all the broken pieces of me, but that doesn't mean she won't keep trying to get me to move past some of them.

I press my lips to hers, which doesn't do anything for my straining erection, then move across her cheek to her ear. "D-d-do they have a ba-ba-bathroom in this place I can t-t-take you into to f-f-fuck you?"

Her eyes widen, and she slaps me playfully on the shoulder. "Stop it."

Before I can reiterate my intentions, Enzo approaches from across the bar and smiles at Finley. I'm man enough to admit when I'm jealous, and this smooth, handsome fucker makes me tighten my arm around her at my side possessively.

"Excuse me." Enzo clears his throat, shifting uncomfortably under my glare. "Ms. Banks, can I have a word?"

She glances at me briefly before pushing to her feet and following Enzo off to the side of the room to speak in private. I keep an eye on them, twisting my beer bottle in my hands when what I really want to do is smash it and use the pieces to remind him that she's mine.

Parrish approaches, his gaze darting from Finley to me, and he slides into the chair she just vacated.

I glare at him.

"Don't worry, fucker. I'm not staying long. She can have her seat back."

I snort and shake my head.

"I just wanted to say thanks again for all your help in getting the shitstorm that's been going on around here resolved. And for finally ending the Yankovich problem."

That final shot acted as a catharsis for all the anger and anguish I've held onto so tightly for so long. I completed the mission—and got the girl. So, while I may not like Parrish or the way he acted like I was his own personal mercenary, I still appreciate that if it weren't for him, I wouldn't have Finley.

I incline my head in acknowledgment of his thank you, and he slaps me on the shoulder and rises.

"I'm hoping I won't ever have to see any of you guys again. So, tell Reaper the same, but if you guys are ever in New York, you're always welcome here."

As annoyed as I am with how things have gone down since I got here, I appreciate the sentiment and offer him a nod of agreement.

"Back to the silent treatment, huh?"

I don't bother answering him, just return my focus to Enzo and Finley. The longer they stand together, talking, the more I want to walk over there, scoop her up, throw her over my shoulder like a damn caveman, and then bend her over the bar and bang her in front of everyone to prove who she belongs to.

All I can do is curl my hands into fists to keep myself from doing just that because he's a client and she *is* mine.

Forever.

She's helping me write my future on that cracked, broken slate, one that no one will be able to wipe away this time.

FINLEY

ENZO LEADS me over to the side of the room, as far as we can get from the raucous crowd of bikers and their women all over the bar.

He smiles sheepishly and glances at Jude, where he still sits at the table, glaring at us in a way that makes my lips twitch. "I just wanted to come over and thank you for all you did for me. I know I wasn't the easiest client."

I flash him a grin. "That's only because you had trouble following directions when it came to our witness." My gaze drifts to the bar, where Danica waits for him, watching us closely. "It all worked out, though."

"Yeah"—he nods—"I guess it did."

Enzo was an absolute thorn in my side as a client—willfully violating the terms of his bond and potentially destroying our defense by being personally involved with the key witness—but considering the fact that I somehow fell in love with my *own* client, I really can't be too hard on him.

"You have my number, but I don't want you to ever have to use it again. You're a good guy, Enzo. It'd be a shame if you wound up being a pain-in-the-ass criminal like your old man."

At the mention of his father, Enzo's eyes dart around the room in search of Wolf. He sits at the end of the bar with Maria's arms wound around his neck, smiling back at his wife, relaxed and happier than I've ever seen him since Schwartz pulled me into this crazy world of the Satan's Knights.

Enzo shrugs with a laugh. "Eh, he's not that bad."

I snort and shake my head, about to argue that fact, when my gaze locks with Jude's where he sits with Parrish, looking like he's either going to strangle the man next to him or come over here and do it to Enzo.

Normally, a man's jealousy might annoy me and make me think he needs to work on his own self-esteem issues, but Jude's eyes blaze with so much heat that I actually squirm and press my legs together against the throb there.

Hell.

He's going to *prove* that I'm his—and it wouldn't surprise

me if he's going to do it somewhere in this building where people are sure to walk by and either see and/or hear us.

As Parrish leaves his seat, I step away from Enzo and make my way back over to where Jude's waiting, but instead of sliding into my chair, I nudge him back from the table so I can sit on his lap.

His semi-hard cock presses against my ass, and I raise an eyebrow at him. "I thought you were just joking about doing me in the bathroom."

He shakes his head, grinning slightly, his hand moving up my exposed lower thigh and higher under the hem of my dress. "Oh, n-n-no. I n-n-never j-j-joke about anything like th-th-that."

I rest my head against his shoulder, squeezing my legs together to pin his hand and prevent it from going where he so clearly intends it to. "Were you jealous just now, seeing me talking to a former client?"

He stiffens under me slightly and shifts his weight, like he's uncomfortable with the question. I pull my head up and look at him.

"Not gonna answer me, huh?"

Jude remains stoic, not giving away anything, but it's all the answer I need.

"You know, I have to talk to other men to do my job, right? I can't just represent female clients because you're jealous."

Schwartz chuckles across the table.

Apparently, I didn't speak quietly enough.

My boss glances between Jude and me. "I mean, I guess I could assign you only female clients, and I could take all the men."

I glower at him. "Fuck you, Schwartz."

"You've already done that." His eyes dart over to Jude.

"But now that you have this guy, I know it'll never happen again."

"About time you figured that out."

He turns away from us and rejoins his conversation with Charlotte, where she sits holding her new baby.

I wrap my arms around Jude's neck and snuggle into him, intentionally rubbing my ass against his cock to feel it grow harder under me.

"Wh-wh-what g-g-game are you p-p-playing, Finley?"

"No game. I'm just thinking it's time we get out of here."

He shakes his head. "No. H-h-here. N-n-now. I'm not w-w-waiting another s-s-second to get ins-s-side you."

Hell.

That growly, demanding man thing shouldn't be so hot, but it is. The fact that he's willing to tell me exactly what he wants and needs from me and isn't embarrassed by the way it comes out anymore warms my heart to match the heat spreading between my legs.

Jude climbs to his feet, letting me slide down until mine hit the sticky floor, then takes my hand in his and drags me past the dozens of people mingling in the bar to the side door that leads out to the patio.

The crisp early fall air hits the bare skin on my exposed legs, and Jude drags me under the tent erected over the old wooden deck and to the far corner—about as much privacy as we'll ever get around here with so many people milling about. It will only be a matter of minutes before someone stumbles out of the bar to have a smoke, so we're either going to have to accept that we will have an audience, or we're going to have to work fast.

Something tells me that isn't going to be a problem.

Jude is so tense and tightly wound that there isn't any way he intends this to be anything other than hard and fast. Which is fine by me. I'll take him any way he wants me, anytime. I want to spend every last minute I have here with him since it's going to be almost a week before I can head down to Baltimore to see him again.

It's going to feel like an eternity after being with him practically every day for a month, but it's time for him to go home, to return to the life he has there with his friends and his business.

He tugs me over to one of the rickety, old tables set up under the tent, grabs me by my hips, and lifts me easily, setting me on the top and instantly reaching for his waistband. The cold metal bites against my thighs, and he frees his hard cock and forces the skirt of my dress up around my waist, exposing me to him and the cold air—not to mention anyone who walks out after us.

That thought makes my pussy clench, and he uses the fingers of one hand to shove my thong to the side while the other strokes his length, pre-cum already beading at the large tip.

My mouth waters to suck him between my lips, but there isn't any time for that now. He lowers his head and kisses me deeply, dragging his cock through my wetness and slipping inside me easily. I gasp into his mouth, clinging to the back of his neck as he tugs my hips to the edge of the table to get even deeper.

"I w-w-want you to f-f-feel me inside y-y-you every f-f-fucking second th-th-this entire w-w-week while we're a-a-apart." He pulls his hips back, then sinks into me again, sending the table creaking and skittering slightly across the worn wood of the deck. "Every t-t-time y-y-you w-w-walk, I w-w-want you to f-f-feel my c-c-cock between your l-l-legs and remember that y-y-you're *mine.*"

"God, yes, Jude. Yours. All fucking yours."

Because I am his.

All his.

No matter what he does at night.

No matter who he was before.

I know who he is *now.*

He's the incredibly complicated man who knows how to reach a part of me I didn't know needed it. The one who made me see beyond my career to something else. The only one who will ever hold my heart.

Each drive of his hips cements our future even more. Each groan and grunt and moan of pleasure, the sounds of us committing to making *this* work, whatever it takes.

His thrusts become harsher, more erratic, and he jerks my head up to devour my mouth again as I squeeze around him and spur him to move faster with my hips meeting his. The grind of his pelvis against my clit finally sends me flying, lights flashing against my closed lids, my lips falling open on a strangled moan of release. He pumps into me relentlessly, chasing his own orgasm, and dips his head to dig his teeth into the soft flesh of my collarbone.

The bite of pain mixing with the ecstasy engulfing me drags out my bliss longer, and he empties himself into me on a groan and tightening of his hands at my hips.

Jude Lawson just marked me—in more ways than one.

I belong to him and his mouth, forever.

EPILOGUE

SIX MONTHS LATER

MOUTH

"Is this what normal looks like?" Chaos inclines his head toward where Viktoria, Avery, and Finley sit near the fire pit, laughing and sipping their margaritas.

The early spring weather is a welcome change from the snowy cold winter we've had. Being able to get out here and enjoy the outdoors allows us all to breathe some fresh air while we have a few drinks and some burgers thrown on Reaper's grill.

I shrug and glance at Reaper on the other side of me in our deck chairs. "I d-d-don't know. What do you th-th-think?"

He chuckles. "I mean, I guess it is." He spreads his arms wide, motioning to his yard, which hasn't quite come fully back to green after the long winter. "Just three normal guys barbecuing while their women gossip about God only knows what."

Only most guys didn't just come straight here from eliminating two men who robbed a liquor store, killed the clerk, and walked out of court scot-free...

I bark out a laugh and shake my head as I take a drink of my beer. "I c-c-can only imagine wh-wh-what those th-th-three are talking about."

Probably none of it good, considering how well those women know us and what loose lips they seem to have when they're together. It's incredible to see how quickly they've all bonded. Even with Finley only being able to come a couple times a month, they're three peas in a pod, like they've known each other their entire lives. Undoubtedly, Avery and Viktoria know far too much about our sex life and everything else that should stay just between Finley and me. But I suppose that's just the price you pay for having love in your life—from a good woman and good friends.

Chaos shifts in his seat, suddenly stiff and awkward when he's been so relaxed since we arrived. "So, guys…"

We both turn toward him, my gut churning slightly at the sudden shift to seriousness in his tone.

"Watch the girls and tell me if you notice anything unusual."

I narrow my focus on them, trying to see what he does that has him so concerned. The last thing we need after so many months of relatively uneventful life is for another major drama to come up—especially when this is one of my weekends with Finley. I don't want to be distracted by anything else so I can concentrate on spending every waking moment with her.

Viktoria, Avery, and Finley whisper conspiratorially, occasionally glancing our way as they try to pour Avery's drink into their glasses.

I jerk my head toward Chaos. "I-i-is she pr-pr-pregnant?"

He grins and nods, and Reaper leaps from his chair and

pulls Chaos off his, embracing him and clapping him on the back.

"Holy shit, man! That's amazing."

Lumbering to my feet, I offer him a hug. "C-c-congratula-tions. You guys d-d-deserve it."

"Did they just figure it out?" Avery yells across the yard, giggling.

Chaos nods to her. "Yep, took them long enough."

Avery rolls her eyes and laughs. "And I thought you guys were supposed to be super observant."

We burst out laughing as the women all climb to their feet and make their way over toward us, smug looks on all their faces.

Viktoria appears incredibly pleased with herself. "I told you these assholes wouldn't notice. It took my keen cop eye, which none of them have."

"Hey, I f-f-figured it out."

Finley slides next to me and tucks herself under my arm, staring up at me with a grin. "Yeah, but I knew the minute we got here and I saw her. She's practically glowing."

I shrug. "H-h-how the h-h-hell am I supposed to kn-kn-know what a pregnant w-w-woman looks like?"

Something flashes in Finley's eyes that makes the blood rush straight to my cock.

Fuck.

I dip my head down to brush my lips over her ear. "H-h-how about we f-f-find somewhere inside for me to t-t-try to put one in y-y-you?"

She jerks her head back, her mouth opening and closing a few times before she finally manages to speak. Finley is usually the last one at a loss for words, but I've managed to render her speechless. "Yeah…"

"Yeah?" I raise an eyebrow at her, laughing at the stunned look still on her face.

Even though it's only been six months, and we haven't ever really talked about it, the thought of seeing her belly growing with my baby inside it, of being a father, just feels right. Like that's what's meant to happen and what all the turmoil we've been through has all been about.

"E-e-excuse me, g-g-guys. Finley n-n-needs to show me so-so-something in the h-h-house."

They all give us smug, knowing looks as I grab her hand and drag her toward the two-story bungalow Reaper and Viktoria bought on the outskirts of Baltimore.

We step in through the back door, and Finley releases a giggle, squeezing my hand.

"Are we really doing this?"

I lead her into the downstairs bathroom and push her up against the door. "Y-y-you telling me you r-r-really want a baby with m-m-me?"

Uncertainty flashes in her gaze. "I don't know. Jude, it's only been six months."

"The ha-ha-happiest six m-m-months of my l-l-life. My n-n-new one. The o-o-one that is my f-f-future, n-n-not about the p-p-past. I w-w-want to fill my h-h-head with all n-n-new memories, w-w-with you at the c-c-center of all of th-th-them."

Her expression softens, and she presses her palms against my face. "I love you so much."

"I l-l-love you, t-t-too. N-n-now, about p-p-putting that b-b-baby inside you."

She giggles, her head falling back, exposing her neck, almost in offering. I lean in and kiss her there, and she fumbles with the button and zipper on my jeans to finally free my cock.

It wasn't really an answer to my question, but we've come to the point where we don't even need words. Ironic since

I'm finally becoming more comfortable with actually talking again.

I slip a hand down under the hem of her dress, expecting to find something blocking my path, but my fingers only brush against moisture already covering her pussy.

"N-n-no panties?"

She grins and shakes her head. "When I'm down here visiting you, I much prefer the easiest access possible. If we're only going to see each other a few days a month, we need to make good use of them." Something twinkles in her eyes that makes my cock jerk. "Especially with this new goal in mind."

Fuck yes.

I never thought I'd be the guy who gets off on thinking about knocking up his woman, but I don't think I've ever wanted to be inside her more than I do at this very second. "I c-c-couldn't agree m-m-more."

FINLEY

OUR NEW GOAL.

A baby.

A tiny version of Jude walking around with my attitude and his father's big heart.

It's crazy.

It's far too much, far too fast.

We shouldn't even be considering this when we haven't discussed it. When I'm still living in New York and he's down here. When we've only been seeing each other a few days every month when my schedule allows me to come down or his missions give him time to come to New York.

A baby?

Anyone who saw us would say we're crazy, that we're just caught up in the joy of Avery and Chaos' moment, that we're just horny for each other because of the time we spend apart and that all of this will come crashing down around us violently when we take time to consider what we're doing.

Jude and I have a history of making rash decisions and jumping into things without looking, yet, the moment he said those words to me, it just sounded...right. Just like everything with him has felt once I worked past my own guilt over us hooking up while I was representing him.

Jude drags the head of his cock through my wetness and sinks inside me in one long stroke that feels like coming home.

Every time we're together, all the stress of work and traveling back and forth disappears and it's like we've never been apart. I cling to his neck, and we move together fluidly, knowing each other so well, knowing exactly what the other likes and needs, like pieces of a puzzle fitting together, completing a perfect picture that was always meant to be.

A picture in my mind that suddenly has more than just the two of us in it.

All this talk about making a baby has me hotter for him than I've ever been, my blood burning like fire through my veins, rushing to all the places he touches me—desperate for something I never knew I wanted.

A family.

A man worshipping me.

I always thought my career was my partner, that no one would ever understand the amount of time I have to work, the amount of stress I have, the weight that holding the lives of my clients in my hands puts on me. But Jude gets it. He gets me. He understands exactly what I need in the bedroom and everywhere else, and he'll do anything to give it to me.

He drags back his hips and plunges into me again, then

pulls us away from the door and turns to set me on the counter, placing me at the perfect height to pound into me relentlessly.

His hands at my waist keep me from slamming against the mirror behind me with his aggressive thrusts, and I roll my hips up to meet each one, rocking against him and digging my nails into his nape.

With one violent tug, he moves me closer to the edge so he can pump deeper, push harder, force himself all the way into me. I drop my head back on a moan, every cell in my body heating and exploding with the pleasure he always brings me. That sense of rightness that's always there.

One of his large, calloused palms finds my cheek and tilts my face to his. He crushes his lips to mine, kissing me with the same passion and need as he did that first night when I wasn't willing to give in, wasn't willing to admit that I was incapable of resisting what was happening between us.

Everything I risked was worth it for this moment.

We have a future full of friends and happiness and the knowledge that everything's going to work out. If Jude could make it through everything he's had to face to get here, then nothing can stand in our way.

I return his kiss, with every ounce of love I hold for him, and grind on his cock, squeezing him the way I know makes him insane.

It doesn't matter that the others know exactly what we're doing in here or that they can probably hear us.

I don't care.

Let them hear me scream.

Let them hear exactly what this man does to me.

I couldn't care less.

Jude reaches between us and finds my clit, rolling his thumb over it expertly, and I come like a freight train barreling down the tracks, unable to stop. It slams into me, drawing out a gasp as he holds me steady and pounds into me, a man on a mission—apparently to knock me up.

His other work might raise some lingering questions, but this is a mission I am fully on board with. One I'm more than willing to let him succeed in because Mouth is my future, and I'm his new reality.

He finally comes on a groan, somehow plunging impossibly deeper into me, and he stills with his face buried against my neck.

We remain like this panting for a few moments, our hearts thundering against each other before he finally lifts his head and takes my face between his palms. "J-j-just seeing y-y-you on the w-w-weekends isn't enough."

"I know. I've been thinking about it for a while, and I'll move down here. I'll take the bar in Maryland, and I can still take a few cases in New York if I want to. I have to stay until Schwartz's suspension is over to handle things at the office. But then, I'm coming back here to you forever."

The scars and ruins of his past have made Jude what he is today. He might be broken and battered by what happened to him, by what he's suffered, and those wounds may never heal. But even if it means spending the rest of our lives working for it, one day, he's going to find his voice again and won't be afraid to tell other people how he feels about them the way he does with me.

One day soon.

I hope you enjoyed the Scarred Heroes Series. Want more from the suspenseful and gritty world? Check out The Inland Seas Series and The Deadliest Sin Series, all part of the same Sins of the Mafia World as The Scarred Heroes.

Squall Line - Book 1 of The Inland Seas Series
GET IT FREE: books2read.com/SquallLine

Finding Sin - Prequel to The Deadliest Sin Series
GET IT FREE: books2read.com/FindingSin

Sign up for Gwyn's newsletter to stay up to date on releases
and other news: www.gwynmcnamee.com/newsletter

ABOUT THE AUTHOR

Gwyn McNamee is an attorney, writer, wife, and mother (to one human baby and two fur babies). Originally from the Midwest, Gwyn relocated to her husband's home town of Las Vegas in 2015 and is enjoying her respite from the cold and snow. Gwyn has been writing down her crazy stories and ideas for years and finally decided to share them with the world. She loves to write stories with a bit of suspense and action mingled with romance and heat.

When she isn't either writing or voraciously devouring any books she can get her hands on, Gwyn is busy adding to her tattoo collection, golfing, and stirring up trouble with her perfect mix of sweetness and sarcasm (usually while wearing heels).

Gwyn loves to hear from her readers.
Here is where you can find her:
Newsletter:
www.gwynmcnamee.com/newsletter
Facebook:
https://www.facebook.com/AuthorGwynMcNamee/
Twitter:
https://twitter.com/GwynMcNamee
Instagram:
https://www.instagram.com/gwynmcnamee
Tiktok:
https://www.tiktok.com/@authorgwynmcnamee
Bookbub:

https://www.bookbub.com/authors/gwyn-mcnamee
FB Reader Group:
https://www.facebook.com/groups/1667380963540655/
Website:
https://www.gwynmcnamee.com